THE SEAFARERS

The ship was an old East Indiaman, thick of hull, sailing out the last of her useful days with a sturdy dependability. There were long days and nights of uneventful sailing, days and nights of storm, long talks as they stood at the rail watching the prow cut through the swells of the Indian Ocean.

Landfall engendered emotions in Jon that he had not suspected. There was a bittersweet tang to being home, for home meant that he would, sooner or later, see his stepfather and his mother. But the Australian air had a comfortable feel, the sun a kind warmth, almost as if they were a part of Jon's being. He had come home, and it was high time.

Other Books in THE AUSTRALIANS series
by William Stuart Long

VOLUME I   The Exiles
VOLUME II   The Settlers
VOLUME III   The Traitors
VOLUME IV   The Explorers
VOLUME V   The Adventurers
VOLUME VI   The Colonists
VOLUME VII   The Goldseekers
VOLUME VIII   The Patriots
VOLUME IX   The Empire Builders
VOLUME XI   The Nationalists

VIVIAN STUART

Writing as William Stuart Long

The Seafarers

Volume X of The Australians

Futura

A Futura Book

Published by arrangement with Dell Publishing Co., Inc.,
New York, New York, USA

First published in the United Kingdom by
Aidan Ellis Publishing Ltd., Henley-on-Thames

This edition published in Great Britain in 1990
by Futura Publications,
a Division of Macdonald & Co (Publishers) Ltd,
London & Sydney
Reprinted 1991

ISBN 0 7088 4436 7

Printed and bound in Great Britain by
BPCC Hazell Books
Aylesbury, Bucks, England
Member of BPCC Ltd.

Futura Publications
A Division of
Macdonald & Co (Publishers) Ltd
165 Great Dover Street
London SE1 4YA

A member of Maxwell Macmillan Publishing Corporation

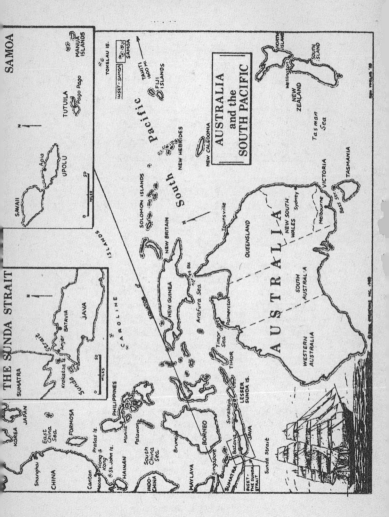

SAMOA

MANU'A ISLANDS
TUTUILA
Pago Pago

TOKELAU IS.
INSET-SAMOA
SAMOA
TAHITI (900 MI)
FIJI ISLANDS

SAVAII
Apia
UPOLU

ISLANDS

AUSTRALIA
and the
SOUTH PACIFIC

NEW CALEDONIA

South   Pacific

SOLOMON ISLANDS
NEW HEBRIDES

NORFOLK ISLAND

Wellington
NEW
ZEALAND
SOUTH
ISLAND

Tasman
Sea

NEW BRITAIN
NEW GUINEA

Townsville

QUEENSLAND

NEW SOUTH
WALES
Sydney

VICTORIA
Melbourne
BASS STR.
TASMANIA

A U S T R A L I A

SOUTH
AUSTRALIA

WESTERN
AUSTRALIA

Palmerston

Arafura Sea
Timor Sea

TIMOR

LESSER
SUNDA IS.

THE SUNDA STRAIT

SUMATRA

BATAVIA
Anjer
Krakatoa I.
Sunda Str.
JAVA

MILES
0   50

C A R O L I N E

CHINA
Shanghai
East
China
Sea
KOREA
JAPAN
FORMOSA
Canton
Hong Kong
Pratas Is.
St. John Is.
HAINAN
South
China
Sea
INDO-
CHINA
MALAYA
Singapore

PHILIPPINES
Manila
Palawan

BORNEO
Brunei

Surabaja
Batavia
JAVA
SUMATRA
INSET-THE SUNDA STRAIT
Sunda Strait

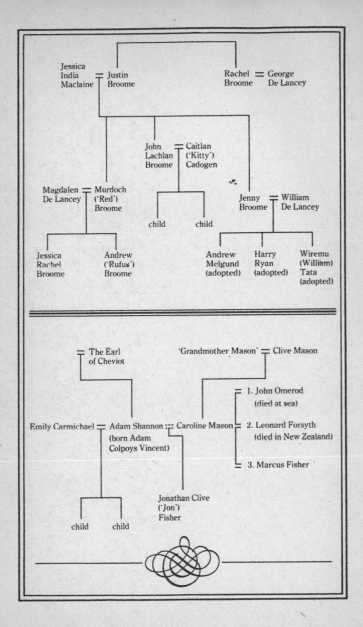

AUTHOR'S NOTE

The *Cutty Sark*, one of the last tall ships of the extreme clipper design to be built, never had a mate named Samuel Gordon. In some instances, her well-documented voyages are moved about in time in order to fit within the framework of this fictional story. A few of the incidents herein depicted as having happened on *Cutty Sark* are based on happenings on other ships. The author claims fictional licence for his effort to reflect a way of life, clipper sailing, in this book. The *Cutty Sark*, having been the quintessential clipper ship, seemed to be an ideal vehicle to accomplish this purpose.

PROLOGUE

November 22, 1869

Although Jock Willis's smile was hidden by his long white bushy beard and his full moustache, his satisfaction was evident in his eyes and his ruddy cheeks. The burly Scotsman was dressed in a dark swallow-tailed coat, a white vest, gleaming linen, and the pale beaver topper that had earned him the nickname "Old White Hat." He stood in the ship's bow—*his* ship's bow—with the fingers of one hand thrust into his trousers pocket as he surveyed a goodly portion of the population of Dumbarton. Pressing with upturned faces all around the construction gangway now doubling as a christening platform, the crowd on the foreshore below had braved the Scottish winter to witness the time-honoured ceremony that had brought Jock up from London. He was the yard's owner, and the ship about to be launched was, in his opinion, the best he had ever built.

Launching days always attracted a crowd, but not usually as large as this. Ships had been launched into the Leven River near its conjunction with the Clyde for centuries. The twin peaks of the Rock of Dumbarton had been witness to the comings and goings of Roman galleys, medieval carracks, stout East Indiamen, and, most recently, the sleek, low, twin-paddlewheelers that had been Clyde-built for speed and stealth to run the blockade of the United States Navy into the ports of the embattled Confederate States of America. The men of Dumbarton were carpenters, dubbers, joiners, caulkers, riggers, and fasteners. Shipbuilding was in their blood; and, of course, all those who had been involved in the building of this new ship were on hand, for this was not just another ship. She was slim and graceful, as sleek as a sea otter as she poised on her bed of keelblocks.

She was a clipper. She had risen slowly from the jumble of

11

timber and iron, the remnants of which still littered the yard. She had been formed of oak and metal and teak—no softwood for her, as would be the case in America, where oak was scarce. Old Jock had insisted on the finest materials, oak from the Forest of Dean in Gloucestershire and the New Forest of Hampshire, where once a retired admiral had wandered, pockets filled with acorns, to plant oaks so that England would never be shy of that durable wood. Old Jock's wishes—for pressing business now kept him in London—had been followed to the smallest detail by his building supervisor, Captain George Moodie, who would have the honour of taking the ship to sea.

Old Jock was a businessman, and a good one. He had known hardship, having been sent to sea as a boy. He had worked his way up to captain, and he had taken tall ships into the far ports of the world. His years at sea had hardened and wisened him, and he was a man who was careful with a pound—but a fair man, and a ship from John Willis & Son never left port without Old White Hat, Old Jock, on the wharf to raise his topper and call out, "Goodbye, my lads." A true son of Scotland, he was a man of many seasons—sailor, businessman, family man, and, in his secret heart, a poet—or, at least, a lover of poetry. For every event, for every mood, there was a verse stored away under the beaver hat. Once, when his young designer, Hercules Linton, had been preparing a materials list for the clipper, Old Jock had quoted Longfellow:

Choose the timbers with greatest care;
Of all that is unsound beware;
For only what is sound and strong
To this vessel shall belong.

Of course, the American poet had been inspired by a clipper being built by the master craftsman of Boston, Donald McKay, whose *Flying Cloud* still held the record for a one-day run, an incredible 374 miles at an average speed of fifteen knots, and that had been a factor in Old Jock's decision to build a composite clipper with strong iron ribs and mast mountings teamed with the finest English oak, for he had a long memory and more than his share of pride. The fact that Donald McKay, the American shipbuilding genius, was in truth a Scot—he had been born in

12

Nova Scotia, after all—eased the pain somewhat, but he was still thought of as an American, and it was time to show the upstart ex-colonists who, after all, was mistress of the seas.

It was shame enough to have McKay's Boston clippers holding all the speed and run records; worse still—despite the years that had passed—was the memory of the American *Oriental*, which had slipped out of Hong Kong harbour in August 1850, to arrive in London just ninety days later. Bringing tea from China was a British trade, and to have an American ship reach port with the first cargo of the season, and thus realize the highest profit, was gall to Old Jock's thrifty, patriotic heart.

But Old Jock harboured other, fresher grudges. Of late, a rival British shipowner, George Thompson, had been showing too much cockiness about his newest clipper, the *Thermopylae*, launched the previous year. While it was perhaps true that the *Thermopylae* was the fastest ship afloat, she had not yet proved herself, and before she began to set records, she'd have competition. Still, her first homebound crossing from China had taken just ninety-one days.

Jock glanced down at the teak planking beneath his feet. This ship, this little love, would best that. Of that he was sure. His new ship, and her captain, George Moodie, would topple the gilded rooster from the *Thermopylae*'s mainmast, and then the world would see who was the cock of the walk.

There were those who questioned Jock's decision to build a clipper instead of another steamship, but Jock did not have to be a visionary to know that steamers could not carry enough coal to reach Australia and the Far East, and he had no wish to be at the mercy of remote coaling stations run by God knew who. Tea from China and wool from Australia and New Zealand were still cargo for the tall ships, and Jock believed that his new ship would pay off and even show a tidy profit before the impending opening of the Suez Canal altered the current situation. Suez would make a difference in the long run, but for the foreseeable future the tea and wool clippers would carry their clouds of canvas around the Cape of Good Hope, into the area of storm and continuous wind known to all sailing men as the Roaring Forties, and thence, homeward bound, into that endless, heavy swell of the Southern Ocean where the Cape Horn greybeards rolled and surged and built crests of more than fifty feet. In such seas this ship would be in her element, and the winds that blew from the west with a reach that was global would be gathered in her three-quarters of an acre of canvas and converted to the driving force of three thousand horsepower. This ship would not foul God's clean air with the stench of coal smoke; her 212-odd feet would be accompanied only by the murmur of the wind in the rigging and the hiss of the foam as she cut the waves, not going over, but through. No bruising, battering battle against the sea for her.

A shout attracted Jock's attention. Young Hercules Linton, the ship's designer, was standing further forward in the bow, waving his topper. Beside him the chief draftsmen, John Rennie, stood with one hand on the shoulder of Captain Moodie. Jock took his hand out of his pocket and waved back. Moodie, using a brass hailing trumpet, bellowed an order to the workers below. All along the ways, workmen with sledges readied themselves. At Moodie's next shout the men lifted their tools, and then, with the final shouted order, the sledges thudded against the wooden dog shores that held the ship's relatively light tonnage clear of the greased ways.

The sound of the heavy sledges echoed from the hills, became a staccato thunder. Scarcely heard above the hammers was the smash of a bottle of the finest wine against the jauntily raked cutwater of the ship. Jock's eldest daughter had broken the bottle with the first swing, and as the ship creaked and began to move, she cried out, "I christen thee *Cutty Sark*."

Stern-first, she slid smoothly, gaining momentum, until she ploughed into the waters of the Leven with a mighty splash. A cheer went up. Jock let out his breath as the hull was engulfed by water, bobbed briefly, then settled into a smooth drift, hiding all but the top few feet of her copper plating—copper was dreadfully expensive, but the only way to keep a ship from becoming quickly fouled with barnacles. Jock looked around at the smiling faces and waving dignitaries on the bow. One face was missing.

He had to shout over the sound of bagpipes on shore. "Where's young Sam?"

The *Cutty Sark* was still drifting, waves generated by her launching racing outward. The man standing next to him pointed. Jock looked forward, at the stump of the bowsprit, to see his niece's son, fourteen-year-old Samuel Gordon, dangling precariously from the chain shrouds and reaching with one hand toward the Junoesque figurehead that protruded at the extremity of the *Cutty*'s raked bow.

Sam Gordon had done a man's work during the construction of the clipper. He was a bonny lad, large for his age, his still-growing body lean and smoothly muscled, his hair a wild mop of Scot's straw. From the time he had reached the age of ten, Old Jock had had high hopes for the lad. John Willis & Son was a family firm—Jock himself had taken over from his father—and there would definitely be a responsible place for young Sam someday.

"What's the lad doing?" someone asked.

Old Jock's half-hidden smile crinkled his florid cheeks and squinted his eyes. Sam was being delicate, careful not to touch the figurehead's bare breasts. He had hooked his legs on the chains and now was hanging upside-down, with one hand clutching the wrist of the figurehead's outflung left arm.

There was, of course, a verse for that, too. The good Scottish dialect rang in Old Jock's head as he watched his great-nephew accomplish his objective. Scotland's own Bobby Burns had taken an ancient legend and spun it into lilting verse—the story of Tam O'Shanter, a bit dazed by good Scotch whisky, watching a beautiful witch dancing, clad only in a short chemise, a "cutty sark." Not everyone was aware that Old Jock had taken the name for his extreme clipper from the Burns poem—or at least they had not made the connection—and not everyone who saw young Sam Gordon dangling dangerously from the bowsprit shrouds knew the significance of the boy's actions as he wedged a hank of rope, one end frayed, into the left hand of the voluptuous figurehead.

Old Jock roared, briefly frightening the men standing nearby. "Well done, lad!"

Sam Gordon heard him and, after pulling himself upright, waved and grinned as tugs began to gather in the *Cutty* and push her dockside, where, in the next few weeks, her towering spars would be mounted and her ten miles of standing and running rigging put in place.

Jock thought again of the poem, of how Tam O'Shanter, enchanted by the provocatively dressed witch, had cried out, and how, in the chase that ensued, the speeding young witch, fleet as the wind, had come close enough to grab Tam's horse's tail, pulling it free. The rope, frayed to resemble a horse's tail, was a symbol of swiftness, of the speed of a racing witch, and by putting that symbol into the hands of the *Cutty*'s figurehead, Sam Gordon had endowed the ship with that witch's swiftness.

Helping hands lifted Sam back to the deck, and Jock edged his way forward to congratulate the boy.

"Uncle Jock," Sam said, his face flushed with excitement, "I must sail with her!"

Old Jock chuckled. He could see himself in the lad, as he had been long ago, more years past than he cared to count. He had been even younger than Sam when he first went to sea, and in those days conditions aboard ship had been far more primitive. He had worked for fifty shillings a month and had lived on biscuit, burgoo, biscuit hash, and salt meat. In his early days as a midshipman he had done his time on an ice-coated yard, his fingers frozen and his nails torn off, standing on a swaying footrope a hundred feet above a pitching, canted deck. That experience would, in all probability, come soon to his great-nephew, for it was still necessary for the tall ships to weather Cape Horn, still necessary for the men who served on them to work in white, frigid water swirling across the decks, to live in a fo'c'sle that was often awash with water sloshing around the bunks, to be never really dry, never really rested, always gaunt-eyed with the need for sleep.

For a few moments he envied the lad, for he would know the tramping thunder of sails, the feeling of speed as a good skipper drove a fair ship hard with her lee rails under.

"You'll need gear," Old Jock said.

"I've saved money from my wages," Sam returned without a second thought.

Jock waved a hand dismissively. "I'll ha' none o' that," he said. "Make it a wee gift from your uncle." He cut off the boy's stammered attempt at a reply. "Save your hard-earned money, lad."

"You mean I really can join the ship, uncle?"

"You'll 'prentice directly under Captain Moodie. If your ma and pa will not be objecting, mind. And don't think it's family favouritism, or that I'm doing you a favour, for Moodie is a hard man, and you'll have to snap-to lively to please him."

"I shall work ever so hard, uncle!" Sam said.

Old Jock's smile faded. Fancy schools and the company of women had refined young Samuel's speech and manners, perhaps too much. He was a handsome lad, clean-cut and personable, though perhaps, God forbid, just a bit too soft—not in body but in temperament—for the sea. Certainly he'd take guff from the other foremast hands, for a clipper's crew had more than its share of drunks, criminals on the run, and shanghaied landsmen—a rough lot, with only a few true seamen mixed in. But, no, this lad would do fine.

Jock put his hand fondly atop the mop of straw-coloured hair. Yes, he thought, this boy would prove himself, just as his forebears had had to prove themselves in the past, and then, God willing, he'd be a man and would, perhaps someday, take over the helm of a John Willis & Son clipper.

January 22, 1879

Being a junior officer in the service of Her Majesty the Queen in Natal Colony was not, Lieutenant Jon Fisher had found, altogether unpleasant. True, the southeastern African sun was often unbearably hot, the climate dry, the dust churned up from Lord Chelmsford's army at times a choking miasma, but there was a grandeur to the landscape that could fill the heart. Just a few weeks before, after having joined his regiment with a fresh draft of twenty recruits green from England, Jon had travelled inland from the shores of the Indian Ocean with one of the army's supply trains, in the congenial company of two fellow Australians—sutlers in charge of the supplies. They had caught up to the army just before it crossed the Buffalo River at Rorke's Drift, and Jon had been immediately assigned to the Second Battalion, 24th Regiment of Foot.

Now, on the morning of the twenty-second of January, five companies of the First Battalion and the company of the Second Battalion to which Jon belonged were camped almost casually on the slopes of a brown and grassy mountain called Isandhlwana. It was, truly, a day made by God, a morning of low mists on the plains, cobalt blue skies, a gentle breeze, a warming sun. The tin cup in Jon's hands radiated warmth, the Chinese tea in it supplied by the Australian sutlers who provisioned the army from their

17

long wagon train. Around him, his fellow officers were having a leisurely breakfast. The general, Lord Chelmsford, was not in camp, having ridden before sunrise with a small force in support of a scouting party. To Jon's surprise, Chelmsford had divided his army of five thousand British troops and more than eight thousand native levies even before crossing the Buffalo, and into not two, but three, columns. That unorthodox decision, in fact, was the topic of a desultory conversation under the awning of the officers' mess tent. The officers themselves, good soldiers all, were hesitant to question their superior, but the civilians, Andy Melgund and Harry Ryan, with the impudence that seemed to be the mark of colonials, were not so respectful of the good general's character.

"Does he fancy himself to be General Robert E. Lee, splitting his forces in the face of the enemy?" Harry Ryan asked.

"And this encampment," Andy Melgund said. "Look at it! I'm no military genius, but it seems to me it would be a good idea to at least laager the wagons, perhaps have the chaps do a bit of entrenching."

"Really," a somewhat dandified subaltern said. "What enemy? Black men with spears? I hardly think that this Cetshwayo will lead his fellows into a British square of fire. What can such savages do against a modern army armed with Martini-Henry carbines?"

Melgund cast an amused look at Ryan. "I've heard such remarks before," he said, "about the Maoris of New Zealand. They, too, were called savages, and they spilled a good deal of blood before our so-called modern armies cooled them down a bit."

Jon was listening with only part of his attention. He was a sturdily built young man of medium height, with well-turned legs and a thick chest. He was strong of face in a way that, even at his tender age of nineteen, had proved to be attractive to more than one young lady. In his neatly pressed uniform, he looked like a soldier on a recruiting poster. His red coat had stood the dust well. His webbing and belt gleamed whitely in the early morning sun, and his cork, coal-scuttle helmet was pushed back slightly, enough to reveal expressive blue eyes and a broad sweep of forehead.

Before him the parched, arid land swept down and across a swale to peak in a buttress of exposed stone at the end of a long, flat ridge. Behind, Isandhlwana rose smoothly upward to its crest from the campsite. There was a feeling of immensity in the view, a hint of the breadth and depth of the African continent, an indication of the barrenness that lay to the northward.

"They're out there somewhere," Harry Ryan was saying.

"The sons of old Shaka himself," Melgund added. He lifted his cup and gazed over the rim into the face of the officer who had questioned the fighting ability of the Zulus. "They can fight, all right. They'll come, when they come, in a black wave of death. You'll hear them before you see them. Beating on their shields in unison, chanting, like low thunder, or a train in the distance getting up steam slowly as it climbs a grade."

"This is an empty, hard land," the officer said.

"Empty because of the Zulu, because of Shaka. When he conquered it he depopulated it," Ryan said.

"We have here," the officer said, "a colonial student of African native history."

"Might pay," Ryan said coldly. "It's good to know what one is getting into, isn't it? Fight? Ask those that Shaka drove out. If a man is known by his enemies, as they say, the Zulu has a certain standing. One of the Zulu chiefs that Shaka drove out was Mzilikazi. All he did was kill hundreds of thousands to establish a new kingdom in Matabeleland."

"We are not dealing with some superhuman Zulu," the officer said.

"No," Ryan returned. "You'll be facing Cetshwayo. He kills men who merely look at him. He'll come at you with twenty *impis*, two thousand warriors to the *impi*, forty thousand men."

"This cheerful conversation," the officer said, putting aside his plate, "is giving me the gripe."

A jangle of harness and a rumble of wheels caused Jon to look up as a caisson rolled past. Behind it, with a small group of mounted officers, rode Colonel A. W. Durnford, bush hat-brim cocked, non-regulation in uniform; he was the officer left in command of the encampment by Lord Chelmsford. He carried himself with a confidence that made Jon forget about Harry Ryan's pessimistic appraisal. Jon, too, found it hard to believe that natives armed with shields and spears would dare face sixteen hundred British soldiers and twenty-five hundred Africans.

Down the slope, soldiers were filing slowly past steaming kettles, getting their morning porridge. Joh could recognize most of the men in his section, although he had been with the army for only a short time. He was proud of the way the men had accepted him, in spite of his lack of experience. Some of them were twice his age, men who had been hardened in battle in the Crimea and in India, men who had been "a-serving of the Queen" before the colonel, Jon's grandfather, had arranged his entrance to Sandhurst, the military college that produced the majority of young officers for Britain's far-flung colonial armies.

During Jon's eight years in England, his often provincial thinking had been altered. He was in fact and in his heart still Australian but, without being overtly arrogant about it, was more cosmopolitan in his views than, for example, either Harry Ryan or Andy Melgund, and decidedly more so than his stepfather, Marcus Fisher, whose name never entered Jon's mind without a hint of distaste. Although Marcus Fisher had had a brief military career, Jon had almost certainly not chosen military life because of his stepfather. Fisher's military service was shadowed by shame, tainted with cowardice. Fisher had become a wealthy and politically powerful man, but he had never succeeded in gaining Jon's admiration. In Australia, Jon could have lived a life of ease and comfort, but he would have been living on Marcus Fisher's money. He wanted nothing from Fisher, and now he was content with the army. Here, in the service of the Queen, he would make his mark.

He anticipated the coming of the Zulu with a mixture of apprehension and exhilaration. A young officer had to be seasoned by battle, had to inhale the fumes of the guns, had to fight bravely and, if possible—if the enemy offered the coveted opportunity—with distinction. As Harry Ryan had said, a warrior is judged not only by the men he has killed, but by the quality, the bravery, of his fallen enemies. Jon half prayed that the Zulu would be brave, that the warriors would come in their thousands, for then he would, God willing, be given the opportunity to distinguish himself, and from that beginning many doors would be opened to him.

At first no one in the camp noticed the sound. It came as a distant hint of thunder and faded. Men were still queueing for their breakfast. In the officer's open mess men were still eating. When the sound came again, seeming to surge up from the rolling hills, directionless, Jon cocked his head and remembered Harry Ryan's words. Indeed, the sound was like that of a distant train struggling uphill, rising and falling with distance. Others heard it now, and the low murmur of voices was hushed.

A closer sound drew Jon's attention. A red-coated rider burst up over a rise, spurring hard. Dust flowered upward from the hooves of the labouring horse. The rider was waving one arm, shouting something unheard in the distance as men turned to watch.

Jon's heart leaped as he first caught the meaning of the rider's shouts.

"Well," Harry Ryan said, calmly finishing off the last of his breakfast, "speak of the devil."

The keen, silvery voice of a bugle galvanized the entire camp into frenzied motion. Men grabbed kit and weapons, jammed on helmets, saw to their neatness as they fell into their assigned positions in order of rank. Officers and sergeants bellowed orders.

"I say," an officer touched his elbow, "Jon, old boy, will you please look up a private or two to guard the food until we get back? I haven't finished my breakfast, you know."

'You might have to eat on the run for a while," Andy Melgund put in.

"Not likely," the officer said. "We've had these scurries of false alarm before." The man was off, and after quickly rounding up a commissary private to guard the mess tent, Jon hurried to his own company, taking in the scene as he trotted down the slope.

It was, in addition to being his first battle alert, a magnificent show to behold, the Queen's might on parade: rank on rank of red coats, crossed by gleaming white webbing and belts; lines of white helmets and shouldered rifles as orderly and as straight as a new picket fence. The distant sound, that slow moving, huffing train, had ceased.

Jon was in position and checking his own gear when the enemy showed himself, and with a suddeness that made his heart leap. Beyond the distant swale bodies sprang up as if from the ground itself, arrayed in a straight line of black just beyond the reach of the British front rank's Martini-Henrys.

"Interesting beggars," said Captain Harper Bell, Jon's

immediate superior and a seasoned India hand. He was old enough to be Jon's father.

Interesting they were—fascinating. The Zulu warriors seemed to be of uniform size and carried shields made distinctive each from the other by various patterns. Leggings of feathers covered their black skin at the ankles.

"They'll put on a show for us now," Bell said. "They'll posture a bit to show us how virile they are."

Almost immediately the Zulus began to beat on their shields rhythmically. A sound of deep-voiced humming came across the parched grass that separated the ready and waiting redcoats from the black wave that had sprung up from a deep ravine. Black warriors leaped forward, brandishing their short, iron-tipped spears, the Zulu *assegai*, reported to have been developed by the mighty Shaka for hand to hand fighting.

"That will be the head of the buffalo," Bell said. "They're taunting us, trying to get us to move against the head so that the horns of the buffalo can then strike us on either flank. They're quite predictable, you see. That small force to our front is the head of a fighting bull buffalo. There and there"—he pointed to either side of the encampment—"will be equal and larger forces—the horns—and behind the head there will be the main body, the loins of the beast. We're supposed to charge the head, and then, with our attention engaged, the horns would sweep in from either side to engulf us, while the loins, the main body, move forward over the fallen bodies of the head."

Although Colonel Durnford was not in sight at the moment, discipline was splendid. The rows of red-coated soldiers moved into position swiftly to form firing squares. Jon's company was deployed at right angles to the ranks opposing the visible Zulus; somewhat to his disappointment, he was facing nothing more than sun-seared, dead grass on a descending slope.

With a deep-throated droning, a chant that sounded like a mispronounced, repetitive use of the name for the tribe, the head of the buffalo charged, with black warriors seeming to flow effortlessly across the distance separating the two armies. At one hundred yards, Martini-Henrys spoke en masse as the front rank of redcoats fired, then dropped to their knees to reload while the rank behind them fired over their heads.

The Zulu died by the score, great swaths of emptiness temporarily parting the black wave sweeping toward the camp. Still they came, pouring up from the concealing ravine in their hundreds, their white feather leggings flashing in the sun, contrasting with their gleaming black skin. Jon was beginning to fear that his company would not even have a chance to fire. The black horde swarmed onward to die, to pile body atop body as they came in range of the deadly marksmanship of the ranks. Then Zulus materialized to Jon's front, and there were more targets than there were rifles; his ears were quickly numbed as the company's weapons rang out in concerted volleys. The horns of the buffalo were closing on the flanks. There was a stench of sulphur, a roar of sound, the throaty humming of the swiftly gliding warriors who now numbered in the thousands and sped toward the British ranks from three sides.

Hearing the rattle of gear behind him, Jon turned his head to see an officer moving black troops into a supporting position to the rear of the ranks facing the charging head of the buffalo.

"Ammunition," a voice bellowed over the din of the rifles. Men scuttled forward carrying containers of bullets. Jon walked behind the ranks, his pistol in hand, observing the marksmanship of his men. They were good, as cool as could be, firing and loading with a competency that was building a low mound of black bodies all along their front.

"Ammunition," bellowed a sergeant. Captain Bell was standing near Jon.

"Where are the bloody ammo bearers?" Bell shouted.

Zulu warriors vaulted over their piles of dead, and now, before the withering fire of the company stopped the bravest of them, they were near enough for Jon to see that they wore shell or teeth necklaces and odd little crownlike circlets atop their heads. He could see the contorted, shouting mouths, the gleaming white teeth. An *assegai* flew, and just to his front a man shouted in surprised agony and crumpled, the wicked spear buried deep in his stomach. Jon raised his pistol, fired through the gap in the line, and saw a Zulu warrior fall. It occurred to him vaguely that he had actually killed a man.

"Where's the bleedin' ammo?" a sergeant bellowed.

The ammunition had not been wasted. By Jon's judgment, a

23

surprisingly large ratio of hits had been made. There were simply too many Zulus, Zulus by the thousands. How many had Harry Ryan said? Forty thousand? Twenty *impis*? It seemed to Jon that a full half of that number were pouring toward his company. He jumped when Captain Bell yelled in his ear.

"Fisher, to the rear! See what's holding up the bloody ammunition."

He ran through what seemed to be chaos but what was, actually, well-coordinated activity. Companies of men, black and white, were being moved to more advantageous firing positions. He caught a glimpse of Colonel Durnford on his fine horse, a pistol in hand. Behind him the head of the buffalo had swarmed through the intense fire to close on the red ranks, and he heard an agonized scream as a man died. Powder smoke obscured the scene. He ran full tilt into a bellowing sergeant and didn't stop to apologize as the man cursed and went on his way. From a distance a bugler blew a call that was carried away in the tumult. He ran past a surgeon's wagon. Wounded men were lying on the ground. His foot splashed into a puddle of blood, and he regained his balance to run on.

When he reached the ammunition wagons he skidded to a halt. A line of angry, cursing men was yelling to the quartermaster sergeant on the wagon to hurry, to forget the bleedin' formality and toss down a box of ammo.

"This ammunition is crown property," the quartermaster sergeant yelled back, as Jon looked on incredulously. "Only those authorized to draw ammunition will receive ammunition."

Angry men closed in on the wagon. Jon saw, at a distance of perhaps a hundred yards, some of the Australian sutlers' vehicles, recognized one as an ammunition wagon, and ran toward it. He would save time that way, instead of trying to fight his way to the quartermaster wagon through the crowd.

In the brief time it took for him to run the distance, the firing behind him had grown sporadic. He turned his head for a quick look and couldn't believe his eyes. Zulus had overrun the forward positions and were pouring into the square. He ran on and reached the wagon to see that Harry Ryan was on the driver's seat, urging the team of oxen into motion.

"Harry!" he yelled.

24

Ryan pulled back on the reins.

"Ammunition," Jon gasped.

"Surely the quartermasters can't be out," Ryan said.

"Ammunition, damn you," Jon yelled, ripping at the canvas flap at the rear of the wagon. Andy Melgund appeared at his side and helped him open the flap. The ammunition was packed for transport in sturdy boxes, each with a tightly fastened lid reinforced by steel bands. Jon half ripped off one of his fingernails as he struggled to open a crate.

"You're a bit late," Harry Ryan called back from his seat.

"Give me a hand," Jon said. "Help me carry—"

"Look behind you, man," Melgund said.

"So much for our noble black allies," Ryan said.

A section of the square held by native troops had disintegrated. The Zulus were pouring in, using their short thrusting spears with deadly effectiveness. Jon looked quickly toward the position of his company and, to his despair, saw that only a few rifles were firing. They were out of ammunition. Bayonets parried *assegais* as the fight became hand to hand.

"Hurry, man," Jon shouted, still wrestling to open a crate of ammunition.

The wave of black death rolled past the disintegrating ranks of British, and the entire encampment was a melee of struggling men. Dust and gun smoke obscured Jon's vision.

"It is time, Lieutenant, that we exercised the better part of valour and got the hell out of here," Harry Ryan said.

"How can you think of saving your precious merchandise at a time like this?" Jon yelled in desperation.

"Actually, I'm thinking more of saving my precious skin," Ryan called back. "It happens that we can move faster and further by wagon than by foot. Are you coming?"

"I have to get back," Jon said, seizing a heavy crate and starting to stagger off. Melgund pushed the crate off Jon's shoulder. It smashed to the ground intact.

"Be sensible, man," Ryan called. "Chelmsford did this. It's not your doing. Chelmsford did it when he split his forces in the face of a forty-thousand-man army."

"My company—" Jon was frantic.

"They're dead, or dying," Melgund said. "There'll be another chance for you to face old Cetshwayo."

Jon bent and tried to pick up the crate of ammunition. The cries of dying men rang in his ears. The shouts of Zulu triumph were bitter, harsh music. He didn't see Melgund bring his fist up from the height of his thigh, didn't even feel the impact as the fist contacted his chin. He felt only a ringing sensation and then blackness.

There was a muted rumbling in his ears. He tried to move and his head pounded. He opened one eye. He was being bounced around atop a layer of ammunition crates inside a wagon. He clasped his aching head and jaw and crawled forward. The wagon was moving over rough ground, the team of a half dozen yoked oxen trotting heavily. Harry Ryan and Andy Melgund were on the driver's seat, Melgund clutching a rifle.

"Welcome back, old boy," Ryan said.

"If you have a slight headache," Melgund said, "consider yourself fortunate to have a head to ache."

"Where are we?" Jon asked.

"Three hours on the way to the Buffalo River," Ryan said, "where, God willing, there'll be a few redcoats to hold back the Zulu who are, quite surely, following our tracks."

"My men—"

"Jon," Melgund said, 'they're gone."

"All of them, my God?"

"All of them. We had one last look back from the top of a rise. The Zulu were looting. They'll have quite a few rifles next time you meet them."

"All of them?" Jon repeated the question hollowly, unable to believe the answer.

"There they are," Melgund said. He was standing up, looking back over the covered top. "Just coming over that ridge. At least a hundred and moving fast."

"I'd trade the whole dozen of these damn cows for one fast horse," Ryan said.

"Three fast horses, if you please," Melgund returned. "Perhaps, if you ask these cows sweetly, they'll actually break into a run."

"Not likely," Ryan said.

"If my memory serves me correctly," Melgund said, "the river is

26

just beyond that next rise. Perhaps if we run for it?"

"A Zulu warrior can run fifty miles in a day and fight an engagement at the end of the run," Ryan said, tight-lipped.

Melgund had no reply.

"The quartermaster wouldn't release ammunition," Jon said, remembering.

"They'll send a salvage team to Isandhlwana to pick up the brass casings," Ryan said. "And someone will be held to account for every round, for every casing."

"They could have held," Jon said. "They could have held if they'd had ammunition."

"Cetshwayo didn't commit his main forces," Ryan said. "The loins of the buffalo, the main body, was not even in action. If Chelmsford hadn't split his forces, perhaps his entire thirteen thousand could have held—if the natives hadn't broken as they did back there."

"There it is!" Melgund said, as the wagon breasted the ridge and the waters of the Buffalo River became visible down the slope.

"Bloody hell," Ryan said. "Cetshwayo split his forces as well."

Across the river, on the far side of the drift, a stockaded house was being besieged by a horde of Zulu warriors. An outbuilding was burning. The sound of scattered gunfire came to their ears.

"We can get across the drift and sneak past them," Melgund said.

"Sneak? With a dozen oxen and a wagon with squeaking wheels?"

"It's something to talk about," Melgund said.

"There!" Jon pointed.

A small force of horsemen was riding hard up the far bank of the Buffalo. As they came near the stockaded buildings, their guns began to make white puffs, and the sound of the concussions came a second or so later.

"No worries, mate," Ryan said. "Her Majesty's brave blue-jackets have come to our rescue. Looks like some of the naval brigade."

The heavily laden wagon was bounding down the rough track to the river. "That lot to our rear is gaining," Melgund said.

"Could you just clamber back in the wagon and pot a few of them?" Ryan asked.

27

"I'm not much of a shot." Melgund grabbed a rifle from behind the seat. "But I'll try."

"Here—let me." Jon took the rifle and quickly crawled back. He opened the rear flap. The Zulus were running smoothly and seemingly tirelessly, overtaking the wagon. He targeted the leader, a tall, well-muscled warrior, and saw the man's life go out of him in an instant as he ran nose-on into a bullet. He dropped four more in short order, reloading smoothly and quickly, and then the oxen were splashing into the shallow drift. The pursuers fell back out of range of his rifle. The wagon splashed through the water, but as the oxen struggled up the far bank, a rear wheel dropped into a rocky hole with a jar. Jon heard a crack of splintering wood as spokes gave way. He had to catch himself to keep from falling against the canvas side of the wagon.

"Perhaps we can talk Her Majesty's lads out of some horses," Ryan was saying as Jon jumped out of the rear of the wagon and checked to be sure the Zulus were not crossing. He walked through the last few feet of shallow water to the bank.

"Speaking of which," Melgund said, as horsemen pounded toward them from the direction of the smoking stockade.

"Ahoy, there!" Ryan called out, then turned to his friend. "Limejuicers it is."

A surprisingly neat-looking naval officer wearing the insignia of an ensign pulled his horse up at the head of the panting team of oxen. "Have you come from Lord Chelmsford?" he asked, with a distinctive Scottish accent.

"By now Lord Chelmsford is probably dead," Ryan said, "along with those he sacrificed at Isandhlwana."

"What's that?" the young ensign demanded.

"If it's all the same to you, young sir," Ryan said, "I'll answer your questions later." He nodded toward the far side of the river. Zulu warriors were streaming into the shallows in silence, shields hiding all but their faces, *assegais* at the ready.

The young ensign began to shout orders. His force dismounted and took firing positions. Soon the Buffalo River was running red, as Zulu warriors fell before the expert marksmanship of the naval detachment. Jon positioned himself with a supply of ammunition close at hand and fired from a kneeling position. The Zulus in the river were being reinforced by others who had come leaping down

28

the slope. They were dying by the dozen in the shallow water, but their numbers were being continuously replenished.

"Admiral," Harry Ryan said, tapping the young ensign on the shoulder, "perhaps we might consider making a run for it. Three of your horses could carry double."

"There's only one problem with that approach," the ensign replied. "When we rode in here we were being chased by, I'd say, roughly three hundred of those fellows."

"And now they're between us and the east?" Ryan asked.

"I'd say not more than ten minutes behind us."

"Not any longer, sir," a sailor said, pointing.

From the sparse greenery that bordered the river a line of Zulu warriors burst forth in silence, running toward the group on the riverbank. A shout came from the warriors who were still trying to ford the river.

"Alternate men, reverse your field of fire," the ensign ordered.

Half the sailors turned and began to fire on the Zulu force that had them trapped now, on the river's bank. The rifle fire took a toll, but the Zulus came on. Half a dozen of them reached the group, *assegais* protruding from behind the shields. Without orders the sailors leaped to meet the attack with bayonets. The young ensign was in the lead, wielding a cutlass with practised skill and a great deal of power. Already three Zulu warriors lay dead from the ensign's curved blade, but a half dozen others were closing on him as Jon raised his rifle, ignoring the Zulus approaching from across the water, and lowered the odds against the ensign.

"Well, gentlemen, we're in for it," Ryan said. There was no time left to reload. Jon emptied his service revolver, then threw it down and leaped to his feet, bayonet outthrust, to sneak the cold steel past a shield and feel it enter human flesh. He jerked the weapon back just in time to parry an *assegai* thrust. At his side Andy Melgund grunted, as if in effort, and out of the corner of his eyes Jon saw him fall, saw blood springing up from a gaping wound to the stomach. With a wild swing of his rifle butt he killed the *assegai*-wielding warrior.

The young ensign was backing toward Jon. They were surrounded by Zulus. They turned back to back, the ensign with his cutlass, Jon with his bayoneted rifle. At least five of the sailors and

29

Melgund were down. Harry Ryan had formed a small square with the remaining sailors.

"Who is it I am about to die with?" Jon asked, as he jerked his bayonet from a Zulu's chest.

"Samuel Gordon, at your service, sir," the ensign said.

"Pleasure, Mr. Gordon," Jon said. He settled into the grim reality of taking as many Zulus as possible with him. He had never liked the bayonet; he thought it was a fiendish weapon, knew in his heart that it was not all that different from a Zulu *assegai*, and his flesh crawled at the thought of the penetration of that pointed steel blade into his own body. His vision was clouded with effort and with the sweat that ran into his eyes. An *assegai* bounced off his helmet and sent it flying, leaving him bareheaded. He had a brief impression of sun, glaring, hot, pitiless. He thrust and then slashed, the blade of his bayonet opening the throat of a Zulu with a handsome, young face. Blood spurted onto the front of his coat, a different shade of red. He knew that he was near death, and he began to imagine that he heard the guns of his company, the reassuring, deadly, sharp reports of rifles. A powerful Zulu in full manhood threw himself toward him, ran head on into the bayonet, and the blade stuck, embedded in bone. He tugged, put his foot on the fallen man's ribs and kicked. He was helpless, weaponless. He could hear the rifle fire, closer now, and looked up to see the remaining Zulus running for the river as a full company of Natal Light Horse, a Boer unit, came riding down the riverbank spreading swift death before them.

Andy Melgund was dead. Harry Ryan had a deep *assegai* slash across his chest. Jon removed his jacket, which was soaked with Zulu blood, and threw it in the river. It floated for a long time as he watched it drift away.

Benjamin Disraeli, first minister of Her Majesty's cabinet, stood before the Parliament, his head bowed. The news from Natal Colony had been the last straw to topple his uneasy government.

"Who are these Zulus?" he asked, his usually vibrant voice muted so that the back benchers had difficulty in hearing him. "Who are these remarkable people who convert our bishops and who, on this day, have put an end to a great dynasty?"

CHAPTER I

The De Hartog house sat on a slight eminence overlooking a remarkably crumpled, folded valley on the outskirts of Pietermaritzburg. It was an African house, low, rambling, red-roofed with Mediterranean tile that had come all the way around the Cape of Good Hope in the hold of a sailing ship. There were sheltered courtyards, wide, airy verandas roofed against the burning African sun, and a profusion of flowering plants. Jon Fisher sat in a comfortable wicker chair on a veranda overlooking a formal garden that was filled to bursting with huge red blossoms so fleshy that their impact was almost sensual.

Jon lifted his left leg. At the end of the fighting on the banks of the Buffalo River he had thought first of the others, of Harry Ryan's deep *assegai* slash across the chest, of the dead Andy Melgund, and of the wounded sailors. It was not until a young Boer officer, tall, blond, and brusque in manner, had inquired as to his condition that he realized he, too, had been wounded, not once but twice. A blade had pierced his thigh a few inches above the knee, and another had slashed across the back of his left shoulder. Both wounds were healing well, without infection.

At the sound of footsteps he looked up and saw the young Boer officer, dressed in civilian clothing now, come around the corner bearing a tray on which sat a bottle of English gin and a pitcher of water.

"The sun is a healer," said Dirk De Hartog.

"The peace and beauty of the setting are also restful," Jon said.

Dirk put the tray on a table, poured, squeezed lemon juice, and added water. "But this," he said, "is the finest medicine of all."

"A Boer drinking English gin."

"To the English," Dirk said, drinking, "and to the beverage that has made possible the conquest of all far and tropical places."

31

The bite of the gin, tempered by water and lemon juice, was a fine sensation. Jon said, "Ah."

"If British generals were as excellent as their gin—"

"Are you speaking of anyone I know?" John asked with a pained smile.

"Now he is a hero of the realm," Dirk said. "Now he has won, and I quote, a brilliant victory."

"You will tell me, I assume, in your own hard-headed Dutch time," Jon said.

"He cornered old Cetshwayo at Ulundi, with over four thousand rifles *and* artillery."

"Indeed brilliant," Jon said. "Cannon against *assegai*." He shrugged. "Not that I bleed for Cetshwayo and the Zulu."

"I should think not, having bled literally because of them."

Jon's face sobered. "Look here, De Hartog," he said. "I haven't yet found the words to thank you for arriving as you did in the nick of time, and for hauling my bloody carcass all this way to allow me to heal in such pleasant company and surroundings."

Dirk waved one hand casually, and a new voice spoke. "You can at least have the grace to acknowledge such a pretty speech of thanks." It was Dirk's sister, Anna De Hartog. Neither man had noticed her quiet approach.

Dirk grinned. "What with the shortage of eligible young gentlemen around here, Anna would never have forgiven me if I hadn't brought you here."

Anna blushed. She was a tall girl, her fair hair piled atop her well-formed head, eyes the blue of the African sky. In spite of coming from a Voortrekker family, she spoke English well, and her small-boned body showed signs of good breeding. "Hush, you," she said, taking the chair beside Jon and, her cheeks still flushed, favouring him with a smile.

"To my lovely nurse," Jon said, lifting his glass. "This toast, and my undying gratitude."

"She practised her healing arts on cattle and goats," Dirk said.

Jan De Hartog, father of the two handsome people, had come to Natal with Andries Pretorius to aid in avenging the massacre of Piet Retief and sixty settlers attempting to establish a Boer settlement in Zululand. Polite and discreet questioning on Jon's part had revealed little about the old man, other than a hint that his departure from his native lowlands in western Europe had not been totally voluntary. Obviously, De Hartog had done well since his arrival in the Natal colony in 1838. The family's land extended over and beyond the convoluted valley that the great house overlooked, and Dirk had dropped hints of business activity other than farming. Both the De Hartog children had attended English-run schools—unusual for Boers—and Jon was certain it wasn't because of their father's love of the British.

Jon's memories of his first days in the De Hartog house were hazy. The journey from the Buffalo River had been swift and difficult for a wounded man, and both he and Harry Ryan had travelled in a haze of fever and pain. His first memories were of the serene and blemishless face of Anna, of those cobalt blue eyes, her naturally glowing cheeks, and her smile.

"I'm pleased, if what he says is true"—Jon glanced at Anna—"that a British officer responds to the same treatment given a cow or a goat."

"My brother exerts himself to be the *enfant terrible*," Anna said. "Sometimes with great success."

Dirk mixed two more drinks, lifted an eyebrow in question to his sister, and was given a positive shake of her head.

"Your friend has gone into the town," Anna said. "He is not the ideal invalid."

"Harry is the restless type," Jon said.

"An odd man, at best." Dirk handed one of the drinks to his sister and took the other for himself. Jon was still on his first. "Talks up a storm and says nothing."

"He lost a man who was as close as a brother at Rorke's Drift," Jon said. "Andy Melgund and Harry were both orphans taken in by an Australian. Harry's originally from New Zealand. His family was killed by the Maoris."

"How terrible," Anna said.

"I'd say Ryan has done well here in Africa," Dirk said.

Jon nodded his head in agreement. "He seems to have a natural talent for business."

"Mules, oxen, food, ammunition," Dirk said. "Profitable sales to the British army."

"It is a service that someone must perform," Anna defended weakly. "He seems very well educated."

33

"He seems quite young to have experienced all that he talks about," Dirk said. "A sailor, as well? He said that he has been first mate on a clipper ship."

"For what it's worth, I owe my life to Ryan and Melgund," Jon said. He was not willing to tell the De Hartogs the precise circumstances, for growing in him was a melancholy realization that, for all practical purposes, his military career was over. He had left his company in the face of the enemy, and he had only his word and that of Harry Ryan to attest to the circumstances. But it was not the possibility of being called coward by others that occupied his thoughts. Rather it was a sense of gloomy guilt, for he felt that he should be dead alongside Captain Bell and his men. A good officer, he felt, would have found a way to get ammunition to the company in time. He had failed. There would be no distinction for him, no doors opening as the result of his performance at Isandhlwana.

"I shall leave you to the company of your nurse," Dirk said, finishing his gin.

Anna sat in silence for a few moments after he had left, then glanced at Jon through thick, dark lashes. "I have a feeling that you'll be going soon."

"Yes. I must."

"They're re-forming your unit, raising recruits in England."

"Yes."

"Will you go back to it?"

He sighed. The issue had to be faced sometime. "I've been thinking of going home."

Anna's face, in spite of an attempt at control, betrayed her dismay. "To Australia?"

"I haven't seen my mother in some years."

"Jon, you could not have stopped what happened at Isandhlwana," she said.

So quickly did her words stab to the core of his guilt that he felt a flash of anger. He looked away, saw Dirk striding toward the stables.

"Mr. Ryan told me that you had no choice, that the position was already overrun, that all the soldiers were either dead or dying and that even then they had to render you unconscious."

Jon did not want to talk about it. "Harry has asked me to

34

become his partner in certain trading ventures," he said.

Anna stood quickly. He leaped to his feet and stood facing her. He had not failed to notice that she had become fond of him. "Anna," he said, "I have to go."

"Go, then!" she flared. "Quickly." She swept her skirts in a circle as she turned and half ran down the veranda to disappear into a doorway. Jon stood, arms hanging loosely at his sides. He owed her, and Dirk, more than that, but for all his gratitude, he was not ready to speak seriously to a woman, not even a woman as lovely as Anna De Hartog. There was a restlessness in him that would never be confined to a landholding in Southeast Africa, something that Dirk had assured him could be arranged. Like Harry Ryan, there was too much in his past that could not be resolved. Ryan had his nightmare of having seen his family butchered by Maoris; Jon had his own cross, the memory of standing there, helpless, while his men and his fellow officers died. Then there was his mother. He knew she had never been truly happy, married to Marcus Fisher. Perhaps, having failed his men, Jon could redeem himself by bringing some joy and comfort to his mother.

He was still awake when Harry Ryan returned from Pieter-maritzburg. He heard Ryan come into the room next to his, stumble over something, stifle an oath. Then there was a knock on the connecting door.

"Are you awake?" Ryan asked.

"I am now," Jon said.

For the late hour, Ryan looked jaunty, his eyes speaking of the consumption of too much alcohol. He grinned as he sat on the foot of Jon's bed. He had never shown his grief over the death of Andy Melgund, except, perhaps, in a heavier than usual dedication to drink, and in moments of black moodiness. Now he was cheerful.

"I dined with some of the stalwart merchants of this fair city," Harry said. "The talk was intriguing. I think there is a definite possibility of profitable trade here."

Harry seemed to be obsessed with making money, with making a mark for himself as a merchant trader. Yet he was recklessly generous with whatever cash he had on hand, gambled often, had spent many evenings drinking with common soldiers and sailors in the pubs of Pietermaritzburg.

35

"Jon, my lad, there's a fine ship sailing tomorrow, direct to Sydney, in God's own country. Straight across the bloody Indian Ocean and home."

Jon didn't answer immediately.

"You are coming? You have written that letter resigning your commission?"

"I have not written the letter," Jon said, somewhat testily.

"Perhaps, if you're not feeling up to it, you could dictate it to your lovely nurse." Harry's smile held a suggestion.

"I'm fully capable," Jon said, controlling his temper; it was just Harry's way. Early on Harry had done his best to arouse Anna De Hartog's interest, had been always making flirtatious advances that were coolly and politely rejected.

"Then do it, man. The world awaits," Harry said breezily.

Jon slept little that night. Feeling still tired when he awoke, he had difficulty keeping up a conversation at breakfast with the De Hartog family and let Harry do most of the talking.

Anna, it was clear, sensed that a decision had been made. After the meal she singled him out, and he followed her to the veranda. It was another perfect, cloudless day, although there would be heat later.

"When is it to be?" Anna asked, not looking at him.

'This afternoon. Harry has arranged passage for us on a merchant ship."

"So soon," she said, still not looking at him. He waited. When she turned to face him, her deep, blue eyes were moist. "I would be interested in hearing of your travels, your experiences."

"Yes, I'll write."

She jerked her eyes away and gave him her trim, feminine back.

"It's so lovely here," he said.

"But not for you."

"Not now, Anna."

"So, you come into my life, and you go out of it."

There was nothing more for him to say. He touched her lightly on the shoulder and went to find Harry, who was saying good-bye to Dirk. Dirk's handshake was firm. "Take care," he said.

"And you," Jon told him. "I'll never forget what you've done for me."

36

The ship was an old East Indiaman, thick of hull, sailing out the last of her useful days with a sturdy dependability. The cabins were comfortable, as ship's cabins go, and the weather favourable. Harry and Jon were the only paying passengers, and Harry soon struck up acquaintances with members of the ship's company, then spent his time playing brag for whatever stakes the low-paid sailors wanted to risk. There were long days and nights of uneventful sailing, days and nights of storm, long talks as they stood at the rail watching the prow cut through the swells of the Indian Ocean. Jon had accepted Harry's invitation to become a business partner, and he was an avid listener as Harry related the opportunities of trade between Australia and New Zealand and Hong Kong, Singapore, Samoa, and countless other lands and ports. Harry promised to teach Jon everything he needed to know and assured him that his fortune was made if only he could come up with some capital to invest with Claus Van Buren and his sons, owners of the trading company with which Harry was associated.

Apparently—Jon didn't really doubt anything Harry told him, because Harry was his friend—Harry had, before becoming a sutler following Lord Chelmsford's army in Natal, worked as first officer and supercargo for the Van Buren firm, sailing to the Asian mainland and to the islands of the southwestern Pacific.

That Harry was a knowledgeable officer was attested to when the captain of the ship began to talk with him as an equal and, on occasion, inquire as to his opinion about the running of the ship. Indeed, Harry seemed at home on the sea, cheerful, active, and in his element.

"Why did you give up being a ship's officer?" Jon asked him one day when the ship had travelled two-thirds of the distance to Australia.

"Simple," Harry said. "There is no real wealth to be had being a sailor. Success comes to the traders, to the financiers. You'll learn that quickly, my boy. And I'll warrant that your earnings will be much more than your pay as a lieutenant in Her Majesty's army."

Landfall engendered emotions in Jon that he had not suspected. There was a bittersweet tang to being home, for home meant that he would, sooner or later, see his stepfather and his mother. But the Australian air had a comfortable feel, the sun a kind warmth, almost as if they were a part of Jon's being. He had come home,

37

and it was high time. He wanted to see his mother as quickly as possible, but Harry had other plans.

"It's important for you to meet the right people," Harry said, upon their stepping ashore in Sydney.

"These are the right people?" Jon asked as Harry led him into a seaman's pub near the waterfront—that being their first stop after depositing their bags at a clean but rather crude hostelry.

"First things first," Harry said. And, within a few hours, Jon knew something about his new friend that gave him pause, for Harry had disappeared with a young woman, winking at Jon on the way out, leaving him to find his way back to the hotel by himself. He was awakened when Harry returned late, the fumes of rum strong about him. As Jon lay awake, distinctly annoyed, he was beginning to have second thoughts about his business partner. Strong drink and women had been the ruination of many a good man, and Jon had no taste for sitting around pubs with the dregs of the waterfront, while his friend amused himself with women obviously of low virtue. However, with the morning, Harry was a different man. Their best clothes had been freshened and pressed by a maid, and, dressed in morning wear, Harry looked quite respectable.

He guided Jon to a respectable teahouse, a dim, pleasantly scented, panelled room with neatly linened tables. A rosy-faced middle-aged woman showed them to a table, produced tea with almost magical speed, and suggested a hearty Australian breakfast.

"We will be joined by a young lady," Harry said, to Jon's surprise. "Perhaps we'll order then."

They did not have long to wait. The young lady swept through the door, a smile on her face, heading directly toward their table. Her thick, auburn hair was winged over her forehead and hung in curls at the rear, with a single curl at each temple. She wore white, and wore it very well, so well that Jon felt his throat constrict in reaction to her beauty as he leaped to his feet. Her face was framed by her sun hat and a high, tight, lace collar extending upward from a frilled blouse.

"Harry, it's so good to see you," she cried, throwing herself into Harry's arms.

Jon was shocked. This one was obviously a lady of quality. But

38

then he noted quickly that the embrace was more sisterly than passionate, that the young woman offered Harry only her cheek for a quick peck before seizing his hands and standing back to examine him. "You're looking well," she said. "Africa agreed with you."

"I liked Africa so well I brought back a token." Harry beamed, indicating Jon. "Miss Jessica Broome, I'd like you to meet Jon Fisher, late of Her Majesty's red-coated service."

"My pleasure," Jon said, making a slight bow.

"Actually, Jon's an Australian," Harry went on. "He just got lost in England and in the army for a while before he came to his senses."

Jessica removed her hat and took a seat. The hostess hovered near, placing a cup in front of Jessica almost immediately, and as she allowed that she was, in fact, ravenous, the three of them accepted the hostess's suggestions and glutted themselves on hot rolls, poached eggs, golden-fresh butter and a wonderful orange marmalade.

Gradually, Jon began to piece together the relationship between Jessica Broome and Harry Ryan. He felt left out, for he found himself, at the breakfast, as well as later, in the midst of what he could describe only as an extended old-boy network, among people who had known one another for decades, and who seemed to know everyone and everything that had happened since the first convict settlements had been made at Botany Bay.

By the time he attended a memorial service for Andy Melgund in a little chapel near the Elizabeth Bay home of Jessica's father, Commodore Red Broome, he had the various relationships more or less pieced together. Both Harry and Andy Melgund had spent part of their youth with the Broomes; thus, in effect, Harry and Jessica Broome had grown up together. Harry and Andy had been adopted by William De Lancey, the brother of Red Broome's wife, Magdalen.

Jon, of course, had heard of both William De Lancey and Commodore Red Broome. He had heard his stepfather speak disparagingly of both men, and, knowing Marcus Fisher as he did, he was thus prepared to like anyone who was disliked by him. Broome, his red hair laced with grey, cut an impressive figure, dignified, quiet, and confident. He took it on himself to welcome the newcomer after the memorial service and insisted that Jon join Harry and the family for dinner. It was an Australian dinner, with a generously laden table and a comfortable lack of formality. Jon found himself seated between Magdalen Broome and another man of whom he had heard, the commodore's bearded brother, the journalist Johnny Broome.

"Our Harry tells me you were with the Twenty-Fourth at Isandhlwana," Johnny said.

"I was there," Jon admitted.

"Terrible disaster." Johnny shook his head ruefully. "I wonder why English generals come in only two varieties, being either of genius calibre or complete nincompoops."

"That's an interesting question," Jon said noncommittally.

"And you're going to go venturing with Harry?" Johnny asked.

"Yes, sir."

"Before you do go off wandering around the world," Johnny went on, "I'd consider it a great favour if you'd allow me an hour or so of your time to talk about Isandhlwana. It's old news, of course, and the Zulus have been pretty well tamed, but I think my readers would enjoy getting another view of what some have called the worst defeat for British arms in colonial history."

Jon felt suddenly cold. the last thing he wanted to do was talk about Isandhlwana. He looked around, seeking a good excuse, saw that Harry was seated next to Jessica, engaging her in animated conversation, and took time to admire the mature beauty of Kitty Broome, Johnny's wife.

"I note a certain amount of hesitation," Johnny said.

"It's just that I'm not sure there'll be time," Jon said.

"Johnny, do leave the gentleman in peace," Magdalen said, leaning forward. "It must have been a horrid experience. I don't blame him for not wanting to talk about it. Besides, Harry's all too willing to give his account of the action."

Johnny laughed. "I have already been given the idea, by our Harry, that he did his best to warn Lord Chelmsford of the dangers."

The conversation moved to safer ground, thanks to Magdalen's husband, who alluded to one of the more ticklish issues of Australian politics. "I understand that your home is in Victoria, Lieutenant Fisher."

"That's right, sir," Jon said.

"What are your views on the question of land rights for newcomers?" Red asked.

"Sir, I've been out of the country for so long I'm afraid I'm not qualified to speak on Australian issues."

"The lad's cut out to be a diplomat," Harry put in, laughing. "It's the same old battle, isn't it? Too much of the land is owned by ranchers for grazing, or under licence by squatters."

"You make it sound so trivial," Jessica said. "It's a serious question. If the country is ever to grow and become totally self-sufficient, we've got to get land into the hands of small farmers."

"Excuse my ignorance," Jon said, 'but wasn't something done about land reform back in the fifties?"

"Not enough," Johnny Broome said. "Some progress was made with the Grant Act of 1865. It opened up some two hundred thousand acres for cultivation, but there are hordes of landless people, people who deserve land. More is needed, but the graziers and the squatters want firmer title, not to sell. In cases where there *are* land sales, there are abuses. The squatters peacock the land, and—"

"I beg your pardon?" Jon interrupted.

"They hang on to the choice land—the runs, water holes, creeks, so that what is offered for sale is totally useless. Or they circumvent the law by dummying." Johnny raised his hand to stop Jon's question. "Dummy owners. They'll buy land in the name of every member of the family, friends, even fictitious persons."

"I think," Jon said, "that Harry was right. It's the same old question. I know that my stepfather was quite agitated about the question of land reform before I left to enter Sandhurst."

The word *stepfather* seemed to trigger a reaction in Magdalen Broome's memory, for Jon saw her pale visibly. "Fisher," she said to herself, under her breath. "Lieutenant Fisher, would your stepfather happen to be Marcus Fisher, your mother the former Caroline Forsyth?"

"Yes," Jon said. "Do you know them?"

A momentary coldness froze Magdalen's face, then her smile was back. Red Broome had exchanged a quick glance with his brother, Jon noticed. It was, indeed, a small world, a small country, and Jon suddenly realized that he should have expected

41

such a reaction. Surely Marcus Fisher's reputation extended beyond Victoria; he had lived a short time in Sydney, Jon now recalled, and colonial society was anything but close-mouthed. If those at the table knew anything, however, they kept it to themselves, for Red again deftly changed the subject, and a short time later Magdalen rose and the dinner party divided, the women going off to the withdrawing room, the men settling down to port and cigars. Jon rose and stationed himself at a window over-looking the harbour. Across the room, with little coaxing, Harry was telling Johnny Broome his version of the events at Isand-hlwana, and his account, Jon was relieved to observe, seemed to reassure the listeners that Jon had indeed been following orders when he left the field in search of ammunition.

A short time after the women had rejoined them—Jessica and Kitty had disappeared—Harry rose and made as if to leave. Jon got to his feet and expressed his appreciation to his host for a fine meal, then repeated his thanks to Magdalen Broome. Harry walked beside him to the front veranda and patted him on the shoulder. "Do you mind going back to the hotel alone? I'm going to try to have a word with Jessica."

"Not at all," Jon said, although in truth he was somewhat annoyed at what seemed a ploy by his friend to get rid of him.

Harry found Jessica with Kitty Broome in the drawing room. He stood just inside the door, hands locked behind him, teetering forward and back on his toes while the women talked animatedly. When Kitty looked up, she smiled and said, "I think there's something on your mind, Harry."

"No," he said. "It's been a fine evening. A pleasure seeing all of you again."

"Well, I think it's time I made myself available for leaving," Kitty said. "I'm sure that Johnny's ready to go."

Alone with Jessica, Harry was at first reticent and unsure of himself, an unusual condition for him around a female. It was Jessica who suggested that they walk in the garden. He felt quick relief and steered her through the house to the back veranda. There he stopped. The moon was full, lighting the well-tended gardens with a soft glow.

"I've had a lot of time to think while I've been away," he said. "I hope you won't be offended, Jess, if I tell you that you were the subject of most of my thoughts."

Jessica smiled and said lightly. "Even last night, when you were in a seaman's bar in the Rocks?"

Harry twisted his mouth ruefully. "I keep forgetting what a small town this is." He faced her, undeterred. "It was a long voyage home, Jess, and we were quite dry."

Jessica's voice was serious. "People will talk, Harry. You should know that. It's hardly my place to give you advice—"

"I am interested in anything you have to say."

"You know, Harry, that you and Andy have always been very dear to the family."

"I'm grateful for that. No one could have been kinder than you and your family."

"My father, and Uncle Johnny as well, think that you have a great future."

"I have plans, Jess. I do. And if I am not speaking prematurely, you have a place in those plans."

She was silent for a long moment. "Please don't say anything that we'll both regret." She put her hand on his arm. "You've been like a brother to me."

He shook his head. "And if you have come to mean more to me than a sister?"

"Harry, please."

"Jess, I'm sorry. But you were with me every day and night. At sea. In Africa. I won't ask you to make any serious decision at this moment, but I must ask you to be aware of the fact that for some time now I have looked on you as a beautiful woman, not as the girl who was once like my sister. Consider that. See if you can see me in a different light as well. Will you do that?"

"I will consider it," she said.

"I will not push you. And to prove it, as an old friend, in a sisterly way, would you do me the kindness of riding out with me tomorrow, and then having lunch with me?"

"I'd like that," she said.

Magdalen, consumed with feminine curiosity, had found the first opportunity to seek out her husband after they had both said good night to Johnny and Kitty. She brought Red a nightcap, fine

43

French brandy worth almost its weight in gold after having been transported halfway around the world, and took a chair opposite him in the study.

"I thought that boy looked familiar," she said.

"Yes," Red answered, staring at the empty fireplace. "I should have picked up on it sooner myself. The name, Fisher."

"But his looks were the giveaway," Magdalen said. "The eyes, especially. When I looked into them I was looking into the face of Adam Shannon himself."

"He has his mother's hair and nose, however," Red said. Rousing himself from his thoughts, he took a sip of the brandy. "He gives me the impression that he's not too fond of his stepfather."

"I wonder if he knows," Magdalen said. "I wonder if he knows that Colonel Forsyth is not his father?"

Red shrugged. "I imagine that Caroline would have been reluctant to admit to her only son that she had taken up with a handsome young officer while married to her first husband. If anyone has told him, I'd imagine it would be Marcus Fisher. It would be like him to throw it up to the boy that he was conceived in an adulterous love affair."

"Surely not even Fisher would stoop so low," Magdalen said.

"With a man like Fisher, one never knows."

"Ah, our poor country!" Magdalen rose and came to kneel beside her husband's chair, putting an arm around his broad shoulders. "With men like Fisher holding such wealth and power, it's a wonder we've come as far as we have."

Red squeezed her hand reassuringly. "And I daresay we'll survive Marcus Fisher as well," he said. "And so will the boy, if I'm any judge of character."

CHAPTER II

As a port of call for the Royal Navy and the ever-growing merchant fleet sailing under the maritime version of the Union Jack affectionately known as the red duster, Port Jackson Harbour was not often empty of the tall spars of the great ships. Harbour watchers, Red Broome among them, could identify individual ships by their rigging and hull shape and could, when a newcomer arrived, associate her with her point of departure—England, the China coast, the islands. When Red spotted the distinctive lines of a topsail schooner that traded between New Zealand and Sydney, he didn't give the vessel a second thought until a familiar figure came striding up the walkway to the front veranda. Red was in the midst of enjoying a well-earned leave at home with his family, and it was not unusual, when he was in residence, to have unannounced callers. The Broome family was well known in the young country, and there were not a few men who, before engaging in any activity that might run head-on into governmental interference, sought out the advice of Red Broome. Red, as a naval officer, tried to stay as far removed from politics as possible, but was—Magdalen kept reminding him so often that he had to admit it with some reluctance—not without knowledge and influence.

This caller caused Red to spring from his chair with a vigour denying his mature years. He met the visitor on the steps, hand outstretched. "Adam," he called out. "What an unexpected delight!"

Colonel Adam Shannon of Her Majesty's Colonial New Zealand Militia was dressed in the dark blue tunic of a senior officer. Over his wide shoulders was slung a grey cape with a black fur collar. His white helmet gleamed with the gold of his rank.

Adam's smile became even broader when Magdalen Broome swept her skirts across the veranda with little running steps to greet

45

him. "Adam," she said, "you become more handsome with every passing year."

To Magdalen, a practical woman at heart, Adam Shannon—or Adam Vincent, as he had been born, the youngest son of Major General the Earl of Cheviot—represented the ultimate in military chivalry or, alternatively, male folly. As a young naval officer, Adam had sacrificed his career rather than expose the unfaithfulness of the wife of his captain, a more than honourable gesture that, Magdalen often thought, was out of place with the times. Adam had endured the suffering and ostracism that came with disgrace, had been court-martialled and cashiered from the Royal Navy, and, after changing his name and enlisting in the ranks of the army, had risen purely on his merits to his present status. He was the holder of not one, but two Victoria Crosses, the highest award for gallantry in the British empire.

"But where's Emily?" Magdalen demanded.

"In her condition," Adam said, "we deemed it best that she stay in Wellington."

The morning passed in talk. New Zealand, Adam's adopted home, was separated from Sydney and New South Wales by well over a thousand miles of ocean, and it was a rare pleasure to have an old friend drop in to bring news of the people the Broomes knew there. In general, the news was good. An uneasy peace had settled over the North Island, where tribal rebellions had been spilling blood for two decades. Adam, who had seen his share of fighting against the Maoris, had earned his army commission in the desperate battles of the late 1860s, when *pai marire*, an eerie mixture of Christian and primitive beliefs, had been used by Maori leaders such as Te Kooti to inspire fanaticism in his warriors. Te Kooti had never been finally defeated, and he had retired to the King Country, in the mountainous wilds of the North Island, to concentrate on founding still another religious cult, *ringatu*. Since that time, the regular British regiments had been pulled out of both New Zealand and Australia, and Adam's commission had been transferred to the militia.

"Thank God the fighting has ended, at last," Magdalen said.

"Yes, but now another kind of fight begins with the Maori," Adam said with a sigh. "Private land transactions are now legal between settler and Maori, for all that most of the best land is

46

already in the possession of the settlers. It bodes no good for the future of relations between our races."

"Sad, but perhaps inevitable," Red said. "What's Julius Vogel been up to?"

Vogel, the colonial treasurer, maintained frequently and publicly that New Zealand was bursting with potential, needing only capital and labour to exploit it and make the colony rich.

Adam laughed. "Mr. Vogel believes in good news," he said, "even if he has to fabricate it."

"I take it, then, that you wouldn't recommend investment in New Zealand at the moment?" Red asked.

"Oh, but I would," Adam said, "although I make no claims at being an economist. Vogel's optimstic speeches will be read in England and Europe, so I'd say that there'll be an influx of both capital and people. Land values will go up, but I think it will be an artificial boom, a speculator's boom. If you want to invest money, choose wisely, let prices rise, and then get out."

Magdalen, listening to the business talk with only half an ear, was engaged in some private speculation. In Adam Shannon's handsome face she saw the lines of his son, Jon Fisher. She admired Adam without reservation, knowing him to be an honourable man, and knowing that his marriage to Emily was a success, and that he loved his two children by her with an almost doting fondness. Why should he have to deny himself the pleasure of knowing his first son? And, conversely, why should Jon be denied the strong and good influence of his father?

"Adam, I'd like nothing more than to lay on a small dinner tonight, in honour of your visit," she said.

"Mercy," Adam said, smiling and spreading his hands. "A small dinner would be most appreciated. I'd certainly not want to put you through too much trouble on my account, though."

"Not at all. Just Johnny and Kitty, and Harry Ryan and a young friend of his."

"And Jessica?" Adam asked.

"Of course," Magdalen said. "My daughter I take for granted, I'm afraid. She'll be delighted to see you."

Later, when Adam had taken his leave to attend to business in town, Red looked at his wife with a raised eyebrow. "Aren't you taking the ship into shallows on a lee shore to have Adam and Jon

47

present at the same dinner?"

"But that's the idea," Magdalen said.

"Woman's curiosity? You're dying to know whether Jon knows, aren't you?"

"I'll have to admit to some curiosity," she said, "but actually I think it's a shame that those two fine men don't know each other."

"And where *are* the young people?" Red asked.

"I let them take the victoria. I didn't think you'd mind."

With Jon in the driver's seat, the top folded back, and Harry and Jessica in the rear, Red Broome's handsome carriage had rolled through the outskirts of Sydney not long after sunrise and, after traversing country roads, was at present sitting empty on a knoll overlooking the vast expanse of Port Jackson Harbour. Jessica had prepared a picnic, and with the sun at its zenith, the three of them were sprawled on blankets on a grassy slope. Jon felt pleasantly full, to the point of drowsiness. Harry was animated, however, talking animatedly, filling the air with tales of the sea and far places.

"If you must talk," Jon said, "please do so in dulcet tones. there's a man trying to take a nap here."

"In that case, Jess," Harry said, "there's only one thing to do. Let's leave the fellow to his peace."

He took Jessica's hand and led her toward the water. Jessica was silent and not at all eager to accept the invitation, for an incident had occurred during the drive out of town that had disturbed her. She knew that Harry had been taking Jon to gamble in Sydney's sporting houses and to dine in the town's best rooms, and she knew, also—for her father had insisted that the two young men move into spare rooms in the Elizabeth Bay house—that they often came in late, and that Harry was almost always the worse for drink. Jon, on the other hand, was—on such occasions when Jessica looked out of her window, awakened by the arrival of a hansom cab—the steadying influence, steering an unsteady Harry up the stairs, urging him to be quiet.

In his brusque way, Harry had already stated to her, more than once, his intentions of their future together, but she had been evasive. She was fond of Harry, true. It was not inconceivable that they could manage a life together. Her father was certain that

48

Harry would be successful. Her father, being a man and, perhaps, having overindulged in strong drink himself at times, seemed to overlook what both Jessica and her mother considered to be a streak of wildness in Harry. But Jessica could not bring herself to overlook what had happened when, the road being temporarily blocked by a lumber dray, Jon had drawn the victoria to a halt in front of an inn on the way out of town. A red-haired woman, obviously dressed in the clothes of the previous evening, had hailed Harry with a broad and knowing smile.

"I think that person is trying to get your attention," Jessica had said.

Harry had thrown one disdainful glance at the woman and looked away, but she had stepped toward the carriage, put her hands on her hips, and said, in a loud, brash voice, "So, ducks, you don't know me in the daytime?"

Harry had tipped his hat and said, "Of course. Good morning, Bess."

"You knew me last night, luv," the woman had said, with a suggestive grin. "But old Bess understands. I can see that you're wiv a lady of quality, ducks."

Now, with her hand in Harry's, standing alone overlooking the sparkling water, Jessica was searching for words to tell him that it was not time to consider a permanent attachment.

Harry turned to face her. "Jess, we'll be going off soon, Jon and I. No pressure, mind you, but have you been thinking?"

"Yes," she said, still unable to tell him that she could not love him.

He waited, and his face went sombre. "You've never been the indecisive, silent type."

"Harry, I don't think now is the time to speak of such matters. Shall we just drop it, please?"

Harry's face showed his quick anger; he had always been easily hurt by what he considered a slight. "If it's no, just say so," he said curtly.

"If you insist on an answer at this moment, then it is no."

"So—" He turned to walk a few paces away, then turned back. He spoke loudly, so loudly that Jessica feared that Jon would hear. "So I'm not good enough for the daughter of the respectable Red Broome?"

"Don't be crude," Jessica said, in the way she had once employed to teach a young boy from New Zealand his manners.

"Sorry," Harry said, falling back for the moment into an old habit of deferring to her.

"Aside from the fact that, as I've told you, I look on you as a brother, there are other reasons," she defended.

"I'd like to hear them."

"Are you sure?"

"Of course," he said, coming back to stand near her.

"As you sailors say, I'm going to go round the Horn." Jessica could not meet his gaze. "Be patient. I have had suitors, Harry. I think you know that."

"With good reason," he said. "You are the most beautiful girl in Sydney."

"I've given no man my promise. For one, I'm not ready. Some might say that I'm looking for a man like my father. Perhaps that's true."

"You could do worse," Harry said.

"But I'm not some dotty girl with stars in her eyes. I've had the good fortune, through my family, of knowing some good men, Harry. My uncle Johnny, Adam Shannon, Uncle William."

"And I don't fit into that category?" he asked, obviously offended.

"Frankly, not yet," she said. She held up one hand to stop his rejoinder. "We're both young. My father says that a young man needs time to find himself. I don't know how to put this delicately, but here it is. I would not be content to watch you squander yourself the way you're doing."

"Ah, the drinking."

"Yes, the drinking. The gambling. And—" She paused, blushing.

"That woman," he said.

"I am not accustomed to being embarrassed in public."

"And if I stop drinking, stop gambling, stop living, then what?" he asked sullenly.

"Since you feel it necessary to express it in such terms, I see little future in a relationship other than that we've known, as friends," she said.

Harry turned abruptly and started walking back toward the

victoria. Jessica followed at her own pace. Jon was awake, and he helped Harry gather up the picnic things. The drive back to the Broome house passed in cold formality, with Jon obviously puzzled by his friend's behaviour.

That evening, Harry did not show up for dinner. Jon was introduced to a man he had heard about in connection with the New Zealand wars, Colonel Adam Shannon.

Adam, who had been talking with Red, was in unusually good spirits as he shook Jon Fisher's hand. He had gone a long way toward accomplishing his purpose in Sydney and was looking forward to getting back home to his family. He was in full dress uniform, and although he did have the distinct impression that the younger man was somewhat ill at ease—indeed, Red had informed him that Jon probably still felt a bit guilty for having left the service—Adam liked what he saw. Fisher stood eye to eye with him and was well built, long-muscled for strength and endurance, and his eyes met Adam's squarely. The significance of the name Jon Fisher had been dismissed by Adam as coincidence, especially since the young man's accent, plus what Red had told him, indicated that Jon was from England, not Australia. Besides, Fisher was a common name. There was only a vague feeling of displeasure as he was reminded of Marcus Fisher, and then Magdalen was being the good hostess, steering the conversation, bringing out some of Adam's experiences in fighting the Maoris. Adam asked Jon a question or two about Isandhlwana, and Jon answered as briefly as possible. It was not until they were seated at table and Johnny Broome was talking, as usual, about politics and business, that Adam stiffened with the realization that he was indeed sitting directly across from his own son, the son born of his youthful affair with Caroline Omerod.

Barely able to accept his own folly in not having the recognized the truth sooner, Adam put down his knife and fork and glanced briefly at Magdalen Broome, who quickly looked away from him. Clearly *she* knew, Adam realized.

His voice did not belie his inner turmoil when he spoke. "You're from Victoria, Mr. Fisher?"

"I spent some little time there," Jon said. "Actually, I've been away, in England and in Africa, almost as many years as I lived in Victoria."

51

"I believe I know your mother," Adam said.

"Do you?" Jon asked politely.

"Yes, I met Caroline first in England. In fact, I sailed as first officer under her first husband. I also knew Colonel Forsyth."

"My father, then," Jon said. He was beginning to look discomposed. When he next spoke, his tone of voice as well as his words made it clear how he felt about Marcus Fisher. "My stepfather adopted me and applied his name to me when I was too young to protest."

Magdalen Broome came to the rescue, mercifully changing the subject, and Adam, as relieved as he was for her intervention, felt his hand tremble as he picked up his fork.

The rest of the dinner went smoothly enough. Afterward, Adam managed to seclude Jon in the parlour, intending to find out more about the young man.

He could see, now that his eyes had been opened, the resemblance of Jon to both Caroline and to himself. He had not been so moved in a long, long time. He had an almost uncontrollable urge to put his arms around the young man and say "Son." But he had lived with urges before, and deeply ingrained within him was the same sense of honour that had led him, some twenty years earlier, to allow himself to be thrown out of the navy rather than bring disgrace upon the woman with whom he had been carrying on an illicit love affair. It was that same sense of honour that stayed his tongue now. The boy obviously believed that Forsyth had been his father; there was no reason, no excuse, to cause him pain, to tell him that, rather than being the son of an army colonel who had died bravely for his country, he was the bastard son of a young lieutenant who had been court-martialled and had subsequently changed his name.

As he questioned the young man, Adam took great pleasure in Jon's assurance, his poise, his maturity. He listened with great interest as Jon told him of his plans to enter the shipping business with Harry Ryan. And then, all too soon, it was time to break off the interview, lest the boy grow suspicious of his attentions.

Later, Red and Magdalen stood with him on the front steps as a carriage was brought round.

"Thank you, Magdalen," Adam said with heartfelt conviction. "I truly mean that."

"You're always welcome at our table," she answered innocently.

"For the dinner, also," he said with a kind smile. "Admit that you engineered this so that I could see—this young man."

"Admitted," she said.

"Lord, he's a splendid lad, isn't he?" Adam's eyes were gleaming.

"I'm favourably impressed," Red said.

"What happened at Isandhlwana must not be allowed to colour his life," Adam said. "I don't want him to have to go through what I went through. I wish I could help, that I could smooth the way for him."

"I think he's capable of riding his own waves," Red said. He glanced at his wife for her opinion.

"I'm sorry," she said, "but I'm afraid I can control my curiosity no longer. Forgive me, but I must know. Did you tell him, Adam?"

"No," Adam said.

"I'm a prying, busybody of a woman," Magdalen said, "but . . . won't he find out, somehow? Thanks to Marcus Fisher, it's not exactly a well-kept secret. There are many who know, or who suspect."

"I wondered about that," Adam said. "I'm astounded that Fisher hasn't told him himself. It would be his style. But, no, I didn't, and I won't tell him. Pray God he never knows. What happened to him in Africa was a blow to his pride, seeing his entire command wiped out, being the sole survivor, not even taking part in the final fight. I would spare him this further blow."

"I like the boy," Red said. "I'll do my best to exert what influence I can to steer him into calm waters."

"I'll be in your debt," Adam said, "even more." He looked up at the sparkling sky, saw the familiar stars, stars to steer a tall ship by, and quickly sent a prayer up for the sake of his son. "I haven't mentioned it, but one result of my talks today may see me stationed in Hong Kong for a time."

"An interesting place," Red said.

"Will you be taking Emily and the family?" Magdalen asked.

"That depends on Emily's condition," Adam said. "But I have no doubt she will insist on going."

"Please write," Magdalen said. "And I'll keep you informed as to the commercial ventures of our two budding businessmen."

"Thank you," Adam said. "Thank you from the bottom of my heart."

Jon had shed his coat and was unbuttoning his shirt in preparation for bed when a knock came at the door. He opened it a crack and saw the lovely face of Jessica.

"May I come in, please?" she asked.

"Give me a moment." He closed the door, hurriedly rebuttoned his shirt, and drew on his jacket. Her face was serious when she slipped into the room, closing the door behind her.

"I'm sorry to intrude," she said. "It's Harry. I'm concerned about him."

Jon's suspicions that the cold formality of the ride home from the picnic and Harry's absence from the dinner had indicated a disagreement were, it seemed, confirmed. "Oh, I shouldn't worry about old Harry. He has friends everywhere. He can take care of himself."

'Perhaps it's an imposition," she said, her eyes downcast. "But you are his friend."

He sighed. "I take it I am being detailed to search the town and bring our errant Harry back to the fold?"

"Would you, please?"

"Of course," he said, and almost added, *"How could I refuse a request from one so lovely?"* Indeed, had it not been obvious that his friend had designs on Jessica Broome, Jon might have found it tempting to pay court to her, for all he was a houseguest of the Broomes. But the situation was tangled enough as it was. He was going to be Harry's business partner. Moreover, although Jessica was a lovely young woman, his own prospects were, at this point, hardly assured, and he would rather wait until he had established himself in his new career. In any case, she was not the only beautiful woman in the world.

"I shall bring back our Harry with his shield or on it," he reassured her as she moved to the door. She cast him a stricken look. "Sorry," he said. "Bad joke."

He walked briskly into the part of town called the Rocks, on the opposite side of Sydney Cove, on the theory that Harry, being upset over something Jessica said, would seek comfort in the form of a cold bottle and a warm, feminine body. From his earlier

54

excursions into the Rocks with Harry, he recognized some faces, and the proprietor of the second pub at which he stopped proved helpful. "Aye, gov'ner, old Harry was here. Try the Comb and Whistle."

The Comb and Whistle, one of Harry's favourite haunts, was a seaman's bar. Roughly constructed, it was dingy and dark and, like other establishments in the Rocks, more than slightly dangerous to a well-dressed stranger. Jon stood just inside the door, letting his eyes adjust to the smoke-filled dimness, the fume of cheap rum in his nostrils. He heard a feminine laugh and walked a few steps among the tables. Harry was in a booth with the red-haired woman who had hailed the carriage that morning, the one called Bess. Their backs were toward Jon. He could see only the top of Harry's head, but that was enough to recognize him, even without the loud Harry-voice telling an off-colour yarn. Jon sighed. Harry seemed to be in good form, not yet too intoxicated. It would be exceedingly awkward to go up to him and attempt to pry him away at this point.

Jon moved to the bar. "What'll it be, mate?" the bartender asked. The grime on the man's hands made Jon wary of anything that might come into contact with them.

"Ale," he said, putting a coin on the counter.

"Your mate's at yonder booth." The bartender nodded toward Harry.

"I know. He seems to be occupied." Jon forced himself to grin. "We won't bother him just yet, will we?"

He took the ale and sat at a small table not too far to the rear of the booth. The tone of Harry's voice had changed. He sounded bitter, and the subject was women.

"They're prigs, all of them," he was saying. "All satin and laces and sweetness and innocence. God knows, the way women around here talk, how the race propagates itself, them all being virgins."

"I'm a 'maculate conception meself," said red Bess. "Me mother was virgin—in the left ear." She roared with laughter. Harry did not join in.

"She had the gall to call me to task," he said. "And she—allowed to go as she pleases, flaunting her virtue—"

Jon felt a flash of anger. Whatever had happened between Harry and Jessica, Harry had no right to be speaking of her in such

55

a tone, and with such insulting words . . ."

"Tossed you over, ducks, did she?"

"Makes me wonder if she doesn't have someone else creeping through her window when the lights go out," Harry said. Jon rose, set to put an end to the conversation, even if it meant angering Harry. Harry's next words froze him, however, and he came to a halt directly behind the booth, where he couldn't possibly help but hear everything with numbing clarity.

"Now that's a proper house," Harry had said. "Arranging a meeting between an adulterer and his bastard son."

"You mean it?" Bess said. "The Broomes?"

"Hell, everyone who's been out here for any time at all knows all about it. Such a blasted hero, bloody Colonel Adam Shannon, or Vincent, or whatever he chooses to call himself at the moment. Why, when he was a naval officer, he seduced his captain's wife and was court-martialled for losing his ship! And my friend Jon Fisher is the issue of that deceit. You've seen him, Bess. The poor digger doesn't even know it!"

Jon had calmed. It was an obvious lie. He was the son of Colonel Leonard Forsyth, who had died in New Zealand . . .

"His mother, Caroline Omerod Forsyth Fisher—how's that for a name?—is a good example of what they call quality, my fine, darling Bess. While her first husband was at sea, she got in a bit of slap-and-tickle with the handsome young first mate, and then when she found herself in the family way and with a husband dead, she grabbed the first thing that came along—one of Her Majesty's bleedin' marines this time, a man much older than herself."

Jon knew that if he heard more he might do something violent, and he was not yet ready to confront a drunken Harry Ryan. He went back to his table and drank his ale. Oddly, he even had trouble remembering the first name of the marine colonel who had been his father. Forsyth—Leonard Forsyth—had always been a shadowy, almost imaginary figure in his life. His mother had never volunteered information about him, rarely spoke of him fondly, and when Jon himself had asked questions, she often as not would dismiss them casually. He knew only that Colonel Forsyth had been a man of honour and had died on the field of battle. *Of course* he was Colonel Forsyth's son.

And yet . . . Jon recalled his maternal grandmother, who had been dead for some years, God rest her soul. She had been a fine, loving woman, who in his early years in England had given him the love and attention that were often lacking from his otherwise preoccupied mother. He'd always thought, rather fondly, that Grandmother Mason had been just a little mad. She had loved mystery. To her the blue of a robin's egg was a delightful enigma, the coming of a storm a token of the devil. Life itself was a puzzle to her, she had been fond of stating, one she had never solved, and as a result she was wont to be vague.

Jon remembered, as he sat there in the dingy pub, that she had had a tendency to speak in incomplete sentences. He could almost hear her, and he stiffened as, from somewhere in the dim recesses of memory, words came back to him:

"*Things are not always what they seem, Jon . . . A person may not be what he seems, just as you——*" With chilling clarity there came to him one of her favourite statements: *Oh, my darling boy, what a secret will be revealed to you one day.*"

He had never before seen any meaning to such talk from his grandmother, had never associated her hints and allusions with a mystery personal to him. But now the slightly eccentric prattle of a woman long dead caused his blood to chill. He actually shivered.

He rose, thinking to confront Harry, to demand the source of Harry's statements. He walked to the booth. Harry was being sick. Bess was holding his head. There was a sour reek in the air, and Jon's stomach turned. He knew that he had to get out of the place. Harry looked up, wiped his mouth weakly, and said, "Aye, shipmate!"

"It's time to go home, Harry," Jon said.

"'ere," Bess said, "who are you to be giving orders?"

"Go home, Harry," Jon repeated.

In imitation of Bess, Harry said, " 'ere, who are you to be giving orders?"

"Then go to blazes," Jon said, turning on his heel. He was almost running when he hit the street. He went back to the Broome house to find it dark. He used the key that had been lent to him to enter, made his way quietly to the room he had been occupying, packed his few things with careless haste, left a brief note, and was going down the hall when he saw a light come on under the door of Jessica's room. He was not up to seeing her. He felt only a tinge of

57

regret as he hurried to the front door and closed it behind him. Jessica was a fine young woman—all the Broomes were fine people, the backbone of Australian society; but at the moment Jon resented them, for if what Harry had said was true, then the Broomes must have engineered the meeting between Adam Shannon and him. To let the adulterer look over his bastard son?

Twice the next day, while he was scouring the waterfront before finding a small, bedraggled coastal sloop heading south, he was informed that Harry was looking for him. He stayed in the public room of a down-at-the-heels inn until it was time for the sloop to weigh anchor, and then he was at sea, in cramped quarters, for he had to know the truth. He was not of a mind to question relative strangers, such as the Broomes; but there was one source of which he could be sure. His mother.

The voyage down the eastern coast was uneventful, with trading stops at small fishing villages to break the monotony of sailing. Jon went ashore only to stretch his legs, and when the sloop was under way he spent a lot of time on deck, willing the wind to fill the sails more strongly. For all that the burning question of his parentage was ever in the forefront of his mind, his thoughts ran the entire course of his life, and he found that he could recall things from his childhood that he had not thought about in years.

He considered his mother to be a beautiful woman. He remembered how, as a boy, he had found pride in knowing that she was striking, that people admired her for her beauty. But to his surprise, he found that he had few fond memories of her. His maternal grandmother held a more secure place in his heart, as far as love was concerned. Love his mother? Of course he did. And yet she was not always a vivid figure in his memories. He could recall and name a series of nannies, some with fondness. He could remember childhood friends, and his memories of Marcus Fisher were quite vivid, but . . . his mother always seemed to be on the fringes of his life, a beautiful, sweet-smelling figure dressed in an elegant gown, leaning to kiss him gingerly on the forehead and to say, "Be a good boy, Jon." She always seemed, in his memories, to be leaving, to be off to some gala party, or on a trip that kept her away for days.

He spent much time thinking of his mother during the trip down past the southeastern headlands through the Tasman Sea, into the

Bass Strait with Tasmania to the south. By the time they had reached broad, calm Phillip Bay, with Melbourne, the jewel of the south, spread before them, Jon had sorted out his life as he had never taken the time to do so before and, as a result, had reached several conclusions that, although he didn't fully realize it at the time, had far-reaching consequences for his future.

If he had been asked, at the moment, while he waited for the old sloop to move gingerly to dockside, he might have said that he now honoured his mother, forsaking the word love. By no means did he consider himself the unhappy product of an abusive parent; that English mothers of Caroline's standing and social pretension had a tendency to look upon their offspring as little more than small pets who could be trying, albeit occasionally entertaining as long as they were tended by an efficient nanny, was no revelation. Caroline, he had decided, had not been an atypical mother. On the contrary, she had most probably been quite fond of her only son and would most probably have protested mightily had anyone questioned her love for him.

He had also come to grips, during the voyage, with his part in the tragedy of Isandhlwana. He had been able to look on his actions with some detachment. He had done his duty. He had been at his place, with his company, during the initial stages of the Zulu attack and had been ordered away from the action by his immediate superior. His only remaining doubt concerned his decision to go for ammunition to the reserve wagons of the Australian sutlers, instead of storming his way past the headstrong quartermaster, using his rank, or whatever else was necessary, to speed up the distribution of ammunition. But even so, a green lieutenant would probably not have carried much weight with the veteran N.C.O.'s at the wagons. He could only conclude that part of the tragedy of Isandhlwana was due to the British temperament itself, an unquestioning respect for property, tradition, and the rules. The quartermaster was legally and financially responsible for each round of ammunition and for the spent brass casings as well; consequently he and his men guarded each round as if it were worth its weight in gold.

Of course, such qualities had their worth. If, at times, an unwillingness to change caused serious setbacks, the nation always seemed to recover. And it would recover from the memory of Isandhlwana.

The willingness to accept change was, in Jon's mind, the principal characteristic that made men like Lord Chelmsford seem relics to those who had come out to the ends of the world—to Australia and New Zealand. He resolved never to be hidebound. He would not be reckless, seeking change for the sake of change, but he would not push forward to sure defeat in any circumstances simply because of tradition.

Jon hired a carriage to complete the final leg of his journey. Marcus Fisher had done well for himself in Victoria. He had outgrown the old homestead at Urquhart Falls years ago, not long after Jon had left for England. The Fisher estate now overlooked a small lake, a bit of old England transported to the countryside on the outskirts of Melbourne. The house itself, of grandiose proportions, was of red brick with a central tower, ornate parapets, and capped chimney pots. It was surrounded by sprawling, open areas of lawn and by huge, spreading trees that, in spite of their age and health, failed to reach as high as the central tower. Beyond the stables and other outbuildings, pasturelands were dotted with trees and, instead of the usual sheep, fat, healthy cattle.

The woman servant who opened the door looked at Jon blankly, almost insolently. He identified himself, and after giving him a doubtful look, she bade him enter and informed him that Mrs. Fisher was in the morning room. But she did not allow him to proceed down the hallway until she had gone ahead to announce him.

Jon's first reaction, when his mother came running into the hallway, her arms outstretched, was shock. She was not as he remembered her. She wore a loose, wrinkled dressing gown, and her hair was untidy, mostly grey. But it was her face that froze him in midstep. She had aged incredibly in the nine years he had been away. Her full lips had taken an unhappy turn downward, and there were cruel lines on the once glowing cheeks. And in spite of her obvious joy in seeing him, Jon detected emptiness, perhaps defeat, in her once defiant eyes.

She did not smell like mother, either, and he realized with shock, as she kissed him, that her breath was heavy with brandy, for all it was mid-afternoon.

"Oh, Jon, Jon," Caroline cried, "thank God you've come home!

I've been so lonely."

The servant, hovering near, approached Caroline with a concerned look. "Mustn't get too agitated, missus," she said, taking Caroline's arm.

"But my son is home," Caroline said. "And isn't he marvellous, Martha? Just look at him. Just look at you, Jon. So tall, and handsome."

"You're looking well, Mother," he managed unconvincingly.

"You're a sweet liar," she said, "for I know that I must look like the wrath of God." Her smile faded, and her voice took on the harsh tones of his memory, when he had displeased her. "But you didn't let me know you were coming. Shame, to catch me looking like this." She turned to the maid. "Martha, give Master Jon tea in the morning room and then join me, to help me look decent."

She half ran to the stairs and disappeared. Jon followed the maid into the morning room.

"Is it tea you're wanting, then?" the maid asked.

"No, thank you," he said. "You are—?"

"Martha Blevins," she stated, with no further explanation.

"How long have you been with my mother?"

"Six—no, seven years."

Jon had noted the woman's concern. The look on her face in the hall, when Caroline had been pleasantly excited, had been one of fondness.

"Has she been ill, Martha?"

Martha made a sound through her nose. "Ill? No."

"She's changed so much."

Again there was that sound of disdain. "What do you expect, running off and leaving her with—" She paused, as if unwilling to pronounce the name, and looked away.

"I didn't exactly run away." Jon didn't know why he was bothering to defend himself to a servant he had never met before, but he needed information, and she was, at the moment, his only source. "I spent eight years in England, in school and with my grandparents, and then a year in the army." He smiled. "You're fond of her, aren't you, Martha?"

"She's a fine lady," the old woman said.

"She's my mother, and I'm concerned about her, too."

"Better late than not at all," Martha said.

"She's been drinking," Jon stated bluntly.

"Yes, poor thing."

"Why?" he asked.

The old woman seemed to be thinking. Then her face went tight. "She's alone in this house most of the time, with nothing to do and no one to talk to but me."

"And Marcus Fisher?"

"Humph," she snorted. "Him."

"Is there trouble between my mother and Mr. Fisher?"

"There's little else," Martha said. She seemed to have decided Jon was not her enemy, and when she began to talk, the words came rapidly. "He keeps his own place in the town," she said, "and he does not sleep alone, mind you. And when he comes here it's hell for her, him calling her names, and berating her because she seeks a bit of comfort from the bottle now and again."

"You're the only maid in this big house?"

"He won't hear of her hiring anyone else, and with me working my poor old fingers to the bone! As if he would miss the little bit of money!"

"It looks as if he's done well," Jon said.

"*Well?* Humph. He's Mister Big himself. Delegate to the colonial parliament. A shipping company, sugar plantations up north. And God only knows what else."

Carrying from upstairs, Caroline's voice, a cross between anger and pleading, sent Martha scurrying out of the room. Jon, curious now, did a bit of exploring. The house was dusty and smelled of disuse, but it was a rich house, with the finest of French and English furnishings, made more expensive by the difficulty of transporting them by ship across the thousands of miles of ocean. Some of the rooms were closed off. The kitchen was odiferous with spoiled food and unwashed dishes.

He was waiting in the morning room when Caroline swept in, overdressed for the afternoon, but looking better until, close up, he saw that she had overapplied rouge and lip red. Her hair was piled loosely atop her head, giving her, in the dimness of the room, an illusion of youth. When she came nearer, however, Jon saw the wrinkles on her neck.

Martha brought in a tea tray. Caroline sat primly as she poured. "Now you must tell me all—everything that you've been doing."

"That will take a while," Jon said. "Where's Fisher?"

Her face went slack.

The morning room was heavily draped. Jon went to the windows, drew open the curtains, and looked out over the lake in front of the house. It was a peaceful, attractive setting, almost idyllic. Similarly, what he had seen of the rooms and furnishings left nothing to be desired; yet there was obviously no happiness in the house. The place felt oppressive. He longed to leave, but he knew he could not bring himself to desert his mother in her present state, nor could he depart without knowing more about what the state of affairs was between her and her husband. The burning purpose of the trip had been dimmed, surprisingly, by his shock in seeing how his mother had deteriorated; but that question, too, would have to be resolved before he could leave. He was wondering how he could ever broach the subject as he listened to his mother talk on about how empty the house was, how lonely she was, and how happy she was now that he was home.

He saw the dust of an approaching carriage first, then the vehicle itself, skirting the west end of the lake to draw up in front of the house. His throat tightened when he saw Marcus Fisher dismount from the carriage and turn to speak to the coachman. Fisher had put on weight, and it was not becoming. Although his dress was impeccable, it could not hide the sagging muscles and the protrusion of his stomach.

"He's home," Jon said, and his heart went out to his mother when he saw her leap to her feet in obvious agitation, spilling her tea. He went to her, eased her back into the chair, picked up the cup and saucer, and put it on the tea tray. By that time he could hear hurrying footsteps in the hallway, and then Marcus Fisher was standing in the door. He looked unsmilingly at Jon, then at Caroline.

"Sober for a change?" he asked in the drawling voice that Jon remembered only too well.

"Look who's home," Caroline said.

"So it's true." Fisher met Jon's gaze. "I heard in town that you came in on the *Merit*."

"And how are you, stepfather?" Jon asked.

"I heard that you ran at Isandhlwana," Fisher said, in a harsh tone. "I had hoped you'd have enough respect for your mother not

63

to run here in your shame."

Jon controlled his flash of anger with difficulty. He had expected coolness from his stepfather, but not open hostility.

"Marcus," Caroline said weakly.

"Keep out of this!" Fisher snapped.

"If I am not welcome to visit my mother in this house," Jon said, "perhaps we can make arrangements for me to see her in the city."

"Do what you damn well please—"

"Marcus, must you be so mean?" Caroline cut in. "Can't you at least have the decency to allow me the pleasure of being with my son after so many years?"

"Sleep with him, if that's what you want," Fisher said. "That's your prime talent, isn't it?"

"You miserable bastard!" Caroline shot back, to Jon's astonishment. "At least my son didn't try to cover up the truth by attempting to steal the bravery of another man."

Fisher moved with deceptive speed. He had crossed the room before a stunned Jon could realize his intentions, and the back of his arm made a meaty slapping sound as he struck Caroline with a force that caused her to collapse onto the sofa. Jon's reaction was instinctive. As Fisher lifted his arm to strike again, Jon clapped a hand on his shoulder, jerked him around, and put all his anger and strength into a blow that felled the man heavily, sending him skidding on a loose rug. Jon felt pain in his hand, but he knew only his anger for the man who had struck his mother.

The moment seemed to last forever. Caroline was sobbing. Fisher raised his head, shook it, and glared at him with hate-filled eyes. "I won't kill you now," he said.

"Please try," Jon said.

Fisher picked himself up gingerly, rubbing his jaw. "I can expect no more from a bastard and a coward—"

Jon took a quick step forward, then controlled himself.

"I'm leaving," Fisher said. "When I return, if you are here, I will take a horsewhip to you."

"Let him go, Jon," Caroline wailed, as Jon moved forward. "No more! Let him go."

Jon watched Fisher retreat to the front door and climb into his carriage; only then did he turn back to his mother. She was drying her tears. There would be an ugly bruise on her left cheek. Her eye was already swelling.

"You're hurt," he said.

"No. It's nothing."

"Has this happened before?"

"No."

"I'm going to take you out of this house, Mother."

True alarm widened her eyes. "Oh, no," she said. "I—I can't *leave*."

"You can go back to England. Grandfather would be happy to have you."

She shook her head violently. "This is my house," she said. "I had it designed, and I watched it being built. It is my home, my haven, and no one will make me leave it. Not you, not Marcus—no one."

"I think we should get something for that eye," Jon said, but Martha had anticipated him, appearing from nowhere with a cut of fresh beefsteak. Caroline leaned back weakly and allowed Martha to minister to her for a few minutes, then she pushed the maid away.

"I'm afraid you'll have to go, Jon," Caroline said. "It breaks my heart, but it will be for the best. He's not like that, usually."

"Humph," Martha said.

"I'm really very happy here," Caroline said.

"All right, mother. I'll take a room in town."

Martha put the beefsteak back to Caroline's eye and ordered her to hold it there. "If you need me, sir, just call," she said, with a wink. Before she left the room, she whispered into his ear: "Anyone who will knock Himself on his arse can't be all bad."

As soon as they were alone, Caroline's voice was suddenly different, harsh, as if it came from another person entirely. "I asked you to leave, young man. Why are you still here?"

"I'll take you to England," he said. "There are ships here in Melbourne—"

"I have stated my wishes," she said imperiously.

Jon hung his head. Even though she was his mother, he was, after all, unused to dealing with women of Caroline's ilk, and he'd never been involved in a domestic scene quite so unpleasant. "All right. I'll go. But first I have a question for you."

"Yes?" She gazed at him from her one good eye.

65

"I have been called bastard, and not only by Marcus Fisher. Why, do you suppose?"

"I'm not feeling well, Jon. Please go. We can talk some other time."

"Not until you answer me," he said firmly. "I met a man in Sydney just recently, a man to whom I seem to bear a striking resemblance. His name is Adam Shannon, or Adam Vincent. He said he knew you in England."

"The man is a cad and a liar," Caroline said, no longer meeting his gaze.

"As a matter of fact," Jon said, "he's an army colonel in good repute and, I'd venture to say from what I've heard, destined for greater things. Tell me about Adam Shannon, Mother."

"You must not believe vicious lies and scandalmongers."

"I was told, indirectly, that everyone who has been out here for any length of time knows that you and Adam Vincent were lovers, while your first husband was at sea. There was quite a scandal, I've heard, and this Adam Vincent was kicked out of the Royal Navy. Why, Mother?"

"I'm very tired, Jon," she said, rising, letting the beefsteak fall wetly onto the velvet of the sofa. He took her by the arms and looked into her eyes.

"I must know," he said.

"So that you can say that I'm being punished by God for my indiscretions?" Her eyes were wet with tears.

"Because it's my life," he said. "Because I have the right to know!"

She sad down weakly. "Please forgive me, Jon. He hounded me, giving me no peace, pleading at my skirts like a hungry puppy, playing on my natural loneliness while John was at sea. I was so young, and I was—I admit it—weak. I longed for human company and, God help me, I paid for it with my virtue."

"Then Colonel Forsyth was not my father?"

She nodded. Great tears wet her cheeks. Her eyes were closing, and the bruise on her face was becoming suffused with colour. Jon felt an upwelling of sympathy for her.

"I have been told that he . . . that Adam Vincent was a skilled seducer," she went on, "that I was not his only victim. Ah, that such a man could rise to power."

66

"Adam Shannon is my father?"

Her voice was suddenly strident: "Yes, damn you, are you satisfied! Is it not enough that I have to live with my own shame, and the shame of knowing that my husband is a coward and a blackguard, and that my own son is also a coward who ran from his command?"

He was silent.

"Think what you may—I don't care," she said, her voice rising, taking on a hint of madness. "Perhaps it's true. Perhaps I *am* being punished by God. But it was not my fault. God, I did love my husband. And Adam Vincent killed him, and then had the audacity to want me to marry *him*. Oh, he was smooth, so smooth in his talk, in his persuasion—'

Martha Blevins reappeared in the doorway. Jon motioned her in, and she led the weeping Caroline out of the room. Jon was standing in the hallway, some minutes later, when the old woman came back downstairs.

"She'll be all right," Martha said. "Or at least as right as can be expected. I think you've seen that guilt hangs heavily over this house."

"Will you stay with her?' Jon asked.

"I'll look after the poor dear. No worry."

"I'll not be remaining in Melbourne," Jon said, his mind suddenly made up. "But I'll write. I'll address the letters to you."

"You do that. And now you'd best go."

The fresh air seemed blessed after the oppressive atmosphere of the house. He breathed deeply, and as he did, he relived the scene, saw his mother being struck, saw her weeping, and in that moment, knew for certain that Marcus Fisher was not the only blackguard in Australia. What Adam Vincent—or Shannon, or whatever his name was—had done to his mother—and done to him—could not be excused, or forgiven. One day there would be an accounting, both for Marcus Fisher and for the man who called himself Adam Shannon.

CHAPTER III

When Jon left his mother's house he was intent on leaving Victoria as quickly as possible. It was high time for him to get on with his life, and he had committed himself to Harry Ryan and his business associates.

Disturbed as he was by his mother's condition and the state of her marriage to Marcus Fisher, he could not see where he could be of help. His mother was stubborn and set in her ways; he had offered to take her to England, where she would have been welcomed by her aging father, but she had refused. For all her drinking, she was, after all, a rational adult, and consequently he did not see, at present, that he had any further responsibility. Perhaps she was as content as she could be in her red-brick house overlooking the lake. And perhaps she could manage better with Marcus Fisher when Jon was not around.

Actually, Jon was beginning to wonder why it was his fortune to be intimately associated with two people who seemed unable to resist the lure of drink. Perhaps life in the colonies had more snares than he had envisioned. He told himself that Harry had managed well before having met him, that the young man's love of a high time had not seemed to hinder his advancement in business, for, certainly, Harry was further along toward financial success than Jon. Jon was not exactly penniless. He had a small inheritance from his maternal grandmother. He had not drawn on it at all, having been careful to live within his meagre army pay and the annuity that was sent along to him at regular intervals by his grandfather.

He had to admit that one reason he had not committed himself fully to Harry and his venture was his reluctance to risk the principal amount of his inheritance, but, as he checked into a somewhat ramshackle ornate hotel to await transportation back to Sydney, he came to the conclusion that it was time either to commit himself, to risk all, or to forget venture trading and find some other career.

The old hotel was decorated with mementos of the gold-rush days. It had a rustic, serene atmosphere, and the food was excellent. He spent an afternoon strolling Melbourne's broad avenues, fully ninety-nine feet wide, admiring the splendid domes of the law courts and the spires of Saint Patrick's and Saint Paul's. The city named for the second Viscount of Melbourne, William Lamb, was a bustling, growing seaport. Jon, who had read more than a little of the history of his adopted land, wondered if John Batman and John Fawkner could even have dreamed of the rapid growth the city had experienced since 1835, when the two men led a small group of settlers across the Bass Strait to live in bark and timber huts and plough wheat paddocks in what were now broad, pleasant streets.

He could see work still going on to enlarge the deep-water facilities of Port Phillip Bay, and found it hard to imagine that the tall ships and grunting steamers arrayed before him were docked where once had been swampy river flats. Only two decades earlier Melbourne's docks had witnessed the passage of one-third of the world's production of gold, both a boon and a curse that had contributed to the city's frantic, lawless growth, making her the San Francisco of the western Pacific, bringing a flood of gold-seekers from Liverpool, Hamburg, Canton, and countless other cities around the world. Many of those who had come to find gold had stayed, enough to make Melbourne's population somewhere near forty percent of the entire population of Victoria state.

Gold had brought them here, but it was not gold that had made them stay. Indeed, most of the once-rowdy mining towns in the hinterlands had faded into near obscurity, while the fertile grazing land of the interior was now the object for greed and speculation. As elsewhere in Australia, sheep had become king. Former diggers and newcomers, tempted by the promise of crown land, had invested their life savings to get a start farming in the backcountry, only to find that others, more often than not the proprietors of vast sheep runs, had arrived before them and were squatting on the best lands. The crown grants threatened the wealthy landowners—among them Marcus Fisher and a notorious former police superintendent by the name of Leonard Brownlow, who between them owned vast tracts around Urquhart Falls. Fisher and Brownlow, Jon had not taken long to discover, were leaders in the growing battle between the squatters and the would-be small farmers, called selectors, whose cause had been taken up by those who supported land reform—mostly middle-class politicians of the liberal persuasion.

But Victoria's problems were not his—or at least Jon thought—and eventually he found his way to the telegraph office, to send a brief message to Harry, in care of the Broomes, informing him that he was in Melbourne and would be returning to Sydney as soon as he could arrange transportation.

Harry's answer came the next morning, and it caught Jon unprepared. Evidently the commitment he had contemplated would have to be made sooner than expected. Harry had telegraphed: "Waste not trip to Melbourne. Buy wool."

Jon made a wry face. Wool, he knew, came from sheep—but that was about all he knew. Wool was somehow made into warm clothing. And of course there were plenty of sheep in Victoria.

He tucked the telegram in his pocket and went to the dining room of his hotel. It was crowded, with only one small table available. He had just seated himself when he heard his name and looked up to see a spare, sombrely dressed man of the church holding his telegram in hand.

"You dropped this, Mr. Fisher," the man, grey-haired and somehow familiar-looking, said.

Jon took the telegram. "Thank you, sir."

"It was open. I didn't mean to pry."

"Not at all," Jon said.

"Well, then—" The minister began to turn away.

"I beg your pardon," Jon said, causing the man to turn back. "If you were planning to have lunch, sir, I seem to have taken the last table. Would you join me?"

"Kind of you, sir." The minister extended a hand. "Let me introduce myself. I am Evan Bainbridge. I do not insist on being called Reverend."

"My pleasure," Jon said, taking the offered hand. Bainbridge had a strong, if dour face, a ruddy complexion for a minister, and bushy brows over kind, blue eyes. He was of uncertain age, well

70

over fifty but still sure of movement and clear of eye.

"Your name I know, from having read your telegram," Bainbridge said. "By any change are you related to one of my parishioners, Mrs. Marcus Fisher?"

"My mother," Jon said, suddenly realizing he had met Bainbridge once, briefly, before he had left for England. The man had been new to the parish then and evidently did not remember him.

"A fine lady," Bainbridge said. "So you're the young Jon she speaks of?"

"I suppose so," Jon said. "I've just returned from abroad."

The conversation was interrupted as they gave their orders and, only a minute later, were served steaming plates of rich mutton stew. "I didn't know," Jon ventured, "that my mother was a churchgoer."

"I fear that, like many of my flock, she is not overly consistent. However, she and her husband are quite supportive, both in spirit and, ah, financially."

"I hesitate to lay my own personal burdens on a man I scarcely know," Jon said, "but if you could tell me your opinion of my mother's health?"

"Ah," Bainbridge said. "You've seen her, then?"

"Yesterday," Jon said. "I've been far away for nine years at school and in the army. There's been quite a change in her, more than I would have expected in such a relatively short period. She's not exactly an old woman, you know."

Bainbridge was smiling sadly, and his face had softened. "I fear that I, too, have noted a change in her. I am not privy to any personal problems she might have. She has not confided in me, I must say, nor has her husband. When they attend church, though, they seem to be a handsome and compatible couple."

Jon was not ready to confide in anyone what he knew of his mother's troubled marriage. He nodded and applied himself to his meal. Bainbridge, too, was silent for a time, then he said, "Again, I apologize for having looked at the wording of your telegram, but I gather that you are a wool merchant?"

Jon laughed. "Someone is trying to make a wool merchant of me. I confess that I know little of wool."

Bainbridge's eyes twinkled briefly. "It grows on sheep, my boy."

71

Jon gave a wry grin. "Now my education is complete."

"As it happens," Bainbridge said, "I am travelling into the interior tomorrow. As a part of my ministry I am, part time, an old-fashioned circuit rider. It is my privilege to carry the word of God to isolated smallholdings and villages. In fact, the northernmost point in my travels will be, oddly enough, your stepfather's holdings at Urquhart Falls. Since it's shearing time, it would be an excellent time for a prospective wool buyer to have a look at the lay of the land and to talk with growers. You might even get ahead of the competition, as they say."

"I'm beginning to think that we were well met, Reverend Bainbridge. If you can put up with the presence of a total greenhorn, I'd be honoured to accompany you."

"My mode of transportation is an ancient buckboard that came, oddly enough, all the way from America. Although it seems to seek out every stone and bump in Australia, I find it more endurable than riding. If, however, you care to ride, I can suggest an excellent source of rental. As for supplies—"

"I will, of course, pay for my share," Jon said.

"Kind of you. I'll be happy to lay them on."

Jon handed over money, a surprisingly small amount suggested by Bainbridge, and informed his newfound companion that, yes, he would like to have a horse, and then spent the balance of the day buying a few items of clothing suggested by Bainbridge and in visiting one of Melbourne's growing banks to arrange transfer of his London funds to Australia.

Bainbridge's buckboard was indeed ancient, looking as if it had been driven over every track in the outback. It had two seats, leather covered and worn, the driver's seat moulded into a concavity the exact size of Bainbridge's spare bottom. The team of bays, in contrast, were glossy with health and youth, and Bainbridge set a good pace as they cleared the suburbs of Melbourne.

Jon quickly discovered why Bainbridge had not bought much food; apparently the man had friends everywhere. From the first stop outside Melbourne, to well into the north country, he was greeted with friendliness and affection at grand country houses, sheepherders' shacks, and small chapels in tiny, hidden villages.

"There are times," Bainbridge confessed, after a fine meal in the

72

home of a prosperous squatter, "when I feel that my appearance has no other effect than to cause everyone to think it is feed-the-animal time. They push food at me wherever I go."

"I have observed that," Jon said, putting a hand on his own full stomach and smiling.

Bainbridge's sermons, Jon soon discovered, were simple but pithy, often delivered to an audience of two or three, and concentrating on that one main law that was added to the Ten Commandments by the Christ. The message was, almost always, "love thy neighbour," and Bainbridge was delivering it in a land that was becoming increasingly divided. Jon had not realized the intensity and extent of the dispute over land reform, but his travels with Bainbridge were an education. The disparity between the rich and the poor was strikingly evident, and, as they neared Urquhart Falls, Jon was witness to two different examples of the tactics practised by men like his stepfather and Leonard Brownlow.

A selector family was loading their household goods onto a decrepit wagon when Bainbridge's buckboard topped a grassy rise and jolted down a track toward a shack on a pretty little creek. "Here, what's this, Welles?" Bainbridge asked, when a ragged, gaunt man stopped his work and approached the buckboard.

"Well, you see, they've taken it," the man said. "Kit and caboodle."

"Austin, Austin," Bainbridge said. "I warned you about borrowing money from—" He stopped, lifted a hand. "Forgive me. The last thing you need now is someone telling you 'I told you so.' "

"I guess I deserve it," Welles said. "You did warn me, Reverend, but I guess I couldn't believe you . . ."

Gradually, as Bainbridge shared food from their own supplies with the Welles family, Jon pieced the story together. Bainbridge conducted a brief prayer session before Welles lifted his tow-headed brood atop his poor possessions, and the wagon rumbled off toward the south.

Jon had taken to riding in the buckboard occasionally, for the company and to ease the saddle sores on his backside. He let Bainbridge ride in moody silence for a mile or so before saying, "I gather that my stepfather foreclosed on the Welles holding?"

"It's one of the favourite tactics of the squatters," Bainbridge said. "They have the money. They have the best of the land already, and they're not satisfied. They want to keep the selectors out. They wait until a man is in trouble, after a drought, or when crops fail for other reasons, and then they generously offer to lend more money than the small farmer can ever hope to pay back— wait until, inevitably, the loan is in arrears, and then use perfectly legal means to take the man's land."

Jon knew enough, by then, to see that Bainbridge was in an awkward position. It was obvious that his sympathies were with the smallholders and equally obvious that his church in Melbourne, his chapels in the outlying villages, in fact his entire work was dependent on the large contributions of men like Marcus Fisher. Jon had long since decided that if he had to resort to tactics such as those used by Fisher, he would stay poor.

"We are now riding on your stepfather's land," Bainbridge said one morning, after they had spent the night sleeping on straw mattresses in a small farm's barn.

It was fine, wide-open land, gently rolling into the distance, the grass dotted here and there with low-growing brush. Sheep clustered in clumps. Herdsmen and their dogs gazed at the buckboard and rider, the men bearded and blank-eyed, the dogs nervous and alert.

"In view of the bad blood between Fisher and me," Jon said, "I think it best if I rode past and went into town."

"I doubt seriously if your stepfather will be here," Bainbridge said. "And given the size of this holding, 'riding past' may be more than you bargained for. But suit yourself."

Indeed, Marcus Fisher was yet in Melbourne, not at his estate by the lake but at the town house he kept near his waterfront business offices. He was entertaining a guest, a barrel of a man, whose girth was nearly half of his height of a full six feet. Even though the guest was dressed in a dark, expensive evening suit that looked thoroughly English, his stiff bearing, close-cropped hair, and monacled left eye telegraphed his nationality even before he spoke in a harsh Prussian accent.

"My dear Duke," Fisher said, as Maxim Stoltz marched ahead of him into the well-appointed study, "I trust you are enjoying your stay in Melbourne."

74

"I find the facilities quite primitive," Stoltz said stiffly.

"But I trust it is all suitable grist for your pen," Fisher said, showing the duke to a comfortable English leather chair and filling a crystal snifter half full of French brandy. He smiled, for he knew full well that the pose of tourist and writer adopted by the German was just that—a pose. He knew Stoltz to be a rich and powerful man, a familiar at the German court, whose primary interests, no doubt, were to advance his country's, and his own, commercial position in the region. Fisher had his sources, and he knew that Stoltz had come to Australia from Samoa, where Germany was trying to establish a formal colony to consolidate its trading base in the Pacific.

"*Ja*," Stoltz said, after swallowing a gulp of the powerful spirits. "I find that there are odd customs here that will interest German readers."

"I myself would be interested in reading your impressions of Samoa," Fisher said.

Stoltz did not betray surprise at his host's knowledge of his itinerary. "A lovely place" was all he said.

"I have heard that the women are quite beautiful," Fisher continued, with a suggestive smile.

"It is for your countrymen to 'go native,' as they say, with females of an inferior race," Stoltz snapped, glaring through his monacle. "Personally I think the practice is reprehensible."

"Quite so," Fisher retreated. He decided to try another tack. "Did the representatives of Her Majesty's government give you a joyful welcome in Samoa?"

Stoltz stiffened his back even more.

"And, of course," Fisher went on, "the Americans threw open their arms to you. Why, both the British and the Americans would welcome a German presence in Samoa, is that not so?" He was offended by the superior manner of the German and had decided to get to the heart of the matter.

"I do not find that to be humourous," Stoltz said.

Fisher let his face go slack. "I myself have considerable business interests in the South Pacific, sir. I don't find anything humourous in attempts by German merchants to cut into my trade." There came a time, Fisher knew, when one had to stand eye to eye with such a man as Stoltz and keep him off-balance with quick thrusts.

To Fisher's surprise, Stoltz laughed. "Perhaps we will get on, Herr Fisher. I like a man who does not beat through the bush."

"Around the bush," Fisher corrected automatically.

Stoltz shrugged his indifference. "I think, Herr Fisher, that your trade with Samoa is in human cargo, is it not?"

Fisher smiled. "There are Samoan men and women who seek opportunity in Australia and New Zealand. We find it profitable to provide transportation and work contracts to such."

Stoltz drained his snifter and shifted his considerable weight. "Since you are a man who speaks directly to the point, I will do the same. I am perfectly aware that the indenturing of Samoans is nothing more than a legal way of continuing the slave trade." He laughed at his host's reaction, for Fisher had nearly dropped his glass of brandy. "Forgive me, but it is amusing, since it was you British who lamented most piteously over the shipment of black Africans to the plantations of the New World."

"They are not slaves," Fisher defended. "They sign contracts to work for a specified period of time at specified wages—"

"Which amount to just enough food to keep them alive and a place to sleep," Stoltz said.

"Be that as it may, they earn their freedom and a chance to resettle in a new and growing country."

Stoltz adjusted his monacle. "And you use Samoan labour to harvest your sugarcane crops, to cut your trees for timber, adding greatly to your margin of profit."

"I am a businessman," Fisher said.

"As am I. So let us talk business, Herr Fisher."

"It was my impression that such was the purpose of this meeting, which, I might add, is taking place at your request." Fisher rose and poured more brandy for both of them.

"*Ja, gut*," Stoltz said. "So let us examine, in this world that is fuelled by trade, what it is that each of us has that would interest the other."

"By all means, let us," Fisher agreed, but he could think of nothing the Germans had that he wanted. He, on the other hand, had wood, wool, wheat.

"Would you say, Herr Fisher, that the colonial policy of Great Britain, a policy that is aimed at keeping other great powers, such as Germany, out of the Far East and the Pacific is a wise policy?"

"From whose viewpoint?" Fisher asked.

"Ah," Stoltz said. "Indeed. Let me approach this from another angle. Suppose, just suppose, that the German government and the young German nation tires of the overbearing claims of the British that they rule the seas and challenges them, perhaps in the Pacific."

"Then there would be war," Fisher answered bluntly.

"Exactly," Stoltz said. "And who, Herr Fisher, would be damaged most by a sea war in the Pacific? Who would stand to lose the most if German ships blocked the passages at some crucial points, such as the Cape of Good Hope?"

"That is a prospect I hesitate to contemplate," Fisher replied diplomatically.

"You," Stoltz said, "and Australia. How many of your ships would have to be sunk or seized to hurt your business ventures here severely?"

Fisher considered the prospect unlikely. "If you are threatening war, sir, you are talking to the wrong person."

"I?" The German spread his hands. "I am a man of peace. I do not want war any more than you do. I, too, would lose much." He leaned forward. "However, Herr Fisher, it is often left to men of common sense, to the business community, to avert the foolishness of the governments. Their interest is power. Ours, as I think you will agree, is money."

"What do you suggest?"

"I suggest that under certain conditions, ships chosen by you would be welcome in the German ports of Samoa, while others would not."

Fisher was beginning to see the light. What Stoltz was offering him was a monopoly on the kanaka trade—the Samoans and other islanders were referred to, with no little bigotry, by that term—at German ports in Samoa. In a labour-hungry Australia and New Zealand, that meant enormous profits.

"As I hardly need say, sir, I am interested."

"I am sure you will agree that in the event of any armed conflict between Germany and Great Britain, most probably involving the Americans as well, it would be in the interests of Australia to remain neutral."

"Ah," Fisher said, somewhat taken aback. All the man was

asking him to do was to be a traitor to the British empire. Although the idea, in itself, was less than attractive, he immediately began to consider the lucrative possibilities.

"You are a man of some influence," Stoltz continued. "While you are a member of the international business community, an entity that suffers most by war, you are also involved in governmental councils of your own country. As an influential member of the Victoria legislature, you are in an excellent position to advocate the sanity of free trade. A vote here on some tariff matter that would, if passed, heighten tensions, a vote against the confederation of Australia—"

"I am but one man," Fisher said.

"But the fight must begin somewhere. Do you agree that if the liberals win, and there is a confederation, land reform, and all that goes with it, you will lose much?"

"There is firm opposition, of course, to such actions," Fisher said.

"But, also, would not the liberals immediately move to close down your very profitable kanaka trade?"

"I see that you are not a novice on the subject of Australian politics," Fisher said noncommittally.

Again Stoltz spread his hands. "Is not what I have said the basis of our becoming partners and allies?"

"Sir," Fisher said, "since you are so well versed in the affairs of my adopted country, perhaps you also know that there are certain opponents of confederation who could be persuaded, with the proper inducements, to change their stance?"

Stoltz grinned broadly. "*Now* we are on a subject that is familiar to me—the subject of money. We are prepared, Herr Fisher, to assist you and those who stand with you in any way possible."

"With cash?"

"Not in unlimited amounts, but perhaps enough to tip the balance in certain specific cases."

"This cannot, of course, be committed to paper," Fisher said.

"I am a duke of the kingdom of Prussia," Stoltz said. "My word is worth more than a ton of paper. Send your ships to Samoa. You will find that they are welcome there in German ports."

Fisher stood. "I will do that, Herr Stoltz."

"And your bond?"

"I am not a duke of anything," Fisher said. "But in business, my word is my bond."

"Then it is settled," Stoltz said, rising and extending his hand.

Marcus Fisher's sheep station near Urquhart Falls served also as a staging area for labour gangs employed in Fisher's timbering operations. When Jon Fisher and Evan Bainbridge finally arrived at the central buildings, it was midday and a weather change was in the air. Twenty or so kanakas were sitting, lounging, or standing near one of the larger outbuildings. Several women in the group, all of them young and lithe, were dressed in clothing that added an exotic touch to the scene.

Jon, having been away from Australia for nine years, was not aware that the importation of native islanders under indenture had become so prevalent. He was impressed by the size of the men, the natural grace of the women. As he and Bainbridge rode past, he stared at the islanders with fascination.

A man at the main house hailed Bainbridge, who waved in a friendly way. "Wait here, please," he told Jon. "I'll signal to you if your stepfather's here; but I think you're perfectly safe." He turned the buckboard toward the house.

A drover was training a young sheepdog in a pen nearby; the man gave orders calmly and softly as the dog, quivering in its eagerness, drove two lazy-looking sheep from one end of the paddock to the other. From the group of islanders there came a guttural, rhythmic chanting. The sun was at its zenith. Jon dismounted, removed his hat, and wiped his brow, all the while wondering where he was to start in this new venture of buying wool.

Bainbridge had disappeared into the house, but a minute later he emerged with a black-bearded man, not the one who had hailed him. The two of them walked over toward Jon.

Bainbridge introduced the bearded man as Captain Bartholomew Jamison.

"I see that you have a new batch of kanakas," Bainbridge said to Jamison before the man had a chance to question Jon. "I presume that there are Christians among them. They appear to be Samoans."

"No doubt," Jamison said gruffly. He was a bull of a man, with a thick neck, powerful, sloping shoulders, and deep chest. His nose was a harsh beak, his eyes hooded slits under brows as black and profuse as his beard. "You missionaries have always liked the tropical isles, no doubt for the willingness of their women."

Bainbridge ignored the insult. "I trust I have your permission to offer them what comfort I can?"

Jamison waved a hand. "Be quick about it. We'll be moving them out soon."

"You'll be welcome at the service tonight, Captain," Bainbridge said.

Jamison snorted.

An aborigine boy was idling near the sheep pen. Bainbridge motioned to him, and he came on the run. "Will you please see to my horses, Willy?"

"I do, boss," the boy said as Bainbridge handed him a copper coin.

Jon followed Bainbridge to the group of Samoans. For the first time he noticed the fatigue and confusion on the broad, dark faces. One of the women was obviously ill, lying on the baked ground with nothing under her.

"How many of you understand English?" Bainbridge asked. A few men and women indicated their understanding. "If one of you will please translate for me?"

A strong-looking young man stepped forward. "We will welcome the words of Christ from you, reverend sir. I will translate."

Bainbridge spoke slowly, of love, and hope, and of the eternal rewards of salvation. The young Samoan translated the words with generous gestures. A woman began to sob softly. At the end of his brief sermon Bainbridge led the group in a hymn, and the strains of it had scarcely died away when Jamison, with a cat-o-nine-tails in his hand, appeared with a half dozen rough-looking men.

"Now that you've purified their souls," Jamison said, 'it's time we put them to work." He yelled harshly in the Samoan tongue, and the group huddled into a rough formation, preparatory to being marched off. The sick woman was helped to her feet.

"Captain Jamison," Bainbridge said, "I don't think that woman is in any condition to make a march to the forests."

80

"You stick to their souls, Bible pounder," Jamison said. "I'll take care of their bodies."

"Sir," Bainbridge pressed, "I must insist. That woman needs medical attention." He moved forward and took the woman from the two men who were supporting her. With a snarl, Jamison moved with a quickness surprising for his size and bulk, seizing Bainbridge by the collar of his coat, jerking him away, and sending him sprawling. As if for good measure, he laid a quick backhand blow of the scourge across the woman's shoulders. She cried out and almost fell, then managed to stagger to safety within the group of Samoans. Jamison wheeled and, raising the whip, stood over the fallen Bainbridge.

"That will be enough," Jon said, moving forward.

Jamison's slitted eyes darted to Jon. "And who in Hades are you to give me orders?"

"I don't see where that concerns you," Jon said. He extended a hand to Bainbridge, who, still dazed, was sitting up. He had dust on one cheek. Jamison stepped between them, his shoulders hunched. "I asked you your name, pup," he snarled.

"I'm Jon Fisher."

An openmouthed laugh revealed blackened, broken teeth behind Jamison's beard. "Well, well," he said. "As it happens, I've just come from a chat with your stepfather in Melbourne."

"Very interesting," Jon said. "Now, if you'll please stand aside and let me help Reverend Bainbridge."

"I think not," Jamison said, slapping the cat-o-nine-tails against his palm. "Your stepfather had some unkind things to say about you, bucko."

"I'm sure he did," Jon said. He moved to step around Jamison, but the man again blocked his way.

"Among other things, he said that if you ever put foot on Fisher property again you'd be horsewhipped."

The Samoans had cowered into a tight group at a distance, and Jamison's men were gathering around Jon. It was, Jon realized, a hopeless situation. "I was unaware that my stepfather's threat extended to my crossing a grazing in the outback," he said. "Now, if you'll excuse me, I'll just—" He tried to step around Jamison again, only to stiffen with sudden pain and leap aside as the cat stung his shoulders with a sound like that of a cleaver swung

81

flat-side down onto a fresh cut of meat.

"But this is not the tool for the job," Jamison said, tossing the cat aside. One of his men threw him a coiled bullwhip. Jamison caught the leather handle neatly, jerked the long lash behind him and, in a flick of the forearm, sent it popping toward Jon's middle. Jon was narrowly able to leap aside to avoid the lash. Jamison coiled the whip again. Jon retreated and circled at a distance, trying to judge the reach of the whip. When it next snapped, it came dangerously close to his face; a flick of that flying tip into the eye and he would be blinded, he realized. With desperate courage, he abruptly dashed forward, thinking to tackle Jamison, but the man was too fast for him. The lash caught him on the side, just above the belt, and he felt the vicious sting and a swift runnel of blood as he leaped backward out of range.

Once, twice, the bullwhip snapped, only inches from his chest. The cut in his side was painful. At first, when he heard his name, Jon could not place the source; then, on the repetition of it, he glanced aside and saw that Bainbridge was on his feet, a short stout stick in his hand. Jon caught the tossed stick deftly and danced aside, only to feel the tip of the bullwhip slash his trousers, leaving fire on the upper part of his left thigh. Again the whip hissed toward him. It was sheer luck that he got the stick in front of him, directly into the path of the lash, so that the tip struck, curled, and for a moment made the lash taut as Jon pulled. Then he had a hand on the lash, and he cropped the stick to grip the leather thong with both hands and pull himself up as if he were climbing a horizontal line.

"He aims to close quarters, Cap'n," a man yelped in laughter.

Jamison clung to the handle of the bullwhip, trying to jerk the lash out of Jon's hand, and then Jon was near, smelling the feral breath of the bearded man, his right fist flying to land solidly on the point of Jamison's jaw, his left still clinging to the lash near the handle. He saw Jamison's return blow coming, managed to duck it, and buried his right into Jamison's stomach. Jamison grunted and landed a blow that rang like a bell in Jon's head and momentarily dimmed his vision. He felt himself falling, but he clung desperately to the lash. His entire weight was on the lash and the right arm of Jamison, who tumbled after him. Jon landed on his back, rolled, felt the lash jerk out of Jamison's hand. He threw the whip aside and leaped at the fallen man, catching him full on the nose with a solid blow as Jamison scrambled to his feet.

Jamison shook it off, however, made it to his feet, and rushed forward, bull-like. Jon knew that he was no match for the man in strength, but at Sandhurst he had had more than a little training in the pugilistic art as championed by the Marquis of Queensberry, and as he fell back before Jamison's fury he landed three quick, jabbing blows, so that Jamison's black beard was becoming matted with blood.

Jamison managed to connect with a powerful blow to Jon's chest, and he feared that his ribs were cracked. He stepped backward, fists up, guarding against Jamison's savage, looping swings. He saw his chance and launched his right fist, with all his body and shoulder behind it. It landed on the side of Jamison's jaw, and the fury went out of the man as he slumped heavily to the ground.

"By God, I wouldn't have believed it!" a man muttered, as Jamison struggled, only to fall back into the dust.

"Come," Bainbridge said, putting a hand on Jon's arm.

"Not so fast," one of Jamison's cronies said, pushing Bainbridge away and seizing Jon's arm. Jon broke the grip and swung, only to have his arm seized by another man, and then others subdued his struggles. He was held firmly be two men, one on either side, as Jamison, shaking his head, and with blood dripping from a cut eye and from his mouth and nose, staggered over to him. He saw the blow coming and could do nothing. Jamison's fist buried itself in his stomach, and the breath went out of him in a whoosh; then the fist was coming again, and when it connected, just below the right eye, he felt a rush of pain and could do nothing but struggle against those who were gripping his arms. Out of the corner of his eye he saw the old minister try to help him, only to be felled with one swift blow. Then Jamison's fist contacted his cheek again, and a dullness overwhelmed him. He had a vague awareness, without pain, that he was being struck again and again.

When he awoke he felt quick panic, thinking that he had been, after all, blinded by Jamison's lash. A heavy weight seemed to oppress him, along with an ache that encompassed his entire body. He groaned as he raised himself on one elbow.

"Thank God," he whispered, as he detected a glimmer of light, struggled to open his swollen eye, and saw that he was in a crude room with an oil lamp.

"Here, you're awake," said a voice that seemed familiar. He turned his head and felt as if his entire brain had slid inside his skull. He saw that Bainbridge was sitting in a chair beside his bed. "Easy lad. Lie back."

"Where—" he whispered, but the effort to speak caused his cut lip to begin bleeding again.

"Easy," Bainbridge said. "He's gone. You're going to be all right."

Jon accepted something to drink, a warm brew that tasted bitter but was nonetheless soothing. When next he woke it was daylight, the morning sun coming in through a paneless window. Bainbridge was slouched on the floor against the wall, a blanket over his legs. The old man had a livid bruise on his cheek below one eye. Jon raised himself to a sitting position and gingerly tested his legs and his arms. He seemed to be of a piece. He moved his legs off the bed, groaning as the movement revived his headache and sent a dull pain shooting through his chest. It took him several minutes to assess the damage. He could only imagine what he looked like, there being no mirror in evidence. Both his eyes were swollen, one closed entirely. His lips had been punished badly. However, although his chest and stomach were sore, there seemed to be no broken ribs. He stood, feeling as if he were scaling a vast height, and then that he was looking down from a mountain peak.

He was standing at the door when he heard Bainbridge moving behind him. The morning sky was glowering. The weather system that had been threatening was moving toward the grazing station rapidly, with vast, towering black clouds almost touching the ground. A distant rumble of thunder sounded.

"Thank goodness," he heard Bainbridge say. The old man was having trouble getting up.

Jon moved stiffly to extend a hand and help him to his feet. "Are you hurt?" he asked.

"Only stiff." Bainbridge began to brush himself off.

"I saw you try to help me. I am in your debt."

"I must confess," Bainbridge said, with a wry smile, "that at the time I was not quite sure that I should try to be my brother's keeper. But I had no desire to turn the other cheek after this." He touched the bruise under his eye.

The aborigine boy who had attended the horses appeared, a loaf of coarse bread and some cheese in his hands. "You eat, boss?"

"Not I," Jon said. "Thank you. Your master, Jamison, where is he?"

"He go," the boy said, waving a hand. "Take kanakas to big trees."

Bainbridge took the bread and cheese and handed over another copper coin. The boy disappeared and returned within minutes, driving the buckboard, with Jon's horse tied behind.

"I think, Mr. Fisher, that we'd best get you into Urquhart Falls and have a doctor look at you," Bainbridge said.

"I'll be all right," Jon said. "You told me that there would be wool to buy in this area."

"Ah, the amazing recuperative powers of the young." Bainbridge climbed stiffly into the buckboard. "I feared that he intended to kill you. Jamison is a violent man, but I suspect that something more was behind his actions than mere anger at my trying to do something for that poor woman and your intercession."

"Captain Jamison saw fit to step into a family quarrel," Jon said, after joining him on the seat. He did not voice his intention to meet with Jamison again; he had no wish to involve the good minister in further trouble. "Wool, Mr. Bainbridge. I came for wool."

And wool he found. The fertile grazing fields of Victoria seemed to have been made by the Creator for sheep, and their wool that year was rich and of the finest quality. He was amused when Bainbridge took a part in his first attempt to buy wool, employing a smooth bargaining technique to bring the price down considerably from the initial quoted offer. Jon was not sure, nor was Bainbridge, that they had struck the best possible bargain until, three successful negotiations later, the prices were so closely grouped that Jon said, "I think we've done well. These graziers know the value of their own product." There had come a point in each of the different negotiations when the growers refused to cut another shilling.

"Well, you'll find out, my boy, when you get back to Melbourne and see what others have been selling their wool for."

At first travel was painful. Gradually, however, the soreness left Jon's body, the bruises began to turn pale saffron, the swellings to fade. By the time they had made the return circuit—with detours for Bainbridge to minister to his scattered, isolated flock—one had to look closely to see the tiny scars of healing around Jon's eyes and lips.

The wool he had purchased was to be delivered by the growers to the Melbourne docks. Jon telegraphed Harry in Sydney, quoting amounts and prices, and received a wire in return congratulating him on his bargaining powers. Then there was nothing to do but wait, and he grew restless. The anger generated by his severe beating was still inside him, subdued for the moment, but it was like a small, fierce animal, waiting for release.

He found himself, one morning, in the vicinity of Marcus Fisher's waterfront offices, and although he was not looking for an encounter, he was secretly pleased when, upon rounding a street corner, he found himself directly in the path of his stepfather.

"You," Fisher said, when Jon halted in front of him.

"I met one of your minions at Urquhart Falls," Jon said.

Marcus Fisher did not attempt to hide his satisfaction. "So I heard. I trust you enjoyed your—chat with the good Captain Jamison."

"Our conversation was interrupted, and I intend to finish it someday," Jon said. "But it is to you to whom I now address my words. I tried to persuade my mother to leave you." Fisher started to speak, but Jon held up one hand warningly. "She would not. I respect her wishes. I tell you this, however, in sincerity and before God. Lay a hand on her again and I swear you will regret it for the rest of your life."

Fisher reddened, and when he made no response, Jon went on.

"I'm going to visit her. Do you have any desire to try to stop me?" He almost hoped that his stepfather would dare to defy him.

But Fisher merely shrugged. "None at all. Not until or unless you make a nuisance of yourself again."

Jon started to speak, changed his mind, and without a backward glance walked on. The very next day he hired a gig to take him to the red-brick house overlooking the little lake. Martha Blevins admitted him and led him to the morning room.

Caroline was dressed, to his consternation, in a somewhat bedraggled ball gown. Her hair was done up in a formal style. "Jon, darling," she said, extending a hand. He took it, pressed it.

"I'll be leaving Melbourne soon, Mother," he said. "I wanted to see you once more." She reeked of brandy.

"How kind of you to call," she said. "Would you please summon one of the servants, so that we might have tea?"

"One of the servants is here," Martha Blevins said, her voice pitched as if she were speaking to a child. Jon looked at her in surprise and dismay.

"Oh, Martha, please ask someone to feed the swans," Caroline said. "They're so hungry. It's so difficult to maintain a manor and an estate these days. Jon, did you see the swans?"

Jon looked helplessly at Martha. She nodded affirmatively. "Yes, they're—quite handsome," he said.

Jon followed Martha out of the room. In the hallway he took the old woman's arm and pulled her to a halt, raising one eyebrow in question.

"Is she like this often?"

"It comes and goes," Martha said. "I humour her. She fancies that she's back in England, the mistress of a magnificent manor. It does no harm."

Jon went back. Caroline chatted, quite lucidly, about the old days in England until Martha served the tea. Once again Jon asked his mother if she would leave with him—to England, if she wished—and once again he was refused.

"Don't concern yourself about me," she said. "I have exactly what I need, and—" Her eyes went dark, and she gazed off into unfathomable distances, "—what I deserve."

He stayed with her for an hour, prompting her to speak of the old days, when she was young and married to John Omerod; he hoped that the memories would encourage her to go to England. In the end, he had to admit defeat. He rose to leave.

"Before you go I have something for you," she said. She swept regally across the room and did not become unsteady on her feet until she had reached a small writing desk. She opened a drawer, turned, and, balancing herself with difficulty, walked toward him, smiling. She handed him a bank draft, made out to his name, for a surprisingly large amount.

"What's this?" he asked.

"For you."

"I will not have one penny of Marcus Fisher's money," he said. He tried to hand it back to her, but she was adamant.

"This is yours, your birthright, from your father."

"My father?"

"From Colonel Forsyth," she said. "It was mine, and now it is yours."

"My father is—"

"Hush," Martha Blevins said from behind him; she had entered the room without his hearing her. "Take it and let her see your gratitude. What she says is true. It's her money."

"Mother, I—"

"Take it, damn you," Martha hissed in his ear. "Do this one last thing for her."

Jon felt a chill. At the moment his mother's eyes had the clarity of sanity in them, and she was smiling. "Thank you, Mother. I shall consider you a partner in my business ventures, and this an investment to be returned with interest."

"How nice," Caroline said. She drifted toward the windows. "Come and see the swans before you go, darling."

He stood at her side. The surface of the little lake was wind-rippled and bare of any life. "They seem to be missing," he said, watching for her reaction.

"Oh, dear, just when I wanted to show them off. But you'll see them the next time, my dear."

Jon told Martha that he would find his own way out. As he left the room, his mother's voice was in his ears. She was talking animatedly about having a great ball, inviting all the best society from London. He halted, turned to go back, and then, with a feeling of inadequacy and sadness tempered—he had to admit—by relief, he opened the front door and stepped into the world that awaited him.

CHAPTER IV

Magdalen Broome was accustomed to having her husband show up at the house shortly before dinner with an unexpected guest. Of late, such guests had tended to be young and, more often than not, handsome as well, so that Magdalen, although she didn't broach the subject with Red, concluded that he might possibly be growing concerned about Harry Ryan's continued courting of their daughter. Magdalen herself was not worried on that score; she knew her daughter well, knew that Jessica was enough like her to show unmistakable signs if she were actually in love with Harry or with anyone. Magdalen knew that Jessica was a thoroughly sensible young woman and that she considered Harry no more than a friend, less than a brother, and certainly not an acceptable suitor.

The latest young man escorted home by Red Broome was obviously, from his walk and his clothing, a ship's officer. Red tended toward such men. He was young, bright-eyed, and cut a fine figure in his dark-blue jacket, brightly shined black shoes, and visored officer's cap, although the latter came off his head politely the moment he entered the Broome house.

"My dear," Red said, "may I present Sam Gordon, second mate of the *Cutty Sark*."

"Welcome to our home, Mr. Gordon," Magdelen said.

"Ma'am, the commodore assured me I would not be an unwelcome intrusion so near mealtime." The young visitor's accent was decidedly Scottish. "Nevertheless, my apologies."

"Nonsense," Magdalen said. "There's always a place for one more at our table. Harry and Jessica are in the drawing room, Red, and dinner will be ready in three-quarters of an hour. So there's plenty of time for you gentlemen to—what's the expression—wet your whistles?"

89

"That's close enough, eh, Mr. Gordon?" Red asked, receiving a smile from the younger man. He led the way into the drawing room. Harry Ryan, resplendent in impeccably tailored garments of the latest London fashion, rose. Jessica looked up from her knitting and smiled at her father, then glanced at the young man beside him; her eyes met her mother's only momentarily, but it was enough for a silent communication to pass between them. Her attention returned to the newcomer, and a flush was visible on her cheeks. Red did the introductions.

"Yes, I saw the *Cutty Sark* come in," Harry said. "She's a beauty, no doubt of that."

"Did you have a swift passage, Mr. Gordon?" Jessica asked after a minute, apparently recovered from her initial shyness at first laying eyes on the visitor.

"Only tolerable, I'm afraid," he answered.

"Too bad," Harry quickly put in. "She seems to be plagued with bad luck, the *Cutty*." Harry had evidently noticed Jessica's blush, and his tone barely concealed the instant antagonism he felt toward the newcomer.

"The sun is well over the yardarm," Red said, striding to the sideboard to pour a healthy measure of brandy for Gordon and himself. Harry already had a glass in hand, as usual.

"I know that man from somewhere," Harry whispered to Jessica, who had taken her seat again but had put her knitting aside.

Red and Gordon soon were engrossed in talk of ships, and Magdalen went off to see to dinner. Harry kept studying Gordon's face without joining in the conversation. Then, suddenly, he exclaimed, "But you are the fellow with the cutlass!"

"I beg your pardon?" Gordon said.

"The cutlass, at Rorke's Drift. The Zulus!" Harry leaped to his feet.

"Yes, I was there." Sam broke into a smile. "Of course! How stupid of me. Sorry I didn't recognize you. You were with the young Australian who was killed, and that redcoat lieutenant, right?"

"I can hardly believe it!" Harry had put down his drink to clasp Gordon's shoulder. "All this fellow did was save our lives, Jess, arriving just in the nick of time, what with a few hundred Zulus on our backs."

"But it took the Boers to save all our necks, eh?" Sam added.

"I was afraid you hadn't made it out," Harry said. "I was a bit fuzzy there toward the end, before the Boers arrived."

"I remember now," Gordon said. "Unlike you, I escaped with only nicks and bruises. But I see you've recovered well."

"Quite well," Harry said. "And that redcoat lieutenant you mentioned is now my business partner, Jon Fisher."

"Glad to hear it," Sam said. "It is a small empire, isn't it?"

"For those who ply the clippers, it is," Red put in. "I'm envious of you for that ship, Mr. Gordon."

"I imagine that old Jock Willis has had a bellyful of being beaten by just about every other clipper in the trade," Harry said without tact, although clearly he was in much better spirits now.

"Yes, Uncle Jock is, quite naturally, disappointed in the *Cutty*'s performance to date," Sam said. "But we're all sure that she'll live up to her potential."

"Have you been in the *Cutty Sark* long, Mr. Gordon?" Jessica asked.

"On this tour, no," Sam answered. "But I was in her on her trial runs and on her maiden voyage. I was a mere apprentice then, of course."

"But you were in naval uniform at Rorke's Drift," Harry said.

"Well," Sam admitted, "Uncle Jock wasn't the only one who was disappointed in the first few trips the *Cutty* made."

"I sense a story there," Jessica said. "Do tell us."

"Actually, there's not much to tell," Sam said. "I was young. I had watched the ship grow from her keel up. I knew that only the finest of materials had gone into her, that my uncle and his supervisors had been so selective that it nearly bankrupted the construction firm. I knew that she had the lines of an extreme clipper, that she was a racehorse, a miracle of design, but—and this is not really a damning criticism—her first captain, George Moodie, was simply not a driver. He was a good man, an honest and fair man, and he taught me all I know about the sea, but . . . it takes a young man, perhaps a somewhat reckless man, to drive a clipper and get the best out of her."

"And there have been those who have driven clippers right under," Harry said.

"No danger of that with Captain Moodie," Sam replied,

shaking his head ruefully. "I wanted so desperately to knock that cock off the masthead of the *Thermopylae*. I guess I was young enough to be ashamed. So I left the merchant service and took a commission in the Royal Navy—thus I was at Rorke's Drift, Mr. Ryan."

"And now back in the merchant service?" Jessica asked.

"And back on the *Cutty* for good?" Harry added.

Sam Gordon answered with a determined nod.

"And will she be in the hands of a driver now?" Red asked.

"I'd venture to say that one day Mr. Gordon hopes to—ah—drive the *Cutty* himself," Jessica answered for him.

"You've divined my fondest dream," Sam admitted. "When I was a lad, I climbed down onto the *Cutty*'s figurehead as she was being launched, in order to place the horse's tail in the hand of the witch. I promised myself then that one day she would be mine."

"You'd best hurry, then," Harry said. "Soon it will be all steam. Already steamers through the Suez are taking the bulk of the China trade."

Red took up the challenge. "There'll always be a place for the clipper, Harry. No one wants to drink tea, for example, that has spent weeks in an iron hull. Gives it a bad taste. And it's still uneconomical for steamers to carry enough coal to make the Australian run."

"It's my turn, please, gentlemen," Jessica put in. "You passed right over some very enigmatic remarks made by Mr. Gordon. What's this about witches and horses' tails?"

"I beg your pardon, Miss Broome," Sam said. "We Scots sometimes mistakenly assume that everyone knows the lore we were brought up with. Let me explain—"

"Jess," Harry said, reluctant to let the newcomer monopolize Jessica's conversation. "I'm sure you've read the Burns poem about Tam O'Shanter."

Sam adroitly skipped over the interruption. "It's not one of his greatest works, perhaps, but my uncle was very fond of it." Moving to Jessica's side, he recited it for her, so that Harry could not cut in, and Jessica responded with delighted laughter as he described how he had risked falling into the icy water to put the scrap of rope into the hand of the *Cutty*'s figurehead.

At dinner, the conversation was general, touching on the sea trade, and British and Australian politics. It was not until it was time for the guest to leave that, with her mother's timely intervention, Jessica contrived to free herself from Harry long enough to speak with Gordon alone. She escorted him to the front door and handed him his hat.

"Thank you for a very pleasant evening," Sam offered.

"We all hope to see you again before you sail," Jessica said. Her eyes met his, and again she felt the swift rush of colour to her cheeks.

"It takes a while to load a cargo of wool," Sam said, with a reassuring smile. "I'll be here for a time."

"Then I'll ask my father to have you to dinner again."

"I could think of nothing I would prefer more." He started out the door, then turned back. "A thought just occurred to me. Would you care to make a tour of inspection of the *Cutty*?"

Jessica hesitated only a moment. "I'd love to," was her answer. "Thank you, Mr. Gordon."

The *Cutty Sark* stood majestically in the Sydney Cove anchorage, a graceful, dark silhouette that rose above the other vessels anchored nearby. Her spars were bare, except for the red duster that folded and rippled in a small breeze, and the lines of her rigging made an attractive geometric pattern against the sky. The gold letters and scrollwork on her stern stood out brightly against the black hull.

"You'll note," Sam said, as he rowed Jessica toward the ship in a dinghy, "that she has a generous overhang at the stern. This gives her a little more bearing in a strong following sea. But she's at her best in a strong beam or quartering wind. In such winds there's not a clipper that can stay with her. Once, under Captain Moodie, we logged seventeen and a half knots."

There was only a skeleton watch on board. Sam let Jessica go ahead of him up the stepped accommodation ladder and joined her on deck. She tilted her head and looked up to the sky through the towering rigging, then accepted Sam's arm. After sending a man ahead to be sure that everything was shipshape and that the few crewmen still aboard were dressed decently, he showed Jessica the captain's luxurious stateroom and the large, skylighted saloon with its long table and benches and elegant maple-and-teak panelling. Just forward of the saloon were the officers' quarters, where he slept—at least when it was possible to sleep, he added—and Jessica didn't giggle, as most landsmen did, when he told her that the hatch forward of the line of fire buckets was the booby hatch.

Good smells were coming from the galley, which was just forward of midships. Jessica asked if she might peep in, and when Sam opened the door for her, she saw a chubby, smiling Chinese man stirring something on the stove. The cook looked up, clearly startled at the female face, until Sam stepped from behind her. "Ah, Missa Mate," he said. "Good tucker this day. You eat, maybe bling lady?"

"I'd love to," Jessica said.

"Leg of lamb Chinese style," the cook grinned.

So, to the delight of the young duty officer, a Mr. Turner, who had expected to eat in solitude, Sam and Jessica joined him in the saloon. The leg of lamb was delicious, perfectly seasoned, but when Jessica tried to worm the secret out of the grinning Chinese cook, she met with little success.

"We don't always eat this well at sea, Miss Broome," Turner said, pouring the last of the claret and sitting back with a smile of satisfaction. "We carry chickens and pigs for fresh meat, but it doesn't always last the voyage."

Afterward, Sam and Jessica stood together at the taffrail, taking in the view of Sydney Cove and Port Jackson Harbour. "The *Cutty*'s a lovely ship," Jessica said. "I can see why you would want to be her captain one day."

Sam made a wry face. "It may be long in coming, I'm afraid. I didn't please my uncle when I left his service to enter the navy."

"You'll do it," she said, with a confidence in her tone that surprised Sam. He was looking into her eyes, noting that there were little sparkles of light being reflected from their blue depths. He swallowed. Although he was no roué, Sam was not totally inexperienced with women; yet he had never had a woman look at him in just that way.

"Why do they call such a beautiful ship unlucky?" Jessica asked.

"She's not unlucky. If anything, the men who have had her have been unlucky."

"That's a fine distinction."

"I think everyone expected too much of *Cutty* too soon," Sam said. "They laughed when it took us a hundred and four days from the Channel to Shanghai on her maiden voyage, but, Good Lord, she was new! It took a while to tune the sails and the rigging, and the crew wasn't familiar with her idiosyncrasies. Still, we had some splendid runs on that first voyage, up to three hundred and sixty miles a day."

Looking back, Sam felt a surge of resentment against all those who spoke slightingly of the *Cutty*, and against those men who had captained her. Of course, other factors had contributed to the *Cutty*'s lack of distinction. For example, her first cargo of tea, on that initial voyage, had paid only half the freight that similar clippers had earned before the opening of the Suez Canal. True, *Thermopylae* had whipped her by two full days on her second voyage to China; but on the third voyage, when the *Cutty* and the *Thermopylae* left Shanghai on the same day, the *Cutty* had surged four hundred miles ahead in the first two weeks of the voyage, before losing her rudder in a gale in the Indian Ocean.

Captain Moodie had shown his mettle then, when most skippers would have limped into the nearest port for repairs. Using a small-scale model of the *Cutty* as a guide, he had ordered the ship's carpenter to fashion heavy planks by sawing up spare spars, had the blacksmith forge iron fittings, and jury-rigged a rudder that allowed her to hobble around the Cape of Good Hope and on to London. And, at that, *Thermopylae* had bested them by only a week.

Sam had been introduced to the sea by the *Cutty Sark*, and she, in spite of her sometimes inept captains, had been a good teacher. There were those who could not understand why a man went to sea, for it was a harsh and unforgiving life, but those who questioned it had never been aboard a clipper being driven with her lee rails under, skimming the sea as if she had been born to it. He had been offered other positions, as first mate on other clippers, as well as on steamships, but he could not bring himself to desert the *Cutty* before she had proved herself as he knew she could. He owed at least that much to his uncle, and to his own pride.

Old Jock had forgiven Sam his bad judgment in going into the navy, but being of the old school, Jock was not one simply to hand

over command of one of his clippers to a comparative newcomer
—even his own nephew—and Sam would have to earn the honour.
He only hoped it would come before the time Jock thought it
appropriate for him to stow his sea gear in the attic and take his
place in the world of business.

Sam was not yet ready for that eventuality. He was still in love
with his mistress, the *Cutty Sark*, although, if the truth were
known, his fidelity was being sorely tested at this very moment, as
a small harbour breeze played with the curls at Jessica's temples.

"After Moodie, they picked another old man to captain her," he
said. "He wasn't a bad man, William Tiptaft, but he was fifty, and
it takes a young man to drive a clipper, a man who can get by on a
couple of hours of sleep, or go without sleep for days."

Sam had left the *Cutty* before her second captain had died of a
heart attack in Shanghai, and so he was not in her when James
Smith Wallace drove her hard and well until, in the Indian Ocean,
the fiery-tempered first mate killed a seaman who he felt was being
slack. Captain Wallace allowed the mate to leave the ship and join
an American vessel in the Sunda Strait, breaking the law and
putting his crew into a righteous rage. Subsequently the *Cutty*
sailed into a calm in the Java Sea with the crew on the verge of
mutiny. Captain Wallace, a severely disturbed man, went overboard in the middle of the night, leaving the ship without a
captain. The crew took her into Singapore, where most of them
deserted, having had enough of what they considered a bad-luck
ship, and it was in Singapore that the *Cutty Sark* was given the
most nefarious captain of her lifetime.

The man selected by Jock Willis, William Bruce, was a short,
pudgy Scot with eyes that seemed on the verge of jumping out of
his head. His voice was high-pitched, almost feminine, and—as
Sam Gordon was to discover when he rejoined the *Cutty*—he did
not refrain from exercising it regularly. Bruce was a man with a
severely split personality. Deeply religious, he frequently haran-
gued the crew with Bible-pounding, soul-saving sermons; yet he
was also a drunken sot. The *Cutty* had taken forty-two days to sail
from Singapore to Calcutta, half again as long as it should have
taken, because Bruce was celebrating his new command with an
extended period of drunkenness and kept ordering the sails to be
shortened.

As fortune would have it, Sam Gordon had joined the *Cutty* in time for her ultimate humiliation. She had left Calcutta with a cargo of tea for Melbourne and, for a few blessed weeks, had made excellent time—with Bruce sober, but immersed in his Bible to the point where the junior officers exercised effective command, she had romped over the waves in smart fashion. However, as they neared the coast of Australia, Bruce had come out of his cabin, put his Bible aside, and promptly shortened sail, allowing the *Cutty* to flounder while he checked and rechecked the navigation of the first mate. A much slower sailer that had left Calcutta a week after the *Cutty* passed unchallenged and beat *Cutty* into Melbourne Harbour.

Jessica interrupted Sam's musings to remind him that it was growing late. He helped her down the accommodation ladder and into the dinghy and rowed to the docks, the troubles of the *Cutty Sark* taking second place in his mind to the pleasure of facing Jessica in the small boat, to be able to study at leisure the delicate lines of her neck, the flattering way she had arranged her hair, her full, red lips.

He was invited to dinner again that evening, and the only damper on his pleasure was that Harry Ryan was once more present. But there were other guests to prevent Harry from dominating the conversation, among them Harry's employer and an old Broome family friend, the trader and shipowner Claus Van Buren. Sam was seated next to Van Buren, and he found that the older man was not at all reluctant to talk. In a soft-spoken, down-to-earth manner—the exact opposite of Harry—he yet managed to recount a stirring tale of his experiences during the Maori wars in New Zealand and spoke of his trading post in the Bay of Islands and of his clipper ships.

Sailing records were a popular topic of conversation at the Broome house, Sam had discovered somewhat to his dismay, for the *Cutty Sark* held no records. Harry, seated across from Sam, did not let this embarrassing fact go unmentioned.

"She's never had the proper captain," Jessica said, coming immediately to his defence and thus earning Sam's gratitude and irritating Harry.

"By all accounts," Claus Van Buren put in, "she should be the fastest ship afloat."

"Nonsense," Harry said; as usual, he had been drinking more than his share and was being cocky, as well as put out by Jessica's attention to Sam Gordon. "Not only are there many clippers that can best her—she could be bested by a steamer."

"Let's not get carried away, Harry," Red Broome intervened, his tone good-natured but firm.

"Take the *Antony*", Harry said, ignoring him. The *Antony* was a new steamer belonging to Marcus Fisher and Leonard Brownlow. "My bet is that she's the fastest vessel in the South Pacific."

"Harry," Jessica said, "you're being rude. Anyway, it's all speculation. But perhaps one day we'll see if a smelly old steamer can beat the *Cutty*."

"If they can get her captain out of church to take her to sea," Harry persisted. "Or out of the nearest pub."

Red Broome frowned. It was common knowledge that Captain Bruce had been preaching fire-and-brimstone to a revival meeting at a small church on the outskirts of Sydney when, by all rights, he should have been seeing to the welfare of his ship after a long voyage and to her loading, instead of leaving such duties to his junior officers. Red sympathized with Sam Gordon. He himself had served under unfit captains, and there was nothing a man could do but do his best and pray for the day when the situation would change.

"Jess," Red said, "I'm sure that our young guest has had enough of sea talk. Why don't you and your mother take him out to the gardens for a view of the harbour by night?"

Magdalen, who suspected that Red had developed a liking for young Gordon, looked quickly at Jessica to see her blush and then smile with pleasure.

"I'll come along," Harry Ryan said, starting to rise.

"No," Red said, "stay with us Harry. Claus has been telling me about this new venture of yours, and I want to hear all about it."

Harry resumed his seat with a look of disgruntlement, his angry eyes following the others from the room. "There's not much to tell," Harry said. "I'll be sailing on the *Java* as supercargo, stopping at Palmerston, and then on to Hong Kong."

"I expect Harry to make me a lot of money," Claus Van Buren said.

"I'm sure he will." Red scrutinized the young man to gauge the reaction to the information he was about to impart: "By the way, Harry, I brought up the subject of your going to Hong Kong for a reason."

Harry looked up, not really interested, his mind still on Jessica and Sam Gordon.

"It hasn't been officially announced yet," Red said, "but I'll be moving the family to Hong Kong shortly. I'm to be the naval attaché there."

Jessica stood in the moonlight, the soft glow shadowing her face in a way that caused a surge of sweet pleasure in Sam. Magdalen, as soon as they had left the dining room, had tactfully excused herself on the pretence of an errand in the kitchen.

"You musn't mind Harry," Jessica said. "I'm afraid he drinks too much."

Harry Ryan was the last person Sam wanted to talk about under such circumstances, but he could think of no way of turning the conversation in other directions without its seeming obvious.

"One can look at the *Cutty Sark* and see that she's a great ship, or will be one day," Jessica said.

"Yes."

"Her time will come, Sam, just as yours will come."

"I pray that is true."

"And when she makes a simply marvellous passage and beats the sails off every other ship on the oceans, you must write to me and tell me about it."

"It would be my pleasure." He smiled. "And if that time is postponed? May I still write to you?"

"Yes," she said, her voice a whisper, for she realized that she had been perhaps too forward. To cover her confusion, she said, "But you'll have to write to me in Hong Kong. My father is being assigned as naval attaché there, and mother and I will be going with him—that's what he's telling Harry at this very moment. It all has to do with Chinese pirates, you see. My father will be organizing some kind of expedition against them, although he's too old to be going into action himself."

Sam felt a pang of loss, for the *Cutty* would be taking her cargo of wool on the long haul around Cape Horn all the way to England. It could be years before their paths crossed again. He opened his mouth to speak, but his lips were suddenly dry. He had wanted to say words to Jessica that would indicate his feelings, his pleasure in knowing her, in being with her, but he couldn't seem to moisten his lips, and his tongue was leaden.

"There's a chill in the air," Jessica said.

"Yes, perhaps we'd better go in."

Jessica took his arm, and for all their disappointment at the impending separation, the expressions in their eyes as they met and held each other's gaze told them all they needed to know.

Jon Fisher's inheritance from his grandmother lay in the hold of a ship, a frail, wooden vessel that would brave the world's most dangerous oceans on the way to deliver the wool to the looms of England. For the next year, or until he earned a return on his investment, nearly all he had to live on was the bank draft in his inner coat pocket, the money from his mother. It was more than enough, certainly, but he was hesitant to touch it. He still felt guilty for having taken the money, but it did, he had to admit, give him a feeling of security. Ships were lost at sea. Ships were burned. If the clipper made it to London, and if England's economy hadn't undergone one of those unpredictable swings for the worse, he would show a good profit on his first trading venture, even after sharing his proceeds with the Van Buren company who owned the clipper.

He made a resolution, there on the Melbourne wharves, as he watched *his* ship being worked out to sea, that he would be very, very conservative with his remaining funds, the money from his mother. Unlike Harry Ryan, he was in no desperate hurry to get rich. He was by nature cautious, and he had learned that he did not like risk, even if only money was at stake.

He made a relatively swift trip northward to Sydney on a coastal trader, to find Harry full of new plans for mercantile success. "Wheat, Jon," Harry said. "The Chinese need wheat for their noodles, and there's space in *Java*'s hold for it."

"I wish you luck," Jon said.

"Not I, *us*—you and me."

"I think not," Jon said. "I'm a bit short, with all my funds tied up in wool."

Harry, of late more secure in his mind about his future chances with Jessica Broome now that she would be living in Hong Kong—distant, but still within reach—and Sam Gordon would be off to England and God only knew where else, arranged a meeting between Jon and Gordon and joined in the talk about the fight on the Buffalo River. That night Red Broome gathered all three of them for dinner and, without anticipating the effect on Harry, dropped a bombshell. At first Harry grinned, for the news involved more bad tidings for the *Cutty Sark*. Her master, busy preaching and drinking, had dallied too long to get favourable rates of freight on wool and instead had settled on taking a cargo of coal to Hong Kong. To a clipper, coal was an ignominious cargo, dirty, leaden in weight, driving her hull so deep into the waves that she had to slog along like a heavy-bodied East Indiaman. It was the second item of news connected with the *Cutty* that caused Harry's neck to redden with anger.

"Jessica and I have decided to take passage on the *Cutty*," Magdalen Broome announced. "The captain has been kind enough to offer us his own stateroom, while he moves in with the junior officers."

Sam Gordon's jaw nearly dropped open, for this was news to him as well. He expressed his astonishment that Bruce would give up the comfort of his own cabin, and admitted he wasn't too pleased to think that, in all likelihood, he would have to share quarters with the first mate, whose own cabin would be commandeered by Bruce.

Red Broome would be taking a naval vessel to Hong Kong, and he had settled on the *Cutty* for his womenfolk because she would be departing only days after his own ship. Red, in fact, announced that he was quite pleased with the arrangement. He had often been separated from his wife and family, for that was the lot of a navy man—indeed, he had not seen his son, Rufus, now finishing naval college in England, for four years—but as he grew older, each separation seemed to be a greater sacrifice. So the sooner Magdalen and Jessica could join him in Hong Kong, the better. And, if the truth were told, Red was not exactly displeased that Jessica and Sam Gordon would have an extended voyage on which to become better acquainted.

When he realized the turn events had taken, Harry was barely able to control his anger. "I had expected that Mrs. Broome and

101

Jessica would accompany me on the *Java*," he said, his words clipped. "We have much more room, and equally comfortable accommodations."

"I appreciate the offer, Harry," Red said, "but Mrs. Broome is eager to join me as quickly as possible. The *Java* will be coasting around Australia, am I not correct?"

"With the luck of the *Cutty*," Harry said, "we could still beat her."

Harry left as soon as the meal was finished, not bothering to join the men for port and cigars in Red's study. Jon and Sam listened to the talk of the older men for a while and then took their leave.

"Shall we join Harry for a nightcap?" Jon asked, as they strolled down toward the town. "He might be needing some consolation."

Sam wasn't exactly eager, for he knew that Harry considered him a rival, but he found that he liked Jon Fisher. Fisher had fought well at Rorke's Drift, and he seemed to have his head on straight. "Why not?" he asked. "But just where shall we join him?"

"He'll be in one of his favourite pubs along the waterfront. Come on, I'll show you."

They found Harry at the first stop; he was standing at the bar in animated conversation with a group of seamen. Harry, already heavy-tongued, greeted them jovially, insisted on treating them, and steered them to a table where he proceeded to down several more drinks while talking animatedly. Sam's fears that Harry might feel resentful toward him seemed to be unfounded, and he was surprised when, without warning, Ryan abruptly turned to him and said, "I'll see both you and the *Cutty Sark* in hell, Gordon."

"Easy, Harry," Jon said.

Harry sprang to his feet and, without a further word, walked out of the pub.

"He's drunk, Sam," Jon said. "He'll apologize tomorrow. Excuse me, but I think I had better set off after him."

Sam was not so sure that Harry *would* feel apologetic in the morning, but he nonetheless followed his friend out the door, intending to mend fences, if he could.

"It's a rough neighbourhood for a man who is going around with a chip on his shoulder," Sam said as they gained the street. Harry was just turning a corner, staggering a bit, striking the edge

102

of a building with his shoulder. Sam was used to dealing with drunken sailors, and although Harry wasn't a shipmate, Sam felt some responsibility for his welfare. "I think," he said, "that it would be good form to tag along and see that he doesn't get waylaid or run aground."

"It's not your concern, but I appreciate it," Jon said.

Sydney, like most seaport towns, could offer a visiting sailor just about any form of vice that could be desired. In the Rocks, to where Jon and Sam found themselves being led, women of the street plied their trade, places to drink were plentiful, and—as if it had come back from dim colonial outposts to haunt the British Empire—opium, that oriental drug of nirvana, was available in at least half a dozen ill-lit dens frequented mostly by Chinese labourers. When Sam and Jon rounded another corner and saw Harry weaving his way across the street toward a particularly notorious opium den, Jon quickened his pace.

"Harry," he called. "Damn it, Harry, wait for us!"

If Harry had heard, he ignored them, if anything quickening his pace. He disappeared into the dark doorway while the others were only halfway across the street.

"That's a bit much, isn't it?" Sam asked.

"A bit too damned much," Jon said.

"Well, we've come this far. I suppose we'd best go in and drag him out."

An ancient Chinese woman in a black tunic and pants accosted them just inside the door. "Gentlemen in wrong place?" she asked, showing toothless gums in a grimace that might once have been a smile.

"We've come to get a friend," Jon said.

"No trouble." It was not clear whether her words were a reply or a warning until a muscular Chinese man, wearing the same dark garments, appeared behind her. He had a plait of black hair hanging down from a flat, round hat, and in his hands was a knife with a blade fully a foot long.

"No trouble," Jon agreed.

He led Sam through a curtained doorway, on the other side of which they halted, for the light was so dim that they could barely make out the forms of men and women, mostly Chinese, it appeared. Along the walls of the room were arranged a series of bunks, and almost all were occupied by motionless forms.

"Keep an eye on that one with the knife," Jon whispered to Sam, as he moved forward. A lissome Chinese girl in bright garments materialized from the shadows.

"Gentlemen want the smoke of blissful happiness?" she whispered.

The air of the room reeked with a peculiar, sweet odour. Through the gloom, the winking, glowing eyes of a dozen pipes were visible as men sucked the deadening smoke into their lungs.

"A friend of ours just wandered in here by mistake," Jon explained.

"It was no mistake," Harry said, from one of the cots near them. He had apparently walked directly to the cot to fall into it; he was holding a pipe in his hand and recommenced drawing hard on it.

"For God's sake, Harry," Jon said, filled with quick disgust.

"Ti li," Harry said to the girl, "give the gentlemen pipes. They're on me, my friends."

"Harry, we're leaving," Jon said. "And we're taking you with us."

"No trouble," warned a deep, heavily accented voice behind Sam. He turned his head to see the big Chinese man, the knife blade glowing in the dim light.

"No trouble," Sam said. "I'm leaving, Fisher."

"No quicker than I," Jon said.

"You bastard," Harry shouted, leaping from the cot, pipe in hand, making a rush for the Chinaman. "You can't throw my friends out."

"Want trouble," the Chinaman grunted. "You get."

Had it not been for Jon's quick action, the knife blade would have met Harry's rush and cut his throat. As it was, Jon managed to get his hand under the Chinaman's arm, diverting the foce of the blow; still, the blade slashed a deep gash across Harry's left cheek. A quick surge of blood flowed from Harry's face as he halted, shocked, to bring his empty hand up to his cheek. Sam, not wanting trouble but knee deep in it now, with the big Chinese turning to threaten Jon with the knife, kicked the man in the back of a knee and sent him down with a yelp of pain.

"Out of here," Jon ordered, grabbing Harry by the arm.

They pushed aside the curtain in time for Jon to take the fist of another Chinaman in the gut. Harry was making little sobbing sounds of pain. Sam lashed out with a fist and caught the Chinaman in the throat, and the man backed away, gasping for air, his eyes bulging. At the same moment, however, Jon was brought down full length, with the weight of the first man, without the knife, on his back. Harry kicked out and grunted as his toes struck the Chinaman's skull.

Sam helped Jon up, grabbed Harry, and was almost out of the front door when the toothless old Chinese woman materialized before them with a screech of hatred and a wicked-looking scimitar with a gleaming, razor-sharp blade. Jon shouted a warning and ducked under a blow that, even though the old woman looked frail, might have decapitated him; and then both the Chinese men were back, attacking with a rush of bellowed threats and fancy arm movements of some Oriental martial discipline. Jon took a blow to the head that made him dizzy even as he caught one of the black-clad men with a boot in the groin, and Sam turned back to hammer the second Chinaman with a series of blows.

The blade of the scimitar flashed again, barely missing Harry and threatening the Chinamen as much as it imperilled Jon and Sam. The muscular Chinaman yelled a hoarse protest and shoved the old woman sprawling through the curtain, and a second later two more black-clad forms appeared from behind the cloth, one of them holding a butcher's knife.

"Run for it," Jon shouted, giving Harry a push through the front door and diving behind him, as Sam narrowly dodged the thrown butcher knife. He, too, dived outside, rolled, and came to rest against a pair of booted legs just as he heard frantically blowing whistles and saw a brace of constables charging full tilt down the street.

"Yellow boy, hold it right there," shouted a constable, his revolver pointed at the biggest of the two Chinamen, who had recovered his knife. The rush toward the front door from inside the opium den halted. The big Chinese withdrew, slamming the door.

Jon and Sam picked themselves up. Harry was kneeling with his hand to his face, his fingers unable to stop the flow of blood.

"Mates, you picked the wrong place," the constable said, with a disapproving shake of his head.

"It was a mistake," Jon said. "We didn't know what kind of establishment it was."

"Your friend's hurt," the constable said.

"We'll take care of him, constable," Sam said. "I'm second mate of the *Cutty Sark*. We'll take him back to the ship, where he'll not be getting into any more trouble."

"We believe in hospitality to visiting sailors," the constable said, 'but mind you, you'd best stay out of this part of town."

"Thank you, constable," Jon said, leading Harry away. The combination of drink and opium had dulled the pain of Harry's cut, and he went without protest. The *Cutty Sark* was trimmed for the night, lights in place, a seaman on watch. The man hailed the boat and, when Sam identified himself, came down the ladder and helped the wounded man up the gangway.

A clipper did not carry a surgeon. Usually the captain was surgeon, minister, sometimes father to his crew. Aboard the *Cutty*, however, the role of minister had so preoccupied Captain Bruce's sober moments that the remaining duties had fallen to others. Sam went into the officers' quarters, got the medical kit, and directed Jon to light two lamps and place them on the table in the saloon in front of a seated Harry. He pulled Harry's hand away. The cut was long, running from the cheekbone to the corner of the mouth, and although it had not gone all the way through the cheek, it was gaping and still bleeding profusely.

"Jon, you'll find a bottle of brandy in the kit," he said, "there." He was preparing needle and catgut.

"Do with a little taste," Harry mumbled, as Jon handed him the bottle. He drank deeply and then tottered on the verge of unconsciousness.

"Hold him tightly," Sam directed.

As an apprentice, Sam had done his share of sail mending. The technique was crude but effective. The skin was surprisingly tough, making little tents before the sharp needle thrust through. He took fine stitches, close together, and counted twenty-three before he had the gaping cut closed. The flow of blood was diminished. Harry had felt nothing.

"He'll be a good German now," Jon said, "with a fine duelling scar."

"I can't bed him down on board." Sam was replacing the items

106

in the medical kit. "If the captain should hear of it, there'd be trouble."

"I don't want to take him to the Broome house in this condition," Jon said. "I'd better take him to my hotel."

"I'll give you a hand."

"Thank you, but you've done enough," Jon said. "I can't ask you to trouble yourself further."

Sam waved a hand dismissively. "The way I see it, I signed on for the voyage back there in the opium den."

They got Harry to the hotel without incident, but when they were leading him through the lobby, under the suspicious eyes of the night clerk, Harry seemed to revive. "Here," he grumbled, "where are you taking me?"

"Just up to the room, old boy," Jon said. "You can use a little lie down."

"I'm not sleepy," Harry said, pulling away, weaving back toward the entrance.

Jon grabbed for him. "I've had enough of this nonsense, Harry." He seized his friend's arm.

Harry lashed out a backhand, and the blow surprised Jon, bringing blood to his lips and causing him to release Harry. Sam interposed himself between Harry and the door. With a bellow of rage Harry charged, his fists swinging. The night clerk had run out of a side door, calling for the police. Sam gauged his blow, aiming at Harry's uninjured cheek, and let it fly. Harry was stopped, but only for a moment. He cursed, picked up a chair, and flung it. Sam ducked, and the chair smashed the glass of the entry door with a shattering din. Jon caught Harry from the rear, all the while trying to talk sense, but Harry elbowed him in the stomach. Two constables came pounding through the door in time to see Harry throw another chair, which smashed a potted palm.

"You again, is it?" a constable said, moving deftly to snatch Harry's arm up behind him in a painful restraining hold "I thought you were taking this one back to his ship?"

"We did, constable," Jon replied, still short of breath from Harry's blow. "We fixed up his cut, but since he'd already paid for a room in this hotel, we thought it would be a shame to do him out of a chance to sleep in a real bed, what with the ship sailing soon."

The constable was unimpressed. "Now see here, we can't just

brush this off. This is a respectable place, not a Chinese opium den."

"We'll pay for the damages," Jon volunteered. The clerk had come gingerly back into the lobby. Jon extended pound notes. "I think this will cover the damage, sir."

The man took the money.

"Well," the constable said, "is it enough?"

The clerk licked his lips as he fingered the pound notes. "It'll do, I reckon."

"Can you get this one to bed, or shall we help you?" the constable asked.

"We can manage," Jon said fiercely, glaring at Harry.

"I'll be a very good boy," Harry said, with an innocent smile.

"My God, Harry," Jon said, when the constables had gone and the night clerk was standing warily behind his desk. "You will come up to bed now, won't you?"

"Why not?" Harry was all cooperation. He turned, his eyes narrowed. "But this one is not welcome."

"He's welcome to me," Jon said.

"This one I want out of my sight." His tone sounded dangerously serious.

"He saved your neck tonight," Jon said. "There were people in that place who would have slit your throat for your pocket change, much less the wad of notes you carry around."

"I don't like you, Gordon," Harry said. "I have never liked you, and I will never like you."

Sam shrugged at Jon.

"Sam—" Jon began.

"Don't be concerned," Sam said. "I'm going back to the ship. Perhaps we can have lunch before I sail?"

"My pleasure," Jon nodded.

"My pleasure," Harry mimicked drunkenly.

Jon watched Sam Gordon stride out the door. He turned to Harry. "You're an ass, Harry, an insufferable ass."

"Is that any way to talk to your partner?" Harry asked, with a grin made lopsided by the growing stiffness in his injured cheek.

"I may not be that for long, Harry," Jon said.

108

CHAPTER V

For a sailing ship, the quickest passage was rarely the shortest distance between two points. The *Cutty Sark*, her graceful hull riding deep in the water under the weight of her cargo of coal, first beat her way northward, breasting the Australian current that swept down toward the eastern coast from the New Hebrides. She sailed into sodden, equatorial heat, an enervating steambath of tropical air that was inescapable. The teak-panelled walls of the captain's cabin sweated. The air inside was stifling.

The *Cutty*'s crew performed their duties with their clothing heavy with sweat, moving with leaden indifference to the high-pitched orders of Captain Bruce. As always aboard ship, water was scarce, and except when a heavy tropical shower swept over their course, Jessica was always thirsty. She and her mother were allowed water to wash clothes twice a week, so that she felt always soiled and sodden.

A freakish, favouring wind gave wings to the *Cutty* in the northern Coral Sea. Bruce, who seemed to suffer as much as anyone from the heat, was seldom seen on deck, leaving the running of the ship to the first mate, James Draker, a man who seemed to be too old for the position; usually the first officer on a ship of the *Cutty*'s calibre was an energetic younger man on his way toward command.

In spite of the heat and discomfort, Jessica took a great interest in the running of the ship and turned out on deck to observe the trimming of sails, the shortening of canvas in a squall, and she was thrilled when, with the skies bright and wind favourable, Sam Gordon, heading the duty watch, filled the *Cutty*'s spars with a white cloud of canvas that gathered the wind and drove her lee rail under so that white water swirled the deck and seamen had to han on to lines as they traversed the ship's waist. For a time, the *Cu*

med to fly through the waves, and the spirit of a high-seas chase
nimated the crew. They snapped to smartly, swarming up the
hrouds and onto the yards to make some minute adjustment to
the rigging, and their voices from aloft were joyous.

Sam came to find her and help her negotiate the canted
quarterdeck to the stern, where two men stood stoutly at the
wheel, their arms straining to keep the *Cutty* on the quartering
wind, which was blowing with the force of a light gale.

"This, now, is clipper weather, ma'am," shouted one of the men
at the wheel.

Two young apprentices, one of them white-faced and obviously
seasick, were standing at the rail, a coiled, knotted line in their
hands. Sam gave an order, and the weight on the end of the line
was cast into the sea. The two youths let the line run through their
hands. Sam was timing the flow of the line, and when it was fully
extended and the two apprentices were straining against the pull of
it, he grinned with unconcealed delight and said, "Seventeen
knots."

The *Cutty* was, indeed, flying. For the moment she was in the
hands of a driver, and Jessica could see for the first time just how
much Sam loved the ship, and how much joy it gave him to see her
performing as old Jock Willis had hoped, and as her designers had
intended. It bothered Jessica not at all that sea spray wet her face
and that foam from the waves breaking over the rail drenched her
feet. For a moment she allowed herself an idle dream, thinking of
Claus Van Buren and his wife, Mercy, who had always accompanied Claus on his frequent sea voyages, and she tried to imagine
how it would be to be the wife of Sam Gordon, and to be a part of
his life at sea. With the wind in her face and the ship flying, it
seemed not an unpleasant prospect.

Her reverie was interrupted by the high-pitched voice of
Captain Bruce, screaming from the door of the officer's quarters.
"*Mister* Gordon," he shouted, "who gave you orders to lay on
topgallants?"

"Sir!" Sam barked noncommittally.

"Is it your intention to drive her under?" Bruce screamed. "You
will shorten sail at once."

The look on Sam's face caused Jessica's heart to leap in quick
mpathy. He went forward, and she heard him shouting orders

110

through a brass hailing trumpet. Within minutes, the *Cutty* was sailing sedately along, her lee rail no longer awash.

They put in on the island of New Britain for fresh water and supplies. The next leg would be a long one, through the Caroline Islands into the Philippine Sea, rounding the north tip of Luzon and then across the South China Sea into Hong Kong. Bruce was, Jessica was sure by now, overly cautious, and when the *Cutty* resumed her voyage, she wallowed along with just enough sail to make the ride uncomfortable. Thankfully, however, they were now sailing north from the equator, and the miserable heat abated somewhat and the winds picked up.

Even with Captain Bruce in command, it was not a bad passage, Jessica was thinking. Except for him and the aging first mate, the *Cutty*'s officers were all bright, eager young men and without exception were pleased to have feminine company in the mess. Mealtime was, for them, a gala occasion. Jessica tried not to show favourites, and Magdalen smiled to see her daughter the centre of attention, although she well knew Jessica preferred the company of the second mate, Sam Gordon.

Sam, for his part, spent as much time with Jessica as his duties allowed him. He was always the gentleman, always courteous and considerate, and ever careful not to compromise Jessica by attempting to see her alone other than on deck. Consequently most of their time together was spent on deck, including moon-lit tropical evenings when Sam was not on watch. But to Magdalen's puzzlement, the relationship did not, during those long, quiet weeks, go past the state it had reached in Sydney. The only possible conclusion was, she decided, that Sam simply was not attracted in a romantic way to her daughter. As for Jessica, her interest in Sam was obvious to everyone, it seemed, but Sam.

"He is such a splendid young man," Magdalen said one day, as the *Cutty* was slopping westward, only days out of Hong Kong. "Your father likes him very much."

"I told him, just today," Jessica said, "that he should leave this ship. I don't think his uncle is a good judge of men, mother. He's had a whole series of captains who understimated this ship or simply did not have the skills to sail her properly."

"Is your concern more for the ship or for Sam?"

Jessica smiled and patted her mother's hand. "Mother, I think you are asking, in your indirect way, if Sam has said anything to me to indicate more than simply a friendly interest. Are you?"

Magdalen returned her smile. "You read me too well."

The expression on Jessica's face changed, indicated mild perplexity. "The answer is no."

"And yet he is very attentive."

"Oh, ever so attentive, and ever so gentlemanly. You'd think I was his younger sister."

Magdalen could see that, in spite of Jessica's attempt at casualness, she was confused and hurt.

"Actually," Jessica went on, with a rueful smile, "I've done everything but throw myself into his arms. Perhaps my next step should be to somehow trick him into my cabin."

"Jessica!" Magdalen smothered a laugh.

"Well, how did you trap Father?"

"Impudence," Magdalen answered after some thought. "Although a touch of perfume behind the ear and a smile were more than enough to trap young Murdoch Broome. Perhaps Sam thinks that he should be further advanced in his career before he takes on the responsibilities of a wife and family."

"Well, I think you're taking this all too seriously," Jessica said, surprising her mother. "I, after all, am not desperate to get married."

"He should, by right, be at least a first mate by now," Magdalen said. "I would imagine that it was the time he spent in the navy that held him back."

"He's been offered first mate on other ships, at least four times, but he won't leave—this witch of a ship."

"Well, dear," Magdalen offered, rather feebly, "you're both quite young. You have all the time in the world."

Harry Ryan had awakened the morning after the fight in the opium den, contrite as could be, eager to make amends to his partner. He did not, however, mention Sam Gordon as he begged Jon to forgive him for his rash actions. Jon, for his part, had been ready to withdraw from his association with Harry, whatever the financial cost. He had, after all, made the transactions in Victoria without Harry's help, and would probably turn a handsome profit. But, with Harry being Harry again, and with the prospect

112

of learning more about what he had decided was to be his ca
trading, he agreed it would be a good idea for him to accompa
Harry aboard the *Java*. His caution held, and he continued to te.
Harry that he had no money to invest in wheat to be carried by the
Java and sold in China at what Harry promised would be a
fabulous profit.

Claus Van Buren's *Java* was a tight, comfortable ship, with an
experienced master, George Mayhew. Jon and Harry shared the
supercargo's cabin, and from the day of sailing from Port Jackson
Harbour there was an air of holiday about Harry that was
infectious. His still-bandaged wound seemed not to trouble him,
and he was on excellent terms with Captain Mayhew, whom he
had previously served under as mate. Indeed, when the ship passed
through the Torres Strait between the pointed northern tip of
Australia and New Guinea, Mayhew called Harry into his cabin to
consult him on navigational problems in the Arafura Sea. Jon
regained a good deal of the respect he had lost for Harry; the man
obviously knew his ships, and he knew the sea.

"I think you're missing your calling, mate," Jon said to him on
one occasion. "You have salt water in your blood. You should be
commanding your own clipper."

Harry laughed. "That's too much work. But I'll hire men, one
day, to push clippers—clippers with the flag of the Ryan Company
on them."

Because she was to make calls at no fewer than half a dozen
ports, including Palmerston, that northern outpost beyond which
stretched a vast and empty land, *Java* would arrive in Hong Kong
several weeks later than the *Cutty Sark*, and it was only the
prospect of picking up a few pounds in local trades and, later, of
enormous profits in China, that kept Harry from fretting. Clearly
the thought that Sam Gordon had Jessica to himself for the long
passage to Hong Kong was eating at him, though he never
admitted as much to Jon.

From Palmerston, the *Java* made her way to the north of the
Lesser Sunda Islands into the steaming Java Sea, her destination
Singapore, on the tip of the Malay Peninsula. Harry was familiar
with these waters, and when he was asked, as before, he pored over
the charts with the captain, for the treacherous currents and reefs
near the Sunda Strait had snared more than one unwary ship.

The *Java*, having added deck cargo at both Timor and Surabaja, was not setting any speeds records. She was ploughing along, the heat making it unpleasant for all her crew, who spoke with longing of reaching Singapore, where they could enjoy a cool bottle. The weather did not cooperate, however, and off the Sumatran coast they found themselves becalmed in a steamy fog, with sails slack and not a breath of air stirring.

"I don't like this," Harry grumbled, as he and Jon stood at the rail, looking out into fog that reduced visibility to mere yards.

"Damnably hot," Jon agreed.

"Oh, the heat's good for the soul," Harry said. "It sweats the poisons out of your system."

"Then what's bothering you?"

"Shoals just to the northwest," Harry said. "Malay pirate waters."

"I shouldn't think we'd have to worry about them at the moment," Jon said. "How could they see us in this?"

"They know the waters. They'll smell us out."

"I see," Jon said, although he didn't. He turned at the sound of footsteps. The calm was so complete that the tread of the captain as he approached was a thudding that seemed to carry great distances.

"Mr. Ryan," Mayhew said, coming to lean on the rail beside them, "have you experienced such conditions in these waters?"

"Never," Harry said.

"I'm considering putting out the longboats."

"In my opinion, that's a good idea, sir," Harry responded. "Besides, Jon and I haven't had any exercise of late. We'll pull an oar for you."

"That's not necessary, of course," the captain said. The supercargo, the owner's representative, was by no means obliged to pull an oar with the common seamen, but Mayhew voiced no further objection as Jon and Harry climbed down a rope ladder to take their places, side by side, in one of the two long boats.

With the captain in the bow calling directions now and then, the crewmen applied themselves to the oars, and the *Java* eased along through the fog so slowly that the only way to tell she was moving was to watch the oily-looking water slide sluggishly along her side and to note a slight swirl in the fog made by her bulk.

"I wonder about you, at times," Jon said, after an hour of backbreaking rowing. He was soaked with sweat and the moisture of the fog, and his eyes stung from the perspiration running down his forehead.

"Good for you, mate," Harry said, puffing as he stroked.

The seamen were singing in time with their rowing.

I thought I heard the captain say,
   Leave her, Johnny, leave her:
You go ashore and touch your pay,
   It's time for us to leave her.

The strong male voices seemed to be swallowed up by the fog. "Mr. Ryan," a man called out, "if we row her all the way to Singapore, do we get a bonus?"

"I'll buy you a bottle and a woman myself," Harry called back.

"A clean woman," someone else yelled.

"I can't guarantee that," Harry said.

But the work was too gruelling, the heat too stifling, to continue bantering and singing. Soon there was only the sound of the oars, the grunts of straining men. Jon had found his second wind and was not breathing as hard, although his uncalloused hands were burning, and he was certain that his arms would, when he stopped rowing, fall from their sockets. He was thinking of his dead grandmother when the sound came to him, so at first he didn't consciously notice. It was not an instrusive sound but seemed to be a part of the sea, the fog, the calm. He remembered how his grandmother smelled, of lilac and old lace, and how she pampered him at teatime with his favourite biscuits . . . anything to keep his mind off the heat and the ache in his hands and his arms and his back; and then the sound came again.

"Harry?" he whispered, for by the tilt of Harry's head, as if his friend were straining to catch the elusive sound, he knew that Harry had heard it, too.

"Rest all oars," Harry called out, just loudly enough to be heard, and the grateful men stopped rowing. Behind them the *Java* loomed up out of the fog, her bulk and momentum bringing her slowly forward toward the boats.

The sound was more a swishing than a splash. It was rhythmic, and it was drawing closer. Jon was straining his eyes toward the sound and he thought he saw something, a dark movement, in the whiteness.

"Turn about," Harry ordered. "Back to the ship, and smartly."

No one asked questions. The men bent to it with a will, and in a matter of seconds the prow of the longboat in which Jon was riding banged against *Java*'s oaken side and Harry was swarming up the ladder. Before Jon gained the deck he heard the captain's voice: "Sound the alarm! Break out the weapons, Mr. Mate. All hands at boarding stations."

Jon felt a movement in the air. A breeze, slight, almost unfelt, was stirring the fog. He could hear the swish-swish of the approaching sound clearly now, and when he peered over the port rail he could see two small, low, dark boats breaking through the fog.

"Pirate *prahus* to port," someone bawled.

Jon ran to his cabin, dug his pistol from his bags and thrust it into his belt and, upon regaining the deck, seized a sword offered to him by one of the mates. He heard a thud and knew that one of the *prahus* had come alongside. As he moved to take a place at the port rail, he heard the blast of a small cannon, knew that a short had ripped through the lower rigging, and saw a severed line fall a few yards to his left. He heard wild shouts and turned the other way to see dark, sinister-looking men pouring over the port rail to be met by members of the *Java*'s crew. He ran a few steps, aimed his pistol, and saw the shot strike a pirate on the bridge of the nose. The man fell into the sea without making a sound.

From the starboard another cannon blasted, and Jon heard wood splinter as the ball struck the *Java*'s stout, oaken hull. Then there was only the chaos of the battle on deck, the sporadic, sharp reports of firearms soon replaced with the metallic clank of swords and cutlasses as more pirates swarmed aboard with deadly-looking scimitars. There was more cannon fire, but then that, too, ceased. Jon faced a slant-eyed, dark man dressed in baggy clothing and wielding a curved blade that lashed at his middle. He countered with his sword and lunged, the blade going deeply into the man's stomach, and then there was a rattle of gunfire behind him as Harry led a number of the crew with the rifles that had finally been broken out.

116

With a thud of contact and bloodthirsty screams, another of the *prahus* came alongside the *Java*, and grappling hooks flew into her rigging and were pulled taut. Harry positioned the riflemen to meet the new onslaught, and no sooner had the Malays mounted the rail than they fell before the withering fire, as the sailors volleyed in turns and reloaded as quickly as any trained foot-soldiers. Jon suddenly found himself facing a particularly large pirate, a brute of a man, who showed enough skill with his blade to send him backing toward the group of riflemen. All around, and even in the rigging, the life-and-death struggle was going on, for the pirates took no captives. The deck swarmed with fighting men, and the planking was slippery with blood.

Jon feinted a slash, checked, then darted in under the murderously swung scimitar, slashing his own sword across the man's midsection; then with not a moment's respite he was turning, yelling a warning as he saw two pirates leaping toward Harry from the rear. But a volley from the sailors drowned his words, and he had no choice but to leap past one of the sailors, nearly bowling the man over, and thrusting his sword over Harry's shoulder to impale an attacker in the throat. He jerked the blade free as Harry, startled, turned in time to discharge his rifle at close range into the chest of the second Malay.

"My gratitude, old chap," Harry said coolly, while reloading his weapon. "I think we've got them on the run. Would you ask the captain if he can put a few men aloft?"

Jon quickly saw Harry's intent, for, unnoticed in the heat of the battle, the wind had sprung up, the fog was lifting, and the *Java*, with four *prahus* attached to her like leeches, was moving, her untrimmed sails snapping in the freshening breeze. Jon killed again, a young man who attacked with fear in his eyes, and then he was beside the captain and the first mate, who had been fighting back to back, a pile of bodies attesting to their skill with cutlass and pistol.

"Wind, captain," Jon panted. Some of the pirates were leaping over the side, hotly pursued by the vengeful crew, for at least six of their shipmates lay on the bloodied deck.

"Mr. Mate," the captain said, "stand to and trim sail, if you please."

There were still isolated pockets of combat on the deck, but a steersman was at the wheel, and men were scurrying aloft at the mate's bidding. The *Java* lifted her head and began to move, breaking away from two of the pirate *prahus*. The other two quickly cut themselves free and allowed a gap to grow before opening up on the *Java* with their small deck cannon. At such close range it was impossible for them to miss, and they aimed to cripple the rigging. The foretopmast was struck squarely, breaking with a rending snap and sending a tangle of spars and rigging crashing to the deck. But the wind was holding, and in a matter of minutes the ship was free of the pirates, moving smartly on the choppy waves.

Harry came to pound Jon on the back. "Bit of a lark, eh?"

Jon looked around. The deck was littered with dead, some of *Java*'s crew among them.

"Saved my life, mate," Harry said.

"My pleasure," Jon said dully, but he was thinking, *Now we're square, Harry Ryan.* What Harry and Andy Melgund had done for him at Isandhlwana and at Rorke's Drift was evened off.

The bodies of the Malay pirates were thrown unceremoniously into the sea, where they were greeted by a pack of hungry sharks. The *Java*'s dead crewmen would be sewn into canvas, weighted, and given a decent Christian burial, but at the moment the captain had other, more pressing problems. The parting barrage of cannonfire, besides the damage it had done to the rigging, had opened several holes in the *Java*'s hull, just at the waterline. The pumps had already been manned, but it soon became obvious that it was a losing battle.

The captain called Harry to him. "Mr. Ryan," he said, "we must lighten ship." Harry nodded grimly. With her cargo of wheat and wool, the *Java* was riding deep in the water, and with the flooding reaching the lower levels of the hold, the sodden weight of the cargo was driving the ship ever deeper in spite of the work of the pumps.

No time was to be lost, and in a matter of minutes work parties had commenced the onerous task. The deck cargo went first, and then, with the main hatch open, men began to try to undo with jury-rigged tackle and sheer persistence what had taken skilled longshoremen, with the help of cranes, days to accomplish in port. One by one, the closely packed bundles of wool were wrestled from the stifling confines of the hold, and Jon watched with morbid curiosity as the first and most easily accessible bundles were tumbled overboard to mark a trail of financial disaster as they floated behind. But even that was not the worst.

The wind was increasing, the swells were building, and the dark clouds on the horizon threatened more than a mere squall. And still the *Java* rode so low that the water continued to enter her, frustrating all attempts to throw makeshift patches over the holes at her waterline. Another work crew had begun tackling the cargo of wheat in the forward hold. It had to be removed by hand, and men dripped with sweat as they shovelled the grain into any container available, while others lifted, and still others sowed the sea with the seed that represented Harry Ryan's money. Soon the layers of sodden wheat were reached, and the work continued through the night, then into a dark morning of glowering skies and fitful winds.

Harry and the captain had been studying the charts. The ship was sailing eastward, away from the Malays' lairs, and it had been agreed that they would make port in Java, perhaps Surabaja, in spite of the exhorbitant charges that would be laid on them by the Dutch authorities there. The alternatives were few, and they would be forced to pay the high port fees only to use the facilities of some broken-down, primitive shipyard to make the needed emergency repairs. The cost of the repairs would be borne entirely by Claus Van Buren, but that was of little consolation to Harry Ryan, who had suffered severe losses already.

The repairs were made, much more quickly than expected, but the passage back through the Arafura Sea and the Torres Strait was a gloomy one. By rights the *Java* should have been in Hong Kong by now, with Harry, a richer man, paying court to Jessica Broome. They put into Townsville, in Queensland, and Harry wired the bad news to the Van Buren office in Sydney. He was instructed to have the *Java* refitted in Townsville, then take on whatever cargo he could.

The outpost founded by Robert Towns in 1865, the northernmost of Queensland's cities, was not exactly a thriving metropolis, but it contained, Jon found, one outpost of civilization. Buchanan's Hotel, three stories of colonial elegance with its splendid ironwork decoration, was a most comfortable haven, the food excellent, and the service very polite. Jon could ask for nothing more save better company, for Harry had been reduced to a black mood by the loss of his cargo and his disappointment in not being with Jessica in Hong Kong. While the *Java* was in the shipyard, Jon, tiring of Harry's melancholy, took it on himself to scale Castle Hill, a granite outcrop that had just fallen short of being a mountain, to see the commemorative headstone of the town's founder at the summit. Then, for a while, he was content to catch up on his reading either in his room or in the Buchanan's comfortable lobby, to break the day with a stroll down to the waterfront to see what progress was being made in the repairs. It was Harry who came up with the suggestion that they take a small boat and shoot a few crocodiles on the upper reaches of Ross Creek, but although the expedition showed them some beautiful scenery, there were no crocodiles. Circumstances had changed from the early days of Townsville, when it wasn't safe for dogs or small children along the banks of the creek.

Jon had been in the town nearly two weeks before he discovered, by accident, that the influence of his stepfather reached into this corner of Queensland. He had known, although it had slipped his mind, that Marcus Fisher owned sugarcane lands in the north. The extent of Fisher's activities had never been clear to him, however, and his curiosity was piqued when he heard two men discussing the sugar business in the lobby of the hotel and they mentioned Fisher's plantations. The very next day, he read in the local newspaper an article about the "financial genius" of Marcus Fisher, and when, shortly afterward, he met a local banker in the lobby, the man asked him if he happened to be related to Marcus Fisher. When he admitted his relationship, the banker rhapsodized about how important the Fisher holdings in cattle, rice, and sugar were to the economy of Townsville. It seemed that Jon's stepfather had been buying land consistently in that narrow strip of coastline bounded on the west by Queensland's cloud-hidden mountains.

Harry, too, had been hearing talk about the production of sugar in Queensland and was actively seeking ways to profit from a cargo of sugar once the *Java* was ready for sea again.

As the days passed, Jon became increasingly restless. It was high time for him to hear—twice he sent inquiries by telegram— whether his own wool had brought a good price in England. In the meantime, he walked the streets, lingered along the waterfront, and it was there that he saw another aspect of Marcus Fisher's enterprises. He watched a scabrous, ancient brig tack into the harbour and tie up at the wharves, and he was standing not a hundred feet away when the voice he heard, shouting orders in an odd language, made the hair stand up on the back of his head. Sure enough, it was Bartholomew Jamison. Feeling a grim satisfaction —for he still had a debt to be paid—Jon found a vantage point and watched as a surprisingly large number of kanakas were offloaded and crowded into groups on the foreshore. With so many of them aboard, conditions on the brig must have been brutal, with its human cargo packed in almost as tightly as once had been the practice on the old blackbirders, the slave ships. The kanakas looked tired, confused.

Jamison, his huge black beard grown even more profuse, directed a group of rough-looking sailors, who herded the kanakas like cattle through the town and beyond, toward the countryside. Jon followed for a while but kept out of sight, knowing that now was not the time to settle his score—not while Jamison yet had overwhelming numbers on his side, as he had had at Urquhart Falls. He turned back near the edge of town.

Later that day, by discreet inquiry Jon learned that Marcus Fisher used a holding only two miles out of town as a staging point for his kanaka labour, and that Townsville was a major port for the indentured kanaka trade.

Jon had told Harry about his encounter with Jamison at Urquhart Falls. When he mentioned that Jamison was in Townsville and described what he had observed at the docks, Harry chuckled. "From what you've told me, this Jamison handled you rather severely last time. Are you sure you want to meet him again?"

"I can think of nothing I want more" was Jon's answer.

"He'll probably have armed overseers with him at the staging station."

"I'll just have to watch for an opportunity to catch him alone," Jon said.

"Chancy." Harry shook his head. "I was thinking that the good crew of the *Java* would welcome an outing in the country."

"I don't want to start a war," Jon said.

"War? It would be a simple holiday for the crew. They beat off four Malay *prahus*, didn't they?" He grinned. "Jon, you know how much a seaman enjoys a good brawl."

"Let's keep the crew out of this," Jon said. "This is between Jamison and me."

"So, vengeance shall be Master Jon Fisher's." Harry walked a circle around Jon, as if appraising his chances. "So be it. I only hope that we don't have to come and carry you home on a hatch cover."

Jon knew he was taking a calculated risk, but he was careful to remain concealed from sight as he made his way past the main house and several outbuildings at his stepfather's staging station. He saw a boiling plant used to reduce sugarcane to syrup, but no one was in sight. Beyond the boiling plant were the huts for the workers, no more than mere hovels. Jon heard an all-too-familiar voice, and as he rounded the first hut, he saw a large group of kanakas—Samoans, evidently—gathered in an open area, facing Bartholomew Jamison and a hard-looking overseer. The overseer had a pistol at his side, and Jamison had his hated whip in hand. A greying, dignified kanaka was standing a few paces in front of the two white men, trying to reason with them.

"Captain Jamison," he was saying, "I have told you we did not sign the papers to work in the cane fields. If you will remember, we asked that you include specifically in the papers that we would work timber or the rice fields, but not the cane fields."

It was common knowledge in Australia that work in the sugarcane fields was backbreaking, poorly paid labour; evidently even kanakas from distant South Sea islands had no illusions on that score.

"When you signed the papers," Jamison said, "you made a contract. If there is one among you who can read, I will allow him to read the papers, to see that there are no qualifications regarding the sort of work you will do."

"Then you lied, Captain Jamison," the old man bravely replied. "Your paper contains things that your words of promise did not. We will not work. We will return to Samoa."

The overseer beside Jamison drew his pistol, but Jamison knocked the man's arm down roughly, then led him away a few steps. Jon thought that the two of them might be leaving, but suddenly Jamison wheeled and the whip snapped, taking the old man across the shoulders and laying the bare skin open.

Jon's anger flared. As the whip sang through the air again and again, he circled quickly around the two whites and approached them, unnoticed, from the rear. Darting from behind a hut, he grabbed the overseer's pistol, wrenching it from the man's hand, and turned it on the two whites. "That's enough, Jamison," he commanded.

Jamison had been about to lay another blow onto the back of the fallen Samoan. He turned, his eyes wide in surprise, and then laughed through his beard. "Well, well!" he said. "Aside from the fact that you're tresspassing on private land, I'm most pleased to see you."

"And I you," Jon said, motioning the overseer back with the pistol barrel. "I'm wondering, Jamison, if you have the stomach to face me man to man, without your whip."

Jamison, however, was glancing to one side, and suddenly Jon realized that he had put himself in a bad position. Two more whites were approaching from the direction of the house, both of them with pistols in hand. Jon cursed his luck and wondered what to do. He couldn't retreat and let the old kanaka be beaten further, likely to death.

"Want us to shoot him, Captain?" one of the two approaching men called. They were moving to either side of Jon, so that he could not hold them both off.

It was at that moment that, to Jon's astonished relief, Harry stepped out of the nearby cane field, with a pistol in each hand. "I think it would be more prudent of you, Jamison," he said, "to call off your dogs and put down your whip." Harry gave a sharp whistle, and five men stepped silently out behind him, all of them armed with pistols and knives. Jamison's mouth closed.

"All right," he said. "Stand easy, men." He tossed his whip aside, and the two approaching overseers lowered their pistols.

"Well, Jon, he's all yours," Harry said. "And he's a big one."

Jon uncocked the pistol he had taken from Jamison's man and tossed it to the nearest sailor, who caught it neatly. Then he took off his coat, laid it on the ground, and stepped forward, lifting his fists. "No one is to interfere," he called out. "I want Jamison alone."

Jamison hesitated only a moment, then showed his blackened teeth in a wide grin and charged to meet a tattoo of swift punches as Jon danced aside. Harry and the sailors whooped in appreciation.

The big man was more careful the next time he moved in, lumbering forward with his gnarled fists up, swinging wildly to find only empty air as Jon stung him with swift, jabbing blows.

Thus it continued for a full ten minutes, Jamison not landing a single solid blow. His eyes were swollen, his lips bloodied, and he was slowing, taking more and more of Jon's quick, accurate jabs. At last he teetered and slipped, but as he went down he took advantage of Jon's momentary laxness and lunged forward, to wrap his arms around Jon's waist and, with a strength born of desperation, lift him from his feet and apply a pressure that had Jon's back bent painfully. A moan went up from Jon's supporters, while Jamison's men yelled encouragement.

Jamison grunted and continued to squeeze, and Jon, helpless with his arms pinned, could not breathe. Forgetting the rules of fair play, he lowered his head and butted, as forcefully as he could, smashing his forehead into Jamison's nose. He felt bone and cartilage give, then felt himself falling free, to land on his back. He rolled and scrambled to his feet, to find Jamison kneeling, holding his face with both hands. Jon took a step back, eyed the old kanaka, who was being ministered to by his people, then walked over to pick up Jamison's bullwhip. He had never used a whip before, and he swung it in the air twice, tentatively, before he got a satisfactory snap.

Jamison saw Jon advance toward him with the whip and started crawling away like a wounded crab. Jon followed, swinging the whip and hitting Jamison's backside with about every second try, until there was blood soaking the man's clothes and Harry was in front of him, seizing his arm.

"Enough, Jon," Harry said. "Enough. You have avenged yourself. Now it's time to go."

The blood haze that had driven Jon to his actions gradually subsided. He looked around. Jamison's men stood silently, glowering at the *Java*'s sailors.

"What about them?" Jon asked, indicating the Samoans.

"That's not our business," Harry said. "Like it or not, indenture is legal."

124

"We can't just leave them here like this. He almost killed that old man."

"Jon, Marcus Fisher would have you in jail," Harry warned. "If you don't like the law, do something to get it changed. You can't fight it.

Jon left with reluctance. His hands were sore, one knuckle swollen painfully from the blows he had administered. Still, the walk back into town, once they were away from the station, was a jolly one. The sailors were in high spirits, and Jon, out of gratitude, took them all to a pub and treated them, leaving them under Harry's less than temperate supervision. Alone again, he went to his room to bathe, and to press his ribs gingerly to be sure nothing was broken. Despite his satisfaction at having beaten Jamison fairly, a black mood crept upon him. What he had done was childish. Had he accomplished anything, except to gain a dangerous enemy and to further alienate his stepfather? And heaven help the poor native workers who would be left to take the brunt of Jamison's vengeful temper. Jon sank into his tub, regretting that he had come on the voyage, and wishing that he could soon be away from Townsville and free of the troubles he had got himself into.

CHAPTER VI

With the *Java*'s refit nearly complete, Jon spent more time at the shipyard. Out of curiosity, he would bring up the subject of kanaka labour with various people. No one seemed to be concerned about the basic unfairness of indenturing native islanders to work for seven years to, in essence, repay the cost of their transportation to Australia. If not fair, it was a perfectly legal practice, with a long history. Once, in England, Jon recalled, he had met a gentleman from the former American colonies, a man who was, he had thought at the time, an inverse snob, stubbornly proud of the fact that his family had been established in the new world by two brothers who had gone over as indentured servants. Perhaps, in the future, some well-to-do kanaka would brag that his grandfather came to Australia under indenture. But that was little consolation indeed for the present victims of a system that profited from human misery.

Jon was at dinner alone when a waiter came to his table, a look of disapproval on his face. "There is a person who wishes to see you, sir. Outside the hotel."

Jon had almost finished his meal; he wiped his lips with his napkin and walked from the dining room, through the lobby, and into the twilight of a fine day. A few people were walking past, but the only one who seemed to be waiting for somebody was a dark, Samoan man in work clothes, standing against the front of the hotel and looking around nervously. When he saw Jon he came forward.

"You wanted to see me?" Jon asked.

"I have come, sir, to thank you for stopping the beating of the old man."

"I appreciate that, but the trip was unnecessary."

"The old man was a talking chief," the Samoan said. "He is dead."

"I'm sorry." Jon shook his head. "I wish there was something I could do, but—"

"We know that whatever is done will have to be done by ourselves," the Samoan said. "We would be honoured, however, if the man who stopped the beating of our talking chief would be present when we bid him farewell."

"Why, thank you," Jon said, taken aback. "But I don't think—"

"The man you fought is no longer there," the Samoan said. "Not all are like him. The overseers will not disturb our ceremony, and you will not be seen."

It was going to be a long evening, another night alone in the hotel. Jon nodded. "I will come," he said. "Now?"

The man nodded.

"Wait here, then. I'll go up to my room and get another jacket."

The evening air was heavy and perfumed with tropical blossoms. Nightbirds called as Jon walked with the barefoot Samoan down the same road he had already passed over twice that day. The man led him around the buildings of Fisher's staging station and on into the forest. He heard the sound of voices chanting softly and mournfully. A fire flickered through the trees.

The old man was laid out on a bed of palm fronds. He looked peaceful and serene. His people had dressed him in a colourful skirtlike garment and a headdress of feathers. The Samoans were grouped around the fire, seated, their upper bodies swaying to the slow, sad rhythm. As Jon came within the light of the fire, heads turned toward him, but the singing continued. A well-built man, his bare chest showing powerful muscles, rose and approached.

"This is our *matai*," Jon's guide said, nodding in deference to the impressive-looking headman of the group.

"I am Molo," the *matai* said. "Thank you for coming."

"I regret the sadness of the occasion," Jon answered.

Molo guided him to a place by the fire. "Our farewell to old Asaoa is almost complete," he said. "We ask your patience."

There were no tears, no cries of grief, only the soft, sad, chanted song that blended the voices of both men and women in a way that was not at all unpleasant. Jon looked around. The Samoans had donned island dress for the occasion. It was a colourful gathering. The women wore simple, one-piece garments that seemed to be almost magically suspended at a line just above the breasts, so that much more feminine skin than Jon was accustomed to seeing was exposed to the flickering light of the fire. They were an attractive people, well-formed, possessed of a natural dignity. Jon could see why the men were prized as labourers, for most were taller and more substantial than the average Englishman or European. The women were, indeed, pleasant to look upon, broad of face, with thick, black hair done in a variety of styles that mostly featured getting the mass of hair up off their necks.

The old man, the talking chief, was to be cremated, and there was much activity in making the nearby pyre just right. When the body was, at last, placed atop the pyre, Molo, the headman, indicated to Jon that it was time to leave. An honour guard of a few young men would stay with the departed until the cremation was complete. The others still sombre, filed away into another clearing in the forest, not thirty yards away. The beat of drums came to Jon's ears, and as he entered the clearing, he heard the twanging of an unfamiliar stringed instrument. Already the appearance of the people was changing as they produced, from somewhere, necklaces of shells, flowers woven in garlands, and anklets of leaves. The transition from mourning to celebration was puzzling to Jon, but he found the music stimulating and the sight of men and women dancing most intriguing. A buxom middle-aged woman produced a bottle of an oily-looking liquid and doled it out generously, the dancers rubbing their bodies with it to make their skin shine in the firelight.

Molo sat beside Jon, and from time to time he would express what sounded like approval of the dancers, although Jon did not understand the words. Skirts swirled, revealing that underneath them the women wore a garment much like that of the men, a broad, colourful loincloth twisted at the waist to stay up.

"They dance well," Jon said.

"They celebrate life," Molo told him. "Old Asaoa is with the saints in Heaven, but we are alive."

"You are all Christians, then?"

Molo shrugged. "The God of the Bible and your Jesus are more acceptable to many than our old gods."

It was, Jon realized, a noncommital answer, and it was not exactly missionary-prescribed behaviour to be singing and dancing so soon after a funeral; still, for some reason he felt pleased. If life was like this on the islands, he wondered why these people had ever left.

Food was served by giggling, smiling women. Jon ate roast pork from a palm leaf, using his fingers for utensils, and it was delicious. He was enjoying himself and, for the moment, was not thinking of the hardships faced by the Samoans. He was nodding in rhythm with the music when his eyes caught sight of, for the first time, the most beautiful young woman he had ever seen. She was moving toward where he and Molo were seated, swaying with the music, her skirt showing a length of smooth brown leg below the knee, her body shapely even under the loose dress. Her hair looked like that of a figure on a Grecian vase, pulled into a high bun at the rear, so that when she turned in profile, her long, bared neck was as graceful as a swan's. Her exposed ears were small, her lips full and moistened, her brows gracefully arched over dark, serious eyes.

Jon could not pull his gaze from her. She came closer, stopped dancing, knelt, and said, '*Jamá.*'

"My daughter, Misa," Molo said.

"*Jamá*," she said—Jon realized that the word meant father—"our guest does not dance."

"Your guest does not know this dance," Jon said, somewhat amused at the idea, when Molo looked at him inquiringly.

"Misa will teach you." Smiling, Molo leaped to his feet to help Jon up.

Misa's hair smelled of flowers, and as she took his hand and led him into the circle, the ornate shell necklace dangling over her smooth, bare shoulders and her chest made faint music in time with her steps. "Come," she said. "One must simply feel the rhythm."

He tried, eliciting a smile from Misa and good-natured comments from the other dancers. Misa's own hips seemed detached from the rest of her, with a life almost their own as she moved with an uninhibited grace that made Jon forget his own stiffness and throw himself into the dance. As he entered into the spirit of the festivities, Misa seemed, as he watched her, a creature from a dream, the incarnation of unself-conscious desire, a wood goddess, a nymph. And when he was swept away from her by three younger, laughing girls who insisted on their turn dancing with the guest, he felt a sense of loss that surprised him.

He danced, none too gracefully, he realized, for some minutes and then, panting, broke away. Molo was now dancing, so Jon sat alone until the young man who had guided him from town came to sit by his side.

"I don't know your name," Jon said.

"I am Tui." He grinned at Jon. "You have made a good impression on our women."

"Not with my dancing, I'm afraid," Jon admitted, laughing.

"That one," Tui said authoritatively, nodding toward a short, well-formed girl with a broad, smiling face, "she is Timu."

"Yes?" Jon asked, puzzled.

"I am acting as *soa*," Tui said, not enlightening him any further.

"I don't know the word," Jon admitted.

"What is the English? *Ambassador?* Yes, I am ambassador. Usually the *soa* is a man approaching a girl on the behalf of a friend.

"I see," Jon said. "And what does Timu want of me?"

Tui laughed. "She is far from home, and she is lonely."

Jon felt himself blush furiously. He had, of course, heard sailors talk of the delights of the islands, of Tahiti, Fiji, and Samoa. He had been so involved in simply watching, in appreciating the beauty of the dance and of the young woman, Misa, that no such thoughts had occurred to him.

"I'm afraid—" be began, intending to say that it was time for him to go, but not voicing the words as a startling thought possessed him. "Perhaps," he said, "you will be my *soa* to that one, to Misa."

"She is *taupo*," Tui said, shaking his head.

"Meaning?"

"She is of noble birth and thus carefully guarded. When she is married, she will present evidence of her virginity."

Jon was astonished at the bluntness of the reply, but Tui did not seem at all offended, his tone actually regretful.

"Well, it was only a thought," Jon said. "Actually, I must be going."

"Timu will be disappointed," Tui said. "If she had smiled at me as she smiles at you, you could be certain there would be love that night."

Jon had no answer. He sought out Molo and expressed to him his thanks for the evening. The older men thanked him in turn, then escorted him out of the firelight and back toward the road. "I will not try to involve you in our troubles, Mr. Fisher," Molo said, "but I sense that you are sympathetic."

"I must confess I can't understand why you and your people left your homes to come here to this," Jon said.

"The young ones see the riches of the white men," Molo said with a resigned shrug. "They see the Americans, the English, the Germans, and they want more than a *lavalava* to wear, more than fish and fruits. The white man makes great promises about the riches to be had in Australia."

"But you? And Misa?"

Molo looked upward, as if seeking to see a patch of stars among the overhanging palm fronds. "Even I am not immune to wanting better things for my daughter."

"And now she will work in the cane fields?"

"No. She will work in the kitchen or a laundry of a white man's house."

Jon frowned, imagining the lovely, stately Misa slaving over a wash pot.

"But I was wrong," Molo said. "I know that now. Captain Jamison, as the dead one said, lied to us. We knew of the cane fields, and we insisted that it be made plain in our papers that we would not work there. But it was not, and now we will be sent to the fields, and it is futile to protest."

"I wish I could help," Jon said, "but I don't know what I could do."

"It is *we* who must do something," Molo said, with unexpected determination. "We will leave, Mr. Fisher. One way or the other. I don't know exactly how. We have no money to buy passage back to Samoa, and we have little food. At home we would know how to live. Here—" Molo shook his head.

"I'm sorry," Jon said. "There's really nothing I can do."

"If we but had a ship—"

"The laws of Australia are against you," Jon said. "You've signed a legal document. If you try to break your contract, you can be put in jail."

They had reached the road. "Thank you," Molo said, lifting his chin proudly. "We thank you for helping us to say farewell to one of our dead." He turned and stalked away.

Jon looked back. From the sound of the drums, he imagined the Samoans were still dancing. Suddenly he thought he smelled the fragrance, the unmistakable aroma, of the girl, Misa. She stepped out of the shadows and smiled up at him. He felt his throat go dry, and his heart pounded.

"Thank you for coming, Jon Fisher," she said.

"It was my pleasure," he said lamely.

"Perhaps, in this country of the white man, we shall meet again," she said.

"Yes," he said fervently, wishing for it, willing it, yet knowing that it was unwise, if not impossible.

"Good-bye, Jon Fisher."

"Misa—"

But she was gone, floating off into the darkness. He watched until he lost sight of her, and then he turned and started down the road, feeling more alone than he had ever felt in his life.

James Draker, first mate of the *Cutty Sark*, died two days before the ship sailed into Hong Kong harbour. He was at the evening meal, talking with Sam Gordon, when he halted the progress of his fork to his mouth, put it down, looked off into unseeable distances, then fell with his face in his plate. He had shown no indications of having a weak heart, but he was dead, and there was a funeral at sea.

"You, mister, are acting first officer," Captain Bruce told Sam. "I will telegraph my recommendations to the owners that it be made permanent when we arrive in port."

Sam had no wish to be promoted under such circumstances, but he made no comment. He took over the running of the ship—for Bruce had sequestered himself in Draker's cabin, apparently mourning the man's demise in a stupor of drink—and drove the *Cutty* into the Tathong Channel under a full spread of sail, putting on quite a show.

Red Broome had taken a house situated high on a hillside overlooking the crowded city and the splendid natural harbour. By the time Sam was free from his duties of seeing the *Cutty*'s cargo offloaded, his temporary appointment as first mate had been confirmed by the Far-Eastern representative of his great-uncle's shipping company.

"How wonderful for you!" Jessica said, when Sam announced his promotion over dinner with the Broomes. Red and Magdalen, too, expressed their delight at the news, but Sam, despite their support and even their apparent eagerness that he spend time alone with their daughter, was silent about his intentions when, the next day, he accompanied Jessica on a sight-seeing tour of the city. When Sam finally took his leave—the *Cutty*'s ultimate destination New York Harbour— it was with a gentlemanly kiss of Jessica's hand. Although Sam cared for her more than he cared to admit even to himself, the *Cutty Sark* still came first.

Upon leaving Hong Kong, the *Cutty* was shorthanded. More than a few of the crew members had had enough of William Bruce and had followed the time-honoured sailor's custom of jumping ship. Those who had deserted would have no problem getting another ship in a busy port like Hong Kong; and for those who stayed, the empty fo'c'sle berths translated into more work and longer hours, until new hands could be hired. For Sam, it meant doing the work of two men, since it had been decided between Bruce and the company representative, that no new third made would be hired—Ned Turner having taken Sam's place as second—until the ship reached New York. Morale aboard ship was not good. Although the crew's pay was not affected by the fact that the *Cutty* left Hong Kong in ballast, without a paying cargo, a sailor looked upon his ship as his home, and when she was shamed, he was shamed. The *Cutty* had already endured more than her share of humiliation.

The *Cutty* was bound for the Philippines, to take on a cargo of jute, a vegetable fibre used for making burlap, twine, and sacking. Since the *Cutty* had been designed to be a tea clipper, the prospect of hauling common fibre in holds already blackened with coal dust did little to improve morale. Moreover, they were sailing in a season when the winds in the China Sea were against them, so that it promised to be a long, gruelling run.

In the first days of the voyage, Captain Bruce, perhaps because of the unseasonably mild weather, appeared on deck more frequently than usual and even took an apparent interest in their progress, not driving the ship, it was true, but keeping enough

133

canvas aloft to make respectable time, under the conditions; but then the temperature plummeted, the seas picked up, and upon the pretext that his Bible called to him, Bruce secluded himself in his cabin. Sam was left in virtual command, a state of affairs perfect to his liking, for all he had no idea how long it would last.

Bruce was not too preoccupied, however, to leave Sam completely at peace. He reappeared on deck once a day for a few minutes, to take sightings and chart a course that, Sam suspected, purposely differed from his own so that Bruce could overrule him in front of the crew. Sam's own calculations consistently placed the ship further to the west than did the captain's sightings, a fact that concerned him, since the *Cutty* was, according to his reckoning, sailing toward toward shoaling water around the Pratas, a group of tiny islands and reefs due southeast of Hong Kong. As night fell, he quietly ordered all lookouts to be especially alert. During the late afternoon, low clouds on the horizon had indicated a weather change, and now long after dark, the rains came, followed by a squall that filled the *Cutty*'s sails with a favouring wind and sent her ploughing through the whitecapped waves at a fair clip. Visibility was severely limited, and Sam, who had rechecked his navigation several times, was uneasy. For all Bruce's assertions, he didn't see how he could be wrong, and if he was not wrong, the Pratas were lying not far ahead.

The light was out in the captain's cabin, and Sam, knowing full well the possible consequences of his actions, quietly gave orders to alter course to south-southeast. The new course sent *Cutty* running before a following sea, which in other ships might be dangerous, but because of the *Cutty*'s flaring, rounded stern, she was much less susceptible to being swamped from astern, or literally driven under a wave. More than one clipper, Sam was aware, had failed to appear in her designated port because her skipper had pushed her too hard in a following sea. But to stay on Bruce's course would be far more dangerous, even suicidal.

Unfortunately, the new motion of the ship awakened Captain Bruce. He came on deck with only his trousers pulled on over his nightshirt, stood silent beside Sam for a few moments, and then went to check the compass. When he came back, his expression was one of hardly contained fury. "Who gave you orders to alter course?" he shouted over the wind howling through the rigging.

134

"Sir," Sam answered, "I considered it best to be prudent, given the poor visibility."

"Prudent!" Bruce's high-pitched voice was like an angry child's. "Bring this ship back on course, mister!"

Sam hesitated. He was sure in his mind that the course laid down by Bruce meant disaster. Cutty was *his* ship, too; how could he let her have her belly ripped out on a reef? On the other hand, how could he disobey a direct order from his captain? With his heart pounding, his hands clenched in frustration, Sam gave the orders. Men scurried up the shrouds into the wind-lashed rigging, and the helmsman spun the wheel. In short order the *Cutty* was back on her old course, her motion somewhat eased.

"Mr. Gordon," Bruce said, "I cannot watch you every minute of every league across the China Sea, the Indian Ocean, and the South Atlantic to keep you from driving my ship to the bottom. Either you will obey my orders or you will make this cruise in irons."

"Aye, aye, sir," Sam answered woodenly.

By God's grace, and to Sam's great relief, the weather cleared before dawn. The wind was still with them, the *Cutty* making respectable speed, and Sam doubled the lookouts, instructing each man to keep alert for shoaling water. He was in the last hour of his watch, a few minutes before sunrise, when he heard the cry from forward, "White water!" His first impulse was to give orders to come about smartly, but he ran forward to take a look for himself. He could hear the breakers ahead, an ominous rumble of tons of water crashing onto a reef, but there was still time. He ran aft as fast as he could and pounded on the captain's door until Bruce stuck his head out. He was wearing an old-fashioned nightcap and a dingy white nightshirt.

"Your presence is required, sir," Sam said.

"I'll get dressed."

"There's not time for that, sir."

Mumbling, Bruce stalked out, barefooted. Sam led him forward. The breakers were more audible now, and they could be seen in the dim distance, a sweething swath of white water.

'Sir," Sam said, "I request permission to change course."

Bruce was jumping up and down, making squealing sounds, in total panic. Sam calmly gave the orders, and *Cutty* swung away on

135

a tack, leaving the dangerous reef behind. They were not, however, in the clear. Bruce's course had taken them square into the Pratas, and as in many of the shoal areas in the China Sea, the reefs there were not properly surveyed.

Bruce was standing silently beside the helmsman. "Sir," Sam suggested, "perhaps you'd like to take the watch?"

"It's still your watch, Mr. Gordon," Bruce snarled. "I can't take over every time there's a puff of wind. I'd never get any sleep. If you can't do your job—"

"Then sir, I request permission to alter course as necessary until we are clear of the Pratas."

"Damn you!" Bruce yelped, his voice again rising in pitch. "First you deliberately, or out of ignorance, almost drive my ship aground, and then you try to make it sound as if it is my fault!"

"I had no such intentions, sir." Sam caught a glimpse of the bo'sun at the helm, who was grinning broadly. Under Sam's eye the grin faded quickly.

"This is going to go on your record, *Mr.* Gordon," Bruce squeaked. "On your record, mind you! That you questioned your captain's navigation and, in so doing, endangered this ship." He whirled with a swishing of his wet nightshirt and disappeared into his cabin.

"Sir," the helmsman, said "when the cap'n was taking his sightings he probably saw two of everything."

"That's enough, Jenkins," Sam said sternly. To allow the crew to belittle one officer to another was an invitation to mutiny.

"Two stars, two suns," Jenkins persisted. "It wasn't you, sir, who steered us toward the Pratas."

"I said that's enough!"

"Aye, sir. Whatever you say."

Jenkins lapsed into silence, and Sam, cursing himself for a fool for sticking with the *Cutty*, strode forward so that he would not have to see the man's grinning face.

It grew hotter, as the *Cutty* sailed down the China Sea toward Luzon and the broad reaches of Manila Bay. After the incident at the Pratas, Bruce left most of the navigation to Sam. The days were of a sameness, the winds light and erratic. Sam instituted water rationing, for the passage was taking longer than it should have.

And then bad luck struck the *Cutty* again. Sam was awakened by the bo'sun, Tom Jenkins.

"Lord, it can't be time yet," he mumbled, feeling leaden, not believing that he had slept through to his watch.

"No, sir," Jenkins said. "But you'd better come with me, sir."

The look on the man's face, the urgency in his voice, dispelled Sam's tiredness. He dressed quickly and followed Jenkins foward to the crew's quarters. A vile stench assaulted his nostrils, and fear sprang up in him. Five men were in their bunks.

"We thought at first, sir, that it was just the sailor's disease," Jenkins said.

Sam crouched to have a closer look at one of the sick men in the lower bunk. It was not unusual for the crew to suffer from diarrhoea after visiting a strange port. Sailors would drink anything and, while drinking, eat almost anything, but this, he knew from looking at the man, from smelling the rankness in the crew's quarters, was not simple diarrhoea. Even as he stood there the stricken sailor moaned as strong cramps bent his legs.

"Are others ill?" Sam asked, looking around to see that the other four men were in equally dire straits.

"The flux," Jenkins. "That's all."

"You?"

"Not yet."

"Jenkins, these men need water. Lots of water. And I'd like you to get a few of the men who are sick but not on their backs yet to clean up a bit in here."

"Sir, is it what I'm afraid it is?"

"I'm afraid so."

Neither of them wanted to say the word, a dread word, cholera, but within the next two days, as man after man was taken to his bunk to experience the excruciating agony of the illness—the cramps, the fever, the constant voiding of bowels and stomach—no doubt remained that the ship was hard hit.

Men struggled aloft, so weak that what was routine work in relatively calm weather was dangerous. One man forgot the old sailor's adage, one hand for you, one for the ship, and lost his hold on a line to fall almost a hundred feet to thud on the deck. Only a few of the crew were well enough to turn out for his burial at sea.

Sam was near despair. After all her other misfortunes, the *Cutty*

Sark was now a pest ship, a funeral ship. The disease was known to be caused by bad food or bad water, and since none of the ship's officers or apprentices had come down with the symptoms, Sam figured it had to be the food, something that had been served to the crew and not in the officers' saloon. He narrowed it down to a batch of chickens that had been put aboard in Hong Kong. While the crew was eating chickens, the officers had feasted on duck, roasted and basted admirably by the Chinese cook.

Now Sam himself, the second mate, and the apprentices had to take on the working of the ship, for nearly every foremast hand was down. The fo'c'sle was a hellhole of stench and suffering. Sam had not been aloft in some time, and he had to remind himself of the basic rules of safety, for he soon discovered he was not as spry as he had been as a lad. During these last days before they finally reached Manila, he slept an average of three hours in twenty-four, and his hands, softened by his years as an officer, were blistered, the nails torn. They buried three more men at sea, besides the man who had fallen from the rigging, and even when the *Cutty* limped into the broad bay, her troubles were not over. As soon as the condition of the ship became known on shore—and Bruce was obliged to report the sickness to the harbour authorities—there was no hope of help. She was an outcast, a pest ship, and no one would be allowed to leave her, or come on board, until the disease had run its course.

However, with the anchors biting deep into the bottom of the bay, there was, at least, no need to work ship, which freed Sam and the others who were well—excepting Bruce—to nurse the crew and try to bring some sense of cleanliness and order to the ill. They were supplied with badly needed fresh water from shore, but still another man died and was sent over the side, with words from the pious Captain Bruce, who had yet to enter the crew's quarters.

Finally, after nearly two full weeks, the condition of the men began to improve, and some of them were even strong enough to move about and help the others. Those who were well enough scrubbed and hosed down the quarters, washed the soiled bedding, and hung it up to dry.

At last the ship was cleared to dock. The men were yet so weak and tired that most of them did not take the usual shore leave but stayed aboard to sleep, rest, and regain their strength. That was just as well, as far as Sam was concerned, for the *Cutty* had already lost four men from her depleted crew, and she could ill afford to lose any more from desertions.

Bruce delegated Sam to supervise the loading of the jute, while Bruce himself disappeared ashore, presumably to see to needed supplies. One afternoon, the Chinese cook, the only foremast hand who had not come down with cholera, approached Sam on the sun-heated deck. "Missa Mate," he said, "not enough food."

Supplies had come aboard, but Sam had left their receiving to the cook. He was soaked in perspiration, tired, and badly in need of sleep.

"Hasn't the captain replaced the food?" he asked.

"Not enough," the cook said.

"Take it up with the captain." Sam turned to yell at the stevedore who had thrown a bundle of jute into the hold without placement, and when the cook padded aft, he gave no further thought to the problem of the food. The *Cutty* sailed with an undermanned crew, most of them still weakened from the disease, but her luck seemed to have changed. With Sam doing the navigation and Bruce staying mostly in his cabin, she made her way through the Palawan passage and the Caspar Strait past Java Head in near-record time. The winds were with *Cutty* clear across the Indian Ocean, and she rounded the Cape of Good Hope and put into Table Bay without a single serious incident. Bruce's orders specified a short call, after which they were to take the ship all the way to New York without making port. Many ships, making the run from the southern tip of Africa to North America, would have put into one of the South American ports for reprovisioning, but the *Cutty Sark* had not been too profitable of late, and Jock Willis would be eager to be paid for the cargo of jute. Once again, in Cape Town, the captain took on the duty of provisioning ship, and once again, on the day before sailing, the Chinese cook approached Sam to say that there was not enough food.

"You said that at Manila," Sam said.

"Men still weak, not eat much at first. We make it," the cook said. "This time not enough. Men eat like tigers after mating."

"I'll tell you now what I told you before," Sam said. "Take it up with the captain."

"Me no take up with captain," the cook said. "He clazy." He was gone before Sam could reprimand him for speaking ill of the commanding officer. The ship sailed, entering a stretch of water that was nearly devoid of islands, with only tiny Saint Helena and Ascension to break the emptiness of the South Atlantic, and then the Cape Verde Islands far to the east off the nose of Africa, before Bermuda in the North Atlantic. Clipper weather sent the ship scudding northwestward, with Sam in control, for Bruce had put in a good supply of Cape brandy and was confined to his cabin, eating little but leaving a trail of empty bottles behind as the long, watery leagues passed at speeds up to fifteen knots. They sailed into equatorial heat and calm. As usual, water was rationed, and although there was no shortage of food in the officers' saloon, there was grumbling in the crew's mess.

Sam, always sensitive to the moods of the crew, could not at first account for the growing sullenness. His orders were obeyed with the usual efficiency, but not with a will. It was only by accident that he saw the first unmistakable sign of the men's discontent. No weapons were allowed to the crew, of course, and usually they were content without them, for they had their rigging knives for use in an extreme emergency. Sam had wandered forward one day, for no particular reason, when he noticed a sailor working diligently on something. He walked over, hands behind his back. The *Cutty* was under a full cloud of sail, heeled over before a brisk wind. The sailor, seeing Sam approaching, tried to hide the object of his attention.

Sam didn't even speak. He motioned with his hand. Reluctantly the sailor showed him a bludgeon made of closely braided leather, with cord hitching worked in neatly.

"Good work," Sam said. "May I see?"

The bludgeon, which was about a foot long, was weighted on both ends, and Sam knew it could break bones or a skull easily.

"Very neat," he said, handing it back; but from that moment on he began to observe the crew more closely. When sailors took time to fashion makeshift weapons, something was wrong aboard. He learned the reason from the bo'sun, Jenkins.

"If you'd ever come into the crew's mess, sir," Jenkins said, when Sam sounded him out, "you'd see. We ain't had nothing but hardtack and salt pork for three weeks now."

140

"I say in Cape Town," the Chinese cook told Sam self-righteously, "not enough food. Sailors eat like—"

"I know, like a tiger after mating," Sam said. He sought out Bruce, who was wan and nervous, having drunk up his supply.

"Sir," Sam said, "I think we had better divert to the Cape Verde Islands for reprovisioning."

"Not likely," Bruce said weakly.

"Sir, we're down to hardtack and salt pork, and not much of that."

"We do not change our course," Bruce said. "I put aboard enough provisions for a full crew in Cape Town. I don't know what they've done with it, but they can pay for their gluttony by tightening their belts until we reach New York."

"Sir, the cook told me in Cape Town there wasn't enough food," Sam persisted.

"I based my purchases on our usage while crossing the Indian Ocean," Bruce said. "There was more than enough."

"The men were still weak from cholera during that time and not eating much," Sam said. "I don't think you realize the seriousness of the situation, sir. There's not even enough salt pork to get us to New York."

"Then let them chew on leather," Bruce snapped. "You're supposed to be on duty, mister, not in my cabin questioning my authority."

Sam wheeled and left, resisting the temptation to slam the door behind him.

Ordinarily a crewman did not concern himself with the ship's position. He was interested, of course, in the speed of a day's run, but mainly he took note of position and time only when the ship neared port. However, most of the men seemed to be aware when the *Cutty* reached the latitude of the Cape Verde Islands, and their sullenness increased when there was no indication of a course change.

The bo'sun led a delegation of four men to the stern, where Sam was standing beside the wheel. "I think there's something on your mind," Sam said.

"Yes, sir," Jenkins responded without his usual smile "We're not making for the Cape Verdes, are we, sir?"

141

"We are not," Sam said.

"The men don't like that, sir. They're sick and tired of nothing but salt pork. They're afraid of the sickness again."

"That's not likely," Sam said.

"Sir, it's a sailor's right to be given decent food."

Sam had no answer to that.

"Sir, I can't be responsible for what they'll do," Jenkins said.

"It is *not* your responsibility," Sam said sternly. "You men are dismissed."

Sam knew that something had to be done, and as soon as Jenkins and the men were out of sight, he went to the galley and told the cook to serve that week's officers' rations to the crew, and to put nothing on the officers' table but hardtack and salt pork. The results were hardly a surprise.

"What is the meaning of this!" Bruce squealed, when he sat down to the miserable meal. "Where's the bully beef?"

"There wasn't much left," Sam lied. "I had cook serve it to the men."

Bruce's face reddened. He rose half out of his chair. "You—you . . . I'll have you—"

"We can still make the Cape Verdes in a week or so," Sam said.

But Bruce would not be moved. He subsided, ate the meal, and left without another word. The *Cutty* raced on in favourable winds toward the northwest, but it was hardtack and salt pork for everyone, and the situation became so tense that Sam, without asking the captain, issued pistols to the second mate and himself, two men against the entire shorthanded crew. The grumbling among the men was eased, somewhat, when he changed course to intercept a sail spotted far down on the horizon, and the proud *Cutty Sark* was reduced to begging provisions from another ship. Twice more, before coming within a few days of Bermuda, the *Cutty* hailed a passing ship and begged. The second and third times were, to a clipper sailor, the ultimate in humiliation, for the ships approached were ungainly steamers, the grunting, stinking bane of every sailing-ship man.

Only a day out of Bermuda, fate dealt harshly once more with the *Cutty Sark*. After a week of brisk winds, with the skysails and studding sails set and Captain Bruce allowing Sam to push the *Cutty* as she was meant to be pushed, dark and ominous clouds suddenly closed over them, and a roaring, chill North Atlantic storm engulfed the *Cutty* in twenty-foot waves and near hurricane-force winds.

It was too much even for a clipper like the *Cutty*, which could use a fresh gale to set passage records. With the huge, icy wave crests flattened by the winds and then shredded to make the sea's surface a miasma of stinging spray and white water, Sam had no choice but to come about, shorten sail drastically, and ride out the storm. For hours the *Cutty* pounded along, her cutwater into the oncoming waves, with the few men on deck chilled to the bone and often waist-deep in the frothing water that cascaded the length of her decks. After nearly two full days of such pounding, the *Cutty* was finally left behind by the storm, with her sails in tatters and her crew wet, cold, and exhausted.

As the *Cutty* wallowed in the long, smooth-topped swells left in the wake of the storm, Bruce emerged on deck, examined the shredded storm canvas with a jaundiced eye, and turned to Sam. "I will not go into Bermuda with rags on my spars," he said. "Why haven't you turned the men to replace sail?"

Sam had had about three hours sleep in the last forty-eight hours, and his eyes burned in his head. Under these conditions, his first impulse, which was nearly irresistible, was to seize William Bruce by the collar and heave him over the port rail. He swallowed. "Sir," he said, his voice hoarse from calling out orders during the days and nights of fighting the storm, "I intended to wait for the men to eat and dry themselves off. Besides, we've been carried too far north. We will have to make straight for New York."

"Very well," Bruce said, with surprising equanimity. "You are relieved of the watch, Mr. Gordon."

The finest featherhead in all of the world would not have felt better to Sam than his bunk. He fell into it fully clothed and was oblivious even as his head sank into his pillow. It seemed as if he had only closed his eyes when he felt himself being roughly shaken. He opened one heavy lid to see the concerned face of the bo'sun.

"Sir, you'd best come on deck," Jenkins said.

Sam moaned and checked his watch. He'd been asleep just thirty minutes. He used some sailor's language, causing Jenkins to grin with one side of his mouth. "Just the same," Jenkins said, "you'd best turn out, sir."

Sam went on deck, pulling on his watch jacket. He heard the angry voice of William Bruce, pitched very high. The crew had been mustered out, even those who were off watch, and were standing sullenly in a group. The second mate and the apprentices were standing behind Bruce, the apprentices looking uneasy. Young Turner was fingering the butt of the pistol protruding from his belt.

Nat Cheevers, sailmaster of the *Cutty*, saw Sam and looked at him pleadingly. Bruce turned, his face red with hardly contained fury.

"Mr. Gordon," the sailmaster spoke up, "I've been trying to explain to the cap'n that we just ain't got the men to change sails, and—"

"Silence!" Bruce yelped. "If you expect to find an ally for your mutiny in one of my officers, you are to be disappointed."

"Sir, we ain't mutineers," a seaman called out.

"You are not carrying your weapon, Mr. Gordon," Bruce berated Sam in a hushed tone, so that the crew could not hear. It was the first time Sam had ever detected fear in the captain's voice.

"I really don't think we'll need weapons, sir," Sam replied.

"Then, mister, since you think so, I will leave it to you to see that my ship does not enter New York Harbour looking like a tramp of the sea!" He turned on his heel and stalked off to his cabin.

"Mr. Gordon—" Cheevers began.

"Hold your tongue, Mr. Cheevers," Sam said. "You men who are off watch, lay below to your bunks." Half the men on deck disappeared as if by magic. "Mr. Cheevers, take two men from the watch and lay to in the sail locker."

Cheevers opened his mouth to protest, but Sam silenced him with a gesture. "As you know, Mr. Cheevers, the spare sails have been stowed for some time. They will be stiff and must be treated with great care. Do you understand?"

"Sir," Cheevers protested.

"Haste could damage valuable sails," Sam went on. "I want you to be very deliberate in your work, Mr. Cheevers. Do you understand?"

An understanding grin appeared and disappeared on the

sailmaster's face. He nodded. "I understand, sir."

Sam grieved for his ship when she sailed into New York Harbour with tattered sails, frayed rigging, a rusted windlass, and a crew whose every bone seemed to show. William Bruce had not been much in evidence during the last days of the voyage, and he disappeared ashore almost as soon as the lines were made fast to the pier. Sam's first action was to instruct the agent of Willis & Son to send aboard the finest provisions that money could buy. The agent, an ex-clipper captain himself, stood on the *Cutty*'s deck and examined her sorry state. He raised one bushy eyebrow at the appearance of the half-starved crew.

"I'd like to talk with you in my office at your convenience," the agent said. Sam nodded.

After seeing that the crew was properly fed, Sam supervised the offloading of the cargo, then gave the men shore leave, adding a perfunctory warning of the illegality of jumping ship. Then he made his way to the agent's office and was soon seated in a comfortable leather chair with a cup of tea in his hand.

"I have already begun recruiting additional crew members, Mr. Gordon," the agent said with a frown. "But I suspect, from the looks of them, that I'll have to find more men than I originally estimated."

"Probably," Sam agreed.

"Mr. Gordon, what is your opinion of Captain Bruce?"

Sam's answer was mechanical. "It is not the function of a first mate to pass judgment on his captain."

The agent shook his head in quick annoyance. "I appreciate your loyalty," he said, "so I won't press you for an answer. But I presume that if you could speak well of him, you would have."

Sam lifted his teacup without comment. If the truth were known, he had been considering telegraphing his great-uncle, to tell him in detail of William Bruce's incompetence. But even though he was related to Jock Willis and had good reason to assume that one day the old man would ask him to take over direction of the company, he could not and would not speak ill of a superior officer.

"I have telegraphed the home office," the agent said, as if reading Sam's mind, "informing them of the condition of the ship and its crew. While you were occupied with the cargo and the port authorities, you see, I took the liberty of interviewing a few members of the crew, including the cook. It is inexcusable to undertake a long journey without proper provisions for the crew. It is inexcusable to let a ship of the *Cutty Sark*'s status get into the condition in which I have seen her."

"We were shorthanded," Sam felt obliged to say. "The crew was recovering from cholera."

The agent waved off the explanations. "When your ship sails again," he said, "she will sail under a new master."

Sam felt his neck heat up, and his heart was pounding. Perhaps, please God, the time had come. He had served a long apprenticeship, and he had no doubt that he was capable. For all practical purposes, it was he who had been running the *Cutty* for the past year. For a brief moment, he let his dreams soar. It was already too late for him to drive the *Cutty* halfway around the world with a load of tea, for the tea trade was being taken over by the steamers; but there was wool. The long, long reaches of ocean leading out to Australia and New Zealand were clipper waters. Perhaps, at long last, he and the *Cutty* would have the chance to prove themselves.

"Now I'm sure you're tired," the agent said. "I will be in touch with you when I have word from the home office."

Sam slept the clock around, felt like the Chinese cook's starving tiger, ate two fine, American beefsteaks, and then luxuriated in a bath with plenty of hot water. His best clothes were a bit the worse for having been stowed in his locker for the long, watery leagues, but they were clean. He went down the gangway onto the East river wharf, and he was contemplating in which direction to walk when he heard his name being called and looked back to see a short man dressed in morning clothes, beaver hat, gleaming white shirt, and cravat.

"Thank goodness—I almost missed you, Mr. Gordon," the man said, hurrying up.

Sam realized with a start that the man was Alfred Childers, a London shipowner; he looked out of place in New York. "Mr. Childers, you're a long way from home." Sam took the extended hand.

"Mr. Gordon, I pray that we are well met," Childers, said. "I won't delay you long, since I'm sure you need *divertissement* after your long—" He paused, then shrugged. "—and somewhat unpleasant voyage."

"No worry," Sam said, using the Australian phrase without thinking.

"I'll make it short." Childers took Sam's elbow and led him down the wharf, away from the *Cutty*. "My *Roamer* is here in port, and she is currently without a captain. I have watched your career, Mr. Gordon. I was pleased to hear that you were promoted to first mate. I'd like to give you another promotion. I'm offering you the *Roamer*. Will you have her?"

Sam's heart leaped. He knew the *Roamer*. She was no *Cutty*, but she was a sweet ship, sleek, well designed, and capable, he suspected, of almost as much as the *Cutty*. He'd seen her under sail, running down the Channel, and . . . perhaps she *was* as well designed as the *Cutty*, with her long, slim clipper hull, the tall spars, and—

"You would be working the wool trade mostly," Childers said, "Melbourne to Liverpool."

Sam was silent. He halted and looked back over his shoulder at the *Cutty*'s sad condition. What he wanted more than anything else, was to be able to make her gleam, to dress her in fresh, white canvas and replace her frayed ribbon, to polish her brass and see her decks so clean one could eat off them—

"Mr. Gordon?"

"Mr. Childers, you honour me with your offer." He smiled. "I am sure you are aware that I have a family connection with Jock Willis."

"Be that as it may, a man has to look to his career," Childers said.

"Thank you, sir, for your offer." Sam stifled a regretful sigh. "However, there is more than my career and family duty at stake." Childers, seeing the direction of his gaze, looked at the *Cutty Sark*. "I saw her keel laid," Sam said. "I rode her down the ways, and on her first voyage."

"Ah," Childers said, "an affair of the heart." He shrugged. "Well, Mr. Gordon, if you should, for any reason, want to reconsider, please contact me immediately."

After the vastness of the sea, New York seemed crowded and

hectic. Sam ate a pleasant meal in an opulent restaurant, looked at the women and the way they were dressed, and thought that not one of them could hold a candle to Jessica. In the afternoon he went back to the ship, to find it swarming with workers who had already started the refitting. He walked back to the agent's office, feeling anticipation. Enough time had lapsed for cables to have been exchanged with Jock Willis. He had to sit in the outer office for ten minutes before being admitted.

"I have good news for you, Mr. Gordon," the agent said. "As it happens, there is another Willis ship here in New York, the *Blackadder*, with a very fine captain. Mr. Frederick Moore will take over the *Cutty Sark*."

Sam tried to control his disappointment.

"But that is not the good news for you," the agent beamed. "Your great-uncle, Mr. Gordon, has ordered me to inform you that you, sir, are to be the new captain of the *Blackadder*."

Sam felt coldness in his stomach. The *Blackadder* was a scow, a heavy-bottomed slogger of a ship, wide and ungainly.

"I would prefer to remain first mate on the *Cutty*," he said.

"Now, now, don't turn down your first chance at command," the agent advised in a warning tone.

But it was not his first chance to command. He had been offered the *Roamer*. "I'd like to send a telegram to my uncle, please," Sam said.

"Of course," the agent agreed.

The telegram read: "Request reconsider. Prefer remain *Cutty Sark*."

Jock Willis's reply was received the next morning, and Sam was not surprised. "Rekquest denied. Take *Blackadder*."

Fifteen minutes later, Sam stood before the desk of Alfred Childers. "Mr. Childers, if your offer to take the *Roamer* is still open, I accept."

"Excellent!" Childers said, coming around the desk to shake Sam's hand. "She's yours, *Captain* Gordon."

Sam sent one more telegram to his uncle. "Sorry. Signed with Childers. Taking captaincy *Roamer*. Ask forgiveness."

Old Jock, upon receiving the telegram that had travelled so far on the underwater cable laid down originally by a British ship, the

148

Great Eastern, leaped from his seat, crumpling the paper and venting his Scottish anger on anyone within hearing distance. Only after a while did he cool down enough to smooth out the telegram and read it again, this time with a grudging smile "So," he said to himself, "the lad has an independent streak. Well, so did I at his age."

CHAPTER VII

Jon Fisher was not yet a rich man, but a telegram from Melbourne, from his bank, informed him that his first venture into wool trading had returned a handsome profit. Even after paying the Van Buren company its share, he no longer had to worry about eating into his capital. The bulk of his original inheritance had been invested into interest-bearing accounts, and the money given to him by his mother was intact.

His good fortune contrasted with the grim state of Harry Ryan's financial affairs. Harry had been desperately trying to raise money to buy sugar to include in the *Java*'s cargo when she sailed for Hong Kong, but he was having little success. The growers simply refused to extend credit. They took enough risks, he was told, in growing their crops, facing possible losses because of unfavourable weather, labour shortages, or pests. When it came to shipping their produce, it was time for the middlemen to take their own risks of having the cargo lost or damaged at sea.

The *Java*'s refit had turned out to be a much longer process than had originally been estimated, owing to shortages of materials and the yard's work schedule, so that to Jon it seemed he had been in Townsville forever. When he received notice of his success in London he began to take closer note of Harry's by now frenzied efforts to borrow money. He still had serious misgivings about Harry, but Harry was, after all, his partner and teacher in the trade. When he offered to take his wool profit and enter into a joint venture in sugar with Harry, Harry was, at first, speechless, then effusive in his thanks and in his assurances that Jon would get his money back more than doubled. So it was decided, and a happier Harry took himself off to haggle with plantation owners for sugar, leaving Jon, once more, restless.

The *Antony*, the sleek, fast steamer owned by Leonard

Brownlow and Marcus Fisher, came into port and began to load a cargo of sugar; rumour had it that Bartholomew Jamison would be her captain for her voyage out. There had been no repercussions following Jon's fight with Jamison, but Jon did not for one minute delude himself about the man. Jon knew he had made a dangerous enemy, and he made it a point to stay away from both the wharf where the *Antony* was tied up and the pub where Jamison was known to spend a good deal of his time while in town.

There was more on Jon's mind than business, however, and the run-in with Jamison. He went to sleep thinking of the young Samoan woman, Misa, and his first waking thoughts were of her. He imagined her slaving in a hot plantation kitchen, or over a boiling wash pot, and such thoughts raised a fever of indignation in him. He tried to convince himself that she was only one person of countless thousands caught up in unfortunate circumstances. There would always be such people, he told himself, as long as man took advantage of his fellows, excusing it by a difference in language, background, or skin colour. He could condemn the kanaka trade in general—and in his mind he did just that—but in practical terms, his thoughts were for the one woman, Misa. In any case, he could do nothing to stop the kanaka trade, for he was only one man; but by the living God, he swore, he could do something about Misa.

So it was that one morning he dressed, withdrew a considerable sum from the bank, and rented a horse. He went first to the waterfront, to see that Bartholomew Jamison was occupied supervising the loading of the *Antony*. Then, wasting no time, he set off at a gallop for Marcus Fisher's staging depot outside town.

He did not arrive at the compound until mid-morning, however, for, questioning his own motives and the wisdom of his actions, he had slowed the horse to a leisurely gait. He was not, he told himself, going because he loved Misa. She was a symbol. She happened to be slim, regal, beautiful, but what was that to him? Love? That was impossible. Perhaps, in the outback, some digger might marry a kanaka, but no gentleman of quality would even consider it. So love was out of the question, and, he concluded, he was making a fool of himself with a futile, almost adolescent gesture. After all, she had chosen to come to Australia as an indentured worker.

151

When he arrived and rode around the main buildings, all was silence. The huts were deserted, some with doors standing open. He saw a man walking among the huts, and he rode up to question him.

"The people who were here," he asked, "what happened to them?"

"If you're looking to buy indentures, you'll have to deal with Captain Jamison," the man said.

Jon realized that the man had no idea who he was. "There was a new batch here just days ago," he said, hoping for more information.

"Them!" The man waved a grimy hand toward the north. "They's on the way to the cane fields."

"How are they being transported?"

The man laughed. "They got legs, ain't they?"

Further questioning revealed that the kanakas had been marched out of the compound twenty-four hours earlier. Jon thanked the man, then rode off to the north. The trail was easy to follow, for such a large group made unmistakable tracks on the dusty dirt roads. Jon rode hard, stopping twice to confirm the passage of the kanakas by questioning homesteaders. He had to spend the night in the open, but, fortunately, the weather was good, and the only serious discomfort was his hunger. He paid for a breakfast of porridge and bread at a farmhouse and was riding at a trot down a lonely, seldom-travelled track when he saw the stragglers from the column of Samoans. He slowed as he came abreast of an older man who was having difficulty walking. There were open sores on the man's legs, and he was taking each step carefully, leaning on a bent stick as an aid. Some fifty yards ahead was a small group of men and women, two of the men half carrying a woman. Jon rode onward, his anger rising. The landscape opened up into a vast expanse of cane fields, and he could see human figures working, cutting cane and bundling it. A cluster of ramshackle buildings stood in a clearing ahead. The main body of the Samoans was entering the area, and he looked eagerly for the distinctive figure of Misa, saw her, spurred, and then slowed. The kanakas were being herded like a group of animals into a fenced-in area. The fence was not to prevent them from escaping, for even a child could slip over or through the rails; it was simply to herd

152

them like animals. He would have to wait to see her.

An overseer with a pistol in his belt approached him. Jon reined up, keeping a distance from the kanakas and hoping they would not give him away. He said he was travelling through, and the overseer, with unquestioning hospitality, invited him to take "tucker". He ate in the shade of a sideless shed, with three white supervisors, thankful that no one had yet recognized him. He accepted the offer of a bed of sorts for the night in one of the unused kanaka shacks and, as evening came, walked toward the compound where the new arrivals were camping out in the open.

Two white men were leaning with their elbows on the top of the fence, discussing the merits of the new shipment. The old man with the sores on his legs was just then hobbling from one group of natives to another, and the two white men looked at him disdainfully.

"Won't get much work out of that one," one of them said.

Jon walked around to the other side of the enclosure, not caring if the two whites thought him inhospitable. When he spotted Misa, sitting on the ground beside a fire, his breath constricted in his throat. He had forgotten how beautiful she was. Then he saw Tui, closer, and softly called his name, so that the white men did not hear. Tui looked up, rose, and walked casually to the fence.

"Mr. Fisher," Tui whispered. "You have come to help us?"

"In God's name, Tui, I wish I could," Jon answered. "I want to see Misa."

Tui's face went sullen.

"It's not what you think, Tui," Jon said. "I can't help all of you. I, too, am bound by the laws of the land, but I want to help her. I—"

"You want to buy her indenture," Tui interrupted, resentment evident in his voice. "So you can do as you will with her, for even being the whore of a white man would be better than the cane fields."

Jon reddened. "That wasn't my intention, I promise. She will have to work in the kitchens, or in the washing rooms, and—"

Tui spat. "Yours would not be the first promise to be broken."

"Tui, send her to me," Jon begged.

"I will speak to her. Then it is up to her." He turned his broad back, and Jon watched him make his way to the fire where Misa

153

sat. Words were whispered to her, and her face jerked toward Jon. He saw, in the failing light, the large, slightly upturned eyes, the haughty beauty of her face, and then she turned away for a few moments. When she looked back, Jon gestured toward a nearby copse, then walked toward it.

A small breeze stirred the leaves over his head. He sat down on moss, leaned against a huge grandfather of a tree, and waited. Darkness came with the sound of nightbirds and insects. The moon had risen, and the copse was a fairyland of lights and shadows. When he heard movement he leaped to his feet, his heart pounding. It was Tui. He swallowed bitter disappointment until he saw the feminine form emerge from the shadows behind Tui.

"I have come," Misa said.

"Good." Jon moved closer to see her face in the moonlight. "I have told Tui that I can't help all of you. I am not a rich man. What I propose to do is buy the indentures of you and your father. There will be enough money left for you to go back to Samoa."

"My father will never leave his people," Misa said.

"Not even to keep you from working in the fields?"

She was silent. Tui said, "Give us the money. We will use it to buy food as we travel away from this place."

"You can't do that," Jon said. "You are legally bound. They would hunt you." He put his hands on Misa's bare arms, and the contact with her warm flesh sent a tremor of excitement through him. "Listen to me, Misa. Some will die from the work in the fields. Before your contract is satisfied you'll be an old woman, broken and sick."

"Then tell whoever is in authority in this land that the promises made to us have not been kept. Get us out of the fields," she said.

"There is no one who will listen." Jon pleaded, almost desperate. "Let me at least save you and Molo."

"Why me?" she asked, looking straight at him, her eyes reflecting the light of the moon. "Why am I so important to you? There are many others."

The question silenced him. "You won't let me free you?"

"My father won't leave his people. I will not leave my father."

Jon turned away, his emotions struggling inside him. The knowledge of what the mere touch of her had done to him fuelled his desire, as well as his anger at her stubbornness. Without

154

conscious thought he took the money, all of it, from his pocket and thrust it at her. "Take it, then," he said. "Use it as you see fit."

She held the wad of banknotes close to her eyes to see. "It is a great deal of money."

"Yes," he said. "I pray that I am not, with that money, condemning all of you to punishment."

Misa turned and handed the money to Tui. "Go," she told him. "Give this to my father."

"You will come with me," Tui said.

"No," she said. "Not for a little while."

Jon's lips were dry. They stood, not looking at each other, until the soft sounds of Tui's departure were gone. Then, still in silence, she loosened her simple garment and, with a shrug of her shoulders, let it fall to the moss-covered earth. She stood before him, her smooth skin gleaming in the moonlight, dressed only in a *lavalava*, and then that, too, was gone. The beauty of her drove any semblance of shame, or pride, or honour from Jon's heart. With a smothered cry he gathered her into his arms.

He lay on the soft moss, her body beside him, warm in the cool night. Now shame raged in him. At the moment of entry she had cried out, and, even in the dimness of the moonlight, he had seen the dark evidence of her virginity on himself. He had bought her. That had not been his intention, but that was the inevitable conclusion, for she was *taupo*, the daughter of a chief, and now she would never—providing that she ever got home to Samoa—be able to marry and give evidence, according to Samoan traditions, of her purity. Yet, even though guilt surged through him, he knew that if he had it to do again, the outcome would be the same. If he had it to do again, he would take her as swiftly, as selfishly, as he had done. The need had been too great in him. And now, as she snuggled to his side for warmth, he felt his need surge once more, and the second time was lasting and complete, and she sighed with him as he lay beside her beneath the trees.

"This can't be," he whispered. "I will have you for my own."

"I must go," she said.

"I won't let you."

She had risen and was tying the *lavalava* around her loins, and then her breasts disappeared under the loose-fitting dress. He rose,

155

too, quickly dressed, and caught her arm. "Come with me," he said.

"I cannot."

"What will you do?"

"Somehow, with your money, my people will find a way to return to Samoa."

"Let me see to it that you and your father get there. There you can warn others against signing the papers of indenture."

"You have done all you can for us," she whispered. "I will remember. Now go."

He did not try to stop her. She slipped away through the dappled foliage like a wraith and was gone, leaving him to wonder why he had just stood there, and then, aloud, he said, "God help me," for he knew why he had let her go. As much as he loved her, as much as he needed her, he had considered the life he would have led had he forced her to go with him. He would have been just another Britisher who had "gone native", and doors would have been closed to him. He could never have married her; his career, his assurance of a place in respectable society would never have permitted it. Instead, he had let her go, and he would live with his shame.

Jon turned and walked away. He could not stay there, knowing that she was only a hundred yards away, knowing that he had probably only made things worse for her and for all of them by giving them money. He sneaked quietly to the horse pen, singled out his rented animal, and saddled it and rode away, forcing himself not to look back.

Misa was not yet nineteen years old. As she made her way back, ducked under the fence to see that her people were mostly asleep, she, too, knew shame. While love beneath the palm trees was nothing worthy of condemnation for other girls in Samoa, it was forbidden to her, and she had, by giving herself to Jon Fisher, broken a sacred trust. That she had done it for the sake of her people made it no less a blow to herself and to her father. That she had done it because she wanted the white man compounded her guilt.

As the daughter of an important headman, she had always been set apart, and one of the reasons why her father had wanted to

156

work in Australia to earn money had been his desire to be able to have for her the biggest *malaga*, the finest wedding ceremony ever known on the island of Upolu. Now she had given herself to a white man, a thing of shame in itself. It would have been better had she joined the other girls, not burdened with the status of *taupo*, in meeting their young men in the dark of night. It would even have been less shameful to have given herself to a *moetotolo*, one of the scorned night-crawlers who, unable to attract girls themselves, crept from house to house in the darkness, their bodies greased with coconut oil to help them slide through the hands of pursuers if discovered, hoping to find a maiden who, expecting her own lover, accepted the *moetotolo* in a case of mistaken identity.

Never had she braved the night before. Although she did not really believe in ghosts and devils, or evil spirits that could choke one to death, or leap upon one's back and attach themselves so tightly that they could not be shaken loose, she had run back to the enclosure with an occasional glance over her shoulder, just in case.

She saw her father and Tui in conference with other men, all of them seated on the hard ground, their voices low. She went to her place, spread her blanket, wrapped herself in it, and let the tears come. She wished fervently to be back in Samoa, and, to take her mind off what she had done, she envisioned a day in her village overlooking Apia Bay. So vivid was her imagination that she could hear the crow of a cock at daybreak, the shrill cries of birds from the breadfruit trees, the short, cranky wail of a baby being muffled as a mother thrust a warm, swelling breast into its mouth . . .

With morning, there would be talk of bonito fishing. There would be girls giggling as they heard of the narrow escape of some young boy from the home of one of their friends, who would stoutly deny to her stern father that she had expected the boy to sneak into the thatch-roofed house where a half dozen people and a few dogs were sleeping. The half-clad, serene young mothers would be lounging about, babes on their hips. Children would be snatching lumps of cold taro, too hungry to wait for breakfast, and soon the village would be astir with women taking their washing to the water, or weaving mats or preparing food.

The thought of food made her mouth water. The rations of this place left the stomach empty. She dreamed of taro and yams and breadfruit, and stuffed pig smoking from the spit, of a great, baked

157

fish fresh from the sea . . . while the sound of the voices of the men—her father and Tui doing much of the talking—fitfully intruded upon her attempt to escape the reality of what had happened in the copse of trees. She lived through an entire Samoan day, wandered through the village, walked out in her imagination to gather flowers and weave them into a garland, and then dreamed of the night and the fires and the family sleeping.

She started when a hand touched her head. She looked up and saw her father. She had been sleeping, she realized, dreaming that she was younger, no more than eight years old, acting as nursemaid for her younger brothers and sisters. Briefly she smiled at the memory, even as her father shook her awake, for she loved children and wanted many of her own.

A pang of sorrow shot through her. She was ruined now, and she would never have an honourable marriage. She would have to marry some *moetotolo*, or someone of lesser rank from another village.

"Come," her father whispered. "In silence. Gather your belongings."

She could hear hushed movement all around her. The people were up and about in total darkness, the moon having gone into hiding behind clouds. A hand took her arm, and she recognized Tui from his general shape. "We are leaving now?" she asked.

"Before we are scattered into the fields," Tui whispered. "They won't suspect that we would escape on our first night here."

Indeed, the nearby outbuildings were quiet, the windows of the more distant main house dark. One by one and two by two the Samoans slipped over or under the fence at a point nearest the copse of trees where Misa had held her rendezvous with Jon Fisher. She stayed at Tui's side. Molo was heading the way. In the dark it was slow going, and she bumped painfully into the rough bark of a tree, and stumbled more than once. Then they emerged on the other side of the trees and there was a field to cross, then a road and more fields until, on steadily rising ground and with the night beginning to fade, they threaded a path through rough brush and trees that seemed to go on forever. One could speak, then, in a normal voice.

Some of the weaker members of the group were trailing far behind, and Misa had left Tui's side to help them. Tui, who had

158

taken over the lead from her father, finally called a rest. He and Molo sat together, and Misa came to sit beside them.

"Daughter," Molo said, when he had caught his breath, for he was no longer so young. "I am glad to see that you help those who are not as strong. That is good."

"I think she should save her own strength," Tui said.

"Of that I have enough," Misa answered him. "*Jamá*", may I ask where we are going?"

Molo nodded. "We have given that question much thought."

"And your conclusions?"

It was Tui who spoke. "We have this." He withdrew a folded map from his small carpetbag. "When we were aboard ship, I was curious about this land to which we were coming, so I took this from a sailor's belongings." He spread the map on the ground as the last stragglers began to arrive and flop down wearily nearby. He pointed. "We are limited in the direction of travel by mountains to the west, and we do not want to go west at any rate. Therefore, we can go north or south. Since Molo and I both agree that the white man will think our obvious direction would be to the north, away from the city where we landed, we make a circle, thus, pass the city just inland from it, and go down the coast to one of the smaller settlements. There are, according to the map, several small villages. We will go first to the nearest one, called Ayr. There we will try to steal a boat."

Misa shuddered. Already they were fugitives, having broken a legal contract. Now they were to become thieves.

"There will be no opportunity to buy food," Molo said. "We will be hungry. I fear that some of our people will not make the journey."

"Now that they know what awaited them in this promised land," Tui said, "they will find the strength to go home."

"I pray so," Molo replied, his eyes downcast.

The march resumed, but their progress was limited by the slow pace of the weakest, and Molo would never consider deserting any of them. He himself aided the old man with the open sores. Misa tried her best to give the others encouragement, lending an arm to a tired, older woman and later taking her father's place with the old man. As night again fell, they skirted to the west of Townsville, daring for a while to take the open road, on which they made good time. They slept for a few hours in thick forest, and before sunrise Tui appeared with a sheep that he had killed. They quickly built a fire, and in the shelter of the morning mists they gorged themselves on half-raw mutton that everyone agreed tasted better than the finest feast they had ever had. Molo and Tui marched them through the day with hardly a pause, save to mourn the passing of the old man, who died quietly and was buried with whispered songs of farewell.

Several times long detours had to be taken in order to avoid small farms or plantations in the foothills. An entire day passed without food before Tui and another young man killed two more sheep. Although the land was beautiful, it was not fruitful like their native island, where one had but to pick from a breadfruit tree or slake one's thirst with the milk of a coconut.

Somehow they made the march. Molo and Misa kept the remaining group of twenty-three together, and Tui scouted ahead, to look down from a hilltop on the little village of Ayr, situated at the head of a winding inlet. When the others joined him, he pointed, with a satisfied smile, to a small sloop tied up at a rickety dock. It was no longer than thirty feet, but it looked seaworthy. Molo nodded.

"We cannot all go into the village, even in darkness," Molo said, as they crouched down to confer.

"You and I," Tui said, "and perhaps three others. We will take the boat and sail it with the current to the mouth of the inlet. The people will await us there."

"Then we must move them now, today," Molo said. "And there is the question of food. It is many weeks before we will see Samoa. We cannot depend on fish from the sea."

"I have been considering that problem," Tui said. "In talking with men who have been here for some time, at that place where we were first held, I paid special attention to a countryman who was a cook. He bragged that he was trusted to go into Townsville to buy provisions."

Molo smiled at the young man's foresight. "You look like a cook to me," he said.

"But I have not considered how we can carry the amount of provisions necessary," Tui said, hanging his head.

Molo was silent. Only a few hours earlier they had skirted a

160

small farm, where he had seen horses and a wagon. "I have a plan," he said. He called Misa. "Tui and I must go now. You must begin to move the people to the shore." He took her to the lookout and pointed out the cape, some five miles distant, where she and the people would await. "Look for us by moonlight," he said. He then selected three strong, seawise young men and put them in a place of concealment to await his and Tui's return.

It would have been better to approach the farmhouse by night, but both Tui and Molo agreed that their time was limited. The white men who held their contracts would be on their trail, and a blind man could follow the tracks of a group of more than twenty. What was to be done had to be done quickly.

The two men retraced their trail at a loping trot, until the farm came into sight. Crawling through the tall grass, they approached the outbuildings of the smallholding then waited until they were sure no one was about. While Tui watched, Molo entered the barn, found the harness, and had only small difficulty putting bridles on the two old horses that had been munching hay in a paddock. He had a bit more trouble getting the harness on and hitching the team to the wagon, but at last the job was accomplished and he led the horses away from the barn at a walk, looking over his shoulder nervously, for the wagon wheels needed greasing and the horses snorted and the harness creaked and jingled. Tui ran from his place of concealment and climbed into the wagon, and Molo joined him. Soon they were out of sight of the house and on the road into town, expecting at any moment a hue and cry of men in pursuit.

But they arrived in Ayr without incident, encountering not another soul on the road. Despite their considerable apprehension, both men sat proudly erect, having agreed it would not do to act as thieves. Fortunately, there was not much activity in the tiny village. A ragged-looking boy called back his dog as it made a dash for the legs of the horses, and a woman with a swarm of children playing around her simply stared at them as she rocked on the porch of a weathered frame house. They passed a pub with white paint peeling from its rough walls, then no more than a dozen houses before they were at the waterfront and in front of a general store. Tui tied the horses' reins to the hitching rail and walked into the store at Molo's side. The proprietor, a bewhiskered, stout

161

white man dressed in filthy trousers and a faded blue shirt, eyed them speculatively.

"What do you want, kanaka?"

Tui, who had learned to read and write at the mission school on Upolu, had made up a list of provisions. He placed the list on the counter.

"You crazy?" the man said before he had finished reading it. "You think you're in Sydney?"

"Boss man give list," Tui said in intentionally broken English; he had also learned at the mission that, with most white men, it paid to appear stupid.

"Who the hell is your boss?" the store owner asked.

"Boss man Cap'nm Jamison," Tui said. "Take kanakas south. Need grub."

"Did the boss man send cash money?"

Molo took out money, not all of it. The white man looked, reached, but Molo pulled the money away; he had seen the light of greed appear in the man's eyes.

'Cap'n Jamison said you no charge too much. He come talk you," Tui said.

"Well," the man said, casting a look at the banknotes in Molo's hand. "I don't understand why Jamison sends you here. This is a small store. We ain't used to outfitting big stuff. But we'll see what we can do."

A quarter of an hour later, the wagon, laden with salt fish, flour, dried beef, salt, sugar, fresh limes, and tea, rumbled out of the village. One of the three men Molo had ordered to stay behind was detailed to take it to the point at the mouth of the inlet, where the rest of the people had gone. Then Molo, Tui, and the others waited and watched from concealment. Although there was no movement around the sloop that was their target, they waited until well after dark, when all the lights were out in the village and the last few customers had left the pub and staggered off to their homes.

With Molo in the lead, they circled the outlying houses and approached by water, sometimes being forced to wade up to their waists, and then they were under the wharf, the ripples from their movements making small, smacking sounds against the hull of the sloop. Tui lifted himself aboard, crept around to peer into the deckhouse, then hissed a signal to indicate that no one was aboard.

The others piled over the sides in quick order.

In a matter of seconds the mooring lines were loosed. By good fortune the tide was falling, and the current in the inlet carried them silently away from the dock and the shore. The night was calm, the water smooth, and the shore was quiet as they left the little settlement behind. When they were a safe distance away, with Molo at the tiller, one of the other men, who had worked for a time as a deckhand on an island trading schooner, began to sort out the sails and, with some confusion, directed the others in raising the mainsail, which in the slight evening breeze increased their headway and steerage. In less than an hour, the sloop was in sight of the mouth of the inlet, with the wide sea spreading ahead, and from shore a flicker of a campfire directed them to their destination. They came as near to the beach as they dared, then struck sail and dragged the anchor. Tui dived over wearing only his *lavalava*.

On shore the young men used vines to lash together driftwood logs into a makeshift raft, on which the provisions were ferried to the sloop. Those who could do so swam out to be helped aboard, while the weaker ones clung to the raft. By the time the moon had reached its zenith, the sails were set, the anchor had been weighed, and the sloop was moving into the gentle swell of the Coral Sea.

In the full light of day, Misa stood at the stern, looking back to the land they had left behind. The mountains of Queensland were dark masses on the far horizon. It was raining in the higher elevations, and the dark clouds blended with the land until, as the sloop sailed on to the northeast, there was only the sun-spangled, dancing, sparkling blue of the sea. Her stay in Australia had been unhappy and brief, yet for all that, she could not help but feel she had left an important part of her life behind. There, below the horizon now, was the man who had first shown her love, a man she would never see again. As she thought of the brief moments she had spent alone with him, a vast upheaval of sorrow brought tears, and the pain of loss was so intense she bent double, clutching her stomach as she wept.

Tui, who was taking his turn at the tiller, looked at her more with curiosity than with pity. In the past hours he had been more concerned with handling the unfamiliar vessel of the white men than with the girl. Like all Samoan males, he had been born and raised a sailor, although he was naturally more accustomed to his people's graceful outrigger canoes, some even as large as this vessel. Molo had appointed the one among them with the most experience on white men's ships to be boss man, and after some experimentation—including a few moments of crisis when they came around into the wind with a banging of sails and a dangerously swinging boom—a routine had been established, the characteristics of the sloop had become known, and Tui had been chosen from among the other eager volunteers to take a turn at the helm.

"Perhaps I will go to sea for a living," he now said to Misa, as the sloop cut through choppy waters, with the freshening wind giving her wings. "Maybe even sail the great clipper ships and become a captain."

"Perhaps pigs will learn to fly," Misa said, rubbing the tears from her eyes.

They both laughed, but Misa's eyes, as they met his, were red from weeping. "Misa," he asked gently, "what is it that troubles you?"

When she made no answer, he said, "You do not grieve for that land where white men use whips?"

"You overstep your bounds," she told him sharply, but, to his surprise, she did not leave the stern. His mind went back to the night when the white man had given them money. She had remained behind. She was the daughter of the headman, and she knew responsibility. A debt was owed to the white man, a debt that could never have been paid in money.

"I understand," he said softly. She looked at him, her dark eyes welling with tears. "When a debt is settled," Tui went on, "there is not dishonour."

She turned to him, and he saw her shoulders shake. He quickly slipped a lash over the tiller and stood behind her, putting his hands on her shoulder. His guess had been correct. No longer was she *taupo*. And despite his pity for her, he felt a surge of elation, for now she was within his reach. He turned her to face him and saw the great, salty tears streaming down her cheeks.

"No weeping," he said. "We are going home. What happened in that evil land does not matter, not to me, not to you."

164

"I cannot lie," she said.

"No, nor will you have to. We will speak with Molo, tell him of your sacrifice, and then I will speak for your hand."

Her eyes widened. "You?"

"My eyes have loved you since you were this high," he said, indicating a height to her waist.

"No," she said.

"I will cherish you."

She took his hand. "Tui, I would not want to hurt you, but you have always been a good friend, like a big brother—"

"I can be more?"

"But from me there would not be the kind of love you deserve," she said. She was sobbing softly.

He did not understand the meaning of her words until he looked into her eyes. Briefly, jealousy flared. "You lost more than maidenhood in that evil land."

She jerked away and gave him her back.

"Young girl often confuse the first flush of passion with love," he whispered, standing close but not touching her. "What you feel will pass, Misa, and when it does I, Tui, will be there for you."

Misa shook her head violently.

"It will pass, Misa," he repeated. "I will not demand, nor push, nor beg. I ask only one thing. When it comes to a time when you forget, and are ready, consider Tui first."

She controlled her sobbing, wiped her cheeks, faced him, and forced a smile. "That I can promise, my friend, but it would not be fair to you. Because, Tui, I cannot, I *will* not, ever forget what has happened."

CHAPTER VIII

Red Broome was not especially taken with Hong Kong. He had never been. Visiting the port for a brief stopover, as he had done in the past, was one thing, but living there was another. He often felt as if he could not get enough air into his lungs. A combination of the pungent scents of the crowded, dirty city and the knowledge that he was literally surrounded by an alien race—Chinese in their countless millions, teeming in the crowded streets around the harbour and looming like a leaderless host in the mainland behind him—troubled and oppressed him.

Of course, he and his family were well situated, in a fine house on a height overlooking the city and the harbour. Magdalen, solid person that she was, had made the place a home almost immediately, and it was only there that Red felt truly comfortable. As for Jessica . . . well, she seemed to be enamoured of the place and was forever running off, escorted by, mainly, older members of the British community to some occasion or the other, be it a lawn party, the racecourse, or even the Chinese opera, of which she was especially fond. If she was disturbed by the absence of Samuel Gordon, she certainly did not show it, Red felt, for all that she continued to brush aside increasingly insistent attempts by eligible young bachelors to pay her court.

Before taking the assignment to Hong Kong, Red had been well aware of the problems that beset the tiny crown colony. Being the principal British naval station in the South China Sea, Hong Kong was responsible for the protection of British shipping in the region. Alas, such a role, Red had come to realize, was, like most things in the Orient, anything but simple. A glance at a map might indicate that Hong Kong dominated the approaches to the main trading port in China, Canton, but in actuality even an entire fleet of warships would be hard pressed to protect friendly shipping in and around the Pearl River; to patrol what was left of the long, sweeping coastline of Southern China, from Shanghai to Hainan Island, was next to impossible.

Like the Malay archipelago to the southwest, the Chinese coast was a honeycomb of hiding places for brigands and pirates. Shipping losses to seaborne raiders had long since raised the concern of Her Majesty's government, and Red was only the latest in a series of senior naval officers who had been dispatched to deal with the problem. He had no illusions that he would meet with far greater success than had his predecessors, but at least he had the advantage that the army commander with whom he would have to cooperate was an old friend of his. Upon Red's arrival, Adam Shannon, whose regular-army commission had been temporarily reactivated, had briefed him thoroughly. The pirate raids of late, Adam had informed him, were perhaps no more numerous, but they were certainly getting bolder. A powerful warlord ashore had apparently thrown in his lot with one of the larger pirate groups, and as a result the pirates, now better financed and organized, were preying on merchant ships with well-armed fleets of as many as six heavily manned junks.

While Red was still acquainting himself with his new command and taking stock of the resources available to him, he was called to Shannon's headquarters one afternoon to meet Sir Reginald Peckwith of the Colonial Office, who had just arrived in Hong Kong the previous day. Peckwith was still dressed for the English climate, in dark clothes, heavy waistcoat, and, most probably, Red thought, judging by the way the man sweated and squirmed in the tropical heat, long woollen underwear.

Peckwith inquired first as to what was being done about the pirates and listened, wiping his brow, as Adam Shannon explained that he and Red would be mounting a joint operation against the warlord who had become the greatest immediate threat to freedom of the seas.

"You gentlemen seem to work well together," Peckwith commented, after listening to Adam and Red take turns describing their preparations up to the present.

"We're old friends," Red said. "However, Sir Reginald, I think it is best to advise you not to be too optimistic. We have a huge area of shoreline and sea to cover, there are many pirates, and as you know, we have limited resources. Our hope is to make an example of the most notorious warlord, thus giving the others cause to ponder the advisability of their depredations against Her Majesty's shipping."

"Good—I approve heartily," Peckwith said. "I will leave details to you, gentlemen. Meanwhile, there is another, larger matter I wish to bring up. The Chinese pirates are, as I see it, a short-run concern."

Both Red and Adam waited with growing curiosity as Peckwith methodically wiped his brow.

"How aware are you, gentlemen, of the current political climate in Europe?"

"News is often slow to reach us here," Red answered, having no idea of where the conversation was leading.

"I think specifically of the growth of the power of Prince Bismarck's Germany," Peckwith said. "The man has forced unity on all the disparate German states, and his so-called League of the Three Emperors makes him the greatest threat to peace since Napoleon."

"We hear rumours," Adam said, "of German rumblings against Great Britain, but that's all."

"It's more than rumour." Peckwith fingered his tight collar, his face red from the heat. "Bismarck is actively courting the French."

Adam and Red exchanged a puzzled glance. "Surely the French won't forget the Prussian War so quickly," Adam said. "And there's slim chance that Bismarck would agree to return Alsace-Lorraine."

"Don't underestimate the stupidity of the French," Peckwith said. "Of course, that's my personal opinion. In public utterances, I have to pay lip service to the great friendship between Her Majesty's government and the great French nation. But that is beside the point. The point is that we at home expect to see more colonial expansion by the Bismarck government."

"Their shipping is already much in evidence in these waters," Red said.

Peckwith frowned sourly. "Our stand toward German ships at sea is, of course, peaceful. However, that does not mean we are obliged to make it easy for them in their efforts to cut into our trade and to establish German colonies in the Pacific. As of this moment it is not your concern, but I think, as members of the military establishment, you should be made aware that Germany is conducting a programme of expansion in Africa, and, closer to your own interests, in the Pacific. If war with Germany comes, gentlemen, it could very well start in your back yard."

"New Guinea?" Adam asked, his tone incredulous.

"Perhaps. Or maybe Samoa," Peckwith said.

"War, over a group of tiny islands?" Adam shook his head in disbelief.

"Very rich islands," Peckwith said, "with copra and agricultural products badly needed in Germany. I am ashamed to admit that it is estimated that German ships now carry three-fourths of the cargoes originating in the South Seas. We at home intend doing something about this. For one, we will not allow Germany to annex Samoa without a struggle. Nor are we content to sit back and let the United States compete alone for the South Seas trade. Aside from trade, the finest harbours in the South Pacific are in Samoa. The nation that holds those harbours is in a position to dominate the entire area. If Germany should have Samoa, it would put her in a position to strengthen her claim to New Guinea, a far greater prize than any small group of islands."

"We should have annexed New Guinea long ago," Red complained.

"It is being discussed between home officials and the Australian government," Peckwith said. "It's a rather complicated proposition. It would, of course, have to be approved by Parliament." He looked at Red, his gaze steady. "You, commander, have made a name for yourself out here, and I daresay you're a man of influence in your own country. I do not dare to try to initiate foreign policy myself, so this is merely, you understand, an observation. In my opinion, the annexation of New Guinea should be an initiative of Queensland."

Red nodded, knowing that he should remain silent.

"Well, gentlemen, my orders were merely to brief you on the overall situation." Peckwith pushed his chair back. "And I will, of course, be seeing you again before I leave."

"We appreciate your frankness," Adam said, as all three of them rose.

"For the moment, keep your sights on these damnable Chinese

169

pirates," Peckwith said. He wiped his brow once more, with an already sodden handkerchief. "As for me, thank God I'm here only for a visit and soon will be off for London and a sensible climate."

When Peckwith was gone, Red looked at Adam and laughed. "I say, old boy, how do we colonials stand these wretched climates?"

"Old boy," Adam replied, mimicking Peckwith's accent, "we simply take off our blasted long johns and muddle through." He went to the sideboard for a bottle of brandy. "The sun is over the yardarm somewhere in Her Majesty's empire, I am sure," he said. "The old man certainly gave us some food for thought."

Red accepted a drink, but for a moment his mind was elsewhere. "By the way," he said, "Marcus Fisher has arrived in Hong Kong."

"Fisher?" Adam frowned. "What the deuce is he doing here? I thought his commercial interests were with England, besides his dabbling in the kanaka trade."

"Perhaps he's expanding his horizons. But I mention it only because Fisher is keeping some interesting company these days, and Sir Reginald's comments got me thinking. Have you encountered one Maxim Stoltz, who purports to be a journalist?"

"Good God, Red, I have! If he's a journalist, I'm a blessed kangaroo! Fisher and Stoltz, is it?" He mused for a moment. "I wonder. Don't some of Fisher's indentured kanakas come from Samoa?"

"That's what I was thinking," Red said. "Of course it's not illegal to do business with the Germans—but they are known to drive a hard bargain. Still, surely, not even Fisher would sell out his own country, if that's what you're thinking."

"I wonder," was Adam's only reply.

It is a wise young woman who, in the first flush of love, knows her own heart; and Jessica Broome, despite all the outward signs of behaviour that were obvious to her mother, had seemed to have convinced herself that her feelings toward Samuel Gordon were no more than superficial, a simple liking for a personable young man who made for pleasant company without complications. She could even attribute her occasional lapses into melancholy to the change in climate, or to the shock of being suddenly thrust

170

headlong into so different a culture.

Thus she was seated before a window one day, watching the water collect and run from the terrace, thinking that the dullness in her was because of the weather, when she saw a Chinese messenger walk slowly to the front of the house, look around, and then mount the steps. She didn't wait for one of the housemaids to answer the door.

"This Bloome?" the messenger asked.

"Yes, I will take the message," she said, for he was holding a by now sodden envelope in his hands. She recognized it as being from the telegraph office and frowned, for her father no longer received communications at home, since he had established an office. Still, he would be home soon, so instead of trying to explain to the man his error, she gave him a coin and sent him off into the curtain of rain. Only then did she realize that the telegram was not addressed to Commander Broome, but to her, Miss Jessica Broome. Her cheeks flushed with mixed apprehension and excitement, and she felt almost faint as she found an ornate Chinese chair and sank down into it, holding it at a level with her eyes.

Then, in frantic haste, she ripped the envelope open, tearing it unevenly because it was so wet. Her eyes darted to the name of the sender, and she gasped in pleasure, for it was signed "Capt. Samuel Gordon." And the length of the message was an extravagance, considering the rate per word, and that it had come all the way from New York.

"*Altered circumstances allow speaking,*" she read. *Now captain* Roamer *enroute Australia. No immediate Hong Kong. Can you wait? Consider my suit your hand in marriage?*"

For long moments she was stunned. All that time he had been with her in Sydney and in Hong Kong and not a word, and now this—this cold, impersonal declaration. But was it impersonal? Wasn't it, after all, in a way romantic? She leaped to her feet, ran to a window, and looked out at the leaden skies, the steady, drumming rain. But somehow there was a new wonder in the day; there seemed to be more light, and she no longer felt the dampness that had pervaded the house.

Magdalen looked up from her knitting when Jessica entered the room, and then her eyes fell to the piece of paper in her daughter's hand. "What is it, dear?" she asked.

171

Jessica, looking half in a daze, handed her the telegram without speaking. She held two fingers to her lips to hide her growing smile as Magdalen read, then looked up, with a smile suddenly as wide as her daughter's.

"Can you believe men?" Jessica asked. "How can they be so . . . so obtuse?"

"It does seem a marvel sometimes," Magdalen said.

"All that time he loved me! And because he hadn't been given his captaincy, he said nothing!"

"I'm sure, dear, that it was merely because he wanted to be in a position to be able to provide for you."

"But he could have at least hinted!"

"Nonetheless, I am under the impression," Magdalen said, with a sly smile, "that you are willing to wait to, ah, consider his suit?"

Laughing, Jessica lifted her mother from the chair, scattering the knitting, and danced a circle around her. "Oh, Mother!"

"I am so very happy for you," Magdalen said, ending the dance in a hug. "I know exactly how you must feel."

Jessica sobered and pulled away, looking again at the telegram. "But Australia? He said he is coming to Australia, not here."

"Actually," Magdalen said, "if I had my choice for you, I would not have you married to a seafaring man."

"Oh, I don't mind waiting, I suppose."

"You'll mind." Magdalen picked up her knitting. "You'll mind every time he says good-bye and goes off to his first love, the sea." She took her daughter's hand and squeezed it. "But the sadness of parting will be more than compensated for by the joy of his homecoming." She looked into Jessica's eyes. "You're very sure?"

"I've known it from the first time I met him."

Magdalen raised one eyebrow but said nothing.

"We will simply have to move back to Sydney, you and I," Jessica said.

"Not so fast, young lady. Remember that my marriage is to be considered, too. I've done my share of sitting at home, waiting."

Jessica's face fell.

"But we'll discuss it with your father," Magdalen said. "As a matter of fact, he has already broached the subject himself."

When Red was given the news, over dinner, his first reaction was a broad smile. "Fine young man, Mr. Gordon," he said. "I wondered when he was going to summon the nerve to speak up." He smiled fondly at his only daughter. "You realize, of course, that if his ship is to be engaged in the wool trade it might be years before he has a cargo for Hong Kong?"

"Years?" Jessica repeated faintly.

"Your mother and I have discussed the advisability of your, both of you, going home," Red said. "Before you get your hopes up, nothing has been decided, and it will be partly your mother's decision."

"I think we should stay with you, Red," Magdalen said, "until you are ready to sail against the pirates. After all, Mr. Gordon cannot fly around the world, even in a clipper ship."

Red felt a swift pang of loss. And yet he knew that sending them home was the most sensible thing to do. He did not delude himself as to the danger of his undertaking. He was not a young man anymore, and above all he wanted to avoid the possibility of leaving them alone in Hong Kong. Of course there was the British community, but he knew that he would feel better while he was at sea if they were safely back in the comfortable Elizabeth Bay house, among family and friends.

At the Townsville wharves the *Java* and the steamer *Antony* had been loaded almost side by side. It was perhaps inevitable that the *Antony*'s captain, Jamison, would again cross paths with Jon Fisher, but when the meeting occurred, no words were spoken. Jon was walking from the hotel toward the *Java*, and when Jamison rounded a corner and saw him, the bearded man stopped in his tracks, and such an aura of hate came from him that Jon quailed for a moment, but did not halt his progress toward the ship. Jamison followed his every step with slitted, baleful eyes before Jon made the gangplank and went aboard.

"Have a warm chat with an old friend?" Harry Ryan said flippantly, having witnessed the encounter. Jon shrugged. "You're probably going to have to kill that man someday," Harry said in the same casual tone, which somehow made the words seem even more ominous.

"I was told that the loading was complete," Jon said.

"Indeed, my boy." Harry clearly was in one of his ebullient

moods. "And there are other developments. It seems you have a new job."

Jon waited, but Harry merely smiled, determined to make Jon ask. Jon finally gave in. "All right. What new job?"

"You're now supercargo for the company," Harry said. "But don't let it go to your head, because you're going to have to deal with a very stern captain."

"You?" Jon asked, dumbfounded.

"The old man is having a bout of malaria," Harry said. "So you're going to see a ship fly, my boy."

"Good for you!" Jon shook Harry's hand, genuinely pleased for him. He had felt all along that Harry's place was in command of a clipper, not as a businessman.

Soon they were caught up in the last-minute rush of preparations to get under way, and Jon was impatient to finally see the last of Townsville. Easing the *Java* out of the harbour was not a simple task, and it was suddenly complicated when the *Antony*, as if awaiting the opportunity, cast loose her lines and, using her engines, backed directly into *Java*'s path.

"What's that idiot trying to do?" Harry snarled, as the *Antony* approached from windward, sending bilious smoke drifting the length of *Java*'s deck. He bellowed orders, and *Java*'s bow fell away from a near collision with the iron steamer. Harry ran to the rail and yelled through a speaking trumpet, and he did not mince words. On the *Antony*, Jamison nodded coldly.

"Well, that bastard has thrown down the gauntlet," Harry said, as *Antony*'s engines sent her out of the harbour ahead of *Java*. "He's heading for Hong Kong. Let's show him our heels."

Jon looked at Harry, hardly believing he was serious. The *Antony* was the fastest steamer in the Pacific. Races between sailing ships were one thing, but to take on a fast steamer with a clipper was another. Indeed, outside the harbour, in light and unfavourable winds, the *Antony* was soon nothing more than a smudge on the horizon, while *Java* made scant headway. Nor was there any sight of *Antony* as *Java* skirted the northern coast, for all it seemed that Harry could sense the presence of the steamer, perhaps just below the horizon. He pushed the *Java* hard, taking advantage of squalls to send her slicing through the waves with that sleek, racing speed for which a clipper was designed.

174

Jon was more than a disinterested spectator. Besides wishing to best Jamison, he knew that every clipper man doted on passage records, and as the *Java* flew northward through the Coral Sea, he became caught up in the feeling aboard that they had an excellent start toward the swiftest passage ever between northern Australia and China. Harry planned to sail nonstop, while the *Antony* would have to put in for recoaling, most probably in Java. The *Java* was taking the northern route, across the equator north of New Guinea, and then northwestward to round the Philippines into the South China Sea.

The weather was with them, and the *Java* carried all the canvas her spars would support as she ran night and day, past the Palau Islands, then abreast of the Philippines. By the time they altered course to the west, every man on board knew that the *Java* was in the hands of a true master, one who, while avoiding outright brutality or cruelty, yet pushed the crew and himself until all of them were exhausted, bleary-eyed with sleeplessness, but content and even proud in the knowledge that they were sailing the clipper as she had never been sailed before.

Java thundered through the narrow Bashi Channel into the South China Sea. By now, Jon had forgotten the *Antony*. In his mind, the *Java* and her crew were racing the records of the other clippers, not a grunting, snorting steamer. He had come to truly appreciate for the first time the fierce pride of a clipper man, for the *Java* was indeed like a living thing, with a personality of her own.

"I'm going to stand a drink for every man in this crew," Harry said proudly one afternoon, with Hong Kong less than two days' distant. "By god, we *drove* her, didn't we?"

"You did indeed," Jon agreed. "I've told you all along that you had missed your calling."

"A momentary diversion, Mr. Fisher," Harry said, smiling broadly. "Just to show them how it should be done, and to set an example for my own skippers, when I have my fleet."

But perhaps Harry had spoken too soon, for with the Chinese mainland just below the horizon, the winds shifted, then abruptly failed. The *Java* luffed along with no more than a breath of a breeze in her sails, her cutwater hardly making a ripple. Harry chafed, threw on every inch of sail, even had the crew wet down the

175

canvas, the better to catch the faintest puff of air.

The day that remained became two, then three, and on a clear dawn, with the winds still light and unfavourable, and the *Java* on a laborious tack, the lookout spotted a smudge of smoke on the horizon. A steamer was coming up from the south, making for the mouth of the Pearl River and Hong Kong. Harry anxiously examined the distant dot through a glass, and when the steamer was near enough for him to recognize her shape, he exploded with an oath.

"The *Antony*?" Jon asked.

"If the wind hadn't failed, we'd have been in port two days ahead of him," Harry scowled. He put the glass aside and ordered a fruitless trimming of the sails. The *Antony* had changed course and was now making directly for them, and Harry ordered the next tack, planning his approach to the Tathong Channel leading into the harbour.

The distance between the ships closed steadily. The *Java* was crossing *Antony*'s bow at right angles to her course, and according to long-accepted practice, the sailing vessel had right of way. Harry watched with cold eyes as the steamer showed no signs of altering course.

"A bit close, isn't it?" Jon asked, as the *Antony* plowed on, white water at her bow.

"He'll fall off," Harry said.

The *Java*'s duty watch lined her rail, facing the steamer. As the distance closed further they began to cast concerned glances toward the stern, where Harry stood beside the helmsmen. But already it was too late for the *Java* to take action to avoid what looked to be a sure collision; even if she immediately backed sail, the *Antony* would be on her before her progress could be checked.

"Harry, I don't think he is going to change course," Jon said, growing worried. The *Antony* looked suddenly huge, her sharp bow aimed, surely, at the *Java*'s waist.

"Turn, you bastard," Harry bellowed, although there was no chance of his being heard aboard the *Antony*.

Then, as if by a miracle, the *Java*'s slack sails snapped and bellowed, the wind coming on like a fist out of a clear sky. In one of those sudden changes familiar to all sailors who had spent any time at sea, the *Java*, still with her full set of sail, leaned precariously and surged forward, the *Antony* at the same time coming hard about, but still so near that the sailors along the rail panicked and began to run away from the apparent point of collision. The canvas overhead thundered and flapped as the *Antony*'s bow slid by the clipper's stern, the steep, high sides of the steamer so near that Harry and Jon could see the rust flakes, could look up to see Bartholomew Jamison leaning on the *Antony*'s rail, staring down at them through slitted eyes.

"He tried to run us down," Harry said with total disbelief. "He deliberately tried to run us down."

Now the *Java* was moving, with a stiff and steady wind. Harry turned her onto a northern tack and she flew, leaving the *Antony* in her wake, so that by the time they were in the lee of the mainland, the distance between the ships had widened to about half a mile. Harry kept most of the sails set until the last minute; and after the *Java* had glided into the crowded anchorage, laid all her canvas flat aback, then neatly dropped her anchors in turn, he looked back to see the *Antony* just entering the harbour. He grinned. "Well, we beat the bastard."

"Congratulations," Jon said; but even as he spoke he was reliving the moment when the *Antony* had narrowly missed cutting the *Java* in two with her iron bow . . . seeing in his mind the evil, baleful face of Jamison staring directly down at him. And the words Harry had spoken to him in Townsville came suddenly to mind: "*You're going to have to kill that man someday.*"

Harry wasted no time, once the harbour authorities had made their call and tugs eased the *Java* into her berth. "Do you mind holding the fort?" he asked Jon. "I have urgent business ashore."

The first mate was a good man, but the cargo was the responsibility of the captain and the supercargo. "Do you know where she lives?" Jon asked, knowing that Harry was off to see Jessica.

"It can't be too difficult to find out," Harry replied, his tone one of utter confidence. And indeed, it was no trouble for him to obtain the Broomes' address from the shipping agent who represented the Van Buren company in Hong Kong. Harry rode to the hillside residence in style, being pulled along rapidly by a straining, wiry Chinese, and in short order he was left standing in front of the door with his hat in his hand. It was Jessica who answered his knock. Her eyes widened, and then she smiled.

"Harry, what a surprise! We weren't expecting you for some time."

"Good passage," he said, taking a step forward.

Jessica looked unaccountably nervous. "Do come in," she said, at last stepping aside. "As it happens, I'm here alone for the moment."

"Good," Harry said, in a tone that made Jessica look away in haste. "I want to speak to you alone."

Jessica had hoped that time would have altered Harry's attitude toward her, but apparently it had not. She steeled herself to give him the news quickly.

"I've missed you sorely, Jess," Harry said, trying to take her hand, but she managed to avoid contact and led him into a sitting room.

"Tea?" she asked.

"No, not now. Sit down, Jess, please."

"Harry, have I ever told you I don't like being called Jess? Except by Father, of course. My name is Jessica."

"Jessica. Yes, a beautiful name. Forgive me. Jessica it will be. Always Jessica."

"I think I will have tea," she said, disturbed by the look of obvious adoration in his eyes. She rang a small bell. A bowing, smiling Chinese girl entered, took her orders, and left.

"So you had a good passage?" she asked lamely, as both of them sat down.

"Fastest ever," Harry replied. "I was captain of the *Java*, Jess—Jessica."

"That's wonderful, Harry. I'm so pleased for you."

"It's temporary, and it's my choice that it is temporary. I have bigger things in mind for us. You'll not be a sailor's wife, always waiting in port."

"Harry, don't—"

"Being away from you like this, being on a long passage, wet, sleepless, made me realize how much I do miss you when I'm not near you." He rose and came toward her, but she was already out of her chair and had backed away so that it was between them.

"Harry—"

"Listen to me," he said forcefully. "You said that you didn't love me as a woman loves a man. That doesn't matter. We've always got on well, Jess. You can learn to love me."

He reached for her arms and she darted back, her face scarlet. "Harry, I'm going to marry Sam Gordon," she blurted.

He looked stricken. *"What?"*

"Captain Samuel Gordon has proposed marriage to me, and I am going to accept," she said.

"*Captain* Gordon?"

"He has one of Alfred Childers' ships now—the *Roamer*."

"You're going to marry him?"

"Yes."

Harry's right hand, seemingly without his conscious awareness, had gone to the scar on his cheek. "You say he's proposed—but he was on the *Cutty Sark*, on the way to New York."

"Please sit down, Harry," she said, and to her relief he complied weakly. She stood before him. "Captain Gordon proposed to me by telegram. I have not yet been able to deliver my answer to him, because he's at sea, on the way to Australia. But I am going to tell him yes."

"Jess, a sailor?"

"Yes," she said. "My father's a sailor."

His face darkened ominously. "That's idiotic!" he said. "You're going to marry a man who'll spend two years or more at a time away from you?" He leaped back to his feet, but Jessica held her ground. "Come to your senses, girl! Consider what I'm offering you. I'm offering you a comfortable life. Trading doesn't require that I travel with every shipment. We can have a life together."

"I love him, Harry," she said, surprised at the conviction of her own words. "For the sake of our long friendship, please be happy for me."

"Happy?" He glowered. "Damned if I can say I'm happy!"

"You mustn't use such language to me," she said, her tone harsh for the first time.

He looked at her for a long while. She felt herself redden under his gaze, which had changed from adoration to something that had begun to frighten her. To break the awkward moment she said, "Jon Fisher is with you?"

He nodded.

179

"Father and mother will want to see both of you. We'll expect you for dinner."

Harry was silent. He turned and stalked toward the door.

"Harry, you will come for dinner?" she called after him.

He faced her, and his look was black. Then, disconcertingly, he smiled. "Jess," he said, "I wouldn't miss it for the world."

Jon was bartering with local merchants when Harry came back aboard the *Java*. Harry went to his cabin and did not enter into the negotiations. For the moment, at least, his ambition was taking second place to his jealousy and anger.

"I think it's a very favourable price," Jon said, showing Harry the offer for their jointly owned sugar after the merchants had left the ship.

"You did well, my boy," Harry said. "You've made us a pound or two, and I thank you."

"Is something troubling you?" Jon asked.

"Nothing at all. I'm going ashore for a drink. Care to join me?"

"No, I don't." Jon's reservations about his partner were quickly returning. "And don't you think it would be a good idea if you stayed here as we begin to offload?"

"Are you telling me my business now?"

"No," Jon replied stiffly. "Go ahead. I'll handle it."

"I'll see you tonight at Commander Broome's table," Harry said, "since we're both invited. Tell them I might be a bit late."

"Harry—" Jon had intended to warn him against overindulging, but he was left addressing an empty doorway as Harry disappeared onto the deck, without a backward look.

Despite his concern over Harry, Jon had his duties to attend to, which were more than enough to keep him busy the rest of the day; and later that evening, after he had found his way to the Broome house with some difficulty, he was greeted with genuine warmth by all three family members. While they awaited dinner, Red insisted on hearing an account of the voyage.

"They'll be talking about this for a long time," Red said with evident satisfaction when Jon had finished. "How a clipper beat the fastest steamer in these oceans. And with the *Antony* taking the shorter route through the Sunda Strait."

"I can't tell you how impressed I was by the way Harry handled the ship and the crew," Jon admitted. "Not that I'm an expert, of course."

"The lad's a fine seaman," Red agreed. "He'd have unlimited prospects if he could manage to get his priorities on shore straightened out."

Jon put the best light on the statement. "Well, perhaps he can combine the two—his talent as a captain, that is, and his desire to earn a good deal of money in trade."

The talk remained pleasant, and the room was cheery. When a servant came in and informed Magdalen that dinner was ready, she looked at the clock and said, "Please tell cook to hold it for another quarter hour."

"And that's the limit," Red said, rubbing his stomach. "I'll not have a good meal ruined." He kept checking his watch and looking toward the entrance, and when Magdalen at last asked them all to go in to dinner, he was the first on his feet. He cheered up immediately when the fragrant aroma of duckling seasoned with oranges wafted from the serving dishes, and they were halfway through the meal, forgetful of Harry and attending to Red's account of the progress being made in launching an expedition against the Chinese pirates when a servant appeared in the doorway and started to speak, only to be jerked aside rather roughly by Harry.

"Come in, Harry," Red said, although his tone was far from inviting.

Jon immediately saw from Harry's dazed eyes and slack face that he had been drinking heavily; with quick concern he glanced at Jessica, who had halted the progress of her fork halfway to her mouth. But she was looking past Harry, into the hallway.

"Sorry to be late," Harry said, "but I had to wait for my lady." He reached behind him and pulled a tiny, giggling Chinese girl to his side. "This is Soo Ling, or something of that nature," he said.

Red Broome's face flushed, and Jon looked in helpless frustration toward the ceiling. Magdalen stiffened in her chair, for she, like the men, knew the appearance and dress of a sailor's whore.

Red got to his feet, sending a fork clattering to the floor. "Harry, what's the meaning of this?"

"Meaning?" Harry asked. "Does there have to be a meaning? She's my fourth mate." Harry laughed drunkenly at his own joke.

"Why do you bring this woman to my house, to insult my wife and daughter?" Red thundered.

The little Chinese girl, who had been giggling, shrank back at the display.

"That's all right," Harry said, holding on to her. "Soo Ling doesn't understand English, so you can't hurt her feelings."

Red calmed himself with an effort. "You've had your little joke, Harry. Now take that woman away and—"

"Are you saying that my lady is not good enough to eat at your table?" Harry interrupted, still smiling insolently. "Well, I'm not surprised, since *I* obviously am not good enough to marry into your precious little family."

"Harry, please," Jessica appealed.

Harry put his arm around the girl, cupping one of her small breasts through the gaudy silken material of her garment. "It seems, Soo Ling, that we are not welcome here."

"Get out," Magdalen said. "Get out now, Harry, and take that—that woman with you."

Harry bowed low and almost fell onto his face. The girl caught him and pulled him up. "My regards to all," he said, "and my best wishes for a happy life for you, Jess—a happy life of waiting." He strode out the door, dragging the girl behind him.

Red was still standing, stunned, and Magdalen's eyes were filled with tears.

"I'm afraid it's my fault," Jessica said. "I told him this afternoon that I'm going to marry Sam."

Red vented his breath in a long sigh as he sat down. "Well, let's not let it spoil this excellent dinner," he said halfheartedly.

But for Jon it was already spoiled. He pushed his chair back and stood. "Commander Broome, Mrs. Broome, will you excuse me? I think I'd best go after him."

"He's old enough to take care of himself," Red said.

"No," Jessica said. "Do go to him, Jon."

The hired ricksha carrying Harry and the girl was disappearing down the hill. Jon trotted after it but soon lost it in the maze of the city. He tried a few likely looking waterfront taverns, saw seamen from several nations taking advantage of the liberal opportunites for celebration in the city, then gave up the search as hopeless and went back to the ship. After a fruitless wait for Harry, he finally went to his bunk, and when he awoke the next morning, to the smell of food from the galley, he went on deck and inquired for the captain. Harry had returned to the ship very late and was still sleeping, he was told.

Jon waited. Harry slept until just before noon, and when at last he emerged from his cabin, it was with the unsteady step of an old man. His eyes were bloodshot, his clothes rumpled, his face darkened with stubble.

"Jon, would you please tell cook either to feed me or shoot me?" Harry said with a woeful expression.

Joe went to the galley, and after the food was served, he joined Harry in the saloon. He watched Harry pick at his food, all the while aware of a lingering odour about Harry's clothes that was vaguely familiar. finally Jon remembered the scent of the opium den in Sydney and his jaw tightened. Drink was evil enough.

He waited until Harry had finished and was sipping a second cup of strong, hot tea. "I didn't enjoy that scene at the Broomes' last night," he said.

Harry waved a limp hand. "You know, I didn't either. I thought I would, but I didn't."

"Harry, it's time for some strong words."

"Lay on, Macduff," Harry said.

Jon, knowing how desperate Harry was to be rich, and how not even the profits from his share of the *Java*'s cargo would recoup the losses of the former venture, chose his words carefully. "No threats, Harry, just a statement of how things stand. I will not be associated with an opium user. I will not be the partner of a drunk." He paused and waited for Harry's outburst, ready to welcome it as a vehicle to say more, to end the relationship between them.

"You're absolutely right, old boy," Harry said, with a chastened smile. "I don't blame you a bit."

The reply was unexpected, but for some reason Jon suspected its sincerity. "And you owe the Broomes an apology."

"I do," Harry agreed. "Yes, I do." He squirmed. "I've been dreading that, Jon. Come with me?"

"Harry, I'm deadly serious."

"I know you are. Look, it hit me pretty hard, Jess's announcement that she was going to marry Gordon. I went off, that's all. It

183

won't happen again." He smiled winningly. "Look, we've got a good thing going. I know that I'm a bit behind at the moment, but with the two of us working together, there's no stopping us. Come with me to the Broomes, like a friend."

The visit to the Broome house was a brief one. Jessica and Magdalen were there alone. They met Harry and Jon in the sitting room, both of them standing, Magdalen looking grim.

"I'm rather surprised to see you, Harry," she said coldly.

"Mrs. Broome, Jess—Jessica." Harry had his eyes downcast contritely. "I made a total ass of myself last night. I am here to beg your forgiveness. Can you forget?"

"Harry—" Jessica began, but she was cut short by her mother.

"It was not pleasant, Harry," Magdalen said. "You should be ashamed of yourself."

"I am," he said. "I apologize." He looked up and smiled sheepishly. "With my old friend's help, I'm going to be a new Harry Ryan. Isn't that right, Jon?"

Jon nodded uncertainly.

"Well," Harry said, "once again, please forgive me. Now we'll go."

Neither Magdalen nor Jessica made a move to stop them. Harry paused outside and pulled on his cap. "Do you get the feeling, my boy, that I've worn out my welcome?"

"As Mrs. Broome said, it wasn't pleasant, Harry," Jon answered.

Harry shrugged. "So be it. What do you say we see the town?"

"Thank you, no," Jon said. "There's a merchant I want to talk with, about some silk."

"And now who's the worshipper of the mighty pound?"

"You might come along. The price is right. You have your profits from the sugar."

They both got in the ricksha, which started down the hill. "Look, handle it for me, old boy," Harry said. "Silk, you said? If it will make a profit, buy it. There'll be plenty of space in the holds for it, since we'll be leaving not fully loaded. Maybe we can bargain Van Buren down from the usual haulage."

Jon left Harry with some misgivings. He returned to the ship to find a message from Red Broome, asking him to come to the military garrison—to the headquarters of Colonel Adam

Shannon—at his convenience.

The message jarred Jon from his concern about Harry. During the passage to Hong Kong he had thought often of his mother, and of the man who was his father, but the excitement of setting a record, and then the trouble at the Broomes', had driven all such concerns from his mind. Now his previous misgivings about facing up to his true father returned in force. He did not know why Red Broome wanted him to come to Colonel Shannon's office. Perhaps it was merely a convenient place to meet; but that was hardly likely, he decided. Certainly, if Red Broome was trying to intervene in his life, trying to reconcile him with the man who had so wronged his mother, then it would be Broome who owed someone an apology.

He kept his appointment with the silk merchant, bargained with a stubbornness fuelled by anger—anger at Harry, and at Adam Shannon—and made a favourable deal. Then, and only then, did he head toward the military complex which housed Hong Kong's garrison of army troops.

Seeing the sights of Hong Kong soon palled on Harry. He dismissed the ricksha boy and walked the crowded, noisy streets. More than once he had to fight with himself to keep from going into a bar, for as he passed noisy, open doorways, the aroma of rum, whisky, and other spirits wafted out to him, a siren song that kept saying "What's the harm?" He was also tempted by the practised approach of several prostitutes, but he was not in the mood to enjoy their charms. What he needed most was a few moments of forgetfulness.

He found himself standing on a wharf, watching, farther down the waterfront, bales of silk being loaded aboard the *Java*. The company had already arranged for a partial cargo of assorted durable goods, destination India. The silk might bring a decent price there, but at the moment that did not seem important to him, because, after all, the resulting profit would not be sufficient even to recoup his losses, never mind to make him the man he wanted to be, rich, powerful, respected. He was, indeed, in a black mood and he welcomed the anger that came when he saw the hulking figure of Bartholomew Jamison approaching. For a wild moment he considered having a tussle with Jamison, but he had seen the man fight Jon, and he knew that, without Jon's pugilistic skills, he would not fare so well in such a bout.

"Ryan," Jamison said, from a few paces away.

Harry glared at him without acknowledgment.

"I've been looking for you." Jamison had stopped.

Harry felt a rush of dread and prepared himself. He smiled to hide his nervousness and said, "I wonder, Jamison, if you would really have rammed us if the wind hadn't picked up."

Jamison grinned. "Now, that would have been criminal, Mr. Ryan." He let his face go slack. "Mr. Fisher wishes to have a word with you."

"Jon fisher? I just left him."

"Mr. *Marcus* Fisher," Jamison said. "You'll find him in Room 204 in the King's Hotel."

"Why would Marcus Fisher want to see me?" Harry was surprised that the man would even be in Hong Kong.

"I didn't ask him why," Jamison said, then turned on his heel and strode off.

Harry stood there for a long time in thought. There wasn't much else to do, he finally decided, especially when a man couldn't enjoy even one little drink. He made his way to the hotel, the city's finest, and was ushered up to Marcus Fisher's room. Fisher was dressed nattily in tropical whites and was sipping something tall, cool, and definitely, by the smell, alcoholic. "Come in, Mr. Ryan, come in," he said. "I'm having one of the infamous local concoctions— mostly rum, I believe, with a bit of fruit juice to relieve the rawness. Will you join me?"

Harry nodded. After all, a bit of fruit juice and rum wasn't exactly a drunkard's joy. A servant brought him a glass, and he sat in a comfortable chair that Fisher pulled up for him.

"You had a splendid passage out," Fisher said.

"We had favourable weather," Harry replied tersely.

"Still, I'm impressed. Only a real clipper man could have made good enough time to beat the *Antony*."

Harry shrugged. He wasn't going to make it easy for Fisher to broach whatever subject it was that had caused the man to seek him out.

"The previous voyage of the *Java* was not as successful, I understand," Fisher went on. "In fact, I've been led to believe that you were badly hurt by that venture."

"I'm recovering." Harry downed a large gulp of his drink. "Those things happen."

"It's doubly frustrating when the loss represents all one has, and more."

"You seem to know a lot about my business," Harry said.

"I make it a point to know about business," Fisher's smile was almost a smirk. "That's why I wouldn't be worried at all about the loss of one shipload of wool."

"Good for you."

"Mr. Ryan, I'm always on the lookout for good men, men who see things the way I see them."

"How do you see things, Mr. Fisher?"

As if warming to the subject, Fisher leaned forward in his chair. "I see a lot of ships—clippers, as long as they're useful; steamers in the future. I see ships crisscrossing the oceans from the Pacific to the China Sea to the Atlantic, carrying cargoes that can make a man rich beyond his wildest dreams. I see myself building an organization of good men, men who will share the wealth." He stood and walked to the window, which overlooked the crowded harbour. "Opportunity. There are endless opportunities for those who have the means, Mr. Ryan, and right now you have the means only to pick up pennies from Van Buren's leftovers, to rent a bit of space in a Van Buren hull when there's space available. Why, man, I could take a sloop and travel to India and back and make more money on one small cargo than you'll make in five years operating the way you're operating."

"Opium?"

Fisher shrugged. "I use that only as an example."

"I'm listening." Harry's tone was guarded.

"Understand me—I'm not making an offer," Fisher continued, "merely mentioning possibilities. I don't have to tell you that trade is increasingly competitive today, Mr. Ryan. It's the first cargo of new tea into England that brings the highest prices. And a ship carrying the same cargo as all the others arriving before it faces lowered profits. Information is vital to success. Knowledge is not only power, it is money."

"Meaning," Harry said, "that if you knew Van Buren's plans you'd be in a good position to beat him to markets."

"Van Buren is only one shipowner."

"But he's the only one whose plans I might know."

"I wouldn't try to tempt a man to pass along the secrets of his employer," Fisher said with a smug smile. "But if I were going to, such information would be worth a great deal of money, and the man who delivered it would find many doors opening for him."

Harry finished his drink and stood up. He felt the warmth of the rum in his stomach. "Thank you, Mr. Fisher," he said. "I'm not interested in either running opium or in selling you the business secrets of the Van Buren company."

"Pity," Fisher said. "I've heard that the market for silk in India is down."

"Good day," Harry said.

The door had scarcely closed behind Harry when a balding, monacled man stepped in from an adjoining room. "He will be back," Maxim Stoltz said.

"So, you agree that I'm a good judge of character." Marcus Fisher lifted his drink in a silent good-luck toast and downed the remaining contents.

CHAPTER IX

A spindly-legged sergeant was bawling orders in a cracking, harsh voice that carried well. Red-coated troops marched and wheeled smartly. For a moment, as he entered the army compound, Jon felt a swell of patriotic pride, and with it the return of the old guilt at having abandoned the army, of having seen all his company die at Isandhlwana. That, however, was the past, and he consciously dismissed it, his present errand quickly reclaiming his attention. He inquired for Colonel Shannon's headquarters and was directed toward a frame building that could have been located in any part of Her Majesty's empire.

He halted on the porch, looked back at the troops marching so stoutly on the parade, then hitched his shoulders and entered. To his surprise, a navy rating was seated at the battered-looking reception desk; the man looked up at him. "Sir?"

"Jon Fisher to see Colonel Shannon—or Commander Broome, if he is here."

"Sir, the commander is expecting you." As the man rose, Red Broome himself came out of the inner office, in shirtsleeves and with his cravat loosened, to Jon's surprise. "Mr. Fisher, thank you for coming."

"My pleasure, sir."

Red led Jon into the office and motioned him to a straight chair in front of the desk. "Let me apologize for bringing you here on a personal matter," Red began, after seating himself and venting a tired sigh.

"That's quite all right, sir."

"Good. We helped raise that boy," Red went on, and as Jon realized that the subject was to be Harry, he felt more than a little resentful. After all, he had his own concerns and, of late, had had his fill of Harry.

"I know he's wild, and we try to explain that by remembering that he saw his family butchered by the Maoris. But there comes a time when a man has to outgrow his past and stand on his own two feet." Red paused and eyed Jon closely. "Actually, Jon, I'm asking you for your appraisal of him."

Jon shrugged. "Harry can be a charmer."

"He was not charming last night. Has drink got a strong hold on him?"

"I'm afraid so," Jon admitted. He straightened. "Perhaps you should know that I've told Harry that I will not be a partner to a drunkard." He almost admitted Harry's occasional use of opium, but decided against it. "Harry is a wonderful ship-handler. He has talent and ambition to be very successful in trade. I'm in his debt for what he did for me in Africa, but . . ."

"I understand," Red said. "As with that incident last night, a man reaches his limits, doesn't he?" He repeated his sigh. "Both Mrs. Broome and I appreciate the steadying influence you have on Harry. I won't ask you to do more."

"We're joint-venturing on the trip to India. I've used our profits from Australian goods to buy silk. I'll be with him until, at least, we get back to Australia. I'm fond of him, too. I'll do my best."

"Thank you," Red said.

Jon started to rise, thinking that the interview was over. But Red did not move, still gazing at him. "One moment," he said. Jon lowered himself back into his seat. "Quite soon now Mrs. Broome and Jessica will be going back to Australia. Should the *Java*, by chance, be available, they will not travel on her. No reflection on you, of course."

"I understand."

"There is also, ah, one other matter."

Jon tensed at the change in Red's tone.

"I mentioned to Colonel Shannon that you would be calling on me. We share this headquarters building, you know. He expressed an interest in seeing you."

Jon had not yet decided for himself whether or when he would call on Shannon. Now, however, he nodded, for fate had apparently taken the decision out of his hands. In any case, he was determined that Shannon should know the state of his mother. The man should not be allowed to escape unscathed after inflicting such damage on a defenceless woman.

"Will you see him?" Red asked.

"I will," Jon said, rising.

"Just down the hall, to your right, then. He'll be waiting."

The two of them shook hands, and Jon summoned his courage as he was shown into Colonel Shannon's office.

Shannon rose immediately to greet him. The man, Jon had to admit, cut an impressive figure in his tropical dress uniform of the regular army. His fair hair was just beginning to show a tinge of silver, but he was obviously quite fit and trim.

"Please sit down," Adam said.

"That won't be necessary," Jon answered stiffly.

"I had hoped we could at least work toward establishing a friendly relationship," Adam said.

Jon felt his face flush. "One can be careful in his choice of friends, Colonel," he said, "but unfortunately, such is not the case with blood relations."

"I see," Adam said.

"I'm not so sure you *do* see." Jon had committed himself now, and there was no turning back. "For example, I doubt that you've seen my mother. She's become an old woman, Colonel, a vague, disturbed, old woman."

Adam frowned. "I am sorry to hear that. Genuinely sorry. But Caroline—your mother—rejected me long ago, and I have not since been privy to her personal affairs."

"Perhaps I can't blame you for everything," Jon said warily. "There is much, of course, I don't know."

"One must count one's blessings," Adam said dryly.

For some reason, the remark refuelled Jon's anger, and he could no longer check his tongue. "But it *can* be conjectured that if she had not been seduced, had not been taken advantage of when she was young and susceptible, when she was lonely, that her life might have been different. I can't voice a true opinion of what happened aboard that ship when the man who should have been my father was killed, but I can condemn you for what you did to her, and that I do heartily. You first seduced her, and then, in her hour of trouble, when she was carrying your bastard child, you deserted, abandoned her. I suspect that her marriage to Colonel Forsyth was nothing more than a desperate act of—of grabbing at the first

191

life preserver that was available to her."

Adam had paled visibly, and his jaw clenched as he stared at Jon with an unblinking gaze.

"For what it's worth," he said at last, in a tightly controlled voice, "I have kept myself informed about you through the years, as well as I could. There were times when I wanted to come to you, to tell you the truth."

"Somehow you never got around to it," Jon said bitterly.

"There were reasons. Caroline—I had no idea that it would become general knowledge that Forsyth was not your father. You—if you had, as you apparently did, thought that Forsyth was your father, knowledge of the truth would have hurt you."

"So now, as you grow older, you feel the need to ease your conscience," Jon said. "Well, when I needed a father, I got Marcus Fisher."

Adam had no response to that, and indeed, Jon sensed a deep sorrow in the man's eyes as he looked away. When he finally turned back, his shoulders were slumped, and he looked like a defeated man. Jon almost felt pity for him.

"I would like very much to see you, if and when it is possible," Adam said quietly. "I'd like to get to know you. I promise, there will never be any attempt on my part to play the role of father. I offer you only friendship."

For one brief moment Jon was swayed—but then he remembered how his mother had kept asking him to admire the nonexistent swans on the lake in front of her home.

"I'm asking your forgiveness," Adam said. "For I was young. We both were."

That last addition, as if he were trying to place some of the blame on Caroline, made Jon flare again. "I think, Colonel," he said, through tight lips, "that you and I have only your blood in common, and I wish earnestly that it was not so." With that he turned and strode from the office, not bothering to close the door behind him.

Jon walked swiftly across the parade. This time he did not feel the surge of patriotic pride, or the least guilt. It had been a mistake to see Shannon, he felt, for he could not deny that he had felt sympathy for the man. Even in his still-smouldering anger he had to admit to himself that Adam Shannon was an admirable man, someone he would have been proud to call father under different circumstances. Indeed, he was more than ever in awe of the Adam Shannon who had redeemed himself, rising from the lowest rank to his present status, having fought with bravery and distinction in the Maori wars in New Zealand. No, it was the young Adam, Adam *Vincent*, who prevented any possibility of a friendship, the Vincent who had lured his mother into reckless, wanton actions that had ruined her life. For that, no forgiveness was possible. If he never saw Adam Shannon again, he would not be displeased.

The *Java* beat her way laboriously down the South China Sea and suffered adverse winds and stifling calms in the Bay of Bengal. Still, it was not an unhappy ship. More and more Jon was sure that Harry's true talent lay at sea. He was a natural leader of men, keeping the crew spruce and always on their toes, yet without being a tyrant. For all that, his talk, as always, was of money, trade, influence.

The British presence in Madras, where the *Java*'s cargo was offloaded, appeared at first almost nonexistent. To Jon, India's swarming millions seemed to be congregated in the coastal city, and the poverty and the misery were so overwhelming as to be deadening to the senses. He found it odd to think that India, with its small, dark, sad-eyed people, was a mainstay of Her Majesty's empire. He had never felt more alienated from his surroundings, and be began to long for home with an intensity that burned in him. It occurred to him that perhaps he desired to be back where white faces predominated, where there was little, if any, starvation, disease, or misery; but then, as if to upbraid him for his thoughts, a single face kept appearing in his mind—the regal, proud face of the Samoan girl, Misa. For her he felt a mixture of fierce desire and self-reproach, for on the Madras waterfront a white sailor was rarely seen without the company of a brown-skinned, dark-eyed native woman. Such women, if sailors could be believed, were ideal for instant and temporary pleasure, with no binding ties . . . so why did he remember with such clarity that night under the whispering trees of Queensland, with Misa's soft, pliant body beside him?

Jon, unlike Harry, did not avail himself of the brown-skinned solace of the women of Madras. He immersed himself instead in the age-old activities of the merchant—investigating others' goods, haggling, and making contacts. He had decided, during the passage across the Indian Ocean, that his future definitely lay in trade, and he set about, in Madras, to build himself a firm foundation. Favourable buys and sales often depended as much on whom one knew as on the merchandise. He talked with rapacious-eyed Hindus, with wily Chinese who had set up shop on the shores of the subcontinent, with sweaty Englishmen who tried to offset India's sultry climate with copious supplies of London gin. He kept careful notes, building a directory of tradesmen in a notebook, in groupings headed by the names of their specialties.

He was unsuccessful in selling the jointly owned silk in *Java*'s hold on the English market and had to settle for a much lower price from an Indian merchant who carefully explained, in fine, public school English touched only slightly by the melodious inflections of his native land, that India was a poor country, that most Indians had to make do with the cheaper domestic fabrics for which Madras was becoming known. When Jon told Harry how much the silk had fetched, Harry snorted.

"We are not exactly pyramiding our holdings," Harry said.

"In any new venture there is a period of learning, of adjustment," Jon said. "I'm not exactly a veteran at this."

Harry seemed hardly to hear him. "And what do we take back to Australia?" he asked. "The agents have nothing worthwhile for us." Jon was already aware that Harry, in addition to his personal troubles, now faced that ultimate disgrace of a ship—covering long, watery distances in ballast, with virtually no paying cargo.

"The fabrics of Madras," Jon said. "In fact, I'm negotiating for—"

"Cheap junk," Harry cut in disdainfully.

"There are customers for it in Australia," Jon said. "Not everyone can afford silk."

"Hand-dyed junk." Harry shook his head dismissively. "Well, Mr. Supercargo, I don't think that Van Buren would turn cartwheels over a shipload of dyed cotton cloth; but if you think we can unload it on the Sydney market, have a go at it."

Two days later, *Java*, carrying more stone in her holds than goods, weighed anchor and sailed southeastward, with only the open sea between her and Australia. She sailed with a captain who,

194

in Jon's estimation, was growing daily more uncommunicative and who, despite his unquestioned competence, seemed to have his mind elsewhere. Jon was worried that the loss of the cargo of wool, together with the rejection from Jessica Broome, had indeed ruined Harry, and that his partner had neither the patience nor the will to rebuild his shattered fortunes. More than once, while watching Harry standing immobile on the quarterdeck, staring off into space, Jon wondered what the man was thinking, and whether his increasing bitterness was a sign of desperation.

On many of the Pacific Ocean islands, the native people took pride in the legends of epic sea voyages made by their ancestors. From the Fiji Islands in the south, to Tahiti and the Marquesas in the east, and even on lonely, isolated Easter Island, tales abounded of how the great fathers of the island races had come to their new homes after brave and adventurous wanderings from a distant land far to the west.

On Samoa, however, such stories were scoffed at. A Samoan would laugh at the suggestion that he and his people had not always lived on their home islands.

"The God, Pele, created us here," a Samoan would say.

Yet, there was in the Samoan blood that bold, curious quality that made a seafarer. From time beyond memory, their people, in open outrigger canoes, had made trips that would have seemed incredible to a European seaman accustomed to his sturdy full-rigged ships. Samoans long had navigated by nothing but the sun and the stars, and so it was not by accident that the sloop carrying Molo and his people had made its way safely to the green, dark outline of New Caledonia in less than a month after stealing away from the Australian shore. There, under cover of darkness, and with secrecy made possible by the growing spirit of anti-white sentiment that led native peoples to share a certain sympathy, the sloop had been reprovisioned and sailed onward, still navigating by the stars, patiently waiting out squalls, or broiling in the tropic sun when the winds failed. They had passed the Fiji Islands without stopping, knowing they were now very near home, in familiar waters.

When the peaks of Upolu were at last sighted, after a voyage lasting almost three months, all on board were weak and emaciated from the wormy, stale food left to them; but the tropical rains had supplied them with plentiful fresh water, and even the worst off among them found it hard not to join in the dancing and singing on the deck as the by-now skilled seamen brought them neatly round a point and sailed into a sheltered, secluded bay.

Tui led the way ashore, splashing through the shallows. On the beach, he fell to his face and kissed the soil of his native land. Molo, with greater self-control, stayed aboard the sloop until the others were ashore, some already disappearing into the dense foliage to begin to make their way homeward. Tui came back on board, and with his help Molo sailed the sloop into deep, dark water, in a place hidden from any settlement by a densely treed point. There they furled the mainsail for the last time, dropped the anchor, and opened the scuttles. By the time Tui and Molo had swum back to shore, the deck was awash, and they watched silently as the tip of the mainmast vanished beneath the surface. Now there was no proof that they had become thieves; nor was there much danger of reprisals for having broken their indenture contracts. The documents had been prepared by Germans, and to the Germans, as indeed to most whites, all Samoans looked alike.

Molo, who had known disappointment and disillusionment, had recovered with the buoyancy characteristic of his people. He was at home, and that was enough. He had made an unwise decision in going to Australia, but his subsequent actions had righted it, and now there was nothing to do but to take up life where they had left off.

Molo's most pressing concern was his daughter. She had changed during the trip home. At first she had been as excited as any of them and had even worked alongside the men in setting and trimming sail; but then, with the voyage halfway over, an uncharacteristic melancholy had seemed to possess her.

"We will go home now," Molo told her, after rejoining her on the beach.

"Yes," she said, hanging her head.

"Your brothers and sisters will be pleased to see you. They will roast a fat pig in celebration."

"It will be good to see them." Misa's words were sincere, but still it was obvious to Molo that something was troubling her.

"Would you be smiling if we were working the cane fields in

Australia?" he said in mild rebuke.

"I am happy to be home, Father. It is where we belong."

"When the word spreads that you are back, the young men will come," he said. "It is time, Daughter. It is time for you to choose." He held up a hand. "Of course, with my direction. Do not worry— we will choose well. A headman, or the son of a headman, a man of substance, and soon I will see young ones of my blood nursing at your breasts."

When Misa burst into tears and fled into a grove of coconut palms that grew down to near the water on white, gleaming sand, Molo scratched his head in puzzlement. When Pele created women, he thought, he must have been indulging in coconut beer. Odd creatures, they were, to weep when they were happy.

Red Broome stood on the Hood Company wharf and watched the clipper ship *Thermopylae*, the *Cutty Sark*'s old rival, bearing his wife and daughter away through the crowded Hong Kong roadstead. It was fortunate, he decided, that Jessica, when she had sent a telegram notifying Sam of her acceptance of his proposal of marriage, had not mentioned the name of the ship she would be taking back to Sydney. With one last silent prayer for the safety of his loved ones, and with a whispered "Godspeed," Red turned away and, with a discipline cultivated over the years, placed Magdalen and Jessica in a safe, snug compartment in his mind in order to allow himself to get on with his duties.

As commander of the Hong Kong naval squadron, Red had a new flagship, a steam-screw frigate with an impressive number of well-mounted guns. She lay at anchor farther out in the harbour, the H.M.S. *Royal Victoria*, with the other vessels under Red's command grouped around her. Small boats were plying back and forth to the squadron, ferrying provisions, ammunition, and men.

When Red arrived at the military wharf, Adam Shannon was standing there with his hands behind his back, observing the orderly boarding of small boats by the men of his command.

"G'day, Adam," Red said, nodding.

Adam returned the greeting more formally, for Red was his elder and senior in command. But still, the warm friendship between the two of them was evident in their manner of speaking.

"I trust that Mrs. Broome and Jessica got off in good style,"

Adam offered, eyeing the distant spread of the sails of *Ther-mopylae*, just now clearing the harbour.

Red nodded. "Thank you for supervising the embarkation."

"No worry," Adam said with a smile to show Red that he, too, could sound like an Australian.

The last of the red-coated troops from the local garrison, along with the blue-coated colonial militia, were in the boats. Red gave a little bow, swept his hand and said, "After you, Colonel."

Adam had been provided quarters aboard the *Royal Victoria*. He was on deck as Red, with flag signals flying between ships, took the squadron out of the harbour into the open sea. They had timed their departure to clear the Hong Kong and Pearl River approaches late in the day, so that darkness would hide their subsequent direction of sailing to anyone on shore. Piracy in the China Sea seemed to be organized, and neither Red nor Adam wanted to give an indication of the destination of the small but potent expeditionary force aboard the squadron's ships.

Actually the target Red and Adam had selected for the punitive action was a small island in the Ladrone group, so near the mouth of the Pearl River that the presence of pirates there was an open insult to the power of the European nations whose ships used that vital waterway. Red was especially pleased that the first serious action against the pirates was to be an Australian effort. The crew of the *Royal Vic*, as the men had fondly dubbed the frigate, were mainly Australian, and a good percentage of Adam's foot soldiers were Australian as well, with a sprinkling of veterans of the Maori wars among them.

Of their enemy they knew little, not much more than a name that was as odd to their ears as any Chinese name. Han-Kuang, it seemed, was a bold warlord whose major holdings were on the mainland, inland and south of Portuguese Macao. According to intelligence compiled from prisoners who had escaped from his clutches, Han-Kuang was a criminal of the worst stripe, a worthy target for reprisal, for he was a tyrant in his stronghold on the mainland as well as a merciless murderer at sea.

The next day, the squadron steamed the relatively short distance southwest, to approach the outer Ladrone Islands by nightfall. The ships lay to in the dark, as the soldiers sat silently on the decks, keeping themselves occupied with the various tasks that had to be seen to before going into battle. They cleaned and checked the workings of their rifles or honed their bayonets, while some prayed, and yet others passed the tense hours playing at cards.

Before dawn the *Royal Vic* moved into position, with the three other ships of the squadron in line fore and aft, all lying broadside to the shore. With sunrise the target became visible—an ancient-looking stone fortress perched atop a promontory, at the mouth of a cove in which four pirate junks lay at anchor. Through his glass, just before he gave the orders for all ships to commence the cannonade, Red saw frenzied activity atop the parapets, and even as the guns of the *Royal Vic* began to bellow—small guns puffed atop the fort, sending shot whining through the air toward the squadron, most of it falling short to send up great splashes.

The *Royal Vic*'s gunnery officers soon had the range, and in short order the fort was a smoking, crashing place of death, as high-explosive missiles and mortar shells pounded at the parapets and fell within the walls. The other three ships added to the deadly blanket of fire, quickly turning the four junks in the cove into flaming wrecks and thus cutting off the pirates' means of escape.

Red found Adam standing at a point of vantage examining through a glass the damage being done. "She's not as strong as she looked at first," Red shouted close to Adam's ear, to make himself heard over the pounding of the guns.

Adam nodded with satisfaction. Red knew his friend hadn't been looking forward to storming the fort. The advantage was always with the defence in war, providing that the defenders built wisely. And for all that Han-Kuang's proud fortress was being reduced to rubble, its defenders would still have to be flushed out by troops on foot.

By noon the naval guns had fallen silent for lack of a target. Han-Kuang's fortress was hardly recognizable as a work of men's hands, for the bombardment had transformed it to little more than a rockpile. The squadron's boats had been lowered and were nearing the narrow beach, with Adam in the first boat and Red Broome and a handpicked contingent of sailors from the squadron bring up the rear. There was no opposition at the beach or around the cove. Red, a bit breathless, caught up with Adam halfway up the rock-strewn slope leading to the fort.

"Commander, your post was to be rear guard," Adam reminded

199

him with unusual sternness.

"What, and let you have all the glory?" Red grinned.

As it was, Red's sailors raced the redcoats, seeking to reach the top first, and thus it was a sailor who fell first as scattered rifle fire erupted from the ruins. Progress became slower then. Adam Shannon was not a man who was fond of Napoleonic assaults, and he ordered his men to take cover and advance slowly, moving from cover to cover. The hot afternoon wore on, with the rifle fire from the defenders becoming more sporadic and then nonexistent as sailors and soldiers, the latter with bayonets fixed, went over the top of the rubble together, to find only a few bodies in the smouldering, destroyed fort, and no evidence of Han-Kuang. To Red's bitter consternation, the dark sails of a small junk were sighted disappearing to sea from a small, hidden inlet on the far shore—one that had not appeared on the Admiralty charts.

"Damn it, Adam," Red reproached himself. "I should have anticipated that."

"The charts showed that side of the island to be unscalable cliffs," Adam reminded him.

"Still, I should have had one ship there." Red called a signalman to his side and gave orders, which were quickly semapahored to the squadron's fastest cutter. The steam-sail vessel broke away from formation to circle the island in pursuit of the junk, but even as he gave the orders Red knew it was useless. The island was close to the mainland, and the junk's crew would know the local waters. There were a hundred ways of avoiding the search among the islands and reef-strewn shallows, where the junk could pass but the deeper-draft cutter could not follow.

"At least," Adam said, "they'll carry the word. It will spread. Maybe other pirates will get the message."

Red turned his attention to his men. Two of his sailors were dead, four wounded. Adam's casualties were similarly light, but nevertheless the onerous task remained of transporting the bodies back to the ships, to be followed by the all-too-familiar words of burial at sea.

Red had buried men before, too many men. As a military leader he had long since come to terms with the knowledge that, when war came, or even such a small, almost insignificant action as the taking of the pirate stronghold, men would die. This time, however, it seemed to hit him harder. He condemned himself, not only for his negligence in letting the junk escape, but for the needless bravado that had caused him to lead his sailors to the fore in the assault up the ridge. That had been the army's job, and probably they would have done it better alone. True, the men who had participated in the attack would be looked upon with admiring eyes by their crewmates. Pride, morale were important, too. But was it worth two dead men from his crew? And what had been accomplished? A few dead Chinese had been left to rot on the island, or to be attended by others who, perhaps, had gone into hiding. Adam had ordered a search of the island, but even on such a small island there would be caves and crevices where men could hide and wait, to later reappear, mourn their dead comrades, and vow revenge. For Red was not at all certain that the news of the attack would have a deleterious effect on the remaining pirates. Men being men, he felt it was more likely that the death of their fellows would build in the survivors a desire to strike back.

The China coastline was long, poorly charted, and there were shoals and islands, as well as inlets, that didn't appear on any chart. Rooting out the pirates was going to be, Red feared, a long and dangerous job.

CHAPTER X

Commander Red Broome's suspicion that the attack on Han-Kuang's island would stiffen rather than weaken the purpose of the pirates was, indeed, correct. Even as the squadron was rejoined by the cutter that Red had sent to search for the escaping pirate junk and Red set course for Hong Kong, Han-Kuang was storming about on the deck of the junk, terrifying his underlings with his vile language and fearful temper. The pirate was a large man, standing well over six feet, with a bull-like chest and shoulders. He affected the dress of the Chinese court, but after his precipitous flight from his island fort, as the junk wended its way through narrow straits and managed without much effort to avoid detection, he looked a good deal less than princely. He had fallen several times en route down the steep path that he and his bodyguard had used to escape, and his long, silken tunic was soiled, his silken trousers torn.

As soon as it was clear that the ineffectual British pursuit had been broken off, Han-Kuang ordered that they change course to head for home, which meant crossing the open sea and the approaches to Hong Kong. It was a bold, even arrogant move, and he knew that the small junk, with its puny cannon, would be no match for even the smallest British patrol vessel, much less the four ships of battle that had ruined one of his strongholds.

But the voyage was made safely, and when he reached his fortified palace on Shangch'uan Shan, called Saint John Island by the foreign devil Englishmen, his anger was eased somewhat by the expert ministrations of his favourite concubine. With a clear head, he could now plan ways to satisfy his growing resolution to take a multiple measure of revenge on the British. Behind him, on the mainland, was his private empire, not large in territory, but relatively secure, allied as it was with the government in the

Forbidden City. In his holdings, Han-Kuang's whim could mean life or death. And in hidden coves lay a dozen or more armed junks manned by men who knew the joy of looting the ships of the foreign dogs. Yes, he would have his revenge. The only question was how and when.

Han-Kuang had seen, firsthand, the power of the enemy's guns. He knew that he could not stand up to the British men-of-war at sea, and the ease with which the naval cannon had reduced his strong fort had convinced him that he would never again concentrate any strength in a position exposed to naval guns.

Guns. Han-Kuang spent hours in deep thought on the subject of big guns. He told himself that he would gladly give up his favourite concubine for just one cannon to equal those of the British ships, but as he boiled inside, remembering the humiliation of being forced to run, he knew that his chances of obtaining such weapons were slim. No such guns existed in China outside the hands of the foreigners. But certainly they would not allow him to *buy* such guns, even though his treasury was ripe with gold, much of it earned by the sale of the looted cargoes of his victims. Or would they?

Han-Kuang paced the marble-floored chambers of his palace as his devious brain sought for a solution to the problem facing him. The British especially would not—for any amount of gold—sell weapons that would threaten their supreme power, he decided. However, the British were not the only foreign devils who soiled the sacred soil of China with their unwelcome presence. And perhaps even some British merchants—men of little scruples, with whom he dealt frequently in the lucrative opium trade—might be willing, for a price, to serve as middlemen to help him procure, from other foreigners, what was needed. The first glimmering of an idea came to Han-Kuang, and being a man accustomed to taking action swiftly, he gave orders to prepare for travel. Only hours later, dressed as an ordinary merchant so as not to attract attention, he made the sacrifice of leaving his favourite concubine behind and set out, on the very day of his arrival home, toward Hong Kong.

Europeans had first seen the islands of Samoa in 1722. Those first white men to appreciate the natural beauty of what many seafarers felt were the fairest of all the fair isles of the South Seas were Dutchmen, under Captain Jacob Roggeveen. Since Roggeveen's time, many ships had sheltered in the excellent harbours, the best in the South Pacific, and countless sailors of several nations had witnessed the Samoans' remarkably easygoing outlook on life and found it to be charmingly diverting.

More than a dozen islands made up the Samoan group, not all of them inhabitable. The largest, Savaii, was only six hundred square miles in area, and the amount of level, arable land on all the islands was small, since the volcanic origin of the archipelago made for convoluted, rocky terrain, with some mountain peaks rising as high as six thousand feet. In valleys and along the thin coastal strip the soil was fertile and, since the coming of the Europeans, had fed the native population well with lush crops of corn, beans, peas, and other vegetables. Breadfruit, papayas, bananas, taro, pineapples, and, of course, the coconut palm contributed to a life of relative plenty.

It was only in contrast to Europeans with their fancy fabrics and their manufactured goods that the Samoans were poor; and except for curiosity, it was only the lure of having for himself the riches of the European that made any Samoan want to leave his homeland.

Molo, head of the village of Mata on the second largest of the islands in the Samoan group, had wanted his daughter to be able to wear the fine cotton and silk gowns of the white women, to own the golden jewellery worn by both white men and women. He himself had yearned for a gold pocket watch, for fine knives, for guns. Now, having sampled the bitter fruit of his own folly, he had gone back to true appreciation of what he had in Samoa. Not a day passed that he did not thank several gods—including the god of the white men, whom his daughter had come to accept during her years at the mission—for allowing him to be home again.

Molo had immediately been reinstated as headman of his village, for his eldest son, who had assumed the position in his absence, was all too eager to be relieved of the responsibilities of being *matai*. It was but the work of a few days to erect for himself and his daughter a new, beehive-shaped house with floors of pulverized coral and a living area open to the pleasant climate except in bad weather, when woven blinds were lowered. While putting the finishing touches on the thatched roof, Molo looked down on his village and his people and was content.

Misa was helping other women of the family prepare a meal. The stones in the cooking pit had been heated until they were white hot, and with the ashes now raked away, Misa was laying a bed of green leaves on which the food—fish, breadfruit, bananas—would be baked after being covered with more of the leaves.

Once the house was finished, Molo would begin to build a canoe, for at the moment he had to depend on his sons and others for fish. Although it was his right, he would not reclaim the worldly goods he had distributed to his sons before his departure; he viewed the sacrifice as atonement for his past mistakes. Still, for all the extra work, life was good. He would be able to tell his grandchildren and his great-grandchildren about his adventures in the far lands of the white men, and his advice to them would be grounded in experience. "Stay with your people always," he would tell them. "Do not fall prey to the lure of the white man's gold."

After being home for just two weeks, it seemed to Molo that he had never been away. The small village, only twenty-three odd households, was located a safe distance from the Germans, around the bay, so that villagers seldom saw a white man. Molo was more than happy to keep it that way. Had he wielded godlike power, he would have cast out all the white men and returned to the old ways, when a *matai* had absolute authority and respect, and the young people were not so headstrong and had not been corrupted by the ways of the whites. In those days, a woman's chastity was guarded jealously, and a wayward young woman—such as the ones who were so common now—would have had her head shaved as punishment. Thanks to the gods, however, his daughter was not like those young ones who met under the palm tree as soon as it was dark. She knew her responsibility as daughter of the *matai*, and she was chaste. She respected the remnants of their people's traditions and would, in good time, marry outside the village. Her husband would be a high chief, and the union would be celebrated with ancient rites. Her husband would come, with all his talking chiefs, and make a formal plea for her hand. She would be given her own Place of the Lady, a piece of property in her new village upon which a fine house would be built for her, and her children would in their turn carry on the traditions.

Thinking of the future was pleasant, but it wasn't getting the

205

work done. Molo applied himself to his labours, and by the time the sweet aromas were wafting to him from the cooking pit and the women were preparing to serve the food, he was finished. He ate sitting beside Misa, and, not for the first time since their return, he wondered what was bothering her. She looked drawn. The radiant smile that always pleased him did not come to her lips so easily, and when it did, it was bittersweet and fleeting. At first he had attributed her withdrawn, almost melancholy state to the lingering effects of the long and arduous sea voyage, but now he was beginning to wonder. Had she contracted one of the virulent white man's diseases while they were in Australia?

Misa did not join in the animated talk over dinner. Since their homecoming, she had not joined the other girls and young women in activities in which she had once delighted. Not once had she left the village to gather the blossoms of the *pua* tree to be sewn into a necklace. She did her work, peeling banana bark into pliant strips that would be woven into baskets, and their new house would be well covered with floor mats that Misa had already woven from palm leaves; but she had not participated in the dance of welcome, had not roamed the beach, as she once did, in search of the rare *samoana* shells, nor had he once seen her adorned with garlands of jasmine flowers, of which she had once been so fond.

"We will sleep in the new house tonight," Molo told her.

"It is a beautiful house," she said, but there was not the old joy in her voice.

He looked at her helplessly, praying silently to Pele and the old gods to make her well, to make her happy, and, as if the gods themselves had spoken to him, he suddenly knew the answer. The gods had given man the gift of enjoyment of the flesh, and Misa was, after all, a woman now, no longer a girl. . . .

Molo smiled to himself. As soon as Misa had gone into the house, he sought out two of the young men of the village who were known for their romantic journeys in the darkness of night to neighbouring villages. In a circumspect way—but the two young men understood and smiled—he let it be known that the word should be spread among the neighbouring villages that Molo was back and that this beautiful daughter, Misa, was of marriageable age and that an alliance by marriage was being sought.

The results of Molo's instructions to the two young men were not long in coming. Only four days later there appeared in the village a woman of high blood, wife of the *matai* of one of the more prosperous villages some miles away on the shores of the bay. She let it be known to Molo quickly that she was *soafafine* for her son, who would be *matai* one day. She was that best of all possible go-betweens, the mother seeking a match for her son, and Molo was filled with pride at the prospect of being joined to so fine a family. He told the *soafafine* that his village, his family, he himself and his daughter would welcome the arrival of her fine son and that his suit would be looked upon very favourably.

Then there was only the matter of passing the good news along to Misa. Molo set about to do that the minute the *soafafine* and her party had left the village, but Misa was not to be found.

Misa had left the high-peaked, thatch-roofed house early that day, walking on the white sand through the gracefully bent coconut palms toward the shore. When she reached the water's edge she paused to watch a bonito boat setting out through the surf, the young men bending their back to the oars, chanting in the rhythm of their work. She walked along the strand with her eyes down, but she did not see the beauty of the shells and the sparkling sand beneath her feet, as she had been wont to do in the past.

The sandy beach gave way to rock, and she picked her way farther from the village. Ahead of her, sharp, wooded ridges ran down from the hills to end in bare rock at the edge of the sea. An outcropping in the bay towered into a small peak topped with a few struggling palm trees, while breakers foamed whitely in a familiar, muted thunder. But the grandeur of her surroundings was lost to Misa. Her thoughts were hundreds of miles away, in a wooded glen in Australia where the payment of a debt had swiftly become something more than her youthful imagination, or her heart, had been prepared for.

She knew little of love, and what she did know now was as lost to her as the distant stars, for she was separated from Jon Fisher by more than mere oceans. She was now back in her native land, in her home, and she had one further debt to pay, this one hers and hers alone, for she had violated tradition, and the gods would call her to judgement all too soon. That knowledge, coupled with the sweet memories of something beautiful that was lost to her

207

forever, accounted for her preoccupation, for the withdrawal that so concerned her father. A thousand times she had rehearsed in her mind a way to tell him that she was no longer virgin, that she had sacrificed her honour in gratitude to the man who had made it possible for her, her father, and more than twenty others to escape the man-killing labour in Australia's cane fields. The truth had to be told, but she had not the courage to tell it. Soon she must, for otherwise nature would do the telling for her. Since leaving Australia, she had not bled with the full moon, and although she was young and inexperienced in womanly things, she knew that the absence of the monthly bleeding meant that she was carrying a child in her womb. Moreover, she knew that the fact that it was a white man's child would hurt her father more than losing the chance to celebrate her marriage to a *matai* from another village with a huge *malaga*.

Misa did not suffer personal guilt about what she had done with Jon Fisher, even though she had been educated in the High Upolu Mission School where the kind Methodist English lady had drummed into her, time and again, that, under their God, it was a sin to sacrifice one's chastity outside of marriage. Misa loved God, and she loved the sound of young voices singing his praise; indeed, her days in the mission school were among her fondest memories. Still, in all practicality, the concept of chastity, in the face of what nature had taught her since her youngest days, had to be treated with a certain amount of scepticism. It was clear from direct observation that God did not punish the young ones of the village who met under the palms. It seemed he did not even punish the *moetotolo*, who in darkness stole the favours meant for another. . .

Misa released a long-drawn sigh. Had she been an ordinary village girl, and not the daughter of the *matai*, her indiscretion in the Australian grove would have been accepted. She could have borne her child and would still have been looked on with favour by young men. That the child would be half white would be nothing more than a fleeting embarrassment. But she had tradition to consider. She was not an ordinary girl. She was *taupo*, and even though the white man's law and the Christians had tried to end the practice, she would be expected to furnish evidence of her virginity on her wedding night. Yet already she fancied that she could detect a bulge in the flat plane of her stomach, and if she did not soon tell her father the truth, her stomach would. . . .

Misa had been sitting quite some time on an outcrop of dead coral, moodily staring out to where the white combers broke on the reef, when she was startled to discover that Molo himself had walked up and was standing beside her. She had made up her mind to tell him the truth, but to her added consternation, his excitement over his own news halted her feeble beginning, and she listened numbly as he related in detail the visit of the mother of a fine young man who would someday be *matai* of as large and prosperous village.

"Does not even this make you happy?" he demanded in exasperation, when Misa lowered her head to hide her shame.

"*Jamá*," she said, in a voice so soft that he had to lean closer to hear it over the surf, "you will have to tell them that it cannot be so."

Molo straightend and stepped back in astonishment. "What are you saying?"

Misa felt her eyes swimming with tears. "I am not virgin."

Samoan parents rarely if ever laid hands on their children, and Molo was no different, yet in his sudden anger and hurt he lashed out, his palm ringing against his daughter's cheek. Her head was jerked by the force of the blow, and she felt her lip being cut against her teeth.

"Keep still," Molo said, when she started to speak. "Tell me who, and I will—" He paused, as if trying to check his temper. "How many times?" he asked.

"Once," she said softly.

"So," he snorted, but Misa could tell that the answer had somewhat mollified him. "Only once. We will, then, throw our troubles into the sea."

It was, she knew, his way of saying that he would simply forget the one incident that had sullied her virginity. Misa suspected that it would not have been the first time a *taupo* had lied. There were ways, she knew from talking to others, to give evidence of virginity when that commodity had been long gone.

"That will not do, either," she said.

Molo looked at her sharply.

"I carry a child," she said.

Molo threw his head back and gave vent to a howl of anguish.

"I have decided," Misa continued, "that I shall leave the village."

Molo's anger returned quickly. "No," he said. "You will stay. Choose a man for *avaga*." He spoke of a form of elopement, where everyone knew in advance. "Yes," he said decisively, nodding with vigour. "That is the only way,"

Misa could not keep the whole truth back any longer. "And where do I find a man who will accept as his own a child that is half white?" She wiped her cheeks as she looked up at her father, who stared at her in total disbelief for long moments, then fell to his knees on the sand nearby. He made moaning sounds and dumped handfuls of the sand, coloured with bits of pulverized shell and coral, into his hair.

"Don't, Father," she sobbed, pulling him to his feet.

He, too, was weeping. "When?" he asked. "When did a white man force himself upon you?"

She was tempted to take the means of escape suddenly offered, but she couldn't lie to him. "I gave myself willingly," she said. "At first because that was the only way I could repay the man for giving us the money so that we could come home,"

"You gave yourself for money?" Molo looked incredulous.

"I did not sell myself—not in that sense," she said, summoning the last of her pride. "Jon Fisher gave the money freely. He wanted to buy my papers, and yours, to help us get back to Samoa. I told him you would not leave your people."

"And that is true," Molo said.

"He gave the money. Then we, all of us, were in his debt. Only I had the means to repay the debt, for I could see in his eyes that he wanted me."

Molo's expression softened, and, to her surprise, he took her hands. "It was a brave and honourable thing you did," he whispered. "How it must have pained you to give the white man that which you valued so highly. But, oh, my daughter, I would rather have died in the cane fields."

Misa shook her head. "It is done," she said. "And God saw fit to give me a child as the result of it. I will leave the village."

"But where will you go? You will not go into the white man's town to become a sailor's woman?"

"No," she said. "I will go to the mission. They will take me in there."

"To live and work with the whites? To worship their God?"

"They wanted me to stay, if you will remember," she said. It was true that she had been an excellent student, and had also helped the Englishwoman care for and teach the young ones—orphans mostly, and of mixed blood—that were in the care of the mission. "I might be allowed to work with children like my own, children with white blood. Maybe that is my destiny. It is not the fault of the child that his mother accepted a white man."

Molo studied her in silence for a long time. "Perhaps you are wise beyond your years, Daughter," he said, "I truly pray that you are making the right choice." He held out a hand to her. "Come, we will get your things, and I will accompany you to the mission."

"No," she said. "I will go alone. I knew the way well. I have walked it many time."

So it was that Misa left the next morning, early, carrying her scant belongings tied into a bundle. The mission was many miles inland, the path steep and switching back and forth to climb the forested hills. It took her the better part of the day before she came in sight of her destination, which sat on an airy plateau overlooking Apia Bay. A running, giggling, shouting group of light-skinned children was playing outside the schoolroom, a simple thatched-roofed shed that Misa remembered fondly. She saw the wife of the missionary seated in a rocking chair in the shade of the eaves and, saying a silent prayer, made her way forward through the children.

The sturdy, full-rigged *Roamer* was not a ship to set passage records, but she made excellent time as she seized the prevailing trade winds in her sails, looping close to the Brazilian coast before striking across the South Atlantic toward the Cape of Good Hope and the Indian Ocean. She carried a cargo of light manufactured goods in her hold, after having delivered American cotton to England. She was a tight ship and, unlike the *Cutty*, a happy ship, and the men sprang to the rigging willingly when the great Cape greybeards broke over her rails and sent *Roamer* scuttling along almost as if she were a first-rate clipper.

Captain Samuel Gordon had come to respect his first command.

Initially, on the North Atlantic crossing, he had fretted a bit at her clumsiness; but once he had seen how the *Roamer* responded in heavy seas and the inevitable North Atlantic storms, he began to appreciate her for what she was, a dependable steady workhorse, a ship not to be driven but guided into doing the best allowed by her design.

In Sam's present state of mind, however, no ship would have been swift enough. That modern miracle, the undersea cable, had brought him a message that had speeded him away from New York Harbour longing to be in Hong Kong; and later, in England, another message, delivered to him by Alfred Childers's agents, had brought the day of his reunion with Jessica closer still, for she and her mother were on the way to Australia. Only if he could have travelled as swiftly as those electrical impulses that covered the thousands of miles between England and the North American continent, and connected Europe with the Far East, would Sam have been completely happy.

In the absence of one of those disasters that always hover over a ship, each long passage was much like another. If anything, the *Roamer*'s long haul around the Cape, across the Indian Ocean, and then up the eastern Australian coast to Port Jackson Harbour was notable for its uneventfulness. Hardly a man aboard remembered a passage so serene, with only occasional bursts of weather severe enough to cause *Roamer* to shorten sail.

A packet of letters addressed to Miss Jessica Broome had gone ahead from England on a swift clipper that made landfall a full three weeks before the *Roamer*, so the arrival of the ship in Sydney Cove was not unexpected.

Sam saw Jessica standing on the wharf. He spied her first from a great distance, with his glass, and felt a rush of gratitude and exhilaration. She was wearing a pale blue dress with a bunch of gleaming white lace at her throat, a highly imaginative hat that let her hair spill out in cascades of curls, and she sheltered herself from the sun with a little calico parasol. Only then, at the end of the easiest passage of oceans that Sam had ever experienced, the wind failed completely and *Roamer* drifted in the outer anchorage for a full hour before the harbour tugs got to her.

Sam sent his cabin boy to fetch Jessica aboard as soon as *Roamer* touched the wharf. She came up the gangplank with a smile playing on her lips, her gaze fixed on Sam, and her face flushed. She halted uncertainly as she stepped onto the deck, and Sam leaped forward, took her hand, and bent low, at first unable to form words. He knew that his performance was being watched with good-natured amusement by his crew, as well as by onlookers on shore.

She said only one word—"Samuel"—but in that word was volumes.

He let his fingers stay on her hand as he gazed into her eyes. "I must see that the offloading begins," he said, unable to think of anything better.

"Of course," she said.

"It's good of you to meet me," he said. "It's wonderful, but—" Again words failed him.

"I wanted to."

"Shall I have one of my officers escort you home—until I can join you, of course?"

Jessica almost seemed to relish his discomfort. "How soon can you get away?" she asked. "Needless to say, my mother is eager to see you."

"An hour," he said. "I promise I'll hurry."

"Only an hour? May I wait, then? I'll stay out of the way. I'd like to see your ship."

"Well, she's not the *Cutty*," he said, at last feeling on safer ground. "But she's a fine old girl nonetheless." He beckoned to the cabin boy, a bright English lad of good family. "Give Miss Broome a tour, if you will," he directed. "And then take her to the saloon and let her sample that Brazilian coffee. Have cook grind a fresh batch."

"My pleasure, sir!" With impeccable manners, the boy offered Jessica his arm; he was a head shorter than she, but he seemed to grow inches as he proudly led her aft.

When Sam found time to stick his head into the saloon some ten minutes later, he was relieved to see that Jessica was being well looked after. The third mate, who was off duty, was presiding with eager attention, and Wildeye, the grizzled old Welshman who was the ship's cook, had donned a clean apron and was standing in front of the table, a discoloured coffeepot in hand, explaining how coffee was giving tea a run for its money in America. Sam caught

Jessica's eye and winked, and the undisguised warmth of her return gaze fairly made his knees weak.

It was closer to two hours before Sam finally was free, the first and second mates directing a small army of stevedores, and the company's agents having come and gone with the news that the *Roamer* would have her cargo of wool without delay, for consignment to a London firm as soon as the ship herself was ready. "She's ready now," Sam had told them, for he had done necessary rigging repair en route and had kept her otherwise shipshape. The agents, impressed, would send off to the home office a very favourable report on the *Roamer*'s new captain.

During the ride to the Elizabeth Bay house in a hired carriage, Jessica had no end of questions about the passage. Then Magdalen was greeting him, surprising him with a hug and a kiss on the cheek, and there followed talk and food and company in the form of Johnny and Kitty Broome, until it was long past dark, and Jessica finally led him into the parlour, where they were alone for the first time.

A single lamp burned, giving the room a cozy glow, and Jessica turned to face him. For the first time, Sam sensed that she was somewhat nervous.

"Well, I suppose I must write a book," she said.

"On what subject?" Sam was genuinely puzzled, her tone was so serious.

"I shall call it the odd and interesting courtship of Jessica Broome."

He felt a genuine stab of guilt. "Forgive me" he said, taking her hand. "It's a new experience for me. If I haven't done it well—"

She laughed, and the words died on his tongue. "I wouldn't have had it any other way, Samuel Gordon. It isn't every woman who gets a marriage proposal by telegraph, and with an extravagance of words that must have taken a good portion of your pay." Then, abruptly, she was serious again, and as Sam stood there, still clutching her hand, her eyes seemed to become larger, her lips closer, and the lovely arch of her neck moved as she swallowed. Impulsively, he took her in his arms, holding her with his face inches from hers, staring down into her eyes. "Is it permitted?" he whispered, his voice hoarse.

"There is no moral stigma attached to a chaste kiss between a

214

betrothed couple," she whispered with a hint of a smile, but in an unsteady voice.

Gently, he let his lips touch hers and felt a tremor run through his body. His senses swam with the sweet, moist touch, and she smelled of clean, feminine fabrics and a hint of perfume that would, he suspected, stay with him forever. And then, with a sigh, she clutched him closer, her hands on his back, her body pressing against his.

At length they released each other, and Sam stepped back, his gaze still fixed on her face.

"By God above, I never imagined that anything could be so—so—"

"Nor I."

"My Jessica, I will leave the sea. One kiss and I know that I will never have the strength to leave you."

She smiled, pulled herself back into his arms, demanding an encore of that first, thrilling kiss, and apparently enjoyed the repeated performance so thoroughly that she had to clear her throat and swallow before she could speak again. "You will not leave the sea," she said. "Come, sit by me and please do *not* touch me, or I shall lose my breath entirely."

They sat on a loveseat, the curved back separating them. "I have decided everything, you see," Jessica said. "You will not leave the sea. I will come with you on the sea."

Sam had dreamed of that; yet knowing that the sea could be cruel, that life aboard a clipper was filled with hardships, he would never have suggested as much. He started to protest, but she put her soft fingers over his mouth.

"I know, it's a hard life. But I don't intend to spend years ashore waiting for you, Sam Gordon. I've waited over two years for your already, and my patience is exhausted. So there will be no more discussion, at least for now."

"Yes, ma'am," Sam said, in no mood to argue. "Whatever you say."

CHAPTER XI

Misa had quickly readapted to life at the mission. The hardest part of it was the early morning rising. Like her father and the rest of her people, she could never understand why white men felt that the day was wasted if not begun before the sun. But she followed the rules without question, her compliance made easy by the fact that she enjoyed the work with the children. Her job was to teach them to speak English, and when she was immersed in her work, there were times when she could forget her disgrace, could be unaware of the growing life in her. But gradually her girlish shape began to be distorted, so that by the time Tui came to visit her, many weeks after she had left the village, she was protruding quite noticeably.

When she was told that she had a visitor, she half expected to see her father. She ran from the classroom with a great smile on her face, and the smile faded only briefly when she saw Tui. He, too, was smiling broadly, and the smile stayed on his face even as his eyes fell to her bulging stomach.

"Misa," he said. "You are as beautiful as the sunrise on the sea."

"You look well, Tui," she replied, very conscious of her stomach.

"I would have come sooner, but Molo told us that you had eloped with a man from one of the far islands. Only recently did I learn you were here."

"You see me," she said. "You know why my father feels that it is necessary to lie."

"I was there," he said. "Remember? I left you with the white man, knowing that you intended paying the debt for all of us."

She said nothing.

"Come, walk with me." He took her hand and led her away from the mission to an overlook. In the bay below, a full-rigged ship was moving toward the German port.

She felt comfortable with Tui. "Once you said you would go to sea and someday be captain of such a ship as that," she said.

He laughed. "It took only a few days at home for me to forget such foolishness. I have had enough to do with the white man." He looked at her searchingly. "I suspect that you may feel the same way."

"Our life with the white men is just beginning," Misa said, shaking her head. "The Reverend McDougall, who runs the mission, conducts a class for older students in which he teaches the ways of the white men, and their history. He tells us that we must adapt to the white man's ways. He says that we cannot continue to live in the way we have always lived."

"We must don breeches and do manual labour for a few coins?" Tui's tone was bitter. "Not this one. Not as long as there are fish in the sea and fruit on the trees."

"Things are changing, Tui," Misa said. "I have learned from the Reverend McDougall that the white men of three great nations are contesting for our islands."

"But they are *our* islands. Your words admit it. What right has the white man to contest for them?"

"We don't have great ships," Misa answered. "Nor cannon, nor guns. We do not make things of iron and steel. Our numbers, compared with the people of any one of the great nations who come here, are few."

"They want only our copra," Tui said contemptuously. "And they offer tin trays and glass beads in return. I, for one, can do without the white men *and* their trade goods. I would wear bark cloth, instead of this cotton, if it would make the white man go away."

"They want more than copra," Misa said. "I do not fully understand, but the Reverend McDougall says that the real prize in Samoa is our harbours. He says that the English, the Germans, and the Americans are here for that, to control our harbours, and thus to hold dominion over all the seas around."

"The oceans are open to all who dare to brave them" was Tui's only answer.

Misa was becoming frustrated at his refusal to understand. "The

Reverend McDougall says that there might be *war* over our islands."

"Let them fight, then," Tui said. "We will go into the hills until they have killed one another and all their ships rest on the bottom of the sea."

She said no more. Even after living with the white missionaries, Misa herself understood little of the ways of the white man, and trying to explain them to Tui was next to impossible.

"No more talk of the white man and his foolishness," Tui said, as if reading her thoughts. He took her hands in his. "I have come for you, Misa."

Puzzled, she cocked her head questioningly.

"This," he said, touching her stomach, "does not matter. When the white man's child is born, we will leave it with the good missionaries, who seem to like taking care of the white man's bastards."

This last word was in English and had no meaning in the Samoan tongue, but Misa nevertheless felt her face flush. Abandon her child? The thought had never occurred to her.

"I have loved you long, Misa, and now, since you are no longer forbidden to me, I want to have you. We will leave Upolu and go to one of the smaller islands, where the white man finds little to attract him. There we will live and love and produce children of our own in the manner of Samoa."

She pulled her hands from his and turned her back.

"Here, what's this?" He put his hands on her shoulders and turned her to face him. "Will you not have me, even now?"

"Tui, you are so dear to me," she said in a whisper.

"Then we will go."

"I can't."

"Why?"

"The child. I could never leave my child."

"Then we will keep the white man's bastard."

Again the word pained her. "There is more," she said.

"Once you said you loved the white man. To continue to do so now, when you will never see him again, is stupid."

"Then I *am* stupid," she suddenly flared, surprised at her own outburst.

His face darkened, but only briefly. "That, too, will change," he said. "Come with me, Misa. We can leave today—now."

"I can't. I have a job to do. I can't leave them after they've been so good to me."

"Perhaps it would be best, then, if you stayed here until the child was born. Then you might feel differently, and I will come again for you."

She nodded. "As I told you once before, if I take any man, Tui, it will be you."

Misa's son was born in a small room in the mission house. Had she given birth in her native village, she would not have been alone, as she was, with only the Reverend McDougall's wife, Jane, as midwife. At home all her relatives would have been in the house, eating, laughing, coming to check on the progress of the birth at regular intervals, sitting up all night if the labour happened to be long, as it often was with a woman's first baby. At the mission there was only Jane, a kindly, red-haired woman who expressed continual amazement at Misa's ability to withstand the pain of childbirth without writhing or crying out. But to Misa it was not a difficult birth, although the labour was long, and when Jane lifted the little boy and spanked air into his lungs with a lusty whack on his bottom, Misa looked at the damp, bloody, tiny form and knew that she would never, never give him up.

Jane cut the cord with a kitchen knife. She was smiling and cooing as she put the boy next to Misa.

"Mrs. McDougall," Misa said, as Jane turned to the job of cleaning up, "could you please do something for me?"

"Of course, child." Jane was immediately at her side again.

"The cord," Misa said. "Could you please take it and throw it into the sea?"

"Whatever for?"

"So that he will grow up to be a skilled fisherman."

Jane frowned only briefly, then patted her hand and nodded. Samoans customarily burned the cord from a girl baby under a mulberry tree—from the bark of which cloth could be made—to ensure that the girl would be a good worker. If the cord from a boy was buried under a taro plant, he would be a farmer. Misa was relieved that the missionary's wife saw no harm in humouring her. "Yes, as soon as I'm finished here I will take it and throw it into the sea."

219

By the time Tui came, two days after the child had been baptized, Misa had made up her mind. She told him that she was going to stay at the mission, that it was now her home and would be the home of her son. When Tui left, she knew in her heart that he would not return, that she had refused him for the last time. She knew doubt, then, for life with Tui would have been pleasant. But there was now another element to her thinking. As reluctant as she was to admit it even to herself, she had come to appreciate living with the McDougalls in a real house, with doors and windows. She liked eating off fine porcelain plates instead of a banana leaf. Indeed, under the benevolent tutelage of Kevin and Jane McDougall, Misa was undergoing a transformation that the enforced separation from her village had made possible. As a brown-skinned woman, she could never, truly, be a part of the white society, Misa knew, yet it was equally true that she could never be at home again among her own people.

She had another visitor when her son was two weeks old. Molo came and, with ungrudging affection that brought tears to her eyes, hugged her in his arms as he had when she was a child. Then he looked at her and said, "This life seems to suit you, Daughter."

She showed him the boy. To Misa's sorrow, however, he did not touch his grandson and soon turned away. He did not even ask what she had named the boy. After talking with her a while longer he left, having made but one half-hearted effort to let her know that she was welcome to visit the village at any time.

The days blended into the next, and months quickly passed. Storms came, as they do, and repairing the damage they wrought became almost routine work, as it had been back in Misa's village. By the end of the boy's first year, it was evident that Jon Fisher's blood and the beauty of the Samoan girl had blended well. Though his hair was pitch black, he was of lighter skin than most of the half-breeds at the mission, and after he began to run off his baby fat, he quickly shaped into a most handsome little boy. Jane McDougall doted on him. Misa was as indulgent as any Samoan mother, and the older children, also in the Samoan way, tended him and did their best to spoil him. He grew up a happy child, full of love and laughter.

Misa called him Tolo, in a variation of her father's name, but the McDougalls insisted on addressing him by the name she had

220

agreed upon for his christening, Thomas.

"*I christen this child Thomas Fisher*," Kevin McDougall had said at the ceremony of baptism, and the words had since stayed in Misa's mind and in her heart. But she called him simply Tolo, and never pronounced aloud the child's last name.

After two years of looking forward to her daughter's wedding, Magdalen Broome now had only two weeks remaining before her future son-in-law's ship was ready to sail, and she was harried. When, over dinner with Johnny and Kitty, Jessica announced almost nonchalantly that she was going to be an on-board wife, that she would sail with Sam when the *Roamer* left Sydney, Magdalen gasped and actually dropped her fork.

"I think, dear, that you should discuss this with your father," she managed at last to say.

"That would be difficult," Jessica replied, "since in all likelihood he's somewhere out on the China Sea. I suspect, though, he'll be pleased to see me when and if the *Roamer* makes port in Hong Kong."

"I just don't think it's the right thing for you to do." Magdalen eyed Sam in mute appeal.

"Mother," Jessica said, "Claus Van Buren took Mercy with him on his voyages for years." She drew herself up. "Who knows, I might just become a heroine, like that American woman who took command when her husband fell ill, and brought his ship safely into port after weathering dreadful storms."

"Oh, dear." Magdalen did not look in the least assured. "I do wish your father were here."

"Just think, Mother," Jessica went on, "I'll get to visit England and perhaps New York. You should be happy for me."

In the absence of Red Broome, Red's brother, Johnny, gave the bride away in a ceremony that, at least to Sam, seemed eternal. Claus and Mercy Van Buren had arrived in Sydney Cove only hours before the wedding and showed up at the church with a handsome and distinguished-looking couple whose dress identified them, in the eyes of the well-travelled, as Dutch. The church was packed, and only a few—Magdalen chief among them—were aware of the notable absences: Red, of course, and Jessica's brother, Rufus, and Harry Ryan—although Magdalen, for one,

221

was relieved that Harry was not in Australia.

At the reception, Sam began to get a better idea about just what sort of family he was marrying into; many of Sydney's leading citizens were there—traders, politicians, high-ranking military men.

It was only at the tail end of a hectic afternoon that Sam and Jessica were introduced to Claus and Mercy's guests. Professor Conrad Berg, half English, half Dutch, had studied at Cambridge. He had inherited his height from his Dutch father, along with a thatch of well-kept blond hair. He was of a pleasant mien, spoke English with a cultivated accent, and was obviously proud of his bride of a year, a lovely Dutch woman named Vanya, who was sunny, buxom, blonder than her husband, and had eyes only for him.

"You've come a long way, sir," Sam said, when Claus Van Buren informed him that the Bergs lived at Anjer, on the northwest coast of Java and the Sunda Strait.

"It was a condition of our marriage that Conrad get away from his bugs for a honeymoon trip," Vanya said with a charming accent and a little guttural laugh that caused Conrad to look at her fondly. "But it's taken us more than a year to get around to the honeymoon."

"Bugs?" Jessica queried, not certain she had heard the woman correctly.

"Horrid mosquitoes," Vanya said.

"Perhaps I should explain," Conrad Berg put in. "My field is medicine. Not to bore you with details, but there is some evidence—at least to my mind—that malaria is associated with mosquitoes."

"I tell him," Vanya said, "that if malaria and mosquitoes were connected, then there would be malaria all over the world."

"She keeps me humble," Conrad said fondly.

"Actually I act as his—how do you say?—his devil's advocate," Vanya explained.

"Through the work of Alphonse Lavaran in Algeria, we know that a blood parasite is the cause of the disease," Conrad went on. "I am in correspondence with researchers in several countries—England, the United States, and of course with Lavaran in Algeria. Patrick Manson in England and Ronald Ross in India agree with me in suspecting the mosquitoes, even if my Vanya doesn't."

"It *is* such an unpleasant subject," Vanya said, "especially on one's wedding day. Put away your bugs, Conrad, and I will allow you to kiss the bride—but only softly, on the cheek."

The Dutchman laughed, bent his big, solid frame to touch Jessica's cheek with his dry lips.

Vanya hugged Jessica and whispered, "What a splendid couple you make—nd how handsome is your man!" Before Jessica could reply, Vanya said "Come," took her hand, and led her out of the others' hearing. "Claus tells me that you are to join your husband on his ship."

"Yes," Jessica said, puzzled.

"Ships that sail these seas come through the Sunda Strait sooner or later," Vanya said. "When yours does, both Conrad and I would be greatly disappointed if you did not stop to visit our home. We almost never have visitors, and the setting is quite lovely, really, when one gets accustomed to the easygoing way of the native Javanese and the heat."

"Why, thank you," Jessica said, but she was thinking no further ahead than the next few hours, to the time when the house would be empty of guests and she would be going up to her room—not alone, as she'd been doing all her life—but with a man, with her husband. And like the Bergs, they would have to postpone a honeymoon trip. The *Roamer* would be sailing soon, and the voyage, for all it would be work for Sam, would have to do as her honeymoon.

When, at last, Johnny and Kitty, Kitty with her stomach protruding with child, ushered the Van Burens and the Bergs out, leaving the newlyweds alone with Magdalen, Jessica could not bring herself to look at Sam.

"My, my," Magdalen said, collapsing into a chair, "What a day this has been."

Sam smiled at her. "Mrs. Broome, you have done yeoman's service. I consider myself very fortunate in having such a mother-in-law."

Magdalen motioned to them. "Sit down, please, both of you." They sat side by side, not touching, on a sofa. "Don't worry," she said. "I'll not be keeping you. In fact, in just a moment, I'll be joining Claus and Mercy at their hotel for the night."

Jessica flushed. The two servants would soon be finished cleaning up the remnants of the reception feast, and when they had gone to their quarters, she and Sam would be alone in the house.

"I just wanted to tell you before I go," Magdalen said, "that both Red and I highly approve of our daughter's choice of a husband. I wish you every happiness, it goes without saying. I have to admit, though, Sam—I feel I can call you that now—that I'm not overly pleased with your taking Jessica off, and away from me." She held up a hand to cut off their protests. "But I think that I'll be able to weather that storm somehow. Just you take good care of her."

"I will," Sam said, "You need have no worries on that account."

"Good." Magdalen rose, kissed both Sam and Jessica and went to find her wrap. Jessica accompanied her, clinging to her fiercely in the hallway.

"I'll be home around midday," Magdalen said, squeezing her daughter's hand. "Have a good night, darling."

Sam was holding two fine-stemmed glasses when Jessica came back into the parlour. He handed her one of them and said, "To my wife, who is the most beautiful woman in Australia and, as far as I can tell, the entire western and eastern worlds to boot. May she forevermore be my lover, my friend, my sailing companion, and my life."

Jessica's eyes overflowed as she sipped the wine. Any hint of awkwardness she had felt had been dispelled by those few words. She went to him, took the glass from his hand, and placed herself in his arms for his kiss.

To his everlasting credit, he was not precipitate. He was the soul of tenderness and consideration. When, at last, they were in Jessica's bed, and the last garment separating them had been cast aside, their union was directed by Sam slowly, carefully, and tenderly, and, as Jessica discovered the full meaning of womanhood, she knew finally and with no trace of doubt that she was right in having vowed never to be separated from this man who was now hers.

During the next several days Magdalen felt almost a stranger in her own house. Sam and Jessica were polite and attentive when she spoke, except that they rarely looked at her for more than a few seconds at a time, having eyes only for each other. Magdalen wrote to Red: "Their love burns as brightly as a falling star, making for—how shall I say it?—a rather fervid atmosphere in the house. I am reminded, my dear, of those first few days I spent with you so long ago."

There was, for the lovers, much to discuss. A lifetime of memories was to be shared, and Sam drank in and demanded more of Jessica's childhood, her thoughts regarding a thousand different subjects. She, in her turn, liked to lean on his shoulder in the parlour and hear him speak of his youth in Scotland and his apprenticeship at sea. She was brought almost to tears when he spoke passionately of his days aboard the *Cutty Sark*. His faithfulness to his former ship could have made her jealous, had she not been aware that she herself was his main reason for leaving the *Cutty*. Indeed, she had felt almost guilty when Sam explained that he had accepted the captaincy of the *Roamer* to put himself into a position to marry her.

So engrossed were they in each other that when the Childers Company agents sent a messenger to the house to inform Sam that plans had been changed, he scarcely commented, accepting the new orders in an offhanded manner, then returning quickly to Jessica. *She* was interested, however, since the *Roamer* would not, after all, be going to England. One of the company's fastest clippers would be hauling into Sydney within days, and her greater speed would get the *Roamer*'s already partly loaded cargo of wool to England weeks earlier.

Roamer consequently would have to assemble a new cargo and would spend some time in the Orient, making relatively short hauls. And Sam would have at least another week on shore.

"That's splendid news," Magdalen said. "You won't be so far away, and we'll see each other again much sooner, in all likelihood."

Claus and Mercy Van Buren had been showing the Bergs the sights of Sydney. They spent an afternoon and evening at the Broome house, with Vanya and Mercy noticing, as had Magdalen, that as far as the newlyweds were concerned, the world was empty except for the two of them. When Claus dragged Sam off for a brandy and a cigar in the study, more than likely to exchange sea stories, Mrs. Berg, with her husband's enthusiastic approval, renewed her earlier invitation for Mr. and Mrs. Gordon to visit the

Berg home in Anjer. Jessica, realizing that the likelihood of a visit was now far greater, responded with genuine gratitude—if not eagerness to share Sam's company with someone else. "If it becomes at all possible, we will surely do so."

CHAPTER XII

For Jon Fisher it was good to be back in Sydney. He liked the feel of the place, the air, the vistas of the bay, the friendliness of the people. The voyages of the *Java* had brought her home with a load of tea, and although Harry was not satisfied, Jon was pleased. His working capital had grown, not spectacularly but steadily. However, all his efforts to lift Harry's mood had failed, even when he applied the old saw about one having to crawl before one could walk. To add to Harry's gloom there was no immediate prospect for a paying cargo for *Java* and, therefore, no chance for the young partners to speculate on merchandise of their own.

Harry lost himself immediately upon making port. Jon had decided that no longer was he to be his brother's keeper where Harry was concerned. He would not again put his own life in danger trying to rescue Harry from some dingy sailor's bar or opium den. Instead, Jon sent a note to the Broome house asking that he might be allowed to call and was issued an invitation, returned by the same messenger, to please join Mrs. Broome and guests for dinner. He was in his cabin trying to brush the sea wrinkles out of his clothing when Harry came aboard. Surprisingly enough, Harry was cold sober and, indeed, in a fine mood. His eyes flashed with interest for the first time in months.

"Well, my boy," he said, "have yourself a quick fling, because as soon as we can reprovision we're off."

Jon was intrigued and only slightly annoyed by Harry's presumption. "It would interest me to know where we'll be off to and what we'll be carrying."

"Not much on the way out. Some cotton cloth and bric-a-brac for the kanakas of Samoa."

"Samoa?" Jon's heart leaped with quickened interest "I didn't know Van Buren had trading interests there."

"He doesn't." Harry was beaming. "Since *Java* was to lie idle for God knows how long, I've arranged to lease the entire bottom."

That, Jon knew, was a big order. A few bolts of cotton cloth and trade goods to be exchanged for copra and handicrafts from Samoa wouldn't make for a profitable voyage.

"I hope you'll trust me on this, old friend," Harry went on, "because we're going to have to dig into that war fund of yours just to give Van Buren the advance fee for the charter."

"Since I'm to be the chief financier," Jon said, "maybe it would be a good idea to tell me a bit more about this proposed trip."

"Simple. There's only one cargo worth hauling from Samoa."

Jon's look turned to sharp frown. "You're suggesting that we take the *Java* into the kanaka trade?"

"I'm highly recommending it," Harry said. "In fact, I've committed us to it."

"I should think," Jon said, his temper under tight control, "that you might have discussed that with me before speaking on my behalf."

"Jon, Jon, there's nothing wrong with transporting Samoans. They come here of their own free will."

"After being handed a bag of lies by the recruiters," Jon retorted hotly.

"Well, if you're going to be holier than thou." Harry's tone was surly.

"I'm sorry, Harry. I won't be a part of this. We'll just have to scout around and find another paying cargo."

"Is that your final word?"

"It is."

Harry held out his hand. "Then good luck to you."

Jon didn't take the offered hand for a moment, for he was shocked at the casualness with which Harry was willing to end their partnership. Then he took the hand and shook it.

"I'd imagine that Van Buren can use you as a supercargo on another of his ships," Harry said.

"Thanks, I'll make do."

"If you change your mind, I won't be sailing for a week or so." Harry added before ducking out of the door.

At first, as he packed his belongings and left the *Java*, Jon was puzzled. Not to his surprise there was, beneath his efforts to analyze the situation, a sensation of relief. He felt in full control of his own destiny for the first time since he had left the army. There would be opportunity in plenty; of that he was sure. He left the docks with a swinging, light stride, took a room in a hotel, and it was only later, when he was on his way to the Broome house, that he wondered where Harry was getting the money to charter the *Java* on his own. The suspicion that came to him was too ugly to entertain.

Dinner at the Broome's was, as usual, a lively gathering. Johnny and Kitty were there, and the table was filled out by a fresh-faced naval officer and his recent bride, the officer having served with Red Broome in Hong Kong before taking leave to be married. The young officer, a lieutenant, described the battle at the pirate Han-Kuang's island and reported that other, more major efforts were imminent in the continual skirmishing with the pirates. Throughout dinner no one mentioned Harry. It was only much later, after the lieutenant and his bride had taken their leave and Jon and Johnny Broome were seated on the veranda, feet cocked up, cigars smoking lazily, that the name came up.

"I'm afraid that my budding business partnership with Harry is at an end," Jon admitted, when Johnny asked about Harry.

"Oh?" Johnny said, the curiosity evident in his tone.

Jon thought about it for a moment. Sooner or later he would be asked about Harry, he was sure. He decided he might as well give his side of it before rumours distorted the facts. "The *Java* didn't have an immediate cargo," he said.

"Things are a bit slow. It's the season," Johnny offerd understandingly.

"So Harry is going into an enterprise for which I have no stomach."

"Nothing *too* illegal, I hope."

"Legal as any other trading activity," Jon said. "He's going to Samoa for a load of kanakas."

Johnny's feet fell to the floor with a thud of boot heels. "Claus Van Buren in the kanaka trade?" he asked, in total surprise.

"Not Van Buren, as far as I know," Jon said. "Harry's leasing *Java* outright."

"By God, if old Claus knew—" Johnny paused. "Well, it's not

229

my business, I suppose."

The face of the Samoan girl seemed to swim upward from great distances inside Jon's memory. "Tell me, Mr. Broome, if the kanaka trade isn't the business of a man of your position and responsibilities, whose business is it?"

"Ah," Johnny said, "methinks we have touched upon a sore spot."

"Sorry. I didn't mean to sound belligerent."

"Not at all. I can get rather belligerent myself about this ill-disguised form of slavery." Johnny studied the burning tip of his cigar, his expression thoughtful. "Actually, if you care to dig into some back issues of my newspaper, you'll find some rather stinging editorial stands against the trade. I was thinking of something else when I said that what Harry does with the *Java* is not my business."

"I've seen the kanaka trade in action," Jon said. "I saw a man named Jamison beat an old Samoan man to death with a bullwhip."

"And made yourself somewhat of a legend as a result," Johnny put in dryly.

"Beg pardon?" Jon asked.

"It's a small country, Jon. You're quite famous, in a way. I'd venture that the account of your two set-tos with Jamison have been told and retold thousands of times, growing with each retelling, I might add."

"I had no idea," Jon said truthfully. "But that aside, it's a contemptible thing, this trade in human labour."

"Agreed. And it will be up to men like you and me to end it." Johnny again studied his glowing cigar. "*How* is the problem. At the moment the entire agricultural economy is based on cheap kanaka labour. There's a fight building over it, and it'll be part and parcel of the fight for Australian unification. I'm glad to know that you'll be on,the side of the angels."

"For what it's worth," Jon said without conviction.

"It's worth much," Johnny returned with unexpected vigour. "Claus Van Buren will fight against the indenture trade as well, and that's what's giving me pause at the moment. I would feel guilty betraying a confidence between friends, but I think Claus should know what Harry plans to do with the *Java*. It wouldn't go well, in the future, if opponents pointed out that Van Buren, one of the leaders in the anti-kanaka-trade fight, had a clipper engaged in the trade."

Jon mused. He did not know Van Buren that well himself, but what he knew he liked. "If you feel that it's advisable to inform Mr. Van Buren, I'm sure that you would be able to get the same information along the waterfront. Harry, I fear, is not noted for being able to keep his mouth shut. I'm sure that there are others who know."

"To save myself trouble," Johnny said, "I'll pretend that I've heard it elsewhere. At any rate, I'll keep your name out of it."

Oddly enough, Jon's guess that others knew of Harry's plans was confirmed when he met a business acquaintance in the lobby of the hotel that very night as he was returning from the Broomes'.

"I understand that you and young Ryan are off to Samoa for a load of dark meat?" the man said.

"Not I," Jon said, walking past the man to his room. However, the results of his disclosure of Harry's plans to Johnny Broome were not long in coming. Jon had slept in until the sinful hour of nine and was having a quiet breakfast in the hotel dining room when he saw Harry approaching, his face dark. Harry stopped across the table, threw down a telegram, and stood wordlessly while Jon put down his fork and, still chewing, picked up the piece of paper.

Claus Van Buren had not resorted to telegraphese to shorten the word count: "How dare you even suggest that a Van Buren ship be used in kanaka trade? Your association with this company is terminated forthwith."

Jon put the telegram down. "Harry, I'm sorry."

"You knifed me, my boy," Harry grated. "I turn my back for a moment and you drive the shiv between me shoulder blades."

"Harry, last night a man I scarcely know stopped me in the lobby and commented on our—your going to Samoa for indentures."

"But he didn't send the word to Van Buren in New Zealand," Harry said darkly. "It took my old and good friend Jon Fisher to do that bit of dirty work."

"Harry , we were quits yesterday, aboard the *Java*," Jon said, rising. "I would prefer it to be a friendly parting, so I'm going to

231

ignore the fact that you've called me a sneak and a liar."

"Have I?" Harry smiled. "Not yet. Nor will I, for I've seen your skill with your fists. But this will not be forgotten, my boy. It will not be forgotten."

Jon felt himself reddening with anger. "I will say this only once. I did not give the information to Van Buren."

"But you blabbed it at the Broomes last night." He nodded. "Yes, that's it. Who was there?"

"That doesn't matter," Jon said. "Perhaps it's for the best, Harry. Had you taken the *Java* out of port, Van Buren would have been your enemy for life."

"With friends like you," Harry said, "Who needs enemies?" He wheeled as if to stalk off, then just as abruptly turned back, and this time his smile was the old Harry's, friendly and sunny. "No matter, mate. All's for the best, and all that rot. I've had a better offer, after all."

Jon made no attempt to stop Harry. He sat down, toyed with his meal, but he had lost his appetite. Trying as Harry had been at times, he had still been a friend, and Jon would always be in his debt for what had happened so long ago on the plain before Isandhlwana. Jon's black mood stayed with him until late in the afternoon, when he, too, had a telegram from Claus Van Buren.

"Word is you broke with Ryan over Samoan venture. Would speak with you, New Zealand, your earliest convenience."

Well, he had nothing else to do, he told himself. He set about arranging passage for New Zealand and found, to his delight, that the *Roamer*, Captain Samuel Gordon commanding, was coming in from a trip to Wellington and would be making the return run as soon as she could be turned around. He checked with the Childers agents in Sydney, found some spare cargo room in *Roamer* for the return voyage to New Zealand, and set about trying to figure out a profitable use for it. Oddly enough, he came across some Madras cotton material from India, the same sort of inexpensive merchandise that he and Harry had earlier brought to Australia, and purchased it at a price cheaper than he had paid in India. No enormous sums of money were involved, but he feld that he could at least make the trip to New Zealand pay. He met the *Roamer* at dockside and received a warm welcome from both Sam and his new wife. Jessica looked radiant, even though a deep-sea tan and a

232

new slimness had transformed her considerably.

The voyage to Wellington was most pleasant. Jon had always liked Sam Gordon, and the contrast betwen Sam's solid-mindedness and Harry's impetuosity was striking. It was equally obvious that Sam and Jessica were well suited, and the two of them seemed so happy together that it was, at times, uncomfortable to be with them in the saloon. Jon was almost painfully aware of how he had admired Jessica when he first met her, but had been too preoccupied to press his attentions on her. But it was not envy with which he now observed Sam's blissful state, for it was all too easy for him to picture himself in a similar position married to another woman—one with brown skin and wide, alluringly dark eyes. Misa.

Jon met Claus Van Buren in the new offices of the company in Wellington. Although Van Buren was small in stature, mild-mannered, and unassuming, he had an unmistakable air of confidence and authority—as unlike as could be, Jon felt, to his own stepfather. Van Buren had no necessity to call attention to his wealth and influence, for they spoke loudly through him, through his relaxed stance, his calm, assured voice, and keen eyes that seemed to Jon to be able to guess things about him that others rarely suspected. Of late, Jon knew, the Van Burens had been spending most of their time in New Zealand, expanding on their holdings there that had grown from a small trading post in the Bay of Islands. Once Harry had pointed out to him the Van Buren house on Bridge Street in Sydney, a grand old residence that Jon had always admired whenever he passed it.

He accepted the offer of tea and a chair before a vast, heavy, Dutch-built desk and waited.

"As you know, Mr. Fisher," Claus said, "Mr. Ryan is no longer associated with this company."

"I know," Jon said.

"My inclination, at first, was to terminate any association with you as well."

Jon had a momentary impulse to defend himself, to point out that he had had no part in planning to take the *Java* into the kanaka trade, but on second thought he remained silent.

"However," Claus went on, "men whose opinions I value highly speak well of you. I was told that you warned Mr. Ryan about the inadvisability of transporting indentures on one of my ships."

"I did," Jon said.

"And that you broke your partnership with Mr. Ryan over the question?"

"That is true."

Van Buren rose, walked to a window, and looked out with his hands clasped behind his back. He was silent for a long time before turning to face Jon again. "I was fond of Harry Ryan. I knew that he had a wild streak, but I thought that responsibility and work would drive his recklessness out of him. It was because of him that I allowed you to be associated with the Van Buren company in the first place, because, frankly, I didn't want to have anything to do with a son of Marcus Fisher."

"Stepson," Jon corrected.

"I told myself dozens of times that the simple way was just to say no. Harry vouched for you." He spread his hands. "Now Harry is gone. What am I to think? What am I to do about you, Mr. Fisher?"

Jon swallowed nervously. He wasn't sure what was in Van Buren's mind. Perhaps the man was working up toward telling him that he would no longer be able to work in cooperation with the Van Buren company. However, his nervousness did not show in his voice when he said, "I think the thing for you to do, sir, is to allow me to continue to lease space in Van Buren bottoms. In fact, although I'm still not the most experienced trader, I think it would be in the best interests of both of us if you'd allow me to act as supercargo on one of your ships."

Claus stared at him searchingly and then broke into a warm smile. "I had come to that conclusion myself, young man." He sat down behind the desk. "I have been going over the records of your transactions while you were working with Mr. Ryan. You've done well."

Jon made a wry face. "At least I still have my initial capital and some little left over."

Claus shrugged. "That's business, is it not? Sow your seed grain wisely and then add to it. That's something Harry did not understand. He was always after the quick gain, looking to multiply his money extravagantly in one trade. Except in very rare cases, that simply is not wise or possible. If I had approached life as

234

Harry Ryan did when I was a lip-lap servant, I would either be in prison or still poor," He sighed. "But you did not come here to hear my rminiscences. Now, as you know, we have interests in New South Wales and here in New Zealand. Actually, Mercy likes it here in Wellington, as do my children, and I suspect we'll be spending most of our time here. New Zealand is booming, and there are opportunities for all. However, there are disadvantages to being so spread out. Although I have good men associated with me, men like Robert and Simon Yates—whom you may or may not have met?"

"No, I have not," Jon said.

"There is always a shortage of men with the proper motives to look after my interests. In your case, I am hoping that the profit motive for yourself will be the prime factor in your taking over as supercargo of the *Java*."

"Thank you, sir. I—"

Claus held up a hand to cut off his expressions of gratitude. "Of course we pay agents to obtain cargoes for us. But every port is full of shipping agents, and often they work for more than one shipping line. There is no substitute for a dedicated man with something to gain or lose himself." He paused to offer Jon a cigar and light one for himself. "In Hong Kong and in Madras, while Harry was . . . Well, we won't go into what he was doing. But you were making yourself known to traders and merchants."

Jon was more than a little surprised that Van Buren was so well informed. "How did you—?"

"I have my friends, Mr. Fisher. But never mind—your initiative is exactly the sort of thing I'm talking about. Find the cargoes. Know the shippers, know the merchants. Know your trade, and then money will accrue to you, if that is what you want."

"That is my own view, sir."

"Good. Obviously we think along the same lines. Had you any immediate plans?"

"I've had some small success with wool," Jon said.

"Wool. Yes, of course, but remember that every clipper in these seas competes for the wool trade."

"There is something that bothers me, sir," Jon admitted. "I suppose it might be a matter of national pride, but I don't like the idea of the Germans and the Americans dominating trade in the

South Pacific." He went on hurriedly, seeing that Van Buren was about to object. "It's not something I plan to jump into immediately, but I'd like you to keep it in mind, and if, in the future, we see that there are possibilities for, perhaps, cutting into the copra trade—"

"That might be difficult," Claus said. "The Germans have their eyes on all of Samoa, and they are already well connected in the region. Bismarck is determined to make Germany a great colonial power, and there are many who believe that he's willing to fight a war to accomplish that end. In fact, I have heard rumours that Germany is preparing to announce formal annexation of Samoa. If they do—" He shrugged. "I am not a warlike man, Mr. Fisher."

"Surely the Americans will have something to say about a German Samoa."

"I would think so. And no doubt our own govenments would view such an action as hostile intent. I must admit that I would not feel at all comfortable with Germany controlling a good deal of the South Pacific. But perhaps I'm borrowing trouble. After all, in Australia and New Zealand we have impregnable positions."

"It is my understanding that the Germans are the main recruiters for indentured labourers in Samoa," Jon said, not ready to dismiss the subject.

"Ah." Claus eyed him closely. "I forget. So you don't like the kanaka trade?"

"I think it is a continuation of slavery."

"In that we agree; but the Germans commit other offences against the islands as well. On parts of Samoa, on their copra plantations, they keep the natives working with forces of armed soldiers. I need not add that it is hardly an open market."

"I presume, then, that you would not attempt to compete there?"

Claus shook his head. "Not at the present time; the situation is too volatile. But in the future, who knows? We shall just have to wait and see."

Jon left the interview a pleased man. The *Java* would be his vehicle. He would not, of course, be her captain, but as official supercargo he would be the man to say where the *Java* went and what she carried. Only one area of discontent remained. Any trip to Samoa would likely be years in coming, and he longed to know if Misa had made it safely home. He wondered if he would ever see her again.

He said his good-byes to Sam and Jessica. The *Roamer* was loading a cargo of lumber; increasingly of late, New Zealand's native forests were being hasrvested to open up more pastureland for sheep and cattle. The Gordons congratulated Jon on his new position and, in the captain's cabin, drank a toast to long life, health, and the coming new year, 1883. When it came time for Jon to take his leave, Sam and Jessica saw him to the gangplank.

"Well, Jon," Sam said, offering his hand, "since all ships sailing these waters eventually come to Sydney, I'm sure that our paths will cross again."

"I'm sure they will." Jon shook the hand warmly, said good-bye to Jessica, then reshouldered his seabag. He turned at the head of the gangplank and winked at Sam. "Name the first son after yourself, Sam."

"Plan to," Sam grinned back.

Two months later, as the *Roamer* approached Batavia, Java's major port city, in sticky equatorial heat, Jessica Gordon lost her stomach into a night jar for the third morning in a row. Not for the first time, she recalled Jon Fisher's parting words and made a face.

Jessica had missed her period in early March, and to her the signs were clear. She had always been a good sailor. The *Roamer*'s motion was almost imperceptible in the calm, tropical sea, and she knew she was not seasick. Nor did her morning queasiness abate while the *Roamer* took on additional cargo at the Batavia wharves. By the time they had left port and were approaching the Sunda Strait, Jessica's condition had worsened to the point that she could no longer hide the truth from Sam. When she told him what she suspected, he whooped in joy, then quickly sobered.

"But is it natural for you to be so sick, not to be able to keep food in your stomach?"

"It happens," she said, "I'm hoping it will soon pass."

"I wonder," Sam said, "If it wouldn't be a good idea for you to spend some time off the ship."

It was exactly the response she had dreaded hearing. "No," she said quickly. "I'm sure I'll get over it. In any case, I'll have to leave you soon enough."

"We should be at Anjer in two days," Sam said. "We'll call on Professor and Mrs. Berg. I'm sure, in view of their friendliness in Sydney, that they'll invite you to stay with them. A few days of rest while I take care of business might do you good."

Jessica had to admit that a bed that was not in constant motion, and solid ground under her feet, sounded inviting. "I will be pleased to see Vanya," she said. "But don't get any ideas about my staying in Anjer when the *Java* sails, *Captain* Gordon."

CHAPTER XIII

By 1883 the Sunda Strait had become one of the busiest of all ocean highways. It was a gateway to the Orient for the ships of all the seagoing European nations, as well as for that growing young maritime giant, the United States. Lying six degrees south of the equator, the strait formed a narrow gap between Java and Sumatra, so that any ship travelling eastward from India, Africa, or Europe, or westward from China, the Philippines, Southeast Asia, or many of the western Pacific islands, had to make its way into or out of the Java Sea via the strait, or take a long, circuitous detour. It was not unusual for observers in the Dutch settlement of Anjer to see as many as eight ships in various positions of navigating the strait.

As the *Roamer* rounded Saint Nicholas Point, the weather was fair, and the winds were light. The jungled shores of both Java and Sumatra were visible, and Jessica, after her usual bout with the morning sickness, was on deck, determined to see as much of the world as she could before motherhood forced her to move ashore. It was late when the *Roamer* was secured for the night at Anjer, but Sam, eager to install his wife in more comfortable surroundings, sent off a messenger to the home of the Bergs and was delighted when, not more than twenty minutes later, Conrad and Vanya Berg hailed the ship from the wharf.

Nothing would do, the Dutch couple insisted, but for the Gordons to have dinner with them. By now Sam felt confident in trusting the ship to his officers and crew, and the lessening of temperature brought on by evening made the prospect of dinner ashore, in civilized surroundings, impossible to resist.

The Berg house sat on the side of a hill just behind the main part of town, situated so that it took full advantage of the cooling effect of the monsoon winds that blew from the northwest from

December to March and from the southeast from April to October. The front veranda offered a view of the harbour, as well as the surrounding gardens containing an astounding number of flowering plants. An evening breeze made the dining room airy and comfortable, and there was lively talk as the two couples brought each other up to date on events since they had met at the wedding. The Bergs insisted that they stay for as long as the *Roamer* remained in port, and for both Sam and Jessica it was indeed a luxury to sleep in a full-sized bed with the windows open, for all that a netting was required to protect them from mosquitoes.

With the morning, Sam was off to the ship. Jessica, at his insistence, slept late, and when she awoke she felt better, without the usual morning nausea. She found Vanya on the veranda, sheltered from the morning sun, and joined her for a breakfast of ripe fruit and buttered bread. Finding herself ravenous and the fresh food irresistible, Jessica ate with a gusto that amused Vanya.

"They do not feed you on board your husband's ship?" she asked teasingly.

"Nothing so delicious," Jessica said, but her smile faded quickly as the familiar upheaval began in her stomach and she had to make a run for the bedroom.

A little later, as she stood weakly in front of the washstand, cooling her face with a damp cloth, Vanya came into the room and said, "You don't look ill."

"I'm not, not really," Jessica said."

"Ah," Vanya said, with sudden enlightenment. "How long has it been happening?"

"I think I am three months into term."

Vanya nodded knowingly. "You have not seen my Willie. He is four months old, and when I was carrying him I was sick nearly every morning for four months."

Jessica moaned, thinking she had endless weeks of misery ahead of her.

"But that was before I listened to a very wise old Javanese woman," Vanya said. "Come," She led Jessica into the kitchen, spoke to a tiny, wrinkled native woman who was making preparations for the noontime meal, and soon Jessica was holding

240

a cup of something that steamed, looked oily in its darkness, and smelled of fish.

"I can't possibly," she said.

"Drink," Vanya ordered. The little Javanese woman nodded vigorously and repeated the command.

The mixture, a herbal tea, Vanya informed her, did not taste as bad as it smelled. There was a tang to it that cleared the vile taste from Jessica's mouth, and its warmth quickly eased the roiling of her stomach. By the time she had forced down the contents of the cup, she was beginning to feel almost normal.

"Now you will eat," Vanya said.

"Oh, no". To think of being sick again, having just gained relief, was too much. But she obeyed. She nibbled gingerly on a piece of buttered toast, sampled various fruits, and it stayed down.

"Tell Conrad to forget his mosquitoes and to bottle that magic potion," Jessica said. "His fortune will be made, and pregnant women the world over will bless his name forever."

Vanya laughed appreciatively. "They are a deceptively simple people, the Javanese. I, like you, was reluctant to drink something that smelled as the herb tea smells. But once I did, I cursed myself for my previous stupidity. I will have the cook keep a pot on the stove at all times. If you feel the slightest sickness, run for the kitchen and not the chamber pot. Drink one cup when you first awaken, and then you will be able to hold food. We will put some meat on your bones and give that baby the proper nourishment."

The two women spent a pleasent morning, with Vanya showing Jessica all the varieties of flowering plants that Conrad had collected for their gardens. The day was bright and sunny, but the heat was somewhat moderated by the southwesterly breezes. Conrad brought Sam to the house for the midday meal.

"I've just been in contact with our agent in Batavia," Sam announced. "He's found an eager customer for our lumber. Consequently, we'll be doing some island hopping for the next four months. From here to Singapore, then to Brunei in North Borneo."

"Not Hong Kong?" Jessica asked, thinking of her father.

"Not yet," Sam said. "I've requested that *Roamer* be scheduled for a cargo for Hong Kong, if possible, before August."

"Why August?" Vanya asked.

"No later than August the first the *Roamer* will sail for Australia, so that Jessica can have her baby at home."

"I had hoped that she could have the child here," Vanya said. "By August she will be six months into term. A voyage at that stage would be difficult."

"We have fine doctors here," Conrad added. "And she will be most welcome." He nudged Vanya. "This one gets lonely and tries to keep me from my work."

"Thank you for the offer," Jessica said, "but I will stay with my husband for as long as possible. And I would like very much to be with my mother when the child is born."

"Well, you are not going aboard that ship when it leaves here for Singapore," Vanya said defiantly. "Not when we have only now brought the morning sickness under control."

"Under control?" Sam asked.

Jessica told him about the herbal tea, and he nodded thoughtfully.

"Jessica, I think it would be a good idea if you avail yourself of Vanya's kind hospitality and stay here while I make the run to Singapore and Brunei. I'll be back before the first of August."

"Oh, Sam," she said, the prospect of parting from him not at all to her liking."

"For me," he said. "Do it for me?" He smiled wryly. "How can I run a ship while I am worried about your being ill?"

"It's settled then," Vanya interceded. "We'll send boys to the ship to get your things immediately."

Her first parting from her husband was a wrench to Jessica's heart, but she kept reminding herself that it would be only for a relatively short time. The baby's health was of great concern to her, for in the past weeks she had lost weight by not being able to eat, and she had to admit that her staying behind would be beneficial to the child. Still, she was glum as she watched the *Roamer* take the southwest wind in her sails and swiftly leave Anjer behind.

Vanya's company was some consolation, for never had Jessica known a more cheerful person. Her devotion to little Willie was an inspiration, and Jessica delighted in watching as Vanya assisted the young Javanese nurse in ministering to the baby's needs.

Conrad, too, despite his preoccupation with his work, was a pleasure to be with. Not for one moment did Jessica feel a stranger in a strange home.

In her first week after the *Roamer*'s departure, Jessica met practically the entire Dutch community in Anjer. The Dutch had been in Java since 1596, nearly two centuries longer than the British had been in Australia, and most of the people Jessica met, like Dr. Hans van der Stok and his wife, Anna, and the newly appointed telegraph master, Peter Schruit, were Javanese born. Jessica envied the ability of the Dutch colonials to speak at least three languages—including English more often than not, and at least one of the native dialects.

Anna van der Stok was a regular visitor to the Berg house, and Jessica enjoyed many May afternoons with her and Vanya, the three of them sewing, knitting, and chatting easily. The stores in Anjer provided Jessica with the materials she needed to begin to fashion a layette, which she decided to make suitable for either a boy or a girl, although she was sure that her child would be a boy, a son for Sam. At dinners, Hans van der Stok undertook to teach Jessica something of Java, taking great pride in explaining that the colonial excesses that had been common under the Dutch East India Trading Company and early administrations were no longer practised. He spoke of native revolts, of Javanese peasants rising up against the harsh rule of native princes and the demands of greedy colonial officials, and of how the great Culture System instituted in 1830 had expanded the economy of the country. He bragged how, after fifty years of progress, the Dutch colonial policy in Java was now the most enlightened in the world, and he pointed to peace and contentment among the native population as proof.

"The problem is, you see," Anna van der Stok pronounced in a condescending tone, "that we can't expand the economy as fast as the natives breed. In spite of all our advances, the growing number of people keeps the living standards of the peasants at about the same level. If Professor Berg and his friends should, by any chance, find a cure for malaria, God only knows what would happen, what with the sudden jump in population."

"I didn't know, Anna," Conrad Berg said, "that you adhered to the theories of Malthus."

Hans laughed at his wife's blank expression. "I don't think Anna has ever heard of the honourable Englishman. He, my dear, stated the theory that population will always grow faster than production, not only of food but of material things, and will be held in check by war, famine, and disease. He has fallen into some disfavour because some think that he is an advocate of war as a control on overbreeding."

"Oh, dear," Anna said. "I would not, certainly, withhold any medical advances from the poor wretches. It's just that they do multiply so."

"God must have loved the dark-skinned folk," Peter Schruit said, "for he made them in plenty. I can't understand, Mrs. Gordon, the thinking of your people in Australia. Unlike here in Java, your native population is small, and, I understand, undergoing a natural shrinkage as they are pushed back into infertile lands. And yet now you are bringing in dark-skinned people from the Pacific islands."

"I do hope that Jessica doesn't get the idea that we Dutch are hopelessly bigoted," Vanya said.

"Bigoted?" Hans echoed. "I think not. There is a natural separation between dark and white races. And no one desires this separation more than our natives."

Jessica was thinking of Claus Van Buren, who was of Dutch and Javanese parentage, and wondered what he would have to say on the subject.

"The British, you see, are not the only colonial people who have taken up the white man's burden, the moral and spiritual uplifting of native peoples," Schruit said. "Isn't that so, Mrs. Gordon?"

"I'm afraid I haven't given the question much thought," Jessica replied diplomatically. "Our aborigines have been shamefully treated, Mr. Schruit, and these days we rarely see them in Sydney. And the so-called kanakas are agricultural workers, primarily."

"Watch that they don't outbreed you," Anna van der Stok said.

"Jessica is doing her share," Vanya put in, adroitly changing the subject and provoking general laughter.

As the midpoint of May passed, Jessica found it increasingly necessary to fashion herself a new wardrobe. Vanya made her two loose, comfortable dresses and convinced her of the practicality of spending the hotter afternoons dressed in the native *sarong*.

244

Jessica especially enjoyed the mornings. She had fallen into the habit of sleeping until almost eight o'clock, and on awakening she would join Vanya on the veranda overlooking the town and the harbour for a leisurely breakfast. Often Vanya translated for her articles from the Java *Bode*, the principal Dutch-language newspaper. After breakfast Jessica would retire to her room to write to Sam, although she knew he would, most probably, pick up the letters from her in person. He would have reached Singapore by now, she calculated, and would soon be sailing toward Brunei. Each passing day brought closer the time when she would see him again, and she prayed diligently that he would not be shocked by her growing stomach.

The twentieth day of May was, at first, like all the other mornings Jessica had spent with Vanya. They had finished breakfast and Vanya was reading from the newspaper when, abruptly, the heavy plank floor rocked sickeningly beneath them. Pieces of the delft dinner service bounced on the table, some sliding off to shatter.

"Oh, dear," Vanya said, more disturbed over the loss of her china than the earth tremor. "I brought that set all the way from Amsterdam, eleven thousand miles."

The shaking of the earth, and the porch, had caused Jessica's heart to pound. She looked around anxiously. The day was glorious, with a bright sun, a slight breeze, and a cloudless blue tropical sky. She cocked her head as, from far off, there came a sound like that of a naval cannonade.

"That's odd," Vanya said, as the distant rumbling continued.

"What on earth is it?" Jessica asked.

"Oh, not to worry." Vanya busied herself picking up the broken china. "It's a volcano in eruption, which is quite common here. No one gets alarmed—not even Willie. I was puzzled only because the sound seems to be coming from the northwest. Most of the active volcanos are to the south."

Jessica's nervousness was not eased when the little Javanese cook ran onto the veranda, babbling in her own language. Vanya spoke harshly. The woman subsided but was wringing her hands and looking about her in near panic.

"She says that Orang Aljeh, the ghost of the mountains, is loose," Vanya explained as soon as the woman had departed.

245

Conrad approached across the lawn, from the direction of his laboratory, where, among other things, he kept colonies of mosquitoes. The low rumblings in the distance continued, and windows were rattling in the house.

"Please don't be disturbed," Conrad called as he drew near. "When one has lived here for a few years, this becomes almost second nature. It seems that at least one of Java or Sumatra's volcanos is in eruption at one time or another." He laughed as he stepped onto the porch. "Actually, that's why the most fertile soil in the world is in Java. Volcanic ash makes a splendid fertilizer."

"Well, I must say, you're both taking this very calmly." Jessica found herself gripping the arms of her chair, for the distant, continuing thuds of sound had unnerved her.

"Conrad," Vanya said, "the sounds are not coming from the south."

"Yes, I noticed. I think I'll walk down to van der Stok's. I'd like to take a look at his seismograph."

"If you don't mind, we'll walk with you," Vanya said. "If Jessica feels up to it."

"Just you try to leave me here alone." Jessica rose from her chair and took Vanya's offered arm. "Lead the way, Conrad."

Professor van der Stok, when he admitted the visitors, had a puzzled look on his face. "The eruption is not to the south," he said to Conrad.

"Any indication on the seismograph?"

"See for yourself." Van der Stok had no other comment as Conrad scrutinized the instrument, which was on the stone floor, in a corner. Conrad was speechless as he straightened and looked back at his colleague.

"Am I supposed to become frightened now?" Jessica asked, with an uneasy laugh.

"No, no," van der Stok said, "not at all, dear lady."

"It is Krakatoa," said van der Stok's Javanese houseboy from a doorway, breaking the rule that servants speak only when spoken to.

"Nonsense," van der Stok said.

Peter Schruit arrived. "I have had inquiries by telegram from Batavia," he said.

Van der Stok raised a bushy eyebrow. "So the sounds are heard in Batavia, as well." He smiled at Schruit. "My boy says it is Krakatoa."

Schruit shook his head. "When the first shock came I was on the veranda, I examined all the peaks on the strait through a glass and saw nothing."

"Krakatoa is an extinct volcano," van der Stok explained to Jessica.

"Antoe Laoet, the ghost of the sea, lives there," the Javanese houseboy spoke up.

"Keep your peace," van der Stok snapped at him.

"There are native legends regarding Krakatoa," Conrad informed the others.

"I have heard them," van der Stok said. "They speak of the sea being covered with ash at some time in the past—perhaps two hundred years ago."

"And of a great disaster in the distant past," Conrad added.

"That may be," van der Stok said. "But I have examined the peaks of Krakatoa. She is a burned-out crater, not more than twenty-seven hundred feet in elevation. There are many other cones, more majestic, all along the strait."

However, as the morning passed into afternoon, an ominous cloud formed over the three small islands making up the Krakatoa group. Schruit, Jessica learned from Conrad Berg, had sent a telegram to officials in Batavia stating that Krakatoa was casting out fire, smoke, and ash with explosions and rumblings.

Jessica, Vanya, and the baby remained at the hillside house, with occasional reports from Conrad, who seemed to be growing increasingly excited. Accounts from passing ships had begun to come in, he told them. The mail packet *Zeeland*, having passed near Krakatoa, had reported a dark cloud soaring into the sky, complete with lightning flashes and rapidly repeated explosions. Waterspouts had been forming around Krakatoa, and the *Zeeland* had been covered with volcanic ash. The Dutch steamer *Soenda* had passed so near Krakatoa, he said, that the crew had felt the heat of the eruption on their faces.

Jessica, though still apprehensive, became gradually less worried and even somewhat thankful for the distraction. Indeed, for all the next week, Krakatoa put on a spectacular show, issuing her great cloud that was visible in Anjer and all along the strait.

Woodcutters, trying to land on Krakatoa, spoke of an island in upheaval, of sounds like naval cannon-fire. When a mining engineer commissioned by the Dutch governor-general came to Anjer on his way to take a firsthand look at Krakatoa, he was entertained at the Berg house. Jessica listened with rapt attention as he grew expansive on the subject of famous volcanic disasters of the past, especially Italy's Vesuvius, whose outburst had been described so well by Pliny the Younger. The engineer, whose name was Schuurman, also described eruptions closer to home, in Java.

"Sir Stamford Raffles discovered an inscribed stone, dated circa A. D. 1041, that describes the destruction of a powerful Javanese kingdom, with many fine temples," he said. "And we know that Papandayang did terrible damage when it erupted in 1772—not to mention Tambora, in 1815 on the island of Sumbawa. Tambora killed, it is estimate over twelve thousand people, and thousands of others died of starvation."

"Ah, yes," Conrad interjected. "The year without a summer."

Schuurman nodded. "That is theory only, that the ash from Tambora darkened the sky enough to make 1816 an unusually cold year."

Jessica was wishing that the *Roamer* would suddenly appear in the anchorage. She had had enough of volcanoes, and talk of volcanoes.

Conrad, however, did not appear in the least concerned, as his next words indidcated. "We have no reason to fear such cataclysms with Krakatoa, of course, regardless of her fireworks and thunderings. If it were Karang, or Pulosari, both of which rise above four thousand feet, then it might be different."

The next day, Schuurman was taken to Krakatoa by the Dutch ship *Gouveneur General Loudon*, and the little Dutch community in Anjer, assembled in the town hall, was among the first to hear his observations. The jungles that had covered Krakatoa were gone, replaced by a scorched wasteland, and the entire island group was covered in ash and pumice stone. The clouds of eruption were emanating from the smaller of the three peaks of Krakatoa, called Perboewatan. Schuurman tried to impress his listeners with the grandeur of nature on a rampage, of seething lava, thundering clouds, and masses of stone and ash being hurled into the sky.

Jessica was more than pleased when humble little Krakatoa went back to sleep. The volcanic activity became unnoticeable after May 27. She had received letters from Sam, delivered by a mail steamer, but he, of course, had known nothing of the eruption as he wrote, and his letters were full of reassuringly humdrum news about the day-to-day life on the *Roamer*. He told her to be patient, to rest and eat well, and that he would have her back in his arms sometime in July.

The peaceful days were disturbed only mildly by a thick, dark cloud that reappeared over Krakatoa in Mid-June. Ships passed and made their reports of a quiet, if smoking volcano. In July Krakatoa was examined again, close up, by another mining engineer, which for some reason made Jessica feel reassured.

Meanwhile, at the Berg home, the evenings were rich with the aroma of spice trees, the skies a glory of stars. With only Vanya to be thrilled with her, Jessica experienced one of the first delights of motherhood. Her baby began to make movements, and, as July came, the baby's kicks grew so lusty that the movement could be seen through the material of the *sarong* that had become Jessica's most comfortable day-dress. She longed to have Sam with her, so that he could feel his son's strength, and so that she could feel the touch of his hand, rest easy in his arms, and tell him how wonderful it was to be carrying his child. When, in late July, a telegram was delivered to her by Peter Schruit himself, the news contained in its few, well-chosen words sent her, weeping, to her room.

The *Roamer* was not a new ship. She had travelled all over the world's oceans and had weathered more than a few noteworthy storms. It took only a moderate blow off the coast of southern Borneo to make it glaringly evident that the old lady's endurance had been strained, along with other seams in her bottom, to cause her to limp into Singapore with the crew manning the pumps around the clock. Sam had no choice but to put her in dry dock.

Even a rushed job, just enough to make the *Roamer* seaworthy for the trip back to Java and then Sydney, would be a matter of weeks. And even as he applied pressure to the shipyard, and had Childers's agents do the same, Sam knew the earliest he could hope to arrive back in Anjer would be in late August, almost a full month past the time that the doctor in Anjer had advised him was the last possible date for Jessica to attempt a sea voyage.

His first inclination was to resign from his position and take the first ship headed to Java. He even went so far as to inquire about sailings. There was a steamer leaving Singapore within a few days for Batavia, and from Batavia he could catch a coastal vessel to Anjer. Then it would be relatively simple, given the high traffic through the strait, to find a ship heading for northern Australia. However, uncertainties were involved. The steamer was an island hopper and would take long to reach Batavia. It could be days before he could find as ship for Anjer, and more days—weeks, perhaps—before a suitable passage could be arranged for Australia. And by then Jessica would be nearing the later stages of her pregnancy.

At last, he convinced himself that it was more out of concern for Jessica than for his career that he decided to remain with the *Roamer* until she was properly repaired. Still, each word of the telegram he was forced to write brought him pain and guilt. He should not have waited until the last minute to plan to get Jessica back to Australia. Unforeseeable things happen to a ship at sea, and he had let himself be lulled by the smoothness of the *Roamer*'s recent voyages. He could not even bring himself to smile as he worded the telegram in the most economical way, recalling Jessica's joking reprimand over his extravagance in the message in which he had proposed marriage to her.

"Damage requires stay Singapore. Arrive Anjer late August. Plan baby Anjer. Love."

CHAPTER XIV

Jessica and the Bergs were at lunch inside, having just returned from church, when the first explosion occurred. The initial thunderlike clap numbed her eardrums, so that she felt more than heard the ominous echoing and reechoing across the water, as the sound bounced off hills around the strait. Food was forgotten, and all three of them rushed out to the veranda as Krakatoa unleashed its pent-up forces in a series of explosions that, to Jessica's deadened ears, sounded much like a heavy locomotive climbing a steep grade: *chug, whomph, chug, whomph*. As she watched, dumbfounded, the already towering cloud moved downward, a wall of darkness approaching at awesome speed, and within minutes, it seemed, blackness came to Anjer. Jessica could hardly see her own hand held out in front of her. It was the blackness of nonexistence, the darkness of hell itself, and the air was heavy and noxious. Conrad, with remarkable presence of mind, guided the two women back into the house as the detonations from the volcano became even more violent, a roar of sound that made speaking difficult.

All the native servants seemed to have disappeared. Vanya brought Willie from the nursery while Conrad lit a lamp for them in the sitting room, its light dispelling the darkness only feebly.

"I'm going to the telegraph office," he said.

"Please don't," Vanya begged, cradling the fretful baby in her arms. Her usually cheery face was drawn with fear, and Willie, his face buried in his mother's bosom, was beginning to cry softly.

"I must find out what's going on," Conrad said. "I'll be back within minutes. I promise. You'll be perfectly safe here."

He was gone, and Vanya, Jessica, and the baby huddled together on a sofa as the explosions continued, though now somewhat abated. Time seemed to have become eternal, but

251

Conrad, true to his word, was back in what he proudly announced to be twenty minutes. He must have run all the way, Jessica realized.

"The telegraph lines are down to Batavia," he said, sounding breathless. "Schruit's off to find the break."

"What did you learn?" Vanya asked.

"No more than we can see, which is nothing. Of course there's panic in town, in the native quarters and in the Chinese quarter. The natives are blaming us Dutch for the eruption, if you can believe that. They say we've offended their old gods."

"What must we do?" Jessica asked.

Conrad was lighting another lamp. "Not much we can do, except sit it out. I should think that the air will clear soon." He dusted his clothing, knocking off a fine settling of ash. "Odd thing at the waterfront, though. You can't tell whether the tide is rising or falling. The water keeps coming and going."

Jessica shivered.

"Conrad, should we try to leave?" Vanya asked, clutching Willie to her.

"Where? Into the jungle? I wouldn't know where to turn in this darkness. We could easily become lost."

"By boat?" Vanya asked.

"No one is putting to sea," he said. "Although the Chinese are gathering on the waterfront, with everything they can carry. It's mass confusion. Even if we could leave, I don't think it would be a good idea. Should the natives see us fleeing they would panic totally. And God knows what would happen then. Looting, murder."

The air now smelled of sulphur, Jessica noticed, and the heat was stifling. And to add to the discomfort, the fine, airborne ash was making breathing itself difficult. Jessica had to clear her nose with a handkerchief.

"By the way, poor old Schruit had just found a house, and was planning to bring his wife and children out from Batavia as soon as possible," Conrad said, although it was evident he was trying to make small talk to ease the fears of the women. Jessica looked at Vanya and noticed that tears were making tracks through the dusting of ash that coated her face.

Conrad did not know that Peter Schruit had found the break in the telegraph line. On a canal, between two bridges, a schooner and a score of smaller boats and native *proas* were being lifted and dropped violently by the wildly fluctuating water level, and the schooner's masts had snapped the wires. Nor did Conrad know that all efforts to launch small boats along the waterfront were being frustrated, often with fatal results, as the craft were left high and dry one moment, then tossed by swiftly onrushing water another.

The blackness, made deeper by the coming of night, was broken occasionally by brilliant bursts of fire that would, like an infernal lightning flash, make every detail outside the windows of the Berg home stand out clearly. There was, for Jessica, no possibility of sleep. Everything, outside and in, was covered with a layter of ash. The sulphurous air had not grown cooler with the evening, and breathing it was an ordeal. And still the volcano thundered.

When dawn finally came, it was no more than a grey streak of light at the horizon. Mercifully, though, Krakatoa had gone silent. Jessica knelt beside her chair, easing herself down, protecting her stomach, to thank God. After the hours of noise, the quiet that had fallen was, somehow, almost as nerve-wracking as had been the thundering explosions. The lamps remained lit in the sitting room, and Conrad was dozing in his chair. Vanya's head leaned on the back of her chair, and the sound of her exhausted sleep seemed amusingly loud in the unearthly hush. The baby, stretched out in her lap, slept silently.

Jessica completed her prayer of thanks, struggled up from her knees, and walked to the front windows to look out. She wondered what was happening in town.

Peter Schruit had bestirred himself before dawn and returned to the canal to check on the progress of repairs to his telegraph lines. His line-watcher and his telegraphist were busy with their work of splicing the wires back together. He looked out to the strait just in time to see a wall of water moving toward the canal and the town at frightening speed. He shouted a warning to the two working men, then ran for his life. The wave roared up behind him, smashing the drawbridge, a hotel, homes, and businesses. He was not an especially athletic man, and he could not have remembered when he last ran at full speed, but, with death at his heels, he found the endurance to race on, to rising ground, only to lose his footing and fall. He quickly commended his soul to God, for the roar of the wave was in his ears, but when he had the strength to look around, the wave was receding.

After her waking, restless night, Jessica had finally surrendered to total exhaustion, and she was asleep in her chair when an area of almost twelve miles of rock and earth smashed down into the emptied caldera of Krakatoa. The sound of this final paroxysm was to be heard three thousand miles away, but since the force of the blast was funneled upward, perhaps muted by the thick ash in the air, and because it fell on human organs of hearing already numbed by the deafening noise of the preliminary eruptions, the bellow of total devastation was only a whisper to those in Anjer. Jessica slept on as seawater drained into Krakatoa's vast, empty chamber to meet seething, white-hot magma and expand into superheated steam in an explosion of unbelievable violence. Already thousands had died in the huge waves sent out by the initial stages of collapse, but the wave that now reared up from Krakatoa dwarfed anything that had gone before. A mountain of water, it smashed into the already devastated waterfront at Anjer and climbed the slopes.

Jessica was awakened by the roar, by the crashing of things being broken. She saw the house sway, as if from a giant's blow, and even as she leaped from her chair the wall collapsed and water exploded into the room. In one small moment of time that seemed to be frozen she saw Conrad and Vanya and Willie engulfed and then the wave was upon her, lifting her bodily, pummelling her with flotsam, throwing her against the opposite wall. She had managed to gasp a deep breath before being submerged, and now, frantically, she tried to push herself away from the wall, as she was rolled against it with the force of the water, until she was spewed bodily through an open window. She had the sensation of swift and erratic movement, and things kept banging against her. She felt no great pain, only a panicky need for air as she fought desperately to surface.

Sam Gordon, influenced by necessity, had decided that Anjer would not, after all, be the worst place in the world for his son to be born. He had been very favourably impressed by the town, and as the patched-up *Roamer*, in the predawn dimness, held a course parallel to the east coast of Sumatra, he was looking forward not only to being with Jessica but to seeing the Bergs. Conrad had offered to show him the sights of the area, and perhaps, before Jessica was too far along, they would be able to take some short jaunts into the countryside.

He pictured himself at some time in the future telling his son about his place of birth, about the pleasant bay, the shores with their fringe of coconut palms blending into the dense jungle. "It was a pretty little town," he would tell his son. "The streets were bordered by overhanging trees, so that everything was shady. From the harbour, all you could see were the red-tiled roofs of the houses and the lush, surrounding valley."

Sam's first indication that all was not so serene in Anjer came when the day dawned with strong breezes and heavy skies to the south. The clouds had an odd, threatening darkness, unlike anything he had ever seen at sea. And, as the *Roamer* beat onward, he began to smell what seemed to be smoke.

It was the first mate who called his attention to the barometer. It was rising and falling swiftly and erratically, sometimes changing almost an inch in a quarter hour. Sam was puzzled, for there was no logical explanation for such rapid change in atmospheric pressure. Then, over the sound of the wind, in the rigging, he began to hear dull, distant boomings, like a half dozen warships exchanging broadsides; and with the sounds came ash, light at first, covering every surface of the ship with a fine coating.

Despite growing apprehension, Sam held his course through the morning and afternoon hours, but as the *Roamer* approached the entrance to the strait, premature darkness closed over her. Now bits of warm pumice stone were mixed with the fallen ash, and the deck was covered nearly an inch deep, as if they had sailed through a dense storm of grey snow. Sam had hoped to reach Anjer before noon, take on a pilot, and be reunited with Jessica straightaway, but he had the safety of his crew and cargo to consider. By quick work, the company's agent in Singapore had secured a cargo of coal for the *Roamer*, which was preferable to ballast, and it was

255

destined for the coaling station just outside Anjer. Sam decided, consequently, to anchor and wait out the unusually dark night. The wisdom of his decision was confirmed, even as the seamen were dropping the hook, by the sighting of the lights of another vessel quite nearby, also at anchor. Sam called his signalman and had him flash the name of his ship and an inquiry.

The nearby vessel answered that she was the *W.H. Besse*, and that a volcano, its identity unknown, was in eruption at the other end of the strait.

"Condition Anjer," Sam had the signalman inquire.

"Unknown" was the answer.

For Sam, sleep was out of the question. He prowled the ship, exchanging comments with the men about the unusual conditions and the volcanos in the vicinity. Although the ash was still falling and the distant rumbling of the volcanic eruption was a constant, dull presence, he had no real fear for the ship. It was Jessica who occupied his mind. If the volcano was at the other end of the strait, it was quite near Anjer.

He went to his cabin, pored over his charts—which were unhelpful as to the location of volcanos—and entered the day's events in his log, recording in detail his observations of the conditions. He was sent running back on deck when, with cracks like nearby cannon, lightning flashes began to play around the *Roamer*'s masts. His head and shoulders were pelted by falling fragments of pumice, and the ash shower had intensified. As he watched in horror, a huge fireball of lightning flashed down the mainmast and tumbled about on the deck. He felt a severe, tingling jolt in his arm, and hearing a seaman shouting his name, he turned and made his way aft.

"Look here, Captain," the seaman said, with an awed expression, and pointing over the taffrail.

Sam leaned over to look. The copper sheathing of the exposed portions of the rudder had been heated to glowing. Fearing that the heat would start the rudder's wooden core burning, he immediately ordered seawater to be drawn and poured over the sheathing.

The sky was in foment, one moment an intense, inky black, the next brilliantly lit by the lightning flashes. And always there was the sound of the distant blasts of the volcano.

Sam called his first mate. "Turn out all hands. I want all the rigging and canvas wet down, and I want wet sailcloth lashed over the hatches. I want everything that could burn wet down and kept wet." It would take a great deal of heat to ignite the cargo of coal, he knew, but the fireballs and hot pumice were a definite danger. Sam watched as his orders were carried out, and when he was satisfied, he detailed three men to keep the copper sheathing cooled and to continue to keep the sailcloth over the hatches wet, then sent the others below, for it was by now dangerous and uncomfortable to be on deck. As it was, he and the workers had to protect their faces and heads with cowls of sailcloth as the pumice pelted them painfully.

In the early morning, Sam was back on deck when the detonations from the volcano intensified. The sea rose and fell violently under them, and the wind increased. The barometer continued its wild fluctuations, and the magnetic compass went wild, spinning to point in all directions. They caught one glimpse of a swollen, red sun before it was swallowed back up by dense, dark clouds that blocked out the sky and filled their noses with the stench of sulphur. However, the sound of the distant rumblings had eased.

"Mr. Mate," Sam ordered, "turn out all hands. Off watch to clear the decks of this ash. Set sail for Anjer."

Roamer got under way in strong gusts of wind. Again the sky was growing darker, but occasionally the low clouds would part to reveal chaos above them, clouds spinning and rising and falling with a violence never before seen. The harsh, gritty ash increased, and it was hot enough to be painful to bare skin, so that Sam was sweating, half blinded, and choking on the dust in the air. He kept men scurrying into the rigging, wetting down the sails.

It was midmorning when, abruptly, the *Roamer* seemed to shudder, to halt momentarily in her progress, as a devastating boom of sound swept past her. Sam's mind instinctively formed the orders that barked from his lips. "Clew up all sails. Down anchor. Hop to it!"

The anchor was scarcely on the bottom when what felt like a solid wall of wind hit the *Roamer*, in a burst of hurricane force that heeled her over on her beam ends and threatened to break loose the anchor. Sam ordered a spare anchor rigged, and it was on the bottom quickly, with the men working in a shower of ash that limited visibility to less than a yard. As the wind howled and lightning forked all around them, some members of the crew fell to their knees, praying for their souls.

"Captain," called the first mate, "I estimate that the current is running toward the south at about twelve knots."

It took Sam a moment to absorb the implications of the words. The current of a mighty sea had actually reversed itself, and was apparently running in the direction of the volcano. There was no way that Sam could understand that the surrounding waters were being sucked into the maw of the vast, white-hot caldera, forming in the process the giant wave that was moving, even then, to complete the destruction of coastal towns and communities all along the Sunda Strait. And preoccupied as he was by the catastrophe already enveloping them, as well as by his fears for his wife, he could hardly pay heed to the current as a seaman hurried up to him and said, "Cap'n, I think you'd better come take a look. I'm not sure in all this muck, but I think there's smoke coming from the hatches."

The wave that was the result of Krakatoa's final death throes had all but wiped Anjer from the map. It had come in a darkness so total that those who died knew nothing until they were submerged, buried in an instant beneath the masses of trees, broken buildings, and other debris carried before the mighty surge.

It was a hurricane-force blast preceding the wave that had burst in the walls of the Berg house and allowed the waters to sweep through, carrying Jessica before them. Tossed and tumbled, battered, her lungs aching for air, she had given herself, in one fraction of a second of lucidity, to her God. Now she managed to catch one breath as she was carried to the surface of the chaos, before being submerged again, her body fighting for life even though her mind was numbed. She felt a terrific jolt, sensed sharp objects striking her, and all the while flailed desperately for something to cling to as the waters tugged and twisted her. At last she grasped something solid, and her mouth and nose were in the blessed air, which she gulped in, only to gag and choke on the hot ash. There was a mighty roaring beneath her as the wave receded and left her, housetop high, clinging to a fork in a tree.

Her aching arms could hardly hold her, and half in shock she somehow scrambled down, falling the last three feet to land on her backside with a jolt that cleared her head for a moment. She could see nothing but dark grey haze. The roaring sounds continued, and she started crawling, wanting more than anything to avoid being taken by the waters again. Mud and sodden ash covered the ground, making progress difficult.

Ash was still falling, so hot that it was painful to her back and her tender backside. With a cry of despair she realized that she was naked, that all her clothing had been ripped away. She struggled to her feet and ran blindly, slammed into a tree, and tumbled down a slope into water. She tried to scream, gulped seawater, and, coughing and struggling to breathe, began to swim. Her strength was failing in the swirling waters when something soft bumped into her. She seized it, aware that it was hairy. She clutched for better handholds, and the feel of it told her that it was the body of a horse. She pulled herself across it, lying on her stomach, and the baby—*God in Heaven*, she thought, *the baby*—kicked in protest. She adjusted her position to ease the pressure on her stomach.

She feared that the swiftly moving water was carrying her out to sea, but she dared not leave the carcass of the horse, for it supported her in her exhaustion. When movement stopped, and the water was running around her legs, she realized that the carcass had gone aground. She waited and looked around. The air seemed to be clearing. After several minutes, she could see far enough to determine that she was in a rice paddy. The water was no longer moving but lay about in puddles. She tried to stand. Her legs were weak, and all her limbs were beginning to swell and ache from the pounding they had received. In fear, she put her hand to her stomach, and the baby obligingly gave a gentle little kick.

She had no idea in which direction to move, but it seemed imperative to do something. At each step she sank in mud mixed with ash, but she struggled onward until she found higher ground, where she rested for a few minutes. When she began moving again, she found her path blocked by a huge uprooted tree, and as she felt her way around it, her hand encountered a sodden mass caught up in the branches. It was fabric—a torn and battered *sarong*, she realized, but at least it concealed most of her nakedness as she drew it around her. The air had become cold, and she was shivering. Numbed, and only half aware of what she was doing, she wandered onward until she could not walk another step, then sat down against the trunk of a tree and fell into a sleep of exhaustion.

When she awoke, the visibility had improved greatly. At first she did not know what it was that spread out before her. Then she realized it was the sea, but the water was covered with a layer of floating ash and pumice. And all around was ash, giving the landscape a curious, winterlike look. There was no sign of habitation anywhere within her view. The forest was behind her, rising to the far mountains. She guessed that Anjer was to her left as she faced the strait, and she shuddered to think of returning there. If she continued up the shoreline, she reasoned, she would eventually encounter someone. She had taken only a few steps when she stumbled over something soft and choked back nausea as she looked down on a battered corpse, a native woman. She ran, and what was left of her reason was eclipsed by her pain, her exhaustion, and the horror of having stepped on the dead woman.

It was an untold time later when she became aware that she was still walking, as if in a delirium. She seemed to be hearing voices. She moved toward the sound and saw the heartening flicker of a fire. As she approached, she grew conscious of her own appearance. Her bruised body was streaked with blood and ashes, and leeches from the rice paddy still clung to her bare legs. Three Javanese, two men and a boy, were squatting by the fire. They leaped to their feet.

"May I have some water, please," Jessica gasped, half falling to sit on the ground.

One man approached warily.

"Water, please," she whispered.

The man replied in Javanese, and she caught only a tone of anger, and the word *Dutch*. The man was gesturing to the devastation all around, pointing toward Krakatoa. She remembered that Conrad had said the natives blamed the Dutch for the eruption.

"Not Dutch," she said. "I'm Australian. Please."

The man went back to the fire and returned with a water bag, jiggled it in front of her face. He pointed to the golden wedding band on her finger, then made drinking motions.

"You—you want my ring?" she asked.

He went through the pantomime again. "I can't," she said. "It's my wedding ring." She shook her head. The man glowered, turned, motioned the other two to their feet, and they all left, not looking back.

Weeping, Jessica slumped to the ground, and blackness came to her. When she awoke she saw the leeches, panicked, and began tugging at them. Finally she came to her senses and crawled to the smouldering fire, from which she selected a small, half-burnt stick and used its still-hot end to make the creatures fall off. Her legs were swollen and bleeding, and she realized that they had been burned from the hot ashes. In places her skin was peeling away.

Gathering her strength, she made her way along the shore again, into devastation. She passed parts of roofs, ripped from their houses, dead animals, broken trees, and human corpses—a group of a half dozen of them were lodged in the branches of one huge uprooted tree. She now no longer had the capacity to be shocked, and she was thinking only of the baby. Her own pain was unimportant, and it would not even have concerned her had it not had a direct bearing on the health of the baby. If she died, the baby died. Therefore, she must stay alive.

Her hair had come down, and it interfered with her vision. Her eyes were burning from the ash, although the air was almost clear now, and the sun, thus exposed, made for a heat that sent rivulets of perspiration coursing down her brow and temples. She wiped her eyes, tied her hair into a rough bun, and struggled onward.

At length, she became aware that the day was ending; it seemed that she had been walking forever. For some time, she had been angling away from the shore to rising ground. When she saw the glow of another fire, she thought at first that she might be imagining it, that she was doomed to wander lost in the growing denseness of the trees and undergrowth; but as she neared the light, she saw that it was in front of a native hut, which itself was much worse for the events of the night.

An old, white-haired native man was sitting alone by the fire. Hearing her approach, he leaped up, seized an ancient musket and, levelling it, barked a question in his native tongue.

"Help me," Jessica said in English.

The old man lowered the gun. "Who?" he asked in English.

"Help me," Jessica begged, staggering into the firelight and collapsing.

He put the gun down, bent over her, and shook his head. Hardly an inch of her exposed skin was not bruised or burned. Gently he placed his hand on her stomach, and he sighed when he felt movement under it. He was not strong enough to lift her, but he put his hands under her arms and dragged her toward the hut, her bare feet making trails in the volcanic dust. Inside he wrestled her onto a rude cot. He had water, and he used some of it to clean her face and the worst of her wounds. In the light of one short candle he applied leafy poultices to her cuts and abrasions, cocoa butter to her burns.

During the night the fever came. The old man sat by her side, dripping water into her burning mouth from the same cloth he used to cool her forehead. Now and again he would place his hand on her stomach.

The coal in the *Roamer*'s midship hold had been smouldering throughout the day. Somehow the heat and fire of the volcanic outburst had ignited the cargo, and Sam, after having had men remove the sailcloth covering and open the hatch, had determined through the thickening smoke that the fire was deep down, for the top layers of coal were merely hot to the touch. He had ordered the pumps manned, and he estimated that by now some hundreds of gallons of seawater had been pumped into the main hold; but the fire was still smoking.

Sam was well aware that the situation was critical, for the partial combustion of the coal would be creating flammable gases. At any time the glowing fire could lick into flames and the collecting gases could explode, lifting the *Roamer*'s deck or tearing out her sides.

He had already ordered the lifeboats lowered just in case. Meantime, water was being pumped from the bilges, but not nearly as fast as it was accumulating in the hold. Consequently the *Roamer* was becoming heavy in the water—but that was the least of Sam's problems.

The final wave from Krakatoa had lost some of its force as it moved northward up the strait, but it was still large enough to engulf any ship and owing to the poor visibility, the wall of ash-covered water was not seen by the lookout until it was almost upon them. The warning came in the form of a forced, harsh scream, and Sam looked up, his mind could harly comprehend what he was seeing. A solid curtain of grey, reaching almost to the masthead, was speeding toward the ship and would be upon them before any action could be taken. By God's grace, the wind had swung the *Roamer* on her anchor lines so that the bow was to the wave. A few man scrambled for the rigging, as if in hope of climbing beyond the reach of the wave, but no one got more than a few feet above deck before the *Roamer*'s bow reared upward like the head of a panicked stallion and rose nearly to the vertical on the forward wall of onrushing water. She climbed up, seemingly endlessly, as Sam clung to a line, his feet dangling helplessly, and then, with a sickening whiplike suddenness, she plunged over the top and smashed down in a mighty spray of inky, ash-polluted water.

One of the men who fell from the rigging landed almost at Sam's feet, but his fall was cushioned by the ash on the deck. The smaller anchor had been ripped from the seabed, and *Roamer*, listing heavily, began to swing on the other cable until the anchor found a new hold. The sudden motion of the ship had apparently shifted the cargo slightly, allowing air to reach the smouldering fire, and smoke was now issuing from cracks in the decking.

Miraculously, most of the crew seemed unhurt, and Sam ordered the flow of water from the pumps to be increased. As well founder her as to have her burn, he decided.

During the next few hours, the *Roamer* began to sink deeper and deeper with the water in her, and Sam knew that if another wave of the same size came she would, most probably, be driven under. He had to lighten her. He ordered the stern cargo hatch opened, and smoke rolled out, which meant the combustion had spread. Still, it was just possible for a man to leap down and, half holding his breath, shovel out a few lumps of coal before he had to be relieved because of the smoke and the heat. Sam took his turn with the rest, heaving the coal up with a scoop, hearing it thud into the ash on the deck. Men on deck shovelled the coal overboard.

By late afternoon the visibility was greatly improved. Sam could see the dim outline of the Java shore, and he ached to know what had happened there. He could not bring himself to consider that Jessica might be dead. She was there, and only the fire in his hold was keeping him from her. Thus the fire took on the property of a personal enemy, and he worked without pause alongside his men, taking his turn at shovelling, taking his turn at the pumps.

With the coming of night, the *Roamer* was so deep in the water that Sam had to cut the flow of water into the holds, lest her decks become awash. The smoke, which had not diminished, now seemed to be coming from every crack and pore of the deck and hatches. With a dampened bandanna over his face, Sam went back into the after hold. Now the coal had to be passed up in containers, for the hard, sickening work had removed several feet of the cargo—although not enough to balance out the weight of the accumulating water in the bilges. He worked until he saw patches of red in front of his eyes and was in danger of being overcome by the smoke; then he was lifted out and vomited on the ashy deck.

"Don't worry, sir," a seaman said, "she won't get this ship." The men, like Sam, had come to view the fire as a personal enemy, and not one of them slacked off during the long night that followed. With the dawn, the smoke was not as all-pervasive. Sam cut down again on the water being pumped into the holds and put more men on the bilge pumps, and slowly, through the morning, the *Roamer* began to lift herself. But all that day and into the night the men remained sleepless, staggering in exhaustion, fighting the glowing demon in the depths of the hold. It was just past midnight when the first mate called down to Sam, who was working again, shovelling coal into buckets to be drawn up and cast overboard. "Cap'n, I think we've got her. There's no smoke at all."

An inspection of the midships hold confirmed his words. The coal glistened wetly, and it was no longer warm to the touch.

"Give the starboard watch an hour's rest," Sam directed. "Keep a trickle of water running into the hold. Keep the bilge pumps going until she's riding normally."

"If I may suggest, sir," the mate said, "perhaps you should take a rest with the starboard watch."

"You're starboard watch, Mr. Mate," Sam said. He managed a sooty, narrow grin. "Have a good nap."

It was not until August 28 that the *Roamer* approached the bay at Anjer. Sam was in the bow. There was no sign of a pilot boat, but he knew the entrance to the port well enough. On shore were scenes that filled his heart with fear. Of the buildings of Anjer, not one was intact. The town had simply disappeared, leaving muddy, ashen waste littered with fragments of what had once been hotels, businesses, homes. A Dutch ship was in the bay. Sam signalled.

"Where survivors?"

His heart ached with the answer: "No survivors."

He took the gig ashore, walked through knee-deep mud and sodden ash, and saw men from the Dutch ship recovering bodies, some almost unrecognizable as having once been human beings. He made his way up the slope and was not even sure that he was in the spot where the Berg House had once stood. Two Dutch sailors was coming down the slope with a small burden wrapped in burlap. They halted near Sam.

"A baby," one of them said. "It was caught in a tree, at least twenty feet off the ground. Up there." He pointed. The wave had reached high on the hill.

"This was the Berg house," the other sailor said, in his heavily accented English. He pointed to a stone foundation. "They had a small boy, like this one."

"No one survived?" Sam asked.

The Dutchman looked away. He lifted one hand in a hopeless gesture. "Look around you."

"It is said that it is like this all along the shore of the strait," the first sailor said. "God only knows how many thousands are dead."

"Perhaps some escaped to higher ground inland," Sam said, unwilling to accept the inevitable.

"If so, God help them," the sailor said. "There are wild boars, tigers, deadly snakes. If one did not know the jungle—"

Sam returned to the ship. There was not, of course, any possibility of offloading the remaining coal at Anjer. He lay at anchor for another day, hoping against hope, and when he tried to enlist someone who knew the country to scout inland with him, he was told politely that it was useless. He made one abortive attempt at going into the jungle himself but quickly realized that it would take a lifetime to search the steaming, almost impenetrable wilderness. He could not imagine Jessica going into the jungle.

He felt as if his life had ended. Nothing seemed worth the while—but there was the ship. He had his responsibilities to the ship, to her crew, to Alfred Childers. He took the *Roamer* out into the strait, where the water was still littered with floating pumice, and with a dull heart set a course for Saint Nicholas Point. Perhaps he could offload the remaining coal at Batavia.

The waves had brought destruction to Batavia as well. Eighteen separate waves had been recorded by instruments. Boats had been tossed ashore in the rivers, with many people drowned. The town's quays had been damaged, but, in less than a week after his arrival, Sam had, through agents, sold the remaining coal. He telgraphed to the Childers offices in London that he was taking the *Roamer* back into the Sunda Strait to search for his wife. He was back in Anjer in early September.

CHAPTER XV

The search for bodies was still going on when Sam anchored in the bay. He went ashore, and his black gloom was lightened somewhat when he learned that there had been a few survivors, after all. He talked to a pilot named de Vries who had saved himself by clinging to a palm tree when the mighty waters rolled over the town. De Vries had walked to a nearby village, Serang. He had returned to Anjer to view the devastation.

There was some amusement and no little disbelief among the Dutch rescue workers regarding the story of a native who claimed to have saved himself by climbing onto the back of a swimming crocodile.

Peter Schruit, who had outrun the first of the giant waves, had escaped from Anjer before the final titanic wave destroyed all. Sam listened to his story with great hope, for Schruit had met other survivors at a village where the natives had helped by giving them cooked food. Schruit had walked back to Anjer after the wave to see no trees, no houses, nothing to indicate that a thriving town had stood on the site.

By small boat, Sam went to other sites along the shore. He heard stories of horror, of how the natives, blaming the Dutch for the devastation, had turned away dying white survivors, or had sold food and water in exchange for jewellery. Everywhere he went he questioned the survivors, most of them natives, about a pregnant woman, but no one had seen Jessica. The few white survivors, still stunned, shook their heads. No woman six months into term could possibly have survived, was their opinion. If she had managed to escape the wave, she would have perished in the jungles.

Little by little, from reports by survivors on land and from observers on ships in the area, the picture of the catastrophe began to become clear. The coastline of the strait had been devastated by ash, fire, and water. In southern Sumatra thousands had died, burned by the ash and hot pumice, and elsewhere victims had suffered painful burns. But it was the water that had done the most destruction. The Dutch had dispatched ships to the worst-stricken areas. It would be months before even an approximate estimate of the death toll could be made, but already it was clear that the toll would be in the tens of thousands. More than 160 villages had been totally destroyed, another 130 or more seriously battered.

An investigation of Krakatoa itself had revealed that the entire northern part of the island no longer existed. Where once had been land there were now ocean depths that could not be plumbed with twelve hundred feet of line.

Sam, occupied with his desperate efforts to find Jessica, paid scant attention to the reports. Even with the help of many of his crew, however, the search was in vain. No one had seen or heard of a survivor matching Jessica's description.

There came a time, late in September, when he could no longer justify his staying in Java. The last of the survivors had been found in odd locations along the straits. Two sympathetic Dutchman had accompanied Sam on several short ventures into the hills behind Anjer, but the few natives encountered were more concerned with the loss of their crops—the ash fall had done tremendous damage—than in helping a white man find his lost wife. In the end he stood on the *Roamer*'s deck, took one last look at the Java coast, and ordered the anchor raised, sails set.

When the *Roamer* arrived in Sydney, he found that people there were still talking about the disaster in Java, and that the scientists of the world were busy tabulating statistics. Krakatoa's expelled dust had caused twilight over an area of more than three hundred thousand miles. The sound of her final paroxysm had been heard—and had caused various reactions—in Singapore, Manila, New Guinea, and, most remarkably, on the island of Rodrigues, 2,968 miles away in the Indian Ocean. The tidal waves had been recorded in London, in South Africa, by the German scientific expedition at New Georgia near the Antarctic, and in Australia and New Zealand.

Magdalen Broome, who had been agitating by letter to be allowed to rejoin Red in Hong Kong, had been trying since the news of the disaster reached Sydney to get word of her daughter. "Why haven't they telegraphed?" she kept asking. By looking at maps she had seen that Anjer, where Jessica was visiting the Bergs, was disturbingly close to the volcano, and there were, of course, the horrendous reports of the damage done all along the coastline of the Sunda Strait.

"Why do I not hear?" she asked.

The answer was in Sam's face when she opened the door at his unannounced knock. She had to look at him twice to recognize him. He was thin, his face drawn, his eyes leaden. She embraced him, even as she felt a great welling up of sorrow. For weeks she had denied that which, in her heart, she knew must be true. Jessica was dead. Sam's face, and the absence of reassuring words, told all. She led him into the parlour and he sat down heavily, not able to look at her.

"As long as there was hope," he said finally, and seemed unable to continue.

"Oh, Sam," she said, kneeling by the chair, putting her hand on his arm.

"I looked for her," he said. "God knows I looked for her."

"I know you did," Magdalen said. "I was able to find out through the Childers agents that *Roamer* had delivered her cargo to Batavia and gone back to Anjer."

"Magdalen, I'm sorry. I shouldn't have—"

"Hush," she said. "You will not blame yourself, do you understand? Her place was with you, near you, and in her letters she told me she was enjoying her visit with the Bergs. I know that it sounds empty, Sam, but it was God's will, and even if we don't understand why—"

He made a pained sound and looked away.

"You're hungry."

"No."

"Then you will, this minute, go up, have a hot bath, and get some rest."

It didn't matter. He let her bully him lovingly into doing what she ordered, knew that he would not be able to sleep, but fell into blessed unconsciousness the minute his head hit the pillow.

Magdalen had a painful chore to perform. She laboured over a

269

telegram to be sent to Red but found the words nearly impossible to put down.

"Samuel here. Jessica apparently killed Krakatoa. Not worry about me. Your duty first."

Then she set about writing a letter, and it was many hours before it was finished, for she had difficulty seeing through her tears.

A memorial service for Jessica was held three days later. Sam looked only marginally better, although Magdalen had been successful in coaxing him into eating more or less regularly. Kitty Broome had insisted on being at the ceremony, although she had not yet fully recovered her strength from the birth of a son, christened Patrick Cadogan Broome. Johnny, after the ceremony, when the family party had returned to the Broome house, joined Sam alone in Red's study and offered him a cigar. Sam took it, and Johnny lit it for him.

"I hope you don't mind," Johnny said. "I've interviewed the men on your ship regarding their impressions of the great eruption."

"No," Sam answered dully. "Not at all."

"Quite a battle you had with the fire in the hold. It makes a whale of a story. I've written it. Perhaps you'd like to go over it before I print it, to see if I'm on target."

Sam was remembering how he and Jessica had stood on the deck of the *Roamer* on the approach to Java, smelling the wind-borne scent of a million blooms, the sweet, damp, almost too powerful odour of that verdant land. He shrugged.

"The first mate allowed me to copy your log entries."

"I can't say enough in praise of my crew," Sam managed, and for all that the words sounded hollow, he meant them sincerely.

"Well, the captain also comes off well in my account," Johnny went on. "Here." He handed Sam a sheaf of papers.

The writing seemed to blur to Sam. "Just don't try to make me a hero," he said, and contrived a weak smile.

"No man can make a hero of another." Johnny took the offered papers back. "It's a self-done job. By the way, your first mate said to tell you that there's a cargo of wool for the *Roamer*. England. It will be ready in less than a week."

Sam felt a wrench of pain. He had left Jessica in Java, but here in her home he felt close to her. To think of going to sea without her was, he feared, more than he could bear. Still, he could not stay in Sydney forever, with Magdalen fussing over him, treating him as an invalid. After all, her loss was just as great as his own, if not greater.

Telling himself that life went on, Sam walked to the ship the next day, to find that the crew had removed all traces of the ash and had the *Roamer* looking as handsome as ever. He was greeted with respect and sympathy by his officers, and then he went to work, personally supervising the loading of the wool. The *Roamer* was due to sail in three days when the telegram came from his great-uncle, Jock Willis.

"Congratulations saving *Roamer*," it read. "Time come home. *Cuttysark* Sydney November 1. Take captaincy."

So at last his dream, the dream that had begun even before the *Cutty Sark*'s keelblocks had been laid, was to come true, and the taste of it in his mouth was as bitter as the ashes of Krakatoa. Had Jessica been at his side he might have danced a jig of happiness. Without her, however, his triumph was empty. He had his responsibility to Alfred Childers, who had given him his first ship; but that same afternoon he was relieved of any worry on that score by a visit from Childers's agent in Sydney, who told him that Jock Willis had spoken with Childers and that Childers had, with reluctance, agreed not to stand in Sam's way.

The first mate, who had the crew's respect and was a fine seaman, would take the *Roamer* to England. Sam went back to the Elizabeth Bay house, where Magdalen was delighted to hear that he would be staying for a while longer and that he was to have the ship he loved, the *Cutty Sark*.

"Jessica would be so proud of you," Magdalen said, and the words cut straight to Sam's heart.

Caroline Fisher was awakened by a soft hand on her shoulder. For a moment she was totally disoriented, and then she seemed to swim up from green depths, out of the dreamy world in which she usually found herself, into a moment of painful clarity. Her face contorted as she realized that Martha Blevins had awakened her before eight o'clock. Resentment filled her, because now she would have to face a long, long day, when ordinarily she slept until well after ten.

"I'm sorry," Martha said, "but there are some diggers downstairs and they won't leave."

"Diggers?"

"Or farmers—what's the difference?"

"What do they want?"

"They want to see the mister," Martha said, "and when I told them he was in Melbourne, they said they'd speak to you."

"Send them away," Caroline ordered.

"Haven't I tried?" Martha stepped to the window and peeped through the drawn curtains, and when she spoke with her back turned, her voice was raised so that Caroline could not help but hear. "If she wants them camping out on the lawn all day, then that's her affair."

Caroline did not hurry her dressing. She selected each garment with care and managed to endure the ordeal of getting into everything with the aid of liberal swallows of brandy from a bottle hidden at the back of her wardrobe. However, not even the fiery spirit blurred the harsh edges of her mind. Most of the time she seemed to float in a comfortable sea, a sort of dense, liquid enveloping of her mind that prevented thought, but on this morning she remembered all too clearly that she was a woman alone, for all practical purposes. Marcus came seldom to the house, and when he came there was always unpleasantness.

She staggered weakly down the stairs, clining to the polished handrail for support. Martha was in the hallway.

"Well, are you going to speak to them?" Martha demanded.

"Yes," Caroline said. "Bring them in."

"I think it would be best if you go outside."

Caroline started a retort but, on second impulse, withheld it. She followed Martha to the front door, and when it was opened she saw three ragged urchins sitting disconsolately on the grass. A bone-thin woman stood, arms hanging loosely at her sides, behind the children. On the drive was a well-used farm wagon with odd pieces of furnishings and bundles packed into its bed. It was drawn by a team of horses that looked as if they hadn't been fed in years.

"Good morning," Caroline said. "Just what seems to be the problem?"

"I'm sorry to bother you, ma'am," the woman said, her voice not reflecting the meek and hungry look of her. "It was Mr. Marcus Fisher I came to see, but since he's not here—"

"I have nothing to do with my husband's business," Caroline cut her off.

"Well, I had something to do with *my* husband's business," the thin woman said, "which was farming. Farming our own land, paid for with our life's savings. I saw him work himself to death trying to hang on to that piece of land for me and these." She indicated the children.

"I'm sorry," Caroline said. "But I don't see—"

"I wanted *Mr.* Marcus Fisher to witness what he'd done," the woman said. "But maybe you can look and tell him. My Ralph is dead. First you cut us off from our water, so that we couldn't even drive our cattle and our horses down to drink, and then you came and offered my Ralph a loan of money. I told him not to take it. But he did, and then when we couldn't pay, you came and took our home."

"I had nothing to do with it," Caroline said.

"You, your husband, all of you, all of you grand folk who think you can run roughshod over all like us, you did it. Now these are homeless, and they're fatherless. I just wanted you to see them, so you can tell Marcus Fisher that it's not just land, that there are people, real people, who suffer for his greed."

"I think you'd better go," Caroline said, feeling suddenly ill.

"Yes, I'll go," the woman answered. "But I'll leave behind me the curse of God on you and on your husband and all like you. May you all rot in hell!"

"Charming," Caroline muttered to herself, but there was something in the woman's courage that touched her, and the dirty, pinched faces of the children haunted her jumbled thoughts as the old farm wagon creaked and bounced down the drive. She ate her breakfast obediently, without resorting to the brandy bottle, and as she finished she was thinking more clearly than she had in a long time. She knew that Marcus was not only a coward, but a ruthlessly ambitious man. She knew that he had been investing profits from his trade to expand his landholdings, but she had never before seen the human results of his dealings. For some reason, at that moment, she thought of her son.

"Martha, you and I are going into Melbourne."

"We are definitely not going into Melbourne," Martha replied. "You know that the mister doesn't like you leaving the house."

"It is the mister, as you say, that I am going to see," Caroline snapped back.

She returned to her room and, with shaking hands, applied powder and rouge to hide the ravages of drink and time, and when she came downstairs again she paused to inspect herself in the large mirror in the entry hall.

"Well, don't you look lovely," Martha commented, with a rare sincerity in her tone. She had already had the outside man prepare the carriage, and the trip into town was a pleasant one, with Caroline commenting on passing things with a clarity of perception that she herself found surprising. The driver took them through bustling streets to the building that housed Marcus Fisher's offices. Inside—Caroline had visited only on two other occasions she could recall—there was new wood panelling, adorned with expensive paintings that looked to be from London, and luxurious draperies. A neatly dressed male secretary inquired about their business, and when Caroline gave the man her name, he looked at her with curiosity.

Marcus was standing behind his desk when she was ushered into his office. "What are you doing here?" he demanded.

"It's time we had a few things settled, Marcus."

"The only issues we have in common were settled long ago," he replied; but he looked curious, Catoline noted with satisfaction, even uneasy.

"You're doing very well, it appears." She helped herself to a chair and slowly and deliberately arranged her skirts, enjoying his evident discomfort.

"If it's money you want, that mausoleum of yours is already costing too much to maintain," he said.

"No, there's no need for more money. I had visitors today."

"So?"

"A woman and her children. She cursed me and you for having taken her land."

Marcus was still standing. "For God's sake! You bother me with such trivialities?"

"It wasn't trivial to her."

"Woman, go home," he said harshly. "This is none of your business."

Caroline held her ground. "It becomes my business when people you have wronged put a curse from God on *my* head."

"Get out of here," he said, coming around his desk.

"I'm going." Caroline quickly stood. Despite her temporary panic, words came to her with a force that made her heart surge with joy. "I'm going for good! I'll have my lawyer contact you. I'll be very modest in asking for a settlement." She paused, dizzied by her sudden decision, by her own courage.

"You miserable—you—" Marcus was turning bright red and continued to approach threateningly as Caroline retreated toward the door.

"There are so many things about you that I abhor, Marcus," she said, "but I think it is your pretentiousness that I dislike most."

He raised his hand.

"If you strike me, I shall scream and have Martha call the constabulary." Caroline had a hand on the doorknob, but she did not open the door. Surprised by her own hesitation, she wondered where she was finding the courage to defy him.

"So you want a divorce?" he blustered; then to Caroline's discomfiture, he broke into a smile.

"Yes," she confirmed, still defiant.

"On what grounds, madam?"

"Grounds?" she echoed, and confusion came to her.

"There are several grounds for divorce," he said. "Sodomy, cruelty, desertion. Of which will you charge me?"

"Does it—does it have to be something like *that*?" she asked weakly.

"On the other hand, I could divorce *you*." His smile widened. "You are a drunk, and that is grounds. I have not been in your bed, madam, for over two years, and that is grounds."

"That—that was your—choice."

"Or, perhaps, I can have you confined to a mental institution for five years," he went on, sounding confident now. "No problem there, since you would, no doubt, go through your act as grand lady of the manor and feed the swans before the judge."

"Marcus—" She gasped the word; she wanted a drink so badly that she could taste it on her tongue.

"But, sadly, much as I would welcome it, there will be no divorce," he said. "You will go back to your home, madam, and you will stay there."

"No," she said, the thought of returning to the house suddenly repugnant to her. She regained some of her determination. "We have to talk."

"Talk, then," he challenged.

"Marcus, I feel badly about that poor woman."

He laughed. "That's life, my dear. The weak and foolish ones don't last. They come out here expecting to be able to pick up gold nuggets off the surface, and when they're faced with a little bit of work they start snivelling and begging the government to *give* them gold. They take advantage of the liberal weakness of the government to move into lands that have, traditionally, been grazing lands, and then they weep and moan when they don't have the guts to make it. Don't waste your concern on them. Let them go back to London or Birmingham, to the slums from which they came."

"But you have so much, Marcus. You and the others. Isn't there room for people like that poor woman? All they want is a small piece of land on which they can grow food, run a few cattle, have a decent life."

Marcus's scorn was evident in his expression. "You're speaking of matters that you can't possibly understand. I don't know what's come over you, but I've certainly had enough. Now go."

Caroline's heart was pounding, and she felt unbearably hot. "All right then." She opened the door, then again hesitated. "It is true that at the moment I don't have much knowledge about these matters. I know, however, that there are efforts under way to make a place for small farmers. It has to do with unification. I know. I read the newspapers." Actually, the plight of the smallholders had rarely before entered her thoughts, but Caroline clung to the subject half out of perversity. She knew it infuriated Marcus.

"Newpapers!" He fairly spat the word. "You're soft in the head."

"I don't like what you're doing," she said. "I don't like having poor people come to my house cursing me in the name of God."

"Go home, Caroline." He pushed past her and called Martha, who was standing nervously in the outer office. "Mrs. Fisher is ready to go home," he said.

"Yes," Caroline swept imperiously to the front door. "Come Martha. I've finished my business." But in the carriage she began to tremble, and soon she took a silver flask from her handbag. The bite of the brandy made her want to close her eyes and sleep, but her mind was racing with disconnected thoughts. What had got into her?

They were at home before dark, and as the carriage rolled up the drive, she said, "I don't see the swans, Martha. Where are the swans?"

She was sleeping soundly when Marcus Fisher entered her bedroom just before midnight. He lit a lamp and looked down upon her drink-flushed face, fashioned a gag from some silken scarfs, and before she was awake had stuffed her mouth with it. She sat up, choking, and her eyes went wide. His fist thudded into her torso just below her breasts, slamming her back down.

"So you're going to fight me," he said. He was smiling.

She tried to scream, but the sound was muffled. Martha was three doors down the hall, but she was a sound sleeper. Caroline tried to avoid his next blow, but it landed in her ribs painfully.

"You anger me," Fisher said, still smiling. "You try me to the utmost." He struck with his fists on her thighs, on her stomach, leaving her fearful, in her agony, that she was going to vomit and thus suffocate herself. The blows came so fast that she had no time to prepare. She drifted into a red daze.

"Hear me and hear me well," his voice said.

The blows were no longer falling. She was oddly grateful. She followed the movement of his lips with wide, teary eyes.

"You will not talk nonsense for unification. Do you understand?"
She nodded vigourously, eager to please him, to do anything to keep him from hitting her again.

The woman who had awaited Marcus Fisher in his carriage was buxom, blonde, and young. "You took a long time," she said. "Who lives there?"

"A crazy old woman." He slapped the reins to set the horses in motion, and he drove back into town at an invigourating pace. He dropped the woman on the way to his town house and went to sleep feeling that it had been a satisfactory evening.

Only the next morning, as he returned to his office, did he have second thoughts about the wisdom of his actions. Caroline had seemed almost lucid when she was in his office, and if she had enough courage to report the beating he had given her, there could be nasty repercussions. However, as the morning passed, his thoughts became occupied with other, more pressing, matters. For one, Bartholomew Jamison had recently returned from Samoa with a boatload of kanakas, and their papers had been sold at very favourable prices. The profits would be invested in more land, but he had not yet decided where. Toward midafternoon, one of his newest and more valuable employees asked to see him, and he told the secretary to send the young man in immediately.

Harry Ryan sat down and crossed his legs. "I have the reports on trading activity here, Mr. Fisher."

"Good, Harry. You're doing a splendid job."

"I've managed to find a source in Van Buren's Hong Kong office. Van Buren is contracted to deliver—"

"Don't bother with details at the moment," Fisher said, waving a hand dismissively. "Just leave it with me."

"Yes, sir." Harry started to rise.

"No—don't go just yet." Fisher went to the sideboard, poured two large glasses of brandy, and handed one to Harry. "As I said, I'm pleased with you, my boy. You're a valuable addition to the firm. You do the work you're asked to do, and you don't ask questions. I have some big plans for you."

"Thank you." Harry took a large gulp of his drink.

"Do you know what you're building?"

Harry's face was expressionless, although a hint of colour suffused the scar on his cheek. "What I'm putting together, Mr. Fisher—with your help, of course—is the finest commercial spy network this side of Europe. We will know the movements of every ship in the Orient and the Western Pacific. We'll know what every ship is carrying and, in many cases, what they're contracted to carry in the future."

"*Every* ship," Fisher stressed.

"Yes—although I don't really understand the necessity of keeping track of naval vessels."

"Knowledge is power," Fisher said. "It's just a little bonus of

278

information, that's all. Keeps our men in the various ports on their toes."

"Well, if that's all, sir?" Harry had finished his drink.

"Yes, for now. Keep up the good work, Harry."

When Ryan was gone, Marcus looked over the reports. He himself would separate out the reports of movements of British warships, to be sent to Maxim Stoltz. That information was, in fact, more than a little bonus of knowledge, for Stoltz was paying handsomely for it. Marcus had considered long and hard before agreeing to supply military information to the German, but in the end Stoltz's generosity—and the cumulative benefits of Marcus's other business dealings with the German—had swayed him. After all, anyone who cared to monitor the various ports in that part of the world could have supplied the mundane facts of ship movements. Marcus was sure, in spite of Germany's posturing, that there would not be a war. Bismarck could not hope to win more than a temporary victory in some tropical backwater before the might of the Royal Navy was brought to bear to sweep Germany from the high seas.

Whistling a patriotic tune to himself, Marcus spread the papers on his desk and applied himself to the task at hand.

CHAPTER XVI

Red Broome had known for some time that, as far as the Royal Navy went, the age of sail was over. The use of ironclad steamers in the American Civil War two decades earlier had sounded an ominous knell for sail on ships of war; and the use of screw propeller vessels in the Crimean War had convinced even the tradition-bound Admiralty that the future lay in grunting, stinking steamers. In that odd mother country of his, public opinion often had powerful effects on official policy, and the uproar over the loss of the *Captain* in 1870 had brought definite changes in naval architecture, for in a compromise of design the *Captain* and her sister ship, *Monarch*, had carried, in addition to their steam engines, fully rigged spars and huge spreads of canvas. *Captain* was thus, with all the rigging and heavy turrets for her guns, top-heavy. She had capsized with the loss of almost her entire crew in the Bay of Biscay, and a new ship of the Royal Navy never carried spars after that.

There was not, however, agreement on just what should replace the old square-riggers. The Royal Navy in 1883 was a hodgepodge of experimental designs, with no more than two ships being alike. In distant outposts like Hong Kong, the composite ships—steamers carrying sails—still were the rule, and three of the ships at Red Broome's disposal were of that type. He, however, had been given, only a month earlier, a new steam cruiser, H.M.S. *Calliope*, which mounted four twelve-inch guns in turrets amidship.

It took some time getting used to, not having sails. Red had grown up under the sail, and he missed the canted deck, the whistle of wind in the rigging, the smell of tar and canvas. However, if a man had a dangerous job to do, as he did, he deserved the finest tools available, and the *Calliope* was a fine-edged weapon. Her armor could absorb a great deal of punishment, while her four rifled cannon could deal out incredible destruction. There were, most certainly, no Chinese pirates who had the armament to stand against the *Calliope*.

In the months since he and Adam Shannon had led the attack on Han-Kuang's island, Red's squadron had been kept busy making mostly fruitless sweep and search forays. The Admiralty and the Colonial Office had taken a dim view of the direct assault, citing the losses of sailors and soldiers as reason for confining the battle against the Chinese pirates to the sea. But it was obvious that the strategy was not working. The small junks used by the pirates could slip through waters that were too shallow for the smallest of Red's ships. Meanwhile, British shipping losses were growing. Lives were being lost, for once the pirates took a ship they were merciless. A growing clamour of protest was reaching the top levels of government both in England and in Australia, and Red and Adam had sent joint requests up the chain of command to be allowed to carry the fight to where it would count, to the pirate strongholds. When they received word that Sir Reginald Peckwith was once again coming to Hong Kong, they both hoped that his arrival would signal a change in the policy that had effectively prevented them from attacking the pirates' lairs.

Peckwith had apparently learned to adapt to tropical climates, for this time he was dressed sensibly in white linen. He briefly queried Red and Adam about the recent volcanic eruption in the Sunda Strait—which they could tell him little about, having heard only wild rumours—and then he got directly to the point.

"The government feels that something must be done," he said, pacing Adam's office, "and your recommendation for direct action has been approved."

Red met Adam's gaze and smiled, but neither of them gave voice to what they were thinking—that such a decision should have been made months, if not years, ago.

"I assume, gentlemen, knowing you, that you already have a plan of action prepared," Peckwith said.

Adam rose and spread a map of the China coast on his desk. "Here," he said, indicating a deep, sheltered bay south of Macao. "Here is the headquarters of our old friend Han-Kuang. Piracy is becoming more popular out here, since the Chinese know that we're not going to come marching into their strongholds, and

Han-Kuang is certainly not the only organized pirate leader. But he's the most dangerous, in our estimation, and he seems to exert an influence over the others, who ape his tactics."

Red nodded in agreement. "Taking Han-Kuang will speak loudly to the others."

"I see." Peckwith studied the map briefly, tracing with his finger the location of the other European-controlled ports. "I wonder, gentlemen, if you have any information to indicate that certain of these Chinese, perhaps your Han-Kuang, have leaned toward alliance with any European nations."

Red again glanced toward Adam, then spoke up. "We have observed, as have others, that the increasing success of the pirates would seem to indicate that they have advance knowledge of sailings. They often seem to know exactly where and when to strike." He paused, to choose his words carefully. "Colonel Shannon and I have wondered about this. We've made discreet inquiries, and we have our suspicions; but as yet we have no reliable intelligence concerning the source of the pirates' information."

"Her Majesty's government is rather curious about the comings and goings of a certain Maxim Stoltz," Peckwith said. "Do you know him?"

"Yes, we do," Adam answered. "He says that he's a journalist. I've met him only once, briefly, but we hear talk, of course—mostly from the local merchants."

"Well, what do they have to say about him?" Peckwith prompted when Adam fell silent

"That he's arrogant, for one. The French hate him. Being German is enough—they look no further than that. The Americans . . . well, I don't think they suspect that he could be more than he seems. The Chinese are not so trusting—but they're suspicious of all foreigners. If you're hinting, Sir Reginald, that it could be the Germans, through Stoltz, who are passing on ship sailings and schedules to the pirates, that is a definite possibility. However, since it is British ships, primarily that are being hit, we've considered the possibility of a British informer."

Peckwith scowled. "Unthinkable."

"But possible," Red added. "However, if I may say, sir, we'd prefer to leave the conspiracies and the intrigue to you. I know

Adam is itching for a fight, and I'd like to get busy readying my squadron for sea."

"I think the phrase could be 'with deliberate haste,' " Peckwith said. "And let's make a lasting impression with this operation, shall we, gentlemen?"

Sir Reginald was surprised when, only two days later, the squadron slipped out of Hong Kong Harbour in the dead of night and, for all practical purposes, disappeared into the China Sea. He had not been told that Adam Shannon's troops had been on alert for weeks, and that Red Broome had kept his ships provisioned and ready for the order that, at last, had come.

With powerful *Calliope* leading, the squadron zigzagged through the coastal shipping lanes, a welcome sight to British merchant vessels, at least. To all appearances, it was nothing more than another search expedition at sea, but the following night, as the squadron steamed onward, Red's smallest ship broke away and approached the bay leading to Han-Kuang's mainland stronghold. Adam Shannon was aboard, dressed as a Chinese coolie, with a broad hat hiding his face. Several of his best men were dressed likewise, and well before dawn they and Adam climbed down into a native sampan lowered over the side. The small, flat-bottomed craft proceeded up the bay, and at dawn Adam saw the forts, two of them on opposite shores where the waters narrowed. Using care so that the rising sun would not reflect off his glass, he examined the positions. They had been constructed of earth, which, unlike stone, absorbed the shock of a high-explosive shell. The pirates had learned their lessons well during the attack on Han-Kuang's island.

Beyond the forts, at the head of the bay, Adam could see a village, and he suspected it was the site of Han-Kuang's head-quarters. The approaches to the two dirt forts were steep ridges, and Adam estimated it would take every man he had, plus the sailors, to storm the well-chosen positions, even after the guns of the naval ships had done their deadly work. Swiftly, Adam made sketches, marked the most advantageous landing spots for his troops, and indicated possible routes to the tops of the ridges.

In the captain's quarters aboard the *Calliope*, Red looked over

Adam's shoulder as Adam, working from memory, filled in details of the topography. "I think *Calliope*'s guns will be more than enough to do the job," Adam said. He indicated a spot near the mouth of the bay, equidistant from the two forts. "If you station yourself here, you can lob shells into both fortified positions. I don't think we should—at least not at first—shell the village. I suspect that we'd kill more innocent people than pirates, and I don't think it will be necessary."

"The troops are going to have a tough climb," Red commented.

Adam did not dispute the statement. "Once *Calliope* has silenced whatever guns they have on top of the ridges," he went on, "we can move the three smaller ships into the bay. There their guns can lay down a barrage on the upper slopes to cover the initial stage of the assault."

"I see that you've got me well out of the action," Red observed wryly.

Adam laughed. "Well, we must protect our senior senior officer."

"Don't concern yourself about *my* age, old man," Red countered; but he recognized and accepted the necessity of having the *Calliope* lie well offshore. Her guns had the range, and at closer quarters she would not be able to lob her shells down atop the ridges into the fortified positions. He sighed resignedly. "Well, it's not a question of surprise, is it? If they don't see us coming, they'll know we're here when we start dropping high explosives on their pates. So if you don't object, we'll begin the cannonading at dawn, as soon as we can see. That will give you plenty of daylight to take the ships in after we've silenced their guns."

"I'd like to have my men on the beaches no later than three hours after sunrise," Adam said.

It was a muggy morning, with leaden skies and almost no wind. The *Calliope* approached along the coastline, the three smaller ships, with men ready on their decks, trailing close behind. Near the mouth of the bay, she dashed out to sea to her assigned position, leaving the others nearer shore, ready to make their run into the bay.

It was a good morning for the gunners. Smoke from the first shots went straight up, allowing the gunnery officer to adjust the range well. Red was on the bridge, holding the *Calliope* broadside to her targets, with cotton stuffed into his ears to deaden the concussions from the four big guns. When he was satisfied with the range, he gave the order to fire for effect and leaned on the rail to watch the reduction of the ridge tops. When he heard the approaching whine of a large-calibre shell he at first looked quickly around, thinking that the shell had to be coming from another ship. His twelve-inchers allowed him to stand well beyond the range of anything the pirates might have atop the ridges, so all logic told him that the shells must be coming from a naval ship.

A tower of water rose not thirty yards to sea from the ship, and only seconds later Red heard the rushing, sizzling sound of another incoming round. This one was closer.

Seeing no other ships on the horizon than his own, he swept his glass back to the ridge tops, just in time to see the muzzle flashes of two guns on the southern ridge, followed shortly by the approach of their projectiles. The shells, unbelievably big, landed close enough to rock the *Calliope*, even as her own guns thundered to send missiles hissing toward the forts. Red swept his glass to the northern ridge and saw two more muzzle flashes. The northern guns were aiming at the three smaller ships, closer to shore. Men were massed on the decks, unprotected.

"Gunnery officer," Red commanded, "concentrate on those guns. Signalman, make to Colonel Shannon to withdraw."

He watched as shells blasted down amid the three ships, sending up plumes of water dangerously close. To his alarm, the next shell exploded at mast height over the lead ship, sending spars and rigging crashing down onto the deck, but the ship's engines were chugging, and she was turning, the others following, to seek shelter behind a point of land to the south.

"Get those blasted guns," Red ordered, as *Calliope*'s turrets thundered. He waited for the next volley, then ordered full speed with the helm hard aport, to turn the *Calliope*'s stern to the guns on the ridges. Several minutes after the last enemy shell had fallen in his direction, Red again turned the *Calliope* broadside, now at a distance from shore that represented the maximum effective range of his twelve-inchers. The big guns recommenced firing, the first shots falling short of the ridges, but the gunners soon found the elevation. The three smaller ships had reached safety around the point, and Red intended to show the pirates the *Calliope*'s accuracy at a distance.

Suddenly four shells bracketed the ship with frightening accuracy. Only seconds later, his glass revealed more muzzle flashes, and the swiftness of the reloading amazed Red, indicating to him that weapons aimed at him were at least a match for twelve-inch guns. A shell exploded near *Calliope*'s stern, shaking the entire ship, and in the debris left on deck Red saw a mutilated body. *Calliope*'s answering fire, although it landed all around the muzzle flashes of the guns, seemed to do no damage, for another barrage from shore went down the ship as Red gave orders to come hard aport once again at full speed. Soon he was out of range of his twelve-inchers, and the shells from shore were chasing him with dismaying power and accuracy.

"I'd guess that they're sixteen-inchers," Red told Adam, as they sat gloomily in Red's quarters. One man was dead, another wounded on the *Calliope*, and the falling mast and rigging on the other ship had injured half a dozen men.

"If I hadn't seen it with my own eyes I'd say it's impossible," Adam said. "Sixteen-inch guns in a pirate stronghold on the China coast? I would have guessed that the nearest gun of that size would be at Gibraltar."

"Such guns were not turned in some local Chinese armoury," Red said grimly.

"The Germans?" Adam asked.

Red shrugged. "We have to go get them, you know."

"I know." Adam looked at the map spread on the table before them. "We can land our men out of range, march them up the coast."

"And lose men by ambush before we even get to the ridges," Red said.

"I'm open to suggestions."

"I'm waiting for a damage report," Red answered.

The reports came soon, delivered by the engineering officer. The *Calliope* had not been hurt badly. The debris had already been cleared from the deck of the other ship, and although she would be without the option to raise sail, she could still navigate with her engine.

"Sixteen-inchers are big," Red said, as soon as he had dismissed the officer. "Mounted as shore guns they have a limited field of fire. Those we encountered are emplaced to cover the entrance to the bay and the sea approaches."

"Meaning that they could not be depressed, or turned, to fire down into the bay itself?" Adam asked.

"Exactly." Red turned his attention to the map. "We'll do our repairs. Then your three troopships will enter the bay two hours before dawn, run the narrows, and land your troops to the rear of the guns. *Calliope* will lay offshore and engage the guns beginning at daybreak."

"She'll take a pounding," Adam said.

"She's designed to fight" was Red's answer. "We'll give her that opportunity."

In Han-Kuang's fortresses there was a celebration. Han-Kuang had distributed a moderate amount of rum to his gunners in congratulations, and he was smiling with satisfaction. The foreign devils had been routed, with two of their ships badly damaged. He moved about among his men, a hulking figure dressed in the finest silks, dwarfing his retinue of aides and bulking even larger than the European who was at his side, a portly, close-shorn, white-suited German.

"It is most fortunate, my good friend," Han-Kuang commented, "that you were here for the first test of your fine guns."

"Of course, they are fine guns," Maxim Stoltz replied crisply. "They are German guns."

Despite his air of confidence, Maxim Stoltz was in a quandary. He recalled ruefully the serpentine path that had brought him into Han-Kuang's presence this day. For all his dislike for the Chinese people in general and Han-Kuang in particular, Stoltz had been only too willing to listen when an Australian by the name of Jamison, claiming to be associated with Marcus Fisher, had come to him with information that a Chinese warlord was offering huge sums of gold for good foreign cannon. Jamison, Stoltz had determined without any great effort, acted as Fisher's middleman in the lucrative Chinese opium trade, and Fisher evidently hoped to reap further profit—his country be damned—by seeking the weapons from Stoltz. Since Stoltz, of course, also stood to profit handsomely from the Chinaman's offer—and the guns would, after all, be employed against Germany's greatest rival—he had not hesitated to use his own good contacts to obtain sixteen-inch guns of the highest quality—the finest examples of the skill of the Krupp works, arsenal of the Reich.

However, it was most unfortunate that the British had chosen the time that they did to make their attack. His mission now would be much more complicated. Han-Kuang, having seen the strength of the British again—and having, at least for the moment, successfully dealt with it—would not willingly give up his guns. Nor did Stoltz have the power to take them from him by force. There simply were not enough men aboard the *Antony* to even consider challenging Han-Kuang in his own back yard.

But force was not always necessary, not when dealing with a man like Han-Kuang. As Stoltz accompanied the pirate on his tour of inspection and congratulations, it was clear that the two of them shared one attribute, at least—an indifference to the bodies of those who had died during the bombardment. Stoltz waited until they were seated in Han-Kuang's well-appointed field headquarters, set into the side of the ridge behind one of the forts, before he made his offer.

"I fear, my friend," he said, "that the celebration is premature."

The pirate laughed. "We showed them our power. We devastated two of their ships."

"You broke some spars and damaged a cruiser quite lightly," Stoltz corrected him. "They will be back."

"And we will be here, with the guns, to greet them."

"I had in mind a trip," Stoltz said, "for both of us."

The pirate's face went blank. "You talk in riddles."

"I don't intend to be here when the British ships land hundreds of men, when their cannon begin to rake the ridges and perhaps the village."

"But the guns will keep them at a distance," Han-Kuang said.

"The guns are not going to be here."

Han-Kuang stood, a menacing figure, and glowered down at the seated German.

"Because," Stoltz said evenly and softly, "I am going to buy them from you for twenty-five thousand English pounds."

Han-Luang's face darkened even further.

288

"In gold," Stoltz added.

Han-Kuang sat down and folded his hands. "I will listen."

"The past few months have been very profitable for you, have they not?"

Han-Kuang was silent, and Stoltz pressed boldly on.

"The information I have provided you has helped you gain some very rich prizes. The guns have given you security—up to now. Now the British lion is aroused, and not even four German guns can stand against the Royal Navy, my friend. Even if this one little expedition fails, there will be another, with battleships. It is time to count your gains, to avoid the loss of everything in a futile fight." Stoltz stood. "When the British take those forts—and they will—they must not find German guns there. It is not yet time to challenge them openly."

"I know nothing of your politics," Han-Kuang said. "I know only that this is my place, my land."

"But do you yourself have to fight for it?" Stoltz leaned closer and lowered his voice. "And possibly die for it?"

Han-Kuang's eyes narrowed.

"Twenty-five thousand golden English pounds," Stoltz said, "will buy many luxuries, my friend. Then, when the British have come and gone, you will still have your land, your people." He straightened. "Tonight we will load the guns and leave. You are welcome to come with us."

"No. I do not go to the land of the white men."

"Go wherever you please," Stoltz said. "Leave behind a token force to show some resistance, if you must. Position them on the protected sides of the ridges so that they will not be devastated by the cannonade. Then, after they have killed a few of the British soldiers, let them melt into the countryside to reform again at a later date."

The trace of a smile touched Han-Kuang's lips. "I *had* considered investing in more legitimate enterprises," he said.

"Trading with Germany could be very profitable."

He smiled. "Please continue."

"If we had a friend of your wealth, your influence, your power in Canton, we would find much business for him," Stoltz improvised.

Han-Kuang called one of his aides, a young man who appeared

to be full of fire and pride but not possessed of great intelligence. His name was Chen Su.

"We are going to trick the British," Han Kuang said. "We are going to lead them to believe that they have destroyed us totally. While our main force will be withdrawn, you and a company of chosen men will stay and kill the British from concealment before abandoning these positions to them."

"Abandon all this?" Chen asked incredulously.

"Yes. Please do not trouble yourself trying to understand, my son, for these are matters of policy. Can I rely on you?"

The young man nodded. "I will fight to good account."

"It will not be necessary to fight to the death," Han-Kuang said, "although such sacrifice would not be without honour."

The evacuation was accomplished swiftly, with the men working through the remainder of the day and into the night. The engineer from the *Antony* directed the dismounting of the large naval cannon, and they were moved down the slope to the bay in short order. By midnight, the guns were safely stowed in the large hold of the steamer, which got under way and was well clear of the bay before dawn.

At least one man had not celebrated the defeat of the British squadron. He was acting captain of the *Antony*, serving in Jamison's absence, and he had observed the action from a hillside. Now, as he stood on the bridge, watching storm clouds approach from the east, he was still mulling over what he had witnessed. It was an odd place for a New Zealand lad to be, he kept telling himself—standing by idly as Chinamen fired upon ships of the Royal Navy. Odd place, indeed, considering the man who had chartered the ship was a German whose most fervent wish was for an end to British dominion in the region. But at least the guns had now been removed. When the British squadron came back, as it would—Harry Ryan was sure of that—they would not face the devastating sixteen-inch projectiles.

He was, after all, being paid well. And Marcus Fisher had promised him a ship of his own, a free hand in trade, and a chance to enrich himself.

Harry turned the bridge over to the mate and went down into the hold. The German guns were damned heavy. He wouldn't want even one of them slightly loose belowdecks in a storm. He had personally supervised their lashings, and again he tested the tautness of the lines with his weight. When he was satisfied, he went to find Stoltz.

"We'll be hitting heavy weather shortly," he informed the German.

"As long as the guns are safe," Stoltz growled.

"They will be. It would help, of course, if I knew where we were going." Harry had been told to head straight out to sea, away from the shipping lanes, as soon as they had cleared the bay, but he had no idea where the German was taking the guns.

"You will know soon enough, Captain," Stoltz replied unhelpfully. "As soon as we are away from any possibility of the British squadron sighting us."

Harry went to his cabin, dug out a bottle, and drank deeply. He didn't like Maxim Stoltz. He didn't like the idea that, somehow, he was being used against his own country. But on the other hand, what harm had come? If anything, he had performed a service in helping to remove the guns from the Chinese stronghold. As the motion of the ship increased, he went back on deck, almost grateful for the distraction of the coming storm.

Two days later, after weathering a brief, seasonal squall, the *Calliope* took up position, battened down for a pounding from the heavy shore guns, and began her bombardment. In the bay, the three ships carrying Adam Shannon's men, having successfully run the narrows before sunrise, began disembarking troops on beaches on either shore.

Red, watching his shells pound the ridge tops, waited for the return fire, and when it did not come his puzzlement grew. All he could hear were the guns of his own ships in the inner harbour, carrying out their bombardment. He laid down well over a hundred rounds, and still there was no response. He checked his watch every few minutes, knowing Adam's men would be ashore, and when the time came, he ordered the guns to cease firing. He set a course for the mouth of the bay and was in clear sight of the fort when he heard the first small-arms fire and knew that the land forces were engaged.

The big guns of the three smaller ships were pounding the slopes

291

in advance of the troops, the curtain of fire lifting as the men made their way up the brush-covered hills. Still wondering why the guns were silent, Red watched the soldiers through his glass as they made their way up the slopes, against rifle fire that was taking a toll. He saw a man fall, and in that fall he saw death, for the running figure had gone limp, as if all the bones had suddenly been removed from the body.

Adam Shannon was leading his men up the north ridge, where resistance was surprisingly light. His estimate of the time required to take the ridge had been overly pessimistic, for they were almost to the top and the defenders were retreating, pausing to fire only fitfully. The big guns had never opened fire, but Adam didn't have time to wonder about that. Even light opposition could kill, and it didn't take more than one or two rifle bullets flying about one's head to concentrate the attention. He looked back across the bay and saw that the other force had already reached the top of the southern ridge. A British flag was being unfurled, and the sound of firing there had ceased.

Only a pocket of resistance remained when Adam topped the ridge. About twenty rifles, he estimated, were concentrated in one small area of the devastated dirt embankments. He deployed his men carefully and was patient, letting the sharpshooters do their deadly work, picking off any defender who showed his head long enough to take careful aim.

From his position Adam could see almost the entire bay. The *Calliope* had steamed through the narrows, and a small boat was moving toward the north shore. That would be Red. Adam shook his head in disapproval, though he could not help but admire his old friend. But it would be over before Red could climb the ridge.

Chen Su, the leader of the last small group of holdouts, had seen at least three of the foreign devils fall as he looked over the sights of his rifle, but three was not enough. He and his chosen men had fought with honor, and many of them had died. Now it was time to break off the action, as Han-Kuang had ordered, and flee into the countryside, but somehow he could not bring himself to give the order. He had never run from a foe in his life, and he was reluctant to do so now. He could not understand why Han-Kuang had decided to surrender their home, their land, with only token resistance. It was a shame on their honour; it was a shame on Chen.

"Why do they not rush us?" a man asked.

"They will come," Chen said. "When they have killed a few more of us."

"They are too many," someone else said.

"If you are frightened, run," Chen scoffed. "No blame will be attached to you, only your own shame."

He had made up his mind. He would not be known as Chen the coward. His position in one of the empty gun emplacements had been carefully chosen, and it would cost the lives of many foreign devils to root him out of it.

When Red reached the top of the ridge, there was still sporadic gunfire. He crawled to join Adam under cover of a dirt embankment.

"Keep your blasted head down," Adam spoke harshly, pulling Red back by the coat as he peered over the embankment. "That hair of yours is still red enough to stand out like a battle flag."

A bullet hissing past perilously close was enough to persuade Red to obey the suggestion quickly. "There can't be many of them, Adam. We could take them easily."

"We'll lose men if we rush them," Adam said. "Let's give them a chance to stew a bit first."

One by one Chen saw his men being picked off. Most of them were shot in the head and died instantly, but one had been shot in the neck. He was bleeding profusely and making horrible sounds. Chen glanced to his left and right and saw that the red-coated soldiers were beginning to encircle his position. He would have to make his decision quickly. He counted his remaining men—there were only seven—and decided.

"One by one," he said, "leave this place. I will give you protecting fire."

He lifted his head and, heedless of the hail of enemy bullets, began to fire.

"They're running, sir," a sergeant called to Adam.

"Good," Adam said. "Let them take their chances." He did not

293

want to lose more men rushing the position.

"I got one," a sharpshooter yelled.

Red peered over the bank. "There's only one man firing now, Adam," he said.

Chen had exhausted his ammunition. He crawled to the rear of the ruined emplacement and prepared to run, but his gorge rose at the idea. He had given his men the opportunity to live. Only one of them had been killed in the escape. Not far from him, half covered by debris, was the door to a powder magazine. He had seen the foreign devil sailors remove the huge shells—or at least most of them—from the magazine to take them to the ship. But inside, he knew, there remained a dozen barrels of black powder and a few of the high-explosive shells. He whispered a quick prayer, and with bullets zipping around him, raising little puffs in the dirt, he gained the doorway and leaped inside.

"Let's have a look," Red said, half rising, but again Adam jerked him back. "It's all right, man," he said. "They've gone, or they're dead."

He stood up and trotted forward. He had only his revolver, and it remained in his holster. Adam ran to catch him, but before he could take a few steps the earth seemed to rise under his feet and he was thrown to the ground. Clods of earth tumbled down all round him, and echoing explosions battered his ears. He instinctively put his hands over his head as more dirt and debris showered him, and then there was silence, except for his own voice calling, "Red! Red!" He crawled forward. Red's motionless form was half covered in dirt and debris. Adam began to brush away the dirt, working frantically, and when Red's face was uncovered he saw that the mouth was open, still breathing. Adam could hear nothing, his ears numbed by the blast, but he yelled for a medical orderly. He was holding Red's head in his lap when the orderly arrived, at a run, knelt with his kit, and began to examine Red's wounds.

"Is it bad?" he asked, and he had to lean close to understand the orderly's reply.

"I think he'll be all right, sir," the man said, busily working to stanch the flow of blood from Red's shoulder, where something jagged had torn a deep gash. Adam gently brushed dirt from his friend's unconscious features and whispered a silent prayer.

CHAPTER XVII

Adam Shannon impatiently paced the deck of the *Calliope*. The squadron was at sea, making maximum speed for Hong Kong, but not moving nearly fast enough for his liking. He had just come up from the sick bay, where the ship's surgeon had been attending Red. It had been a time-consuming job, but not too difficult, according to the old surgeon, to treat Red's shrapnel wounds. It was not the visible wounds that puzzled the old man. With Adam also present, he had stood beside Red's bed, looking down on the unconscious form with his lower lip drawn between his teeth in frustration.

"There's no reason for him to be in this condition of coma," the doctor had said. "He's undergone shock, of course, but his wounds do not appear critical." He had examined Red thoroughly, looking first for a head wound, or evidence of a blow to the head. Red's face had been peppered by small fragments, some of which the doctor had had to remove, but those wounds were only superficial.

"We need the facilities of a modern hospital," the doctor had said.

There had been, however, work to be done before the squadron could sail for Hong Kong. Adam had directed the clean-up operation, sent men into the village, dispatched boats to search every cove of the bay. They had found one empty pirate junk and put her to the torch, but Han-Kuang's fleet was not in evidence. Nor had any of the blank-faced, cringing villagers ever so much as heard of a pirate. Adam had stood at the head of the bay, gazing inland, thinking of the vastness of China spread out before him. He had known then that this ancient land, teeming with uncounted millions of people, was a sponge that could absorb any attempt of the Europeans to change it. There might be a hint of

Westernization along the coast, in the trading cities, but beyond was China, almost limitless, its people so different that he suspected they would never understand Western ways, or even desire to. He was ready to go home. He longed for the fresh, clean air of New Zealand, for people he could understand. He wanted to be with his own kind, with Emily and the children, perhaps to retire to a smallholding in the outback and raise sheep.

That mood, however, was fleeting. He was an officer of the empire, and the affairs of the empire extended to the far and odd corners of the earth. As he continued to pace the deck, Adam glanced at the distant shore, wondering when they would reach Hong Kong.

The squadron was only twelve hours from home when Red regained consciousness, vomited up dark blood, and whispered of pain in his abdomen before lapsing into semi-consciousness.

"Internal injuries," was the surgeon's verdict. "I have neither the knowledge nor the facilities aboard ship to do anything about it."

The *Calliope* steamed into Hong Kong with Red running a high fever, unable to swallow anything more than warm tea. He was rushed to the British Hospital, where Adam had to leave him in order to make his reports to the high commissioner and to Sir Reginald Peckwith. At his office he was given a telegram addressed to Red. It was weeks old. He opened it and read it, then sat down heavily. It was from Magdalen, informing Red of the fate of his daughter in Java.

For days Jessica Broome had drifted in and out of a feverish sleep, scarcely aware of the pain from her abrasions, bruises, and burns. She had meekly obeyed the orders of the small, wrinkled, old Javanese man, when indeed, she was aware of him, opened her mouth like a small child to be spoon-fed rice and fruit, or given a drink of water. She had no thought of modesty when the old man changed the leaf poultices and applied cocoa butter to her healing burns. She moaned in protest when she was lifted from the bed and placed on a litter formed of vines, leaves and bamboo, but she was unconscious during most of the slow trip as the old man dragged the litter from the ruined hut near the shore into the interior, to a small village nestled on the lower slope of a jungled mountain.

There came a day when she opened her eyes and saw a thatched roof over her, raised her head in puzzlement, then, thinking suddenly of the baby, placed her hand on her protruding stomach to feel firm roundness and an answering kick. She still felt weak and disoriented and was surprised to discover there were old scabs on her arms and her hands. She put a hand to her face and felt the same condition, but she could not remember what had happened. She ran fingers through her hair. It was loose but not too tangled. She heard a sound and looked up to see an old Javanese man entering the hut, with a wooden bowl in his hand from which emanated appetizing aromas.

"Where am I?" she asked, her voice sounding old, strained.

"Ah." The old man smiled. He knelt beside her, looked into her eyes, touched her brow. "You well, you see. No fever."

Jessica, abruptly realizing that she was exposed from the waist up, clutched for the cotton covering that lay over her stomach and pulled it up to conceal her breasts. The old man laughed.

"You well, you see," he repeated, with a chortle of pleasure.

"Where am I?" she asked, her eyes wide, memories crowding into her mind of the awful night, the water, the mud and ash.

The old man chattered in his own language and made motions with his hands.

"Who are you?" she asked.

"Toa," he said, punching himself violently in the chest with his finger. "Me Toa."

"Toa," she said. "Toa, do you speak any English?" She was so weak that each word was an effort. Toa's answer was in his own langauge. "Oh," she said, and felt sleep rush at her and take her.

Within a few days, however, she was able to walk carefully to the doorway and venture out into a cleared area around which were grouped a few native huts. Toa had provided her with a *sarong*. It bulged over her stomach. Judging from the fact that her scabs were gone, leaving new skin that was losing its pinkness, she estimated that weeks had passed since that terrible night in Anjer. Sam would be looking for her. Her mother would be worried to death. With sudden urgency, she glanced around her, looking for Toa, but he was nowhere to be seen. She walked unsteadily toward the other huts, heard female voices inside one, and called out. A Javanese woman appeared and said something in her incomprehensible language. Jessica, having grown exhausted from her feeble efforts, went back to her hut.

Over the next few days she gained strength steadily, forcing herself to eat as much as she could stand. The old man was with her off and on, and at night he slept on a cot at the other side of the hut. She made a continuing effort to get him to understand that she had to go back to Anjer.

"Anjer," he would say, making motions to indicate that Anjer was no more.

"Where Dutch?" she would ask, and the old man would make the same motions to indicate that the Dutch were no more.

Gradually she worked out a system of communication by hand motions. "The sea," she said, making wave motions with her hands. If she could get to the sea, surely she could find Europeans, or attract the attention of a passing ship. "How far to the sea?" She made walking motions with her fingers.

"Ah," Toa said, showing his blackened teeth in a grin. He held up four fingers, made walking motions.

Four days to the sea. She had kept track of the days since she had begun to be able to think clearly again. She thought it might already be October. She was well into her last months of pregnancy. She could not possibly attempt to walk for four days through the jungle, not knowing whether she could actually reach help once she reached the strait.

"Toa," she said, with appropriate motions, "people go to sea?"

He shrugged, then nodded, seeming to indicate that perhaps, sometime, people went to the sea. She made writing motions. "Take message Dutch?"

"You well, you see," he said, reaching to pat her gently on the stomach.

With a change in the monsoon winds the rains came to northern Java, dense sheets of rain that began to dissolve the volcanic ash, wash it away, and make it a part of the jungle floor. Life in the tiny village slowed to virtual inactivity. Jessica had come to believe that the village was a family grouping, with old Toa one of the most honoured men there. When he spoke, people listened. Women obeyed his orders and cleaned the hut he shared with Jessica. Food was served at specific times, usually brought to her now by a shy, older girl with budding breasts who apparently had been assigned as her servant. The girl took great interest in Jessica's bulging stomach, asking, with raised eyebrows and a look of wonder, to be allowed to feel the baby kick.

Now and then Tao would take Jessica to another hut, where there would be a group of people, special items of food, and much talk and laughter. The girl who tended her and a woman who was, apparently, the girl's mother, began to teach Jessica how to weave mats and prepare food. It was something to do to pass the days of endless rain, and as the days turned into weeks, Jessica resigned herself to the fact that her child could be born in a native hut in the Javanese jungle.

Unless she had been delirious for longer than she had estimated, she thought it was late in November when she felt the first discomfort of labour. She had been in good health, and for two or three days she had been bursting with energy, pitching in to help the girl clean the hut, weaving mats with a mindless vigour, and practising the few words she had picked up in the native language. She was in the company of the girl and her mother when she felt the first severe cramp. Her eyes went wide and her hands became still, then she pressed her hand to her stomach and said, "Oh!"

The girl smiled.

"Ah," the woman said.

The village women, taking charge with an authority that gave comfort to Jessica, ordered Toa out of the hut and mounted a day-and-night watch of her condition, keeping her brow cooled with damp cloths, jabbering and smiling, and, as the labour advanced, occasionally lifting the coverings to check on progress. The village midwife seemed to be as old as Toa, a silent, grim-faced little woman, but with the most gentle hands. It seemed that all the village had contributed items for the baby. There was a Western-style cradle made from some aromatic wood, clean, fresh bedding, and soft cotton sacklike garments Jessica assumed were to dress the baby in. Between labour pains, she felt great love for the small, brown women who were looking after her so selflessly.

"I know you can't understand," she said, having caught the attention of the midwife, the girl, and the girl's mother, "but I am so grateful to you. You've been so very, very kind. When I get back to—" She started to say civilization but did not, even though they would not understand either way. "When I get back I'm going to have my husband send you things. Cooking utensils, beautiful cloth, many useful things."

The child was born at night, during a steady, drenching downpour. Water ran in currents off the thatched roof, a few droplets finding their way through to make the inside of the hut feel damp and sodden. Throughout the ordeal Jessica had managed not to weep, or to scream, but when she felt the great, tearing pain of birth she screamed, just once, and then fell back in a red daze of relief. She heard a brisk slap and then, wondrous, and so beautiful that she wept with joy, the protesting wail of a newborn infant. She saw the child in the midwife's hands, her son, and reached for it. The midwife smiled, shook her head, and said something, handing the baby to another woman to be cleansed.

Exhausted and sweating, but feeling elated, Jessica tried to catch a glimpse of the child. "Give him to me," she kept saying, but the women smiled and chattered and continued to bathe the baby, then to wrap it in clean garments. Old Toa entered the hut a few moments later and waving off the protests of the women, seized the child and began to unwrap it to look at it. He grinned broadly. He approached the bed, carrying the baby gingerly in his outstretched hands. Jessica reached up eagerly.

"Is girl," Toa said. "Is little Java girl."

Toa placed the baby beside Jessica. She looked down into a small, red, puckered face. The baby's eyes were open. They were blue, but Jessica knew that newborn eyes were often blue and might later change. She had, Jessica thought, Sam's nose and chin. "Well, little Java girl," she said, "you are indescribably beautiful, and won't your father be proud when he sees you?"

A light, chill, November rain was falling when Jon Fisher emerged from the railroad station onto the bustling streets of London. The Van Buren clipper on which he was supercargo was discharging her wool at Liverpool, and he would have a few days before his services would be needed again. He had appointments with a London merchant on Van Buren business and an appointment of his own with a businessman who was interested in importing South Seas native crafts.

Jon had not been in London for years, and his first impression was that there were simply too many people, too many vehicles, and too much noise, even in the rain.

He attended to the Van Buren business first and was well pleased with the arrangements for a return cargo. His interview with his own client was equally, if not more, satisfying. The man would take all the native crafts Jon could find, for in London the empire-minded populace was hungry for anything that smacked of the far-flung and exotic. He dined well, on good English roast beef, Yorkshire pudding, mushy pease—a solid, filling English meal— and luxuriated in a fine bed in a hotel just around the corner from Buckingham Palace. In the morning, with a great deal of anticipation, he took a hansom cab to his grandfather's town house. The old man answered the door himself, for he had been informed by telegraph that Jon was going to visit.

Major Clive Mason carried his years well. He walked with the aid of an ornate, gold-headed cane, had a mane of snow-white hair, and a face that still reflected the rigours of the India backcountry where he had once done service. On seeing Jon he dropped the cane and took his grandson into his arms in a display of affection that was not at all typical of him. He escorted Jon into a sitting room decorated with artifacts of empire and seated him before a table already laid for afternoon tea.

"You have made a fine man," Mason said. "A bit taller than most Masons, but—" He paused, letting his eyes feast on his grandson.

"You're looking spry, Grandfather," Jon returned with a smile. He had spent pleasant years in this house, before the death of his grandmother. He looked around. "Things haven't changed much."

"As one grows older one learns to distrust change," Mason said. He called the maid and ordered another setting for Jon. "Good passage?"

"Not bad," Jon said. "Bit of a storm off the Cape slowed us down."

"And your mother?"

Jon hesitated. "You know, I think, from my letters that I tried to persuade Mother to come to London."

"Yes. Is that Fisher scoundrel giving her problems?"

Jon had decided to avoid that subject, for he saw no reason to give undue worry to his grandfather. After all, the old man could do nothing for Caroline unless Caroline was willing to be helped. "No more than usual," he evaded. "She likes her house outside Melbourne very much. He spends a lot of time in the city, which seems to suit her. She has a companion, a Mrs. Blevins, who looks after her. I visit her when I can, which, considering the nature of the work I've chosen, isn't too often."

"In good health, is she?"

"She's showing her age, I suppose." Jon chose his words carefully. "She is getting old."

Mason harrumphed. "Nonsense. *This* is old." He tapped his thin thigh with a clenched fist. "But what about you, my boy? I'll have to admit that I was a bit upset when you left the army—but that was your choice and your choice alone. I learned long ago that I can't live your life for you. Are you doing well?"

"Very well," Jon said.

"But no family?"

A flash of Misa's face came to him. "No, not yet." He smiled. "Are you eager to be a great-grandfather?"

"Wouldn't mind." Mason called for the maid to hurry with the tea things. "Don't they have girls out there in Australia?"

"A few," Jon said. "Don't give up on me yet."

Mason laughed. "One will come along. You're lucky to have escaped the clutches of the females of this world so far—not that I tried too hard when your grandmother set her hat for me." He went silent, and a look of intense sorrow came over his wrinkled face. Then he brightened. "One will come along, my boy, and if she's the right one, as your grandmother was for me, you won't stand a chance."

Tea was poured, and Jon filled himself with cake as he listened to his grandfather describe his ailments and complain about the current government. The two of them talked until well past dark, then sat down to a good meal, followed by cigars and brandy in the sitting room.

"Grandfather," Jon said, "I ran into someone you might have known in Australia."

"Oh?"

"He now calls himself Adam Shannon," Jon said.

Mason sipped his brandy, his eyes narrowing.

"I think you knew him as Adam Vincent," Jon pressed on,

watching for his grandfather's reactions.

"Yes. Lord Cheviot's son."

"*Lord* Cheviot?" Jon echoed, astounded. "Major General the Earl of Cheviot?"

"A younger son," Mason said. "Not the heir."

"My God," Jon whispered. He had a grandfather who had been on Wellington's staff at Waterloo.

"He had a spot of trouble, did Adam Vincent." Mason was eyeing Jon closely. "Know about that?"

Jon saw no reason to mince words. "I know that he's my father."

"So." Mason put down his brandy and sat back in his chair. "So. Did your mother tell you?"

"No," he said. "I had to learn it the hard way. Why didn't you tell me, Grandfather? When I found out, I was reminded how Grandmother used to pass little hints, saying that I had a surprise coming to me someday. I don't understand why *someone* didn't tell me."

Mason mused for long moments. "It's a rather nasty situation, boy. I'm afraid your mother, bless her, was never burdened by an excess of good sense. Husband dead at sea, scandal, all that. Have to hand it to young Vincent, though. He was a thorough gentleman."

Jon flushed, remembering the stories that his mother had told him. "A gentleman? By God, Grandfather, he seduced her, took advantage of her while she was lonely and confused."

"Ah." Mason gave a rueful smile. "So it's that way, is it?"

"What way is that?" Jon demanded. "What are you trying to say?"

"Let me see," Mason said. "I'd imagine that Caroline took no blame on herself?"

"Why should she? Certainly, she was foolish to let a smooth-talking man—I can understand it better now. He was the son of an earl, a glamorous figure. That would have made it easier for him."

"Jon, you're a man now. I think it's time you faced the fact that your mother is—well, less than direct, sometimes, and has the ability to twist, if not alter, the truth." He held up his hand to stop a response that Jon had not tried to make, for Jon was remembering his mother's confusion during his last few visits.

304

"Adam Vincent seduced her, true, but most probably without resorting to tricks or subterfuge, and most probably with her willing help, if not her instigation. He then threw away his career in the navy, and his family honour, to protect my daughter's good name."

Jon felt heat rising to his cheeks and wanted to protest.

"I have never seen such a noble action, and such a foolish one," Mason went on. "He wanted to marry Caroline, and it was because of his efforts to protect her honour that he refused to testify at his own court-martial and consequently was cashiered from the navy *and* disowned by his father. He was suddenly a man with no future, and that gave your mother second thoughts. I, too, was against such an alliance, for I, quite naturally, wanted better things for my daughter than to be the wife of a penniless, disgraced man. When he foolishly—at least it appeared foolish at the time —enlisted as a common soldier, your mother wasted little time in marrying Leonard Forsyth—poor fellow, may he rest in peace. In any case, she desired to have you raised as John Omerod's son, and who was I to stand in her way? Colonel Forsyth always thought you were Omerod's son, although he was a good enough man to raise you as his own."

"Grandfather," Jon began, but he was interrupted.

"Now, if I sound as if I'm judging your mother harshly, remember that she is my daughter, and that I loved her and still do. I admit that I made mistakes in counselling her, but she was a headstrong young woman, and there's blame enough to go around. Vincent should *not* have courted a married woman, but I have no doubt that he loved her, probably more than she loved him."

"He—offered to—wanted to—marry her?"

"Yes," Mason said simply.

Shocked into silence, Jon poured more brandy. The old man, looking at him with concern, let him alone with his thoughts. It was much later, with the coal fire beginning to die in the grate, that Mason said, "I have followed Vincent's—Shannon's—career. He distinguished himself in New Zealand, even won a Victoria Cross. To rise to his present position after a disgrace, to hold the rank of colonel—that takes a man, my boy."

"Yes," Jon said. "Yes, I suppose it does."

Still, in the days that followed, as Jon visited the sights of London with his grandfather, it was difficult for him to change the thoughts of a lifetime, to adjust himself to accepting his mother's part in the folly, and to hink of Adam Shannon not as a blackguard but as a young man in love, and one who had sacrificed his honour and his career for the object of that love.

When it was time for Jon to rejoin his ship, Clive Mason presented him with some family mementos, including a miniature portrait of Caroline as a young woman. She was clothed all in white, and the artist had made her glow with youth and life. Jon was struck by her beauty.

"Of course, all that's left will be yours, my boy," Mason said.

"In the far distant future, I trust." Jon held out his hand. Mason grasped it and shook it warmly.

As he walked away, Jon did not look back, lest he break into unmanly tears. Loneliness seemed to weigh him down on the train ride back to Liverpool. His mother was unhappy and in ill health, and his grandfather was old and might well pass away before Jon could see him again.

Jon thought of Adam Shannon, imagined the so well remembered face of a young Samoan girl, and he felt some comfort. He arrived back aboard ship with two firm resolutions. First, he was going to remove his mother from the malevolent presence of Marcus Fisher. Then he was going to Samoa. The latter seemed foolish, but it was a burning necessity. He had to know if Misa had made it back to her homeland, if she was alive. He realized that, even if she was in Samoa, his chances of finding her were slim. There were several islands, and he didn't even know which had been her home. And if he did find her, it was almost a certainty that she would be married to one of her own. The thought of Misa with a Samoan man, bearing his children, threw him into a mood that made his shipmates wonder what had happened in London to the usually bright and cheerful young man.

CHAPTER XVIII

When Sam Gordon saw the *Cutty Sark* enter Sydney Cove under a full spread of sail, the ache in his heart was subdued for the first time since he had left Java. He was pleased to observe that the man who had been her captain since William Bruce had been fired in New York had cared for her. She was spruce, and she was proud. Some seamen had reattached a frayed rope-end to the hand of the figurehead, the witch, and when he boarded her, Sam saw that her teak decks glowed with polishing and care. Only a few of the old crew were still in the *Cutty*, but Tom Jenkins, the bo'sun, was among them. Jenkins had apparently stirred up considerable curiosity among the crew when the word had leaked down from a mate that Samuel Gordon was to have the *Cutty Sark*. The men, Sam noticed, eyed him with a mixture of dread and awe.

Change of command was accomplished with a handshake; the retiring captain wished Sam the best and took only a few minutes to brief him on the abilities and personalities of the officers and men before dashing off to meet his wife, who was already in Sydney, and to make all speed for a farm he had purchased in Queensland. In those pleasurable moments when Sam inspected the ship, conducting a thorough survey of every major item of gear and checking it against an inventory sheet, he thought of Jessica only a few times, not constantly. There were only minor discrepancies between survey and inventory, and the few items of gear that were not accounted for could be absorbed in normal wear and tear. Sam moved his personal gear into the luxurious captain's cabin and, when he was alone, grinned broadly and whispered, "I told you, old girl, when you were still on the ways, that you were *mine*."

On the shores of the Sunda Strait, the strategic location of the site of the destroyed city of Anjer dictated reconstruction of a coaling and watering station. The telegraph master, Peter Schruit, had been assigned to the newly built office there, but pending the completion of the coaling and watering facilities, there was little message traffic. Schruit had hired labourers to begin construction of a commodious house, using materials salvaged from the destruction, and he now had his wife and family with him. Since most of the Dutch community had died in the waves thrown up by Krakatoa, it was a sad, lonely post, but Trudi, Schruit's wife, was an inveterate gardener, and with the help of the children she was slowly turning the grounds of the half-built house into a botanical garden.

Most of the natives were still reluctant to return to the exposed coastal areas; Krakatoa, after all, still smoked. Schruit had convinced his family that the scientists were certain the volcano had spent its wrath and would slumber for hundreds of years, but the natives were not so easily swayed.

In an effort to find more workers to speed completion of his house, Schruit organized a small expedition into the interior, which his wife insisted on joining in order to collect more botanical specimens.

Travel in the rainy season was not pleasant, and resentment of the Dutch had not lessened since the catastrophe. After visiting two villages, Schruit had recruited a disappointingly small number of workers, and his wife was complaining about being constantly waterlogged. "We will visit one more village," he said, "and then we will go back to our home."

Farther away from the coast, however, the natives proved more hospitable, and the welcome extended to the white visitors at a village some twenty miles from the shore was a mixture of warmth and curiosity. A dozen strong young men agreed to sign on as workers, and Schruit congratulated himself for having decided to make the one more stop before heading home. He and his wife were feasted with roast pig and fruit and had a thoroughly enjoyable evening until the rains came and forced everyone into cover.

The headman himself escorted the Schruits through the rain to their quarters, entered with them, and, in passable English, pointed out the various good qualities of the hut. The amiable fellow showed no sign of being ready to call it a night, so Schruit broke out the tobacco, and the headman took the offered pipe with a wide grin and sat, cross-legged, to smoke it. Trudi questioned him about certain plants she had been seeking, then asked what lay inland, toward the soaring mountains. The headman said there was much jungle, animals, and then the cooler uplands.

"How far to the next village inland?" Schruit asked, wondering idly if it would be worth his while to hire a few more workmen before returning to Anjer.

"Next village two days," the headman said. "Far up mountain."

Too far, Schruit thought.

"Only clan of Toa before mountains," the headman went on, "only few families. This many." He held up eight fingers. "And white woman."

"A white woman?" Schruit asked. "Are you sure?"

The headman shrugged. "So it is said."

"Exactly where is this place where there is a white woman?" Schruit asked. Many of the Dutch women who had lived in the coastal towns had never been accounted for, their bodies never found.

The man waved toward the mountains. "Two days, far up."

"Could you take me there?" Schruit asked.

The headman nodded. "After rains," he said.

The rains would continue throughout the season, well into March. Schruit was tired, and he knew that his wife was eager to get home. In any case, he wasn't sure whether to believe the story; he remembered that after the eruption the natives had called all those who were covered with ash white people.

Next morning, Schruit's family started back toward Anjer. Upon his return, Peter spent two days helping his wife plant the specimens she had collected on the trip, thinking only occasionally about the rumour of a white woman in an inland village. It was not until three days after his return that, in a moment of idleness, and mostly because there had been no messages for two days, he sent to Batavia: "Headman village Banjsak reports white woman small village thirty miles inland."

The *Cutty Sark* had arrived in Sydney at an inopportune time. Her bad luck seemed to be holding, for she was not to be allowed to do what a clipper did best, make the long run to European or American ports, halfway around the world through open oceans. Instead, she was assigned a cargo of culled wool for Canton. The Chinese market for wool was a weak one, and the voyage would be only marginally profitable, but at least she would be at sea. Sam longed to see the *Cutty* heeled over on a stiff wind, her scuppers awash, flying as he knew that she could fly.

And fly she did. From the time she cleared Port Jackson Harbour it was clipper weather, with fresh winds and gales in the Coral Sea.

"*Wooooo-eeeee,*" a seaman yelled, as the *Cutty* reached a speed of seventeen knots and two young seamen had to strain to hold on to the line that was used for measuring the pace. Through the Arafura Sea north of Australia she dashed, and the often calm Java Sea gave her more wind, so that she was past Surabaja in a time that had the crew whooping, for they were sure that no other ship had ever made the Sydney-to-Batavia run so swiftly.

It was not necessary to call in Batavia, and the crew was puzzled when the *Cutty* turned south and made for the harbour. Nor had Sam planned the stop. He had made a last-minute decision, and now he justified it partly by arranging for fresh water, fruit, and produce to be taken aboard for the crew. While this was being accomplished, he paid a visit to the Dutch authorities, who told him that, no, there had been no new survivors of the Krakatoa disaster reported.

As he left the office, Sam told himself bitterly that it was time to stop hoping, time to accept that Jessica was dead, that he had to start a new life without her. He checked in with the Willis agent, joined the man for lunch, and discussed the wool market, the competition that sailing ships were getting from steamers, and was finishing his meal when the agent turned the conversation to the Krakatoa disaster.

"I read your report," the agent said. "Your observations must have been of tremendous value to the scientists. It certainly must have been exciting to witness."

"It's not something I'd care to see again," Sam answered tersely.

"I expect not," the agent said. "Terrible tragedy. They'll never know how many Javanese died, and they're not quite sure about how many Europeans." He flushed, belatedly realizing that he had touched on a sore subject. "My sincere condolences about your wife, Sam."

"Thank you."

"You seem to have adjusted."

Sam was silent.

The agent, still flustered by his stupid blunder, rushed on. "Some who lost loved ones are still searching, against all common sense, in my opinion. It doesn't help, of course, when unsubstantiated rumours keep cropping up about survivors in the jungle. Why, just a few weeks ago the telegraph master at Anjer sent word that natives spoke of a white woman in a village about thirty or forty miles inland."

Sam's blood raced. "Just what did the message say?"

The agent spread his hands. "Just that. Native rumour about a white woman."

Sam said no more on the subject. He excused himself as soon as it was possible, half ran to the telegraph office, and sent a request to the home office asking for permission to detour the *Cutty* to Anjer. He did not wait for an answer, however, and, rushing back to the ship, cut off the reprovisioning before it was completed and made sail for the Sunda Strait.

Peter Schruit remembered the young Scots sea captain who had lost his wife. The Dutchman was more tactful than the Willis agent in Batavia had been, however, and he was careful not to lift Sam's hopes. "Captain Gordon," he said, "you do not know the natives as I do. I am sure that if there had been a white woman inland, she would have found a way to get back to the coast, or at least to send word. Don't raise your hopes, please."

"Will you take me to the village where you heard the report?" Sam asked.

Schruit clearly did not relish the idea and protested weakly that the rains had not yet ceased, but when Sam persisted, he gave in.

It was a miserable trip. Even at a fast pace, it took them two days to reach the village where the Schruits had been entertained. The headman greeted them with pleasure and informed them that there had been no further word of a white woman inland, but he did order a young man who knew the hills to guide them to the village of old Toa. It was another two days through a jungle made almost impassable by the rains, so that they often had to wade through rank, waist-high water, fighting insects and leeches, and were not dry once during the time it took to cover the distance. Only as they neared their destination, at a higher elevation, did the low clouds lift and the rain stop.

Because of the constant rain, the insects, and the lack of a comb or a brush, Jessica had despaired of caring for the unruly tangle of hair atop her head and had asked Batee, the girl who had been assigned to her, to cut her hair. With a relic of a knife, Batee had worked with a will, cropping Jessica's long, thick tresses to a length of a few inches. The constant dampness emphasized the natural curl, so that the remaining hair had become a close mass of curls and was, thus, quite easy to manage. Jessica had been given a precious length of cotton by Toa, her protector, and with Batee's help she had made a new *sarong* that was very comfortable and, according to Batee, quite becoming. Batee had shown an aptitude for learning English, and since Jessica by now had picked up a sizable vocabulary in the native dialect, the two women could communicate surprisingly well.

Jessica had made a crude calendar, using charcoal and a piece of smooth bark, and she crossed off the days, anxiously awaiting the change of season, when travel conditions would permit her to leave Toa's village. She was told by Batee that the moon would wane and wax at least twice more before the fair weather came and the jungle trails dried enough to permit travel.

"You go?" she asked Jessica.

"I must go," Jessica said.

"I go," Batee said. "I your woman."

Jessica put a hand on the girl's cheek and smiled. She had come to be very fond of Batee, with her sunny smile, her willingness to work, and her eagerness to please, but she was sure that the girl would be happier in her own village than she would be as a servant in Sydney. She tried to explain, saying that there would be no young men where she was going to ask for Batee's hand in marriage when Batee grew up, but the girl was adamant.

"I go you," she said. "I your woman."

On a day when the clouds lifted, Batee and Jessica carried the baby's cradle outside the hut, hoping to enjoy the sun. Java, as Jessica had come to call the child, was wriggling happily in the cradle, which Toa had made. Jessica sat down on a log and watched Batee tease the baby with a gaily coloured feather. The afternoon brightened, and when the sun finally appeared through the canopy of trees, its warmth was luxurious. She turned her face to it, closed her eyes, and remembered the blue skies of Australia. She felt such a longing for home, for her loved ones, that she feared she would cry. With each day that passed, her restlessness had grown. She was in good health, and so far she had not been afflicted by any of the tropical fevers that made the jungles so unpleasant for Europeans. She prayed that she would remain healthy long enough to be able to make her way to the coast.

Evening was approaching, the sun fading fast, but it was still pleasant outside. Jessica stood near the cradle, looking down at her sleeping child. Nearby two small children played, making shrill, happy sounds. A murmur of talk came from a group of women sitting in front of a hut, and the jungle, as always, was alive with bird cries, the drip of water, and the buzz of insects. Suddenly, jarring amid those normal, familiar sounds, came the voice of a native man, hailing the village, announcing his arrival. The women fell silent and all faces turned toward the sound as a young native man stepped from the jungle into the clearing and stood there until old Toa called out a welcome. Jessica was as curious as any of the others, and her first thought was to question the newcomer. Perhaps he had had word from the European settlements, for he was not of the village.

"Batee," she said, "go, ask this man—" But the words died in her throat, for two white men had followed the Javanese into the clearing, stepping from the shadowed mouth of the trail, and her heart stood still as she recognized the familiar, lanky form.

"Sam," she whispered, and then "Sam, oh, Sam!" she screamed, her voice giving a start to everyone in the village. Then she was running, the loose *sarong* showing her long legs through its slits, and he was coming toward her, his arms outstreched. She cannoned into him with a joyous power that almost sent them tumbling to the ground, as she cried, "Sam, Sam, Sam."

"Are you well?" he asked, still holding her closely. "Have they harmed you?"

She pulled back and, smiling, took him by the hand. "Come with me." She tugged him, trying to run in her eagerness, but he, a

313

bit embarrassed, walked as they approached a small Javanese girl standing beside a crude container of some kind. Jessica halted, and he looked down to see a sleeping child, a child with white skin and delicate features.

"Little Java girl," Jessica said, tears running down her cheeks, "this is your father."

For four days Red Broome remained mostly unconscious, hovering between life and death. The doctors in Hong Kong had been able to determine that he had two broken ribs, but there was disagreement as to the nature of the internal injuries. One doctor thought that a lung had been punctured by a broken rib, while two others held that if such was the case, the blood Red had spit up would have been a brighter red. Although surgery was no longer held in total disrepute, there were no known procedures that could help in Red's case, and his recovery could only be left up to God and to Red's own body.

Adam Shannon visited the hospital daily, and he was not encouraged. He carried in his pocket the old telegram telling of the death of Red's daughter, but he had not yet sent a message to Magdalen Broome informing her of her husband's injuries. If Red recovered, Adam reasoned, worrying Magdalen would have been unnecessary, and if he died . . . Adam did not choose to dwell on that possibility.

The doctors had bound Red's broken ribs to prevent painful movement and—if indeed one of the ribs was protruding into a lung—to prevent further damage. In the short periods when he seemed partially conscious, he was given broth to drink. Gradually his periods of consciousness became longer, and he was able to speak a few words and hear, from Adam, the details of the clean-up of the pirate stronghold.

"But we didn't get them," he whispered.

"No," Adam admitted, "we didn't. For some reason, they had pulled out. The big guns had been removed. We found the places where they had been mounted—four of them. And we found this." He handed Red a scrap of paper with some faded print, which was unmistakably in German.

"I didn't think even the Germans would give such weapons to pirates," Red said. "We're going to have to find those guns."

314

"We've got the squadron at sea," Adam said. "*Calliope* is under the command of Commander Brighton."

"Good," Red said.

"When you're back on your feet, we'll go after them again," Adam said.

Red smiled weakly, but he was tired, and his eyes closed. He lapsed back into sleep listening to Adam's voice.

The squadron met with good fortune, caught three Chinese armed junks attacking a British merchant ship, sank the junks and captured some of the pirates. They were not Han-Kuang's men, however. An even dozen of them were hanged with due ceremony as a warning to other pirates.

As Red's broken ribs mended he was able first to sit up and then, carefully, while leaning on a strong young nurse for support, to get out of his bed and, for the first time in weeks, attend to his own toilet. He was still having difficulty keeping down food, and he had wasted away. Adam was shocked at his appearance when he returned after a two-week foray against the pirates—having destroyed a stronghold on the island of Hainan.

"Adam," Red said, his voice alarmingly weak, "they want to send me home. They want to invalid me out."

"Well, maybe a little rest, some of Magdalen's fine cooking—"

"They don't know what's wrong with me," Red said. "They use big words and try to look intelligent, but they don't know a thing."

Adam sought out a doctor and was told, "It's obvious there were internal injuries, Colonel. There are several organs that could be affected by the force of a large explosion, by a blow. The liver, the spleen, the kidneys. He is, however, now able to take liquids, and we are encouraged. There's a natural healing process going on."

"He said you were talking about sending him home to Australia."

"In many cases, a man progresses better when he is with his family," the doctor said. "The military doctors say that he is not fit for duty and will not be fit for duty in the foreseeable future."

"They want to invalid him out of the navy, is that it?"

"I am not a serviceman," the doctor said.

Adam felt unreasonable anger, but it was futile to protest.

Besides, there was another matter that concerned him almost as much as the thought of parting with a good companion and a trusted fellow officer. Sooner or later there would be a ship with letters from Magdalen, and he had not yet told Red that Jessica had been killed in Java. When next he visited the hospital, Red had accepted being sent home and was even looking forward to it, for he was eager to see his wife. And, he added, it would be about time for the birth of Jessica's baby, his grandchild.

"I suppose it's high time to raise the anchor one last time," he told Adam, "and plant it permanently in Sydney."

"I'll miss you, of course," Adam said, at a loss for words.

"And I you, my friend."

The old and wrinkled telegram was in Adam's hand, but he replaced it in his pocket. He saw before him a sick man. Red could not make the long voyage home knowing of the tragedy in Java; with Magdalen, at least, he could be given the news much more gently.

As soon as travel orders arrived for Red, Adam went to the telegraph office and dispatched a message to Magdalen, informing her that her husband had been wounded, that he was coming home to Sydney, and that he had not been told about Jessica.

Adam accompanied Red aboard the waiting clipper that would carry him home. Red had been issued a wheelchair, and a medical orderly had been detailed to tend to his needs during the voyage.

"I'll write to Emily as soon as I get home," Red said, once he was installed in his cabin. "The mail between Sydney and Wellington is incredibly swift these days."

"Do that, please."

"She'll want to know why you don't let her come out here with you."

"I've been considering that very seriously," Adam said, "but there are rumours that my colonial contingent will be shipped out of Hong Kong soon."

"Any clue as to where?"

"None," Adam said. "Home, I hope."

Adam stood on the wharf and watched the ship being jockeyed through the congestion of native junks in the inner harbour, and then he went back to his office, made a halfhearted attempt to catch up on some paperwork, then put it aside, for he could not give it his full attention. He was no longer young, but he was not old. He had served his country as a naval officer and in the army, and that service had taken him to me odd places. He thought of Emily, and he envied Red for being on the way home.

At first the feel of a ship's deck under him, the salt air, and the knowledge that he would soon be with Magdalen seemed to improve Red's condition. He was eating more, and he even managed some solid food; but as the trip wore on and the ship leaped and rolled in storms, he began to pass blood. By the time the ship entered Port Jackson Harbour, he had been confined to his bunk for two weeks. He roused himself enough to get into his wheelchair, and then he was holding Magdalen in his arms. In his own bed he rested, and listened to Magdalen talk, and slept with the sound of her dear voice fading slowly.

When he awoke, Magdalen was dozing in her chair. He looked at her fondly. There were traces of grey in her hair, wrinkles at the corners of her eyes and mouth, but she was so beautiful, still the young woman he had wooed and won. She, feeling his eyes on her, awoke and smiled at him.

"It's good to be home," he said.

Magdalen squeezed his hand. "It's not truly home unless you're here, Red."

"Jessica—" he said.

Her smile was suddenly radiant. "So much has happened," she said. "I don't know where to begin."

"Well, is it a boy or a girl?" Red demanded.

"You are the grandfather of a little girl," Magdalen said.

Red tried to sit up, and a wave of pain made his face twist. "Where—" he gasped.

"Please be still." Magdalen put a restraining hand on his shoulder, then reached for a cool cloth, which she used to bathe his forehead. "They're on their way to Canton," she said. "If you hadn't had to leave Hong Kong when you did, you'd have been able to see them."

"A girl," Red muttered, and Magdalen wasn't sure, so weak was his voice, whether he approved or disapproved. As he fell asleep, she almost envied him. He had been spared the worry, the wrenching pain of thinking that Jessica was dead.

The next day, after a doctor's visit, Red felt better. He sat up in his bed and was strong enough to answer Magdalen's questions about Hong Kong, Adam Shannon, and the fight with the pirates. He felt well enough to get in his wheelchair, and as they sat on the veranda, Magdalen told him the whole story of Jessica's experience in Java. She read him Jessica's letters, sent back from Batavia after her rescue, in which she described the eruption, her life in the native village, and the birth of her daughter.

"There's good stuff in that girl," Red said. "She takes after her mother. But what was that she named the child?"

"Java," Magdalen said.

"Well, little Java, after what she was through, must be a tough monkey."

"I don't think I like your referring to our granddaughter in such terms."

"What? Monkey?"

"Tough," Magdalen said. "Little girls are not tough."

"She lived through a volcanic eruption and a tidal wave," Red said, with a laugh. "I'm proud of that daughter of ours."

"Well, she was always healthy and active. But it was God's work, nothing short of a miracle, that she didn't lose the child going through all that."

"Amen," Red said. "I'd certainly like to stay around to see her."

The words stabbed at Magdalen's heart. "Well, let's do," she said, with an intensity that made her voice husky. "Let's both live to be a hundred and become irascible old dragons."

"Seems like a good idea," Red said.

Magdalen tried to read the look on his face as he turned to gaze out over the harbour. A steamer was the only ship moving, her smoke rising in a curved plume falling behind her. He was so pathetically thin. The doctor had told her almost the same thing that the doctors in Hong Kong had said, according to the orderly who had accompanied Red home. It was up to God and to her husband's will to live. She, Magdalen, would have to do her utmost to make him want to stay, if not to the age of a hundred, at least for a long, long time.

CHAPTER XIX

A London wag once said that not even the widow herself knew the extent of the empire over which she ruled, and that not one man in the Colonial Office could make a list of Britain's possessions, on which the sun never set, without consulting another list. Such a list, in alphabetical order, would have begun with Antigua, in the West Indies, and ended with the islands of Zanzibar, off the coast of Tanganyika. From Antigua to Zanzibar, from the Falkland Islands—far south in the Atlantic near the Straits of Magellan—from Newfoundland to New Zealand, from Baffin Bay in the north to Coronation Island just off the Antarctic, and from the Seychelles in the Indian Ocean to Tristan da Cunha, the lifelines of empire were maintained by the ships of the Royal Navy and the British merchant fleet flying the red duster. Not even considering the great land masses—Canada, Australia, India, and the British colonies in Africa the British empire was, in the eyes of many, the greatest work in history of one single nation.

The wealth that poured back over the sea to the small islands off the European coast had made Victoria's Great Britain the world's leading power, even if that eminence was being challenged belligerently by Bismarck's Germany and peacefully, in trade and influence, by that growing young giant, the United States. And only those men who were "a-serving of the Queen" in her far outposts realized just how fragile was the thin red line that girdled the globe.

On the troubled coast of China, for example, Colonel Adam Shannon's small force was, in the event of any real trouble with the native population, in the position of being an irritating flea on the back of an elephant. At sea the small naval squadron that was attached to his command was doing no better than holding its own against the multitude of brigands who, in their small, mobile crafts, could dash out from some hidden cove, attack an unarmed merchant ship, and disappear without a trace. True, after the reduction of Han-Kuang's strongholds, the pirate activity slacked off temporarily, but in the months following Red Broome's departure from Australia, the renewed depredations were once again causing alarm.

In the absence of overwhelming force or the ability to protect every ship that sailed into the South China Sea, Adam had reluctantly decided, with the urging of his civilian superiors, to attempt an alternative course of action. Although he did not have unlimited financial resources at his command, he did have enough to begin to build, with the help of longtime members of the British mercantile community, an effective system of informants. It was from such agents in Canton that he learned that Han-Kuang was now established in that city as a respectable merchant dealing in tea, silk, and, it was rumoured, opium. It was a relief to know that the most potent of the pirate leaders had, in effect, retired from the trade, but Adam wondered if, indeed, Han-Kuang had severed all ties with piracy. He decided to pay a visit to the ex-pirate and, after the proper arrangements had been made, took a motor launch up the river to find that Han-Kuang's Canton home was a rich one, well guarded, but open, he had been told, to a visit from the commander of British land forces in Hong Kong.

Adam had not expected to be treated regally but judging from the banquet laid out by the hulking, smiling Han-Kuang, he apparently qualified at least as a minor head of state. In addition to food and drink, Adam was offered tobacco, women, opium. He refused the women and the opium, accepted a fine cigar, and when Han-Kuang had, with a gesture of his hand, emptied the banquet room of entertainers, concubines, and servants, Adam began to state his business.

"Although we have been at close quarters at least twice," he said, "we have not met before."

Han-Kuang nodded. "Twice I would have enjoyed meeting you, each of us with a weapon in hand." He laughed, with what seemed genuine amusement. "However, Colonel, I have come to believe that I owe you a debt of gratitude, for piracy, at best, was a risky venture, and I find that remarkably similar tactics can be applied in the business world, with more, and safer, profit."

"As a representative of Her Majesty's government," Adam said woodenly, "I have been requested to relay official concerns that you, a leading merchant, choose to deal so closely with the Germans."

Han-Kuang spread his hands. "I am a simple merchant. It is the nature of business to sell to the highest bidder, is that not true?"

"So long as that which is sold is nothing more than goods," Adam said. "Whether either of us likes it or not, the future of China is closely aligned with that of my own country. Dealing with our rivals may benefit you today, but the British empire will not be supplanted in this region. If you wish to continue to prosper, you must remember that."

Han-Kuang spread his hands to indicate the palatial house. "The benefits of today can be more easily enjoyed than those of tomorrow."

Adam despised dealing with such a man, but the directives of his superiors had been clear.

"You would benefit even more if you switched your cooperation to us," he said.

"I will, of course, listen to details of such a proposal." Han-Kuang's thin lips curved into a satisfied smile.

"While it may be true that the Germans pay you higher prices for your goods, the volume of trade with them is limited. With your resources, a greater volume of trade, even at lower prices, would return a greater profit, and, I might add, a more secure one."

"Are you intimating that Germany will not expand its trade with China?"

"I'm saying only that if Germany chooses war in this part of the world, they will surely lose. They are relative newcomers to the oceans, while British bases are securely established everywhere. Our men-of-war outnumber those of Germany considerably. It is a wise man who chooses his allies well."

"Why are you, an officer in the British army, offering me conditions?" Han-Kuang asked. "Why was I not approached by a trade attaché?"

"You will be," Adam said. "But I myself also want something from you."

"Ah." Han-Kuang's smile returned. "And what has the British

army to trade for that which you want from me?"

"Gold," Adam said. "Gold for information."

Han-Luang rang a small silver bell, and a girl appeared to refill his glass. Adam refused to drink and waited patiently, for he could see the gleam of interest in Han-Kuang's hooded eyes.

"Perhaps, whether or not I choose to continue to associate with the Germans, an arrangement could be made between you and me," Han-Kuang said. "If you would care to state your needs and the price you are willing to pay?"

"Five thousand golden guineas," Adam said.

Han-Kuang's reaction was unreadable. "What information do you seek?"

"There were four large cannon mounted on the ridge-tops when last you and I were involved," Adam said. "I want to know what happened to them."

"I can give you a quick and simple answer—" Han-Kuang paused, for effect. "—when you have the gold here, in my hands. And for that price, which serves to establish a relationship between us, I will, perhaps give you more." He spread his hands in a guesture of helpless innocence. "If I should choose to start doing business with the British, I would not want to risk having pirates interfere with my trade, would I?"

Adam felt soiled by his dealings with Han-Kuang, but if, indeed, the man was willing to turn traitor to his pirate friends, the British would be getting much more from him than they had hoped. "If it is convenient for you, I will be back with the gold tomorrow."

"Most convenient."

Their next meeting took place in a smaller room, decorated in reds and golds. Han-Kuang was dressed resplendently. He had on a table before him a map of the Chinese coast. Adam delivered the gold and waited while Han-Kuang summoned two close-mouthed clerks to count it and take it away; then the pirate-merchant leaned over the table, and Adam watched carefully as he began to point out pirate nests along the coast. Adam's eyes narrowed at Han-Kuang's third disclosure, and he let anger enter his voice.

"I did not pay for information that is out of date," he said. "We destroyed three junks there and hanged ten men a month ago."

Han-Kuang looked at him with poorly feigned innocence.

"Perhaps that had slipped my mind." He let his finger slide down the coast, and Adam spoke again.

"And if your information is no more accurate than that," he said. "I think I have wasted my money." He stabbed his finger at an island Han-Kuang had failed to indicate, where informants had reported a pirate headquarters with four armed junks.

"Patience," Han-Kuang said calmly. "How was I to know how much you already knew if I did not try to find out?" He nodded knowingly. "Yes, there are six junks, not four, that use this cove. If you go there and find the cove empty, you will find the junks here." He pointed. The finger continued down the coastline, marking locations. Adam was already planning an expedition in his mind as Han-Kuang talked. If Han-Kuang's information was accurate—and he knew enough from his informants to think that it was—then he would be able to deal a strong blow to piracy throughout the China Seas with one extended expedition.

There was now the other matter, the real reason for having sought out Han-Kuang. "The guns," he said, taking a seat across the table from the pirate.

"They were taken aboard an Australian steamer after your initial attack," Han-Kuang said.

"The devil you say!" Adam exploded. "An Australian steamer?"

"You are surprised? Did you think that your countrymen were above greed?"

"The name of the steamer," Adam demanded.

"That I cannot say. I myself did not see her. I dealt with a man whose name was Stoltz." He smiled. "Needless to say, once I had sold the guns back to this Stoltz, I did not want to be at home when you came calling again."

"Surely you must have heard the name of the ship," Adam protested.

"Perhaps, but you English have such odd names for your watercraft. If I heard, it did not register."

"The name of her captain?"

"I am sorry. That I do not know, either."

"Did you see any of the men who were in her?"

A dry chuckle came from behind Han-Kuang's drooping moustache. "I am afraid, Colonel, that all Englishmen look alike to me."

"But the guns were German, and it was Maxim Stoltz who gave them to you and who took them back?"

"He did not take. He bought. I am, after all, not totally stupid. I was paid, and paid well. I think that Mr. Stoltz wanted those guns very badly."

"Where was he taking them?"

"I asked him that," Han-Kuang said. "I was told it was none of my affair. He said only that there was a need for those guns elsewhere."

Adam rose, eager to be off, away from this man who, so easily and without the slightest trace of conscience, could change alliances and betray his friends.

"It has been a pleasure," Han-Kuang said.

During the next two months the Hong Kong squadron ranged up and down the China coast, their guns levelling pirate strongholds and sinking junks, and in short order the incidence of pirate attacks decreased dramatically. But many soldiers had died in the fighting. Adam himself took a ball from an ancient musket in the fleshy part of his left arm, but no bones were broken, and the wound was healing well by the time he received his orders to embark his colonial contingent to sail home. When he made the announcement to his men, there was a loud, spontaneous cheer, and Adan was sorely tempted to join in.

During Adam's campaign against the pirates, the *Cutty Sark* had arrived in Hong Kong, discharged her cargo, and taken on a load of tea. Jessica was dismayed to hear the news about her father and to learn that they had crossed paths and just missed each other, but Sam consoled her and insisted that she use the time in port to have herself and the child checked by a British doctor. Both mother and daughter were declared in perfect health, and the doctor shook his head in wonder when Jessica described her condition after the tidal wave.

Sam and Jessica also took advantage of the brief stay ashore to have the child baptized and christened Rachel Java Broome—although Jessica insisted on addressing her as Java—and within an hour after the ceremony the *Cutty Sark* was Sydney bound.

Little Java took to the sea well. She was beginning to crawl, and Sam had the ship's sailmaster rig a harness for her so that she could navigate the *Cutty*'s decks in good weather, securely attached to her mother by a line. She was growing to resemble her mother, Sam insisted, and he never tired of looking at her, holding her, and kissing her soft little neck and cheeks to hear her delightful, silvery laugh. That she was the darling of the crew was without question. The sailmaker sewed little sailor's trousers for her and a jumper. Old Wildeye, the cook who had followed Sam from the *Roamer*, and who was not known for the variety of his menus, frequently managed to produce a special treat for the "little lass."

When Tom Jenkins approached Jessica on the quarterdeck one sunny, mild day, to ask if he might "borrow" Java for a minute or two, Jessica was doubtful, but Sam nodded, and she let the hulking bo'sun take the child amidships. A group of the off-duty watch had stretched a canvas between them, and they commenced to bounce Java—not high, but enough to make her crow with delight, and Jessica bit her knuckles in concern while Sam laughed.

"She's changed our luck, she has," a crewman said; and indeed, so it seemed. There were no calms for the *Cutty*. She seemed to draw favourable winds day after day, all the way to the northern Australian coast and into the Coral Sea for the last stretch home. Jessica began to look forward with eager anticipation to seeing her mother and her father, and she hoped Red's wounds were not as serious as she feared they might be.

The *Cutty* would be arriving in Sydney at the beginning of the wool season, with tons of freshly sheared wool being moved from the inland grazings to the docks of both Sydney and Melbourne. Sam had little doubt that the *Cutty* would be off for England as soon as she could be loaded, which meant Jessica would have only a few days with her parents; but she took consolation in the fact that, at long last, she would fulfill a lifetime dream and see England.

Jon Fisher was pleased to reencounter Claus Van Buren in Melbourne, where Claus had come on business concerning wool. Jon reported on the transactions he had arranged in England and accepted congratulations for a profitable voyage, then listened as Claus talked about the reasons for his presence in Melbourne. The competition for the new crop of wool, he explained, would be fierce. It seemed that every clipper ship in the world had been sent into the Australian wool trade, especially since the tea trade was being increasingly taken over by steamers using the Suez Canal, which allowed them to haul cargoes far more cheaply and faster. Three of Van Buren's clippers were booked for Melbourne wool, and Claus offered Jon the post of supercargo for all three, meaning he would travel back to England on the swiftest of them.

"Mr. Van Buren, I'm sorry," Jon said, after hearing him out, "but I don't think I'll be able to accept your generous offer."

Claus looked both surprised and disappointed. "Has someone made you a better offer?" he asked.

"No, it isn't that." Jon wasn't sure he could explain his plans to anyone. The truth was that they simply weren't logical. "I have my mind set on entering the South Seas trade, sir."

Claus shook his head in evident disgust. "The situation has not changed, you realize, since the last time we talked on the subject."

"I know," Jon said. "But I have a market for all the native crafts I can bring into England. I'm afraid I'm dead set on giving it a try. I'd like to make it a joint venture with you, sir."

Claus sighed in frustration, but his voice remained calm and reasonable. "Wool. Wheat. Sugar. That is what makes money. Native crafts are a fad, a fashion. By the time you could get to the South Seas and back to England, the styles might have changed, and you might easily be stuck with a cargo you cannot sell."

"Then I take it you are not interested," Jon said.

"In native crafts, no. In you, yes. If you insist on this folly, I will go along with you. I was young once, and I know that a young man has to make his own mistakes. Yes, I will finance this voyage." He raised a finger. "Not with one of my clippers, mind you. The clippers will race for England, and they will be among the first, so that their cargoes will command a good price."

"I wouldn't want to invest money in something in which you don't believe," Jon said. "Do you have a ship that you could lease to me?"

"You would take the whole risk? Can you afford it?"

It would take, Jon estimated, just about all his capital, but he was determined. For more than a year now he had been haunted by the face of Misa. He knew himself well enough to realize that he would never rest until he went to Samoa and made an effort to find her. It had occurred to him simply to take passage on a Samoan-bound ship, but that was an extravagance he was not prepared to accept. He believed he could at least break even on a venture, and he was determined to give it a try.

"Yes," he said. "I'll take the entire risk."

Claus frowned. "I advise against it."

"Do you have a ship for me?"

"You are a stubborn young man," Claus said. "Very well—there is the *Maori*.

The *Maori*, Jon knew, was not a clipper, but an ancient East Indiaman, broad in the beam, slow, and ready for retirement, but still capable of carrying more cargo than any clipper. With native crafts, speed of passage would not be vital. "I'll take her," he said, and he protested only mildly when Claus stated a lease price that was more than generous, covering expenses only, with no profit.

"I can afford to make a gesture to a young man with whom I hope to be associated for a long time," Claus said, ending Jon's questions. "The *Maori* is now in Wellington, loading wool to be transferred to Sydney for shipment on a clipper to England. When she arrives there, she's yours. I think you will get on well with Captain Farrington."

Robert Farrington, Jon recalled, had been second mate on the *Java* during her ill-starred voyage from Queensland to Hong Kong. It seemed a lifetime ago to him now.

"Yes," Jon said, "I'm sure I will. He's a fine man."

His elation was tempered by the fact that he would have to wait several weeks before he had his ship. But it was just as well, he decided, because he had other duties. Jon had determined that he would remove his mother from Marcus Fisher's malign influence, even if he had to carry her off bodily. He was in his hotel room, preparing to go to his mother's house, when a bellman knocked with a telegram. He opened it, expecting some business communication, and felt a great surge of loss when he read that his grandfather had died shortly after his own departure from England. He sank down onto his bed weakly, in sorrow and grim contemplation. Now he had only his mother left—his mother and Adam Shannon.

With renewed determination, Jon rented a gig and drove to her house, fully intending to leave with her beside him and her luggage in the back of the vehicle. As he turned into the drive he was disappointed to see an expensive-looking carriage parked before the front steps, for it could only be Marcus Fisher. For a moment he considered turning around, to come back when his stepfather was not present, but his anger rose in him and he drove the gig to a stop behind the other vehicle.

There was no response when he knocked. However, the door was ajar, and he could hear loud voices from deep inside the house. He pushed the door open and entered. As he walked down the long hallway, he heard Martha Blevins shouting angrily, then the threatening tones of Marcus Fisher. He accelerated his pace until he found himself in the doorway to the salon. Martha was standing in the middle of the room brandishing a heavy poker from the fireplace. Fisher, his face livid, was facing her. Caroline lay sprawled on the floor, her silken dressing gown askew to show her bare legs.

Martha was the first to see him, and she ran to his side. "Thank God you're here! He's been hitting her, and—"

"Shut up, woman!" Fisher yelled, eyeing Jon menacingly. "You," he hissed. "I told you never to set foot on my property again."

"Constable," Caroline said in an imperious voice, lifting herself to one elbow, "arrest this man. He has forced his way into my house."

"You shut up too, you crazy old witch," Fisher snarled; he was still facing Jon.

Caroline's cheek was red where she had been struck, and she had an odd look. Her eyes were directed toward Jon, but they seemed out of focus. "I have asked you, constable, to remove this man from my home," she said, obviously not recognizing him.

Jon addressed Fisher. "My mother is ill. I'll take her into town to see a doctor."

"You'll do no such thing," Fisher snapped. "You will get out, this minute."

"He was trying to get her to sign some papers," Martha said, "and when she wouldn't he began to hit her." She shook the poker toward Fisher. "The shame of it, striking your own wife! And it's not the first time."

Marcus Fisher was becoming calm; he straightened his rumpled jacket. "It was a simple matter of business, Jon," he said. "I'm

328

afraid I let her vagueness rile me."

"*Jon*?" Caroline's voice had changed. "Oh, Jon." She pulled herself unsteadily to her feet and tottered toward him. "I'm so glad you've come. I want to discuss with you my plans for restocking the woodlands. I'm afraid that so many centuries of poaching and free hunting have depleted the game population."

Jon swallowed uneasily. She was imagining herself to be the grand lady of an English country manor again. He looked helplessly at Martha, who was still holding the poker at a belligerent angle and glaring at Marcus.

"Martha, will you please take my mother upstairs and dress her for travel." Something in the tone of his voice caused Martha to lower the poker.

"Travel?" Marcus asked.

"Stay out of this," Jon warned.

"Now, look here—"

Jon took two quick steps and grabbed his stepfather by the lapels. "I told you that if you ever laid a hand to her again I'd thrash you. Don't try me further."

"Easy." Marcus tried to back away.

Martha led the dazed Caroline from the room.

"Now," Jon said, releasing him, "what papers did you want my mother to sign?"

"It was nothing," Marcus said. He started moving toward a table, but Jon, spotting official-looking documents there, moved faster, snatched up the paper, and held it away from his stepfather's grasp. He scanned the top page quickly, and his face went white. The papers called for voluntary commitment to the Sydney institution for the insane."

"You shameless—" Jon could not find the words.

"It would be for her own good," Marcus said. "They can help her there—get her away from the bottle, for one thing."

"You were going to put mother into an asylum?" Jon took a threatening step, and Marcus again backed away. "Now I want a paper from you," Jon said. "I want you to sit down at this table and write out a clear release of this house and this property to my mother, to be hers until her death, without interference from you."

"You'll never see a penny of my money," Marcus snapped.

"I wouldn't have it any other way. Upon her death the property

329

reverts to you. Do it."

"And if I don't?"

"Then I am going to show you how it feels to be struck in the face with a fist," Jon said. "And I hope that you can stand up to it as well as my mother does."

"Actually," Marcus said, "the house is already in her name, along with funds to maintain it. But she's a sick woman. That old witch doesn't care for her properly and lets her drink herself into insensibility every day."

"I can see that concerns you." Jon herded Marcus toward the desk. "Sit down and write."

"If I do," Marcus said, "then she becomes your responsibility. As far as I'm concerned, I never want to see her again."

"Very well," Jon said.

His face glowering, Fisher sat and wrote, then waited impatiently while Jon had Martha Blevins came down to witness his signature. "You realize, of course, that that piece of paper would be worth nothing in a court," Marcus said when it was done.

"Possibly." Jon took the paper. "But let's just say that this is a contract between you and me. Let's understand that if you ever again bother my mother in any way, I will seek you out, wherever you are, and no court in the world would be able to protect you then."

Marcus swallowed nervously. "For a few pounds I could have you killed in a dozen unpleasant ways."

"Then you'd better do it quickly," Jon said. "Consider, however, what would happen to you should your man miss the first time."

Marcus drew himself up, seemingly once again in control of his emotions. "Actually, Jon, perhaps this is all for the best. Your influence over her may be just the thing that is needed. I have fond memories of what she once was, and I wish you the best in restoring her." He started to leave, walking with his back stiff. At the door he turned. "But walk easy, boy. I've let you speak to me as no other man has ever done, because of what I once felt for your mother. Don't cross my path again."

Jon tried to relax. It had taken all his resolve to keep from hitting his stepfather. Martha Blevins, who had witnessed the last exchange, said, "He may be a coward, but he can be dangerous."

330

"Do you have my mother dressed?"

"No, and it's not my fault. She's in no condition to travel. She can't even stand up alone. She would be sick on the way into town, and she'd probably make an awful scene."

"All right," Jon said after a moment of thought; he had a few weeks before the *Maori* would be in Sydney. "Here's what we're going to do, Martha—"

"God help us," she said, when he had finished explaining.

With Martha's help, Jon went through the house methodically, collecting all alcoholic beverages and locking them in a secure cabinet. "God knows I've tried," Martha said. "I try to limit her drinking, but I guess I'm weak. When she gets bad it seems that there's only one thing to make her better, so I give in and let her drink."

Jon was discovering one symptom of the extent of his mother's weakness for drink. He and Martha found bottles, some full, some almost empty, secreted in the oddest places—under Caroline's bed, hidden among her wardrobe and in her bureau drawers, even outside among the bushes.

"We won't have found them all," Martha assured him grimly. "She can be crafty, that one."

The days that followed were among the saddest, and the most frustrating, in Jon's life. Caroline would awake with a raging headache and demand brandy, and Jon would sit on the side of her bed and talk to her in a soft voice, explaining that it was time for her to get hold of herself, that he was there to take care of her, and that in order to become well enough to travel with him, she would not be allowed to drink. He spoke of the pleasures of sailing the South Seas, of peaceful, tropical lands, of verdant islands smelling of flowers.

At first his attentions seemed to calm her. She slept much of the day, but in the middle of the night the cravings of her body roused her, and she prowled the house, growing more and more enraged when she discovered that her secret caches of drink had been removed. Jon was awakened by piercing screams, rushed down the hall in his nightclothes, to find his mother, her full breasts half exposed, her nightgown soiled by her search through the dark corners of the house, beating her hands against the door of the locked cabinet.

She screamed words at him that assaulted his ears and his sensibilities, words that he never would have imagined she knew. She pummelled him, tried to scratch his face, demanding that he open the cabinet. And that was only the beginning.

There were times, during those first few days, when he wanted to admit defeat, to open the locked cabinet and let his mother drink herself into peaceful oblivion. Her entire body would shake, and she would alternate between tearful begging and screamed threats. She would not eat, and she began to lose weight. She resorted to trying to arouse Jon's pity, crying heartbrokenly, telling him that she would surely die. She would promise anything. She would say that if he would give her just one drink she would never, never touch alcohol again, and that she would go with him anywhere and do anything he wanted her to do.

Finally, at the end of a fortnight, she began eating solid food. She was so thin, so pale, and so fragile looking that Jon feared for her health, but a visit from her regular doctor reassured him.

"It is about time someone took her in hand" was his verdict. "She's eating now, eh? Good. Terrible strain on her system, but not nearly as bad as drinking herself to death."

With the *Maori* due in Melbourne in less than two weeks, Martha had established a routine of regular mealtimes. Caroline, pale and thin, took to dressing for the evening meal, and Jon was heartened, for she seemed increasingly rational, liked to talk of the old days in London, and spoke fondly of her father.

"Once you wanted to take me to London," she said. "When can we go? I do so want to see my father."

She seemed well enough to be told, then, that Clive Mason was dead. She took the news surprisingly well. Her pale cheeks flushed, and she dropped her heat for a moment. When she looked up, her eyes glistened. "So I've waited too long," she said.

"When I last saw him he sent his regards, Mother. He said that he had always loved you very much."

"Oh, damn," she said, breaking into sobs. "How I have wasted it, all of it."

"Your life isn't over," Jon said. He rose, went to her, and put his hands on her shoulders. She seized one of his hands, kissed it, and he felt the fall of her tears.

"Oh, my son," she said. "Oh, how I do love and appreciate you."

He pulled a chair close to her, held both of her hands in his. "We're going to get you out of this house for a time," he said. "You'll be with me. The *Maori* is a solid, comfortable ship. The sea air will do you good."

"There is no one else now, is there?" she whispered. "There is only you and I."

"Yes," he said. "We'll go to Samoa—I have business there—and then to London. We'll put some flowers on Grandfather's grave and go through the things in his house together. He has named me his heir, but with the provision that anything you want is yours."

"That sounds like him," she said. "And he was right, of course, not to trust me with the estate. There's only one thing I'd like, Jon. A portrait."

"A miniature, of you? In a white gown?"

"That's the one."

"I have it in my hotel room."

She smiled. "Does that seem like vanity to you?"

"Not at all. It shall be yours."

She looked around. "But I don't want it in this house. I don't want it hanging here."

"We'll mount it in your cabin aboard the *Maori*."

She looked distressed. "When shall we leave?"

"In just a few days. We'll take the train."

"But there's so much to do. The house—"

"Forget the house. Martha has promised to take care of it."

Late that night, when Jon crept to the door of his mother's room to check on her, as he had done every night, he heard muffled sobbing. He stood by the door for a long time, listening and thinking. He suspected that she was weeping for her father, but he wondered if there were other reasons for her anguish. For the first time in years, he felt an outpouring of love for her.

He thought of Adam Shannon, and how different his own life would have been if his real father had been there. Jon could barely recall Leonard Forsyth, the man he had thought to be his father, and aside from one or two instructors at the military college and, for a brief time, his grandfather, the only man who had had a profound influence on his life was Marcus Fisher. To compare Marcus Fisher to Colonel Shannon was to understand what he had lost, and the thought pained him to his soul. Why couldn't his mother have loved Adam Shannon enough to stand by him in his hour of trouble?

The next day, he took his mother into Melbourne, so that she could buy proper clothing for the trip, and he saw her face light up as she fingered and admired silken gowns. He bought them for her. They dined together in the hotel dining room, and Jon was feeling at peace with the world until, as he left through the front door of the hotel with his mother on his arm, he almost bumped into Bartholomew Jamison. At first Jamison didn't recognize him and started to step back, but then with a snarl on his face, the man pushed forward, shouldering Jon aside and forcing Caroline back against the wall as he hurried past.

"What on earth?" Caroline gasped—but then, seeing her son's face, she fell silent.

"Not here, not now," Jon said under his breath, fury burning inside him as he watched Jamison disappear through the lobby. "Not here."

CHAPTER XX

A steady stream of visitors had been coming to the Elizabeth Bay house for weeks, so many that Magdalen, at first, was concerned that Red would be made unduly tired having to entertain them. The doctor, too, urged limits, but Red insisted on having them all admitted and, indeed, seemed to glory in the calls of various government officials, ship's captains, military officers who had served with him, and, to his great pleasure, a sprinkling of enlisted ranks who would stand at attention until Red waved them to ease and then, sometimes awkwardly, wish him well.

A telegram had come announcing the approximate date of arrival for the *Cutty Sark*, and Magdalen was touched to see that Red was marking off the days on a calendar that he kept beside his bed. The news of the *Cutty*'s arrival in Port Jackson Harbour was brought by Red's brother, Johnny, a full week before she was expected. Red demanded his wheelchair immediately and spent the next few hours on the veranda, using a glass to watch the graceful ship enter Sydney Cove and slowly, with the help of tugs, make her way to a wharf. He was on his feet, holding on to one of the supports for the veranda, when a hansom cab pulled up to the house and he saw Sam Gordon alight, turn, and take a pink-wrapped bundle from someone inside; then he was smiling, with tears forming in his eyes, as Jessica stepped down, waved to him, and dashed forward with quite unladylike haste.

She had regained the weight she had lost in Java, and the only overt signs of her ordeal were small scars on her hands and cheeks. She was weeping with happiness when Magdalen met her halfway down the walk, hugged her fiercely, then turned her attentions to the baby, leaving Jessica to rush onto the veranda and take her father into her arms. She held him for a long time, her heart half broken at his wasted condition.

"Enough of this," Red said gruffly, freeing himself from his daughter. "Let's have a look at the little lass."

Sam and Magdalen, with the baby, joined them on the veranda, and then it was time to greet Johnny and Kitty and to admire Kitty's children, and to talk all at once in joyous confusion, until Red was ensconced back in his chair and the others were grouped around him.

Chairs were brought out, and the talk and the laughter extended into the dusk of evening; but everyone became hushed when Red let his head slump and fell asleep in his chair. Johnny helped Magdalen take him inside.

"He doesn't seem to be recovering too swiftly," Jessica said to Kitty. "What do the doctors say?"

"Not much of help, I'm afraid." She squeezed Jessica's hand. "But I think you and that little girl will be the best medicine he's had yet."

"Kitty, tell me."

Kitty shook her head. "There are days when we have great hope. Like today."

"Kitty—"

"He just seems to be wasting away," she said, her voice low. "Something was injured inside him. He has trouble keeping food down, and when he does eat, he suffers horribly from it."

"But can't the doctors do something?" Sam asked.

"There was some talk of an operation," Kitty said, "but now—"

"Now what?" Jessica demanded.

"Now he is too weak to stand the shock."

But in the days ahead, Red seemed to rally. He spent hours on the veranda, watching Java play, and he eagerly questioned both Sam and Jessica about their experiences.

Adam Shannon's contingent of volunteers arrived from Hong Kong, and Adam lost no time calling on his old friend. Dinner was a subdued affair, with the seat at the head of the table empty, but afterward Red insisted that the men join him in his study for port and cigars, and he seemed as animated as ever as the discussion turned to ships and politics and then, finally, to the circumstances that had caused Adam's troops to be pulled out of Hong Kong.

"We haven't received our orders yet," Adam said, "but I have reason to suspect that we'll be bound east soon. The Germans have been making belligerent noises in the Pacific, as you all know."

"Seems to me the Americans are agitating as much as the Germans," Sam spoke up. He spread his hands. "Of course, I don't have the sources of information you gentlemen have. All I know is what I read in the newspapers."

"Which, unless you're reading Johnny's paper," Red said, "can be quite deceiving."

Johnny lifted his glass in silent agreement.

"The German supply lines will be long and exposed," Adam said. "I can't understand why they would even contemplate a war in the Pacific." He looked at Red. "Especially when they'll be up against another Broome."

Red nodded and forced a smile. Magdalen had informed the others at dinner that her and Red's son was to be assigned to the naval squadron based in Australia. Rufus would be home in a matter of weeks, after an absence of more than eight years.

"Red, you remember those guns of Han-Kuang's?" Adam said.

"How could I forget?"

"It's my bet that they're destined for Samoa," Adam said. "The Americans"—he nodded to Sam—"are apparently making them nervous. Too much competition."

Red mused. "Mounted on the heights above Apia Harbour, those cannon would be a potent force."

"I wouldn't relish having to take those same guns twice," Adam said.

"But why should you have to?" Sam asked. "After all, it's the United States that has treaties with the Samoans, with right to the harbour at Pago Pago. We're third in line on this one. I say let them fight it out."

"It's not so simple," Johnny said. "We have our interests to protect in the western Pacific, and there have been British missionaries on Samoa for ages. And the politicians have got it into their heads that Samoa is the key to the western Pacific. To stand by and let Bismarck dominate the sea lanes, the argument goes, would merely invite more German aggression at a later date. No, we'll be in it, is my guess, and, oddly enough, fighting on the side of the ex-colonies in America."

Red was thinking, *At least Sam Gordon will not be involved.* Sam

337

was a merchant navy man to the bone, and political quarrels went against his temperament—which was fortunate for Jessica and the child. Aloud, however, he said, "Give me a few weeks, Adam, and I'll lead your boys up the hills overlooking Apia, just as I did in China."

"I'll look forward to it," Adam said.

Jessica had put the baby to bed and was in the dining room with her mother and Kitty. Over tea they were comparing the personalities of their children. It was Kitty who brought up a subject that Jessica had been avoiding.

"I envy you," Kitty said, "going to England."

"As a matter of fact," Jessica said, "Sam and I were discussing that just today. We have agreed that it would be best for me to stay here."

"Whatever for?" Magdalen demanded.

Jessica opened her mouth to speak but did not find words.

"If you're thinking that I need help in caring for your father," Magdalen said, "remember that this is not the first time he's been wounded, or ill, and that I managed quite well."

"Mother, it's just that—"

"And if you have any sentimental notions about staying because you're thinking that you should be near him in his last days, forget that, too." Magdalen's voice nearly broke, but she spoke with force. "Your father is going to live to be a very old man."

"And I'll be here to help, if I'm needed," Kitty added.

"Your place is with your husband," Magdalen said. "Be thankful to God that he loves you enough to want to have you with him."

Guilt and joy were mixed in Jessica. It was true that she had been thinking that her mother would need help, and that her father was dying. She still thought as much, but she wanted to be reassured, and wanted to believe. Thus, when Sam came up to bed, smelling of drink and tobacco, she clung to him and told him of the conversation, and he expressed agreement and relief. After the long months of thinking that she was dead, he said, it would be unbearable to have her out of his sight.

"So it's decided, then," she said. "I'm going with you. Isn't that wonderful?"

"At this rate we shall rear a daughter who won't know whether she's supposed to climb a coconut palm or a ship's spar," Sam chuckled.

"You're terrible," she said. "She'll be a perfect lady."

"With the vocabulary of a working sailor?"

"She'll have the influence of her father," Jessica said, "who is, after all, a proper gentleman." Sam had been working his hand under her nightdress, and she, unconsciously, had been responding to his touch. "However, sir," she whispered, "I'm not at all sure *that* is altogether proper."

"We have been commanded to be fruitful," Sam said.

"Who am I to go against a divine command?" she said, melting against him and falling silent in his arms.

Busy days followed, days of family gatherings, days filled with preparations, with friends, and, in Sam's case, with business, as he once said again inspected every foot of the *Cutty Sark*. Sydney's waterfront was a bustling place, crowded with onlookers as well as sweating labourers, for the new crop of wool had, it seemed, drawn half the tall ships in the region. *Thermopylae*, the *Cutty*'s old antagonist, was there, proud and tall, the cock still at her masthead, stating her claim to be the fastest of alal the slim, narrow-waisted ships whose size, grace, and speed still kept alive their claim as queen of the seas. In dockside taverns, officers and men got together for bouts of drinking and bragging about the relative merits of their ships. Of all the crews, *Thermopylae*'s was the proudest, to the point of arrogance, taking every opportunity to remind the men from the *Cutty Sark* of the humiliation of the *Cutty*'s maiden voyage to China, when a broken rudder had allowed *Thermopylae* to beat her to England by a large margin.

"Our problem is, you see," Tom Jenkins told a bos'un's mate from the *Thermopylae*, that we've never had us a captain, until now. But now we have got us a genuine captain, and if you climb high enough in the rigging, you might catch a glimpse of the *Cutty*'s stern, laddie."

Sam couldn't help but hear the talk. When he was approached by Tom Jenkins, who was trying to determine which ship would leave port first, judging by the progress of the wool loading, Sam said, "Tom, the days of the great tea races are over."

"I ain't talking about no tea race, sir," Jenkins said. "I'm talking about a *wool* race. And no broken rudders this time."

"I can't guarantee that," Sam said. Actually, the idea of a race had not escaped him, but it looked to him as if the *Thermopylae* would be loaded first. Which was not all bad, as far as he was concerned. Give her a head start, and she'd feel confident.

The next morning, Sam walked the teak decks from stern to bow, noting that some of his crew were actually helping the stevedores stow the bales of wool in the hull. He could almost feel their impatient excitement, sense their confidence. He stood in the bow and gazed up at *Cutty*'s towering spars, saw in his mind her skysails billowing with the monsoon winds of the Indian Ocean, and, like his crew, felt a thrill of anticipation.

Red was feeling well enough that evening to join the usual grouping at the dining table. The talk was mostly of Adam's imminent departure home to New Zealand, where he would be rejoining his family, at least until his orders arrived.

"Sam," Jessica said, during a brief lull in the conversation, "we're simply going to have to have a talk with my father. It seems that he's put down ten pounds on the *Cutty* in the race."

"What race is that?" Sam asked innocently.

Johnny laughed. "That's the reaction I got from the captain of the *Thermopylae*. It seems that everyone in the British empire knows that the *Cutty* and the *Thermopylae* are going to go head to head again, except the respective captains."

"Oh, I have heard some talk among the men," Sam said with a sly smile.

"He's heard some talk from his wife, too," Jessica put in. "We're going to pin their ears back. We're going to fly by them and reach right out and pull that hateful cock down from her masthead and stew it for supper."

"Hear! Hear!" Adam Shannon said. "That's the spirit!"

"It's a tightly held secret," Johnny whispered to the table at large, "but a crewman of the *Thermopylae* told his lady that she'd be across the bar on the morning tide two days hence."

"An even start then," Adam said. "Isn't that *Cutty*'s sailing date, Sam?"

"Yes. Quite a coincidence, isn't it?"

There was general laughter.

"Not to put a damper on the fun, but I spoke with a gentleman at the telegraph office," Johnny announced. "He says there are daily status reports being sent out. I'm afraid, Sam, that the smart money is being laid on *Thermopylae*."

"Who's not smart?" Red demanded. Magdalen looked at him with sudden concern, for his usually strong voice had been a hoarse whisper.

"Well, that remains to be seen, sir," Sam said. "I'll certainly do my best to see that you're not proved to have been ten pounds foolish."

Red's head was sagging. Magdalen rose and pulled his wheelchair from the table, to take him to the downstairs room where his bed had been set up.

"I'm tired, Maddy," Red said when they were in his room. "Just tired, that's all."

He hadn't called her Maddy since the early days of their marriage, and the sound of it pleased her. She helped him undress and don his nightshirt. He let his head down onto the pillow with a sigh.

"Sit with me for a while," he said. "Let the young ones entertain themselves."

"Shall I read?" she asked, noting that her own voice was unsteady.

"No, no, just talk to me, my dear. The sound of your voice soothes all aches."

"I'll miss Jessica and the baby," she said, taking the rocking chair beside the bed.

He nodded almost imperceptibly. "Did she have any foolish ideas about not going with Sam because of me?"

"Of course she did. She's your daughter. I told her we wouldn't hear of her not going."

"Good girl."

"I told her that when she returns in seven or eight months' time you'll be on your feet and that we'll all take a trip to Wellington to visit Adam and Emily and Claus and Mercy."

"I'd like that. And Rufus. He should be here any day now, shouldn't he?"

Magdalen's throat tightened, for she knew their son would not

341

be home for at least another month; Red had somehow forgotten.

"Yes, darling, though I scarce think we'll recognize him, it's been so long."

Red licked his dry lips, and after a pause, he said, "Could you read that book? The one by that Verne fellow, about going around the world in eighty days?"

"I wasn't sure you like it," she said.

"Oh, I did. Imagine, airships with motors. One day maybe they'll make the trip out from England in a matter of weeks, not months. That would be something to see, eh?"

"You'll never see me in an airship," Magdalen said.

"Never say never, old girl." Red let his heavy eyes close. "We've seen a lot, Maddy. We've watched this country grow up—railways, steamships, telegraphs. If man can send a message across and under oceans almost instantly, why can't he build an airship?"

"Hush," she said.

"Don't go, Maddy."

"No. I'm here." She took his hand and leaned against the bed as his breathing deepened and he slept. Her own eyes became heavy, and after her daughter had looked in to whisper that the guests were gone, she pulled off her shoes and outer clothing to lie beside him.

"*Dear God*," she prayed silently, "*this is my husband, my beloved husband, and he is sorely ill. I ask not for myself, Lord, but for our son and daughter, and for our granddaughter. Please, Lord, let him live.*"

She dozed. When she awoke in the chill, silent morning, Red's breathing had changed. Alarmed, she quickly lit a lamp. His eyes were open.

"Maddy," he whispered, his lips barely moving.

"What is it?" she asked, unable to keep the terror from her voice.

"I've tried so hard, Maddy."

His eyes closed, as if he were going back to sleep, and then his chest heaved, once, twice, three times, and it was as if she could feel, with an inner sense, the life going out of him. Something unseen and yet tangible seemed to brush her—a loving, gentle

342

touch—and then she felt such an anguish of loneliness that the wail came from her throat without her realization.

The words were familiar and sonorous, and they were comforting to hear on a still, beautifully sunny morning.

"*In the midst of life we are in death . . .*"

A good percentage of Sydney's oldest families were there, dressed in sombre mourning.

"*Unto Almighty God we commend the soul of our brother departed, Murdoch Broome, and we commit his body to the ground . . .*"

"He was never called Murdoch in his life," Johnny whispered to Kitty.

"Hush," she said.

"*Earth to earth, ashes to ashes, dust to dust; in sure and certain hope of the Resurrection unto eternal life . . .*"

Adam Shannon, in dress parade, commanded the squad of honour; the harsh bark of the rifles fired in salute brought calls of protest from birds and left the smell of gunpowder in the air as Adam and Jessica escorted Magdalen from the gravesite to a carriage.

"I'll be with him soon," Magdalen said, as if talking to herself.

"Oh, Mother," Jessica said through her tears, "don't say that." It seemed petty to Jessica to be thinking that now, after all, she would not be going with Sam. But he could remain in Sydney no longer. She knew that his crew had been bitterly disappointed to watch the *Thermopylae* put out on the morning tide, leaving the *Cutty*, laden and ready, at the dock. Already the *Thermopylae* had a four-day start, and more than pride was at stake. The owner's money and prestige, and money invested by others were represented by the wool in the *Cutty*'s hold. Sam could not delay his departure any longer, and she could not, in all conscience, think about leaving her mother at such a time.

As it happened, Claus and Mercy Van Buren, who had been in Melbourne, had arrived in Sydney only a day after Red's death. Others had sent their regrets. Rufus, somewhere in the high seas, in all probability still did not know of his father's death. Old friends and neighbours kept the house filled with visitors, however, and Magdalen had been kept busy accepting condolences and, against all advice, playing the hostess.

Later, at the house, Jessica went upstairs to unpack the sea chest that contained Java's clothing. Sam was already aboard his ship, making last-minute preparations.

"Just what do you think you're doing?" Magdalen asked entering the room unbidden.

"You see," Jessica said. "They'll get wrinkled staying in here."

"I see," Magdalen said. "And now I want to see you put those things directly back into the chest."

"Mother—"

"Listen to me," Magdalen interrupted. "The night before your father died, he told me he hoped you hadn't any foolish notion of staying here because of us. It was among his last wishes for you to be with your husband. You'll come ashore soon enough, when Java is older and has to go to school. But you should be with Sam now, and I won't have it any other way."

"But—"

Magdalen shook her head. "Pack those things."

Sam, too, tried to protest, when he returned to the house to take his leave, but Magdalen would not hear of it. So it was that when the *Cutty*'s mooring lines were cast off, Java was seated on Tom Jenkins's shoulders, taking in with wide-eyed wonderment the hurried labours of the sailors and the crush of onlookers ashore.

"You can catch 'em, *Cutty*," a man shouted as the ship was eased away by tugs and sailors scampered into the rigging to begin to unfurl the sails.

"Go to it, *Cutty*!"

"We've got our luck with us this time," Jenkins said to Jessica, swinging the child down and into her arms. "We'll show 'em, ma'am." He looked around, puzzled. "Where's the cap'n?"

"He went forward," Jessica said. She followed the old bo'sun into the bow and looked over. Sam had climbed out on the bowsprit shrouds and was perched precariously over the figure-head, clinging to a line with one hand while he replaced the frayed weathered rope in the witch's hand with a new, longer piece. Jenkins whooped, causing little Java to squeal in appreciation.

"We're in for it now, boys," he yelled. "The man's going to *drive* this ship."

Cutty soon was free of her tugs and, in the wind-blown expanse of Port Jackson, made for the open sea as if she were indeed racing for her very life.

CHAPTER XXI

The Reverend Kevin McDougall stood on a cliff near the mission, looking down onto distant Apia Bay. At his side stood his wife, Jane, and the young Samoan woman who had come to be almost a part of their family, as well the finest teacher they had.

A sleek and deadly looking ship of war was entering the inner harbour, her stack smoke making a smudge in the muggy air. McDougall raised a battered glass and examined her for a long time. "German," he said, at last. "The *Adler*, if my guess is right. She's been expected."

In the harbour already were six men-of-war—three of them American, two German, one British. "I don't like it, Jane," McDougall said. "I don't like it at all."

"They seem determined to have their war," Jane said.

In Apia, the town that lay at the base of the oval harbour, there had been weaponless clashes among German and American and British sailors. Worse, Samoans were dying in senseless factional warfare encouraged by the three nations, each great power backing a different claimant to the Samoan throne. Misa's father, Molo, had sided with the Germans, in spite of the fact that it had been Germans who coaxed him into signing into indenture to go to Australia. Tui, less forgiving of the Germans, and hating all whites of English origin because of his experiences in Australia, now fought on the side of the faction backed by the Americans. Thus, to Misa's great sorrow, members of her own village had been pitted against each other.

"I doubt that they'll bother us," McDougall said.

"I pray to God you're right," Jane whispered.

The words had scarcely left her mouth when a small girl came running from the direction of the mission. She started crying out a hundred feet away. "Germans, Germans!"

McDougall ran ahead of the women back to the compound. He came to a halt, breathing hard, when he saw several armed, uniformed men in the central courtyard, rounding up all the children and the Samoan women who helped care for them. He felt a wave of great fear, combined with righteous anger. A heavyset man in a civilian tropical suit was giving orders, pointing out certain of the older children. Another civilian with him. McDougall moved toward the two men resolutely.

"Sir," the minister said, "what is the meaning of this?" He recognized the heavy man as a German of great influence in Apia and knew his name was Maxim Stoltz. He did not know the other, black-bearded man, who did not look like a German.

"We are going to borrow some of your charges," Stoltz said. "Do not worry, preacher, it is only temporary."

"I don't understand." McDougall looked back to see Jane and Misa running up to join him.

"With all the Samoan men fighting among themselves," Stoltz said, "we are short of labour to process our copra. They will be paid. If you like, I will deliver their wages to you, so that you will be able to use the money for their support in this mission of yours."

"Sir, they're only children," McDougall protested.

"Then it is time they learned the value of work," Stoltz growled. He turned away to continue his selection process. He pointed to a thin but tall girl.

"Not her," Misa cried out. "She is ill."

For the first time the man who was with Stoltz took a close look at the Samoan girl, who was, as her Western garb indicated, a part of the staff of the mission. His eyes narrowed and he whispered to Stoltz, who looked at Misa.

With a start, Misa recognized the bearded man. She glanced around nervously, thinking that she would flee, for the man was the same one who had held her people's papers in Australia. She could now remember not only his face, but his name, Jamison.

"You," Jamison said, pointing at Misa. "Come here."

"Misa is a vital part of our operation," McDougall said, "our finest teacher. I must insist that you leave her with us."

"I said come here," Jamison repeated, ignoring the minister.

Misa turned to run, but a German soldier caught her arm and

jerked her to a halt, then half dragged her to stand before Bartholomew Jamison.

"Yes," Jamison said. "I know you. You were in the group of kanakas who ran away and stole a boat." He looked at Stoltz, who nodded. "Take this one with us. She is legally bound to Marcus Fisher. He'll be delighted to see her."

"Leave her alone," Jane protested, moving forward, trying to tug Misa away from the soldier who held her. The soldier shoved Jane roughly, and she sat down with a thump.

"Here, now," McDougall said, leaping forward not to fight but to assist his wife. He was met by the butt of a German rifle, the blow taking him high on the forehead with a dull thud. He fell, blood springing up to run into his eyes. Jane, helpless, knelt by his side, then took his head into her lap when she saw that he was breathing. She fashioned a bandage from her petticoats, all the while weeping as the older childlren and Misa were marched away.

The men who worked the rigging of the *Cutty Sark* were seldom surprised to look over a shoulder and see the captain himself alongside them on the footropes. With the *Cutty* all but becalmed, Sam was in the rigging inspecting the new wire with which he had replaced the worn hempen braces that controlled the angle of the clipper's mighty yards. They were two weeks out of Sydney, and the *Cutty* was crawling in a mere whisper of a breeze, heading southeast into the vast reaches of the Pacific. When speed was important—as it was in the yearly race to be first to England with a cargo of the new crop of wool—the prevailing winds dictated that a clipper brave the fearsome seas and the cold of Cape Horn.

In those days of calm, Jessica and Java were often on deck. Jessica's heart was heavy, not only for her father, but for Sam and the crew, who were painfully aware that no fewer than nine of the world's finest clippers, including the *Thermopylae*, had left Sydney ahead of them.

When the winds finally picked up, the *Cutty* came alive once again. In the far southern latitudes, clipper weather was the norm, and the *Cutty* was in her element.

"We'll knock that gilded bauble off the *Thermopylae* yet," Jenkins told Jessica and Java, after dropping by the captain's cabin to deliver a pitcher of hot tea. It was the third day of near gale-force winds, and Jessica had not ventured on deck for fear of being washed overboard.

Shortly after dusk, the temperature plummeted and they sailed into snow and hail. Sam was on deck when the disaster struck. The *Cutty* had been running before a steadily building sea, and Sam was about to give the order to shorten sail when a hurricane blast of wind hit them with a fistlike mass, heeling the *Cutty* over on her beam ends and causing distressing cracking sounds. With a boom like a cannon-shot the main royal blew out and was shredded in a matter of seconds. The *Cutty* reeled like a fighter, and in spite of the efforts of the helmsman, she spun and broached to, presenting her side to the sudden, fierce winds and mountainous seas. The main upper topsail split, and in quick succession the main and fore topgallant sails went with sharp cracks of doom. The ship rolled, on the point of foundering as a huge sea flooded over her lee rail.

Sam was racing sternward, fighting the steep cant of the deck, impeded by water that swirled in a frozen torrent to his waist. He heard a crashing sound and saw a lifeboat breaking loose, to disappear into the blackness of the night. By the time he reached the wheel the helmsman was recovering, bringing the *Cutty* back with the wind as the torn sails flapped, disintegrated, and sent pieces of themselves sailing away into the snow and the blackness. The next wave was under her stern, and the *Cutty* lifted herself with a mighty effort to let the tons of green water roll off her deck. For long moments Sam feared he had driven her under, but as the *Cutty* steadied herself, he knew he still had a fighting chance.

"All hands!" he called, and the order was relayed below by a string of strong voices.

The *Cutty* was sorely wounded, her canvas in tatters, her speed reduced to steerage way before the waves. Sam gathered the crew, on watch and off. "There are two things we can do," he shouted over the howl of the wind and the din of flapping, torn sails. "We can heave to with storm canvas and wait it out—"

"No, no," the crew shouted, as if with one voice.

"Or," Sam said, with a defiant roar, "we can go aloft and bend on and reef new sails."

"You heard the man," the first mate thundered. "Hop to it!"

They scurried aloft, to work in sheets of snow and freezing rain, clinging precariously to the slippery yards and doing with a gale behind them what would have ordinarily been done with the ship hove to, its bow into the waves. They worked through the night, their fingers near frozen, their faces numb with the cold, and their eyes stinging from the sleet. Sam was with them, not once leaving the deck for the relative comfort of the cabin, but keeping the *Cutty Sark* racing forward, ever forward, toward the Horn and toward bitter cold and seas that promised to be even worse. Not until after dawn, with the new sails in place, did Sam go below, to greet Jessica with a wan smile and collapse on his bunk with his wet inner garments still on. Jessica, who was bundled into several layers of flannel, undressed him and covered him with extra blankets.

As the *Cutty Sark* approached Cape Horn, the *Maori*, thousands of leagues behind her in the Pacific, loafed her way through the South Fiji Basin with placid winds and tropical skies. At first Caroline Fisher had spent most of her time in her cabin, but as the days continued to be pleasant, and she grew increasingly bored, she now often joined her son on deck. She would take his arm maternally and walk by his side as they made circuit after circuit of the deck, talking of Jon's future plans more often than not. Since being forced to give up drink, Caroline had become increasingly lucid, so that Jon had found her company less of a burden than he had expected it would be.

It was on one such occasion after the two of them had dined with the ship's officers and Caroline had seemed unusually animated, clearly enjoying the give and take of the conversation, that Jon decided to broach a subject he had studiously avoided up to now. He began carefully.

"I must say, Mother, that you're looking much better and seem to be almost enjoying the trip."

Caroline laughed. "At least I no longer get the shakes when I think of a tall glass of brandy. Yes, I am feeling well."

"Well enough to talk about a matter that might be unpleasant for you?"

She looked at him with an odd expression, then smiled nervously. "Whatever could you have in mind?"

Jon decided to take the leap. "I'd like to talk about Adam Vincent."

Her face paled, and she looked quickly away, biting her lips in evident agitation. But she recovered and, having released his arm, levelled her gaze at him. "How much to you know?"

"I've talked with him," Jon said. "He's a very impressive man."

"He always was."

Jon saw that it would be up to him. "I know that he's my father." He watched for her reaction, and to his surprise she took a deep, shuddering breath and released it, as if she had been freed of an enormous burden. Tears formed in her eyes. "It's true, then?" he asked.

"It's true," she said. When he remained silent, staring out to sea, she spoke up, her voice unsteady. "Do you want me to confess all—to give you the details of our love affair?"

"No."

"What, then?"

"I suppose I just want to know more about the man who is my father."

"If you're wondering if I loved him, the answer is yes . . . although not enough, I suppose. I will no longer make excuses, Jon. I made mistakes—too many mistakes. Adam suffered on my account, and what I did to him can never be forgiven." Her voice was hardly audible.

"He recovered well."

"Yes, he was that kind of man." Her tears were flowing freely now, and Jon, in pity, put an arm around her shoulder. "I could have saved him the shame and humiliation of being driven out of the navy by simply telling the truth, but I was young and frightened and I couldn't. I just couldn't. It's obvious to everyone—even me, at times—that I am not a mature woman, Jon. I certainly wasn't then. When he enlisted as a common soldier, I simply did not have the courage to stand by him."

"I didn't bring up the subject to hurt you," he said. "I just needed to learn the truth." He dabbed at her wet cheeks with his handkerchief.

"I should have told you long ago, but it was easier to have you sent away. Will you ever forgive me?"

"There was never any question of that," Jon said.

Caroline was shaking with her sobs, but she took his arm, said "Come, let's walk," and continued their circuit around the deck.

"I don't want the crew to think I'm a mad old woman."

The proud gesture for some reason pleased Jon. "You're finished with Marcus Fisher now," he said.

"Yes. Thanks to you."

"I'm going to have my name changed legally."

Caroline glanced up at him, her wet cheeks glistening in the moonlight. "Will you take your—your father's name?"

"No. I won't cause him that embarrassment. I'll take your maiden name—Mason."

"That would have pleased your grandfather very much," she said, then fell silent until they had finished their promenade and she asked to be taken below to her cabin.

The *Maori* approached the Samoan group from the south, and at Jon's first sight of the mountainous slopes of Tutuila, he wondered why there was so much fuss over this group of relatively insignificant islands. True, the harbour at Pago Pago, which under the agreement of 1878 was controlled by the Americans, was one of the finest in this section of the Pacific, but still it seemed odd to have three great nations contesting for such a small prize. The *Maori* dropped anchor in Pago Pago, and on going ashore Jon was pleased to discover that an American merchant there was expecting him and had set aside a decent assortment of crafts. He concluded his business before he made inquiries for a village chief named Molo, who had a daughter named Misa.

"Sorry, we can't help you," he was told. "We have a saying in the United States that applies here. Seems that there are more chiefs than Indians."

"The girl was educated in a mission school run by the British, I think," Jon said.

"Oh, well, there are missions, of course, on all the inhabited islands. Here on Tutuila we have the Baptists."

"Americans, then?"

"Yes. Fine old fellow, the missionary. Shall I arrange an introduction?"

"No, thank you." Jon was beginning to realize the futility of his quest. He didn't even know Misa's home island, if she had indeed made it back safely to Samoa. He was sure, however, that it had been British missionaries who had taught her English.

Her accent had been unmistakable.

The *Maori* departed from Pago Pago for the two westernmost and largest islands in the group, Savaii and Upolu. Between them there were nearly a thousand square miles of land, and hundreds of villages. Thousands of people.

Caroline was on deck when the *Maori* sailed into Apia Bay. She exclaimed over the beauty of the scene—the emerald mountains rising almost from the shore, the changing colours of the water as the ship passed through a wide opening in the reef into the calm, protected bay. Jon, too, appreciated the tranquil grandeur of the setting, although he was struck by the incongruity of seeing several large warships at anchor, evidence of what he had come to consider a ridiculous rivalry. Jon's contact in Apia, a less than fervently nationalistic German merchant, spoke heavily accented English and assured him that the authorities would have no objection to his purchase of native crafts. Copra, of course, would be out of the question, since it was grown, processed, and transported under a German monopoly.

To Jon's delighted surprise, the man had heard of a chief named Molo, if not of Misa, and he even offered to provide a native guide to take Jon to the nearest British-run mission, where he was certain Jon could learn more.

With hardly contained excitement, Jon sent a message back to the ship, stating he would return within twenty-four hours, then set off with the guide. The Samoan, who worked for the Germans and spoke only broken English, led the way in silence along a flat, sandy beach studded with coconut palms and through a small village of thatched huts. Everywhere, brown-skinned people were unhurriedly going about their daily activities. A group of older boys was unloading the morning catch of fish, which were being cleaned by scantily clad women, some of whom reminded Jon of Misa. Past the village, the trail entered the forest and climbed steadily upward, it seemed to Jon, forever. By the time they reached the crest, he was soaked in perspiration, and the breeze that blew was a welcome relief. As the guide led him toward a group of buildings, he heard a child's voice crying out, "Germans, Germans!" A white-haired man with a bandage on his forehead came to meet him.

"I'm not German," Jon said.

"I can see that, friend. My name is Kevin McDougall."

Jon introduced himself and politely refused the offer of food. "I have to get back to Apia as soon as possible," he explained. "I'm looking for a young Samoan woman. She was educated in a British mission. Her name is Misa."

McDougall's eyes narrowed, and the smile left his face. "What is your interest in Misa?"

Jon's first reaction was joy. The man knew Misa. And then he was trying to formulate an answer to the question. Just what was his interest in Misa? To see her once more? To somehow repeat that experience in the grove in Australia?

"I met her and her father in Australia," he said. "I helped them, as best I could."

"Are you the gentleman who gave them money?" McDougall asked.

"Yes, I did give them some money."

"Well, praise God!" McDougall took Jon's hand for the first time. "Welcome, friend."

"You know Misa, then?" Jon asked, holding his breath.

"I consider her to be one of our greatest blessings." McDougall abruptly frowned. "And at the moment, however, I'm very much concerned for her. Perhaps you've arrived at an opportune time. She has been taken away, you see."

Fear crept into Jon's heart. "What's that?"

"The Germans came to conscript our older children into field labour," McDougall explained. "There was a man with the Germans, an Englishman. He recognized Misa and said that she had cheated him by running out on her indenture and by helping to steal a boat in Australia."

Jon's face flushed. Jamison? Here in Samoa? "Was he a big man, with a dark beard?"

"Yes, exactly."

"Bartholomew Jamison?"

"He didn't bother to tell me his name. But he was with a German, Maxim Stoltz—a very influential man in Apia. And he mentioned taking Misa to someone named Marcus. I forget the last name.

Jon's panic was growing. "And you just let them take her?"

McDougall started to flare but restrained himself. "They came with armed German soldiers. I could not stop them, as you can see." He touched his bandaged head. "I have contacted our diplomatic representative here but was told that if the girl actually did run out on her indenture papers nothing could be done."

"Where did they take her?"

"Into Apia, I'm sure."

"How long ago?"

"Four weeks," McDougall said.

Four weeks. In the hands of men like Fisher and Jamison, that could be a lifetime.

The British chargé d'affaires in Apia was a civil servant who was only months away from retirement, a colourless, thin man who, Jon found out quickly, wanted nothing more than to be left alone. While Jon explained his problem, the man drummed his fingers on his desk, shook his head occasionally, and sighed.

The answer did not surprise Jon. "I'm afraid you are interfering in legal matters that are beyond your depth, Mr. Fisher," the man said through thin lips. "Since you're Australian, you as much as anyone should know that indenture papers represent a legal contract. If what you tell me is true, Mr. Fisher—the *other* Mr. Fisher—has a legal right to hold the girl and to ship her back to Australia to fulfill that contract. After all, the man did invest money in her transportation, in her kit, and in feeding her."

Jon left the office with a sour taste in his mouth. As he walked back toward the wharf where he had come ashore, he gazed out at the warships in the harbour. There were a few merchant ships as well, but he had not recognized any of them as belonging to Marcus Fisher—although, in truth, he had no way of knowing how many ships Fisher owned. He prowled the waterfront, looking for English-speaking sailors to question, and was rewarded by the unexpected sight of Bartholomew Jamison, entering what looked to be a seaman's pub. Intense relief swept over him, for if Jamison was still in Apia, Marcus Fisher probably was too, as well as Misa.

Not yet ready to confront Jamison, Jon wandered on, struck up a conversation with an old Samoan who spoke only a little English, and then with an American naval officer, an eager-looking young man who supplied him with information that the Samoan could not.

"Kanakas?" the American said. "Yes, I know where they're kept before being shipped out." He pointed toward the eastern edge of town, and Jon walked in that direction, until he found a pen much like the ones he had seen in Australia. Within the easily climbable barrier, several Samoans were sitting around fires, laughing and singing, most probably dreaming of the wealth they would earn in Australia. He managed to get the attention of one group, and a buxom young woman came smilingly toward the fence. She spoke only a few words of English and shook her head, smiling all the while, at the names Molo and Misa. He wanted to tell the woman, "Stay at home. Change your mind while you can." But he suspected that even if she had been able to understand his words, her optimism would not have been lessened by any warning.

Jon's next stop was in the office of the United States diplomatic presence in Western Samoa. There, in marked contrast to the British office, he was queried politely about his needs by a crisp, efficient naval rating, then ushered into an office where a man who reminded him very much of Adam Shannon thrust out his hand and introduced himself as Commander James Grey, United States Navy.

"What can we do for you, Mr. Fisher?" Grey was taller and thinner than Jon, and his temples were just beginning to be touched with middle age. Jon found him an attentive listener who asked pertinent questions. "It's a barbaric practice, indenture," Grey said. "I'm surprised you people still condone it."

"Only some of us do," Jon said.

"You think the girl is being held somewhere here in Apia?"

"Unless there's been a ship bound for Australia in the past few weeks," Jon said.

"No, no departures," Grey said, after quickly checking a shipping list. "And who is this Englishman who took her?"

"Marcus Fisher."

Grey raised an eyebrow. "A family matter?"

"He's my stepfather," Jon said. "He's from Victoria, actually, and runs sugar plantations in Queensland."

"I see." Grey looked puzzled. "Why is an Aussie working with the Germans?"

"I wish I knew," Jon said. "But I don't. As I said, I know only that my stepfather's employee was with Maxim Stoltz when they went to the mission and took Misa. Perhaps he bribed the authorities—I wouldn't put it past him."

Grey was frowning. "Stoltz draws a lot of water here. The local German authorities bow and scrape to him, as if he were a representative from old Bismarck himself. He pretends to be a journalist, or something of the sort, but since his arrival here things have gotten increasingly tense. The Germans go around looking for trouble, and some of the American and British lads are more than ready to give it to them. There have been some bloody free-for-alls, and partly as a result, the German governor here has told us that we—meaning us Americans—have one week to clear our ships out of Apia Bay."

"Or?"

Grey smiled thinly. "He didn't say. But there are rumours that German troopships are on the way."

"My God." Jon had not realized the seriousness of the situation.

"Meanwhile, your people don't seem to be overly concerned. I've spoken with your chargé d'affaires repeatedly."

"He's hoping to retire to his Norfolk cottage to grow roses," Jon said with barely concealed scorn.

"Then he had better be on his way. So far it's just been fists and maybe an odd bottle or two, but if the German seamen and soldiers appear on the streets armed—" He shook his head grimly.

"I think that all you've told me makes it more imperative that I find Misa," Jon said. "I don't want her to be caught up in the middle of a war."

Grey studied Jon closely for a moment. "This woman, she means a lot to you?"

Jon hesitated only an instant. "Very much. More than I can say."

"I don't want to get your hopes up." Grey stood up and walked to the window, to glance out. "But we're not without our sources of information here. For a while it looked as if our boys in the bush were going to win the little civil war that's going on among the natives, and so we've built up quite a network of informers. I'll put out the word and let you know the minute I hear something. You're staying aboard ship?"

"Yes," Jon said. "The *Maori*."

"If I were you, I'd have your crew ready to haul out of here on the double if the shooting starts."

"Thank you," Jon said simply.

For long weeks Misa had been confined to a bare room in the rear of a German warehouse on the waterfront outside Apia. She had been given no water for bathing and just barely enough to drink. She wore the same simple day-dress that she had been wearing when she was taken from the mission. She felt soiled and grimy. When she had first been taken to the almost airless room, Marcus Fisher had appeared with Jamison and questioned her harshly, trying to force her to give him the names and the present whereabouts of the men in the group that had run away and stolen the boat. Her cheeks still showed evidence of Fisher's vicious blows, in the form of purpling bruises. But Fisher had not come back since, and Misa assumed he had gone to one of the other islands on business. Surely, if he or Jamison had returned to Australia, she would have been taken on the same ship.

She was lying on a filthy cot, staring at the ceiling, when she heard light footsteps approach; it was, she knew, the old Samoan woman who delivered her meagre daily ration of food. The woman unbarred and opened the door and stood looking down at her.

"Why are you here?" the woman asked.

The question surprised Misa, who had tried to communicate with the woman before, only to give up in helpless frustration when the woman refused to reply.

"I am being held prisoner," Misa said, quickly sitting up. "Would you please contact the Samoan authorities?"

"What Samoan authorities?"

"Some member of the town *aumaga*."

The woman spat. "Those who are of the aumaga are no friends of mine." She looked at Misa suspiciously. "Who is your *matai*? For which of the chiefs do your people fight?"

"Does that matter?" Misa asked. "I am being held against my will. I have been beaten."

358

The woman shrugged. "He did not mark you badly."

"Will you help me, please?"

"That depends."

"On what?" Misa asked desperately.

"On who is your *matai* and on whose side you belong."

Misa thought furiously, wondering how to answer. Clearly the woman worked for the Germans; yet she had said that the *aumaga* of Apia were no friends of hers. That was puzzling, because Misa had heard it said that the *aumaga* of the town were in league with the Germans. Molo, her own father, fought for the pretender to the Samoan kingship favoured by the Germans. Tui, on the other hand, was on the side of the American-supported claimant.

"My brother is Tui," she said, deviating from the truth only slightly, in that Tui was not her brother by blood. "He fights for Fita."

The woman's face seemed to soften. "Ah," she said. "Is it because your brother fights against the Germans that you are here?"

"Yes." Misa prayed it was the right answer.

"I will tell you this. The *aumaga* of Apia will not help you."

"Can you help me get away?"

The woman shrugged. "There are guards, as you know. Here in the building the Germans store not only trade goods, but weapons. I do not think you could manage to escape, not without help."

"Can you send word to the Reverend McDougall at the mission, then?"

"Here, eat," the woman said, putting the woven basket down on the cot. "I will do what I can. It may take time. I have been cautious up till now, because the Germans watch me closely. But then I heard you were to be taken from the islands on a big ship."

The words struck fear into Misa, and her fear turned nearly to panic the next day, when Marcus Fisher was back with his questions. "You will tell me who led the escape," he demanded. "You will talk, if you know what's good for you."

"I knew them only slightly," Misa lied. "They were not from my village. I cannot remember any names."

"I think," Fisher said, leaning over her, "that I won't send you back to the cane fields. I think I'll sell you to a brothel."

"I cannot remember any of their names," Misa repeated sullenly.

Fisher lashed out, and his palm rang on her cheek. She was knocked to her side on the cot. He leaned and touched her breast, and she jerked away, her distaste showing on her face.

Fisher laughed. "So, that is more effective than beating, is it?" He motioned to the German soldier guarding the door. "Hold this one tightly," he ordered. The soldier seized Misa's arms and held her down on the cot, while Fisher ran his hands roughly over her breasts. "This line of questioning would be more interesting if you had a bath," he said, but his hands continued to probe and squeeze, and then one hand moved down and tried to find a way between her tightly held thighs. She lifted her head and spat into his face.

Fisher jerked back and, in fury, hit her once, twice, three times. She lay on the cot, dazed. "Slut," he hissed. "A brothel would be too good for you."

The German soldier still held her, eyeing her greedily.

"You don't understand German, do you?" Fisher asked sarcastically. "Well, I can tell you that this large, meaty oaf wants you. I just might let him have you, and when he's finished, all the others. I'll give you just a bit more time to try to remember some names."

Alone, Misa touched her new hurts gingerly with her fingertips. She was too angry, too deeply frightened, to weep.

CHAPTER XXII

Adam Shannon had embarked in haste from Sydney with a new contingent of colonial volunteers and orders that were, in light of the confused political situation, deliberately ambiguous. He was to take his troops into Apia Bay, land them near the village, and stand by in the event of trouble. "We don't seek conflict," he had been told, "but if it comes, be prepared."

"How many warships will I have in support?" he had asked.

"There is a battle cruiser in Apia Bay," had been the answer. "That is all you can expect."

One armed ship. And the best information available was that the Germans had a dozen ships in and around Samoa. The strength of the Americans was unknown. If, indeed, the Germans intended to annex Samoa, they had to be aware that it would not be accomplished without a fight. They had had months—no, *years*, Adam reminded himself—to amass strength in the South Pacific. Adam had three hundred men and a dozen light field pieces against the might of the German navy.

During his brief stay in Wellington, he had had the uneasy feeling that he would not see his family again. He did not believe in pre-battle premonitions, but he could not shake the nagging melancholy he felt. Already, he was missing old Red Broome. The Royal Navy commander in charge of the small convoy of troopships was eager enough and promised that his sailors would give a good account of themselves in any fight, but he wasn't Red Broome. Red had been seasoned by years of service, by the fighting in New Zealand and the China Sea. He had been a man Adam could depend on, could stake his life on, if necessary.

As the convoy steamed eastward, Adam conducted drills on deck and saw to it that each man's weapons gleamed and were in perfect operating condition. And constant exercise kept all but the most seasick men in shape. Still, the miles passed under the keels slowly, and the tropical sun heated the men's sleeping quarters to such unbearable temperatures that most of them sprawled in any available space on deck, not even bothering to go below during the brief and often fierce tropical showers, welcoming the rain, in fact, for its temporary cooling effect.

There was plenty of time to think. Adam found himself going back over his life—another bad sign for a soldier going into a fight. At first he resisted the urge to become nostalgic, but as the days seemed to grow longer and hotter, and the lassitude bred by inactivity held him in its grip, he no longer resisted the thoughts of his boyhood in England, of his apprentice days in the navy. He relived his court-martial and found himself thinking that if he had it to do over again he would do the same thing. He remembered the lashing he had received at the hands of Marcus Fisher on the way to Australia, and although he was not a vindictive man, he still wondered if Fisher would ever, in this life, suffer even a small measure of the pain he had inflicted on others. Such as Adam's own son, Jon.

He thought of Caroline, and although the memories were—or became in the light of a tropical moon—quite vivid, he did not regret her loss, for Emily was, had always been, all the woman that Caroline was not.

Emily. God, how she had stood by him. *If I–no, when I get back, my dear Emily,* he promised, *I shall make known to you just how much you have meant and yet mean to me . . .*

He did have one regret, however—that he had never had a chance to get to know his son. Even under Marcus Fisher's malignant influence, Jon had grown into a fine, courageous lad, and Adam would have liked to spend months with the boy—no, with the man, for Jon was no longer a boy—to get to know him, know his aspirations, his dreams. But that seemed hardly possible now.

The convoy was but two days out of Apia Bay when the skies began to darken to the northwest. The sporadic winds picked up, became gusty, and carried with them slashing flurries of heavy-dropped rain. Overhead, the low clouds were dashing toward the southwest, hurrying by like ghostly ships of the sky. The air grew heavy, even more oppressive.

Throughout a long and miserable day the weather worsened. The transports, heavy in the water and ungainly in even moderate seas, wallowed, pitched, and rolled, so that even many of the troops who had been to sea before became sick.

Commander Alfred Seymour, leader of the naval contingent, sought out Adam with the approach of darkness. The wind had continued to increase and now was near gale force. The steamers' auxiliary sails had been taken in, and the convoy proceeded at the pace of the slowest in growing, white-capped waves.

"I had thought we'd sail out of it," Seymour said. He was the younger son of a baronet, Adam knew, and had a grandfather who had served under Nelson at Trafalgar. "But that seems hardly likely now."

"You think we're in for a heavy blow, then?"

Seymour nodded. "Did you notice the clouds before dark?"

"I did," Adam said. "They were moving unusually fast."

"Yes. I was in the edge of a typhoon once myself. Damned frightening, you know. One could lean half over against the wind."

"Are you expecting a typhoon?" Adam asked with sudden concern. His short-lived naval career had never taken him to the Pacific, although he had heard tales of killer-typhoons.

"Actually, out here they're called hurricanes," Seymour explained. "From the Indian word, courtesy of the Spanish, you know."

"It hardly matters to me what one may choose to call it," Adam said. "Are we in for one?"

"Not yet, old chap. When you look out and see the tops of the waves flattening, or there's so much airborne water that you can't even see the waves, *then* you're in for a hurricane."

"It's imperative that we get to Samoa," Adam said.

"It's odd when you think of it," Seymour continued, oblivious of Adam's last statement. "North of the equator, the beggars whirl in a counterclockwise motion. Down here they're opposite, blowing in a clockwise direction. They can cover an area five hundred miles across. So south of the equator, if you stand with the wind on your back and extend your right arm in line with your shoulders, you're pointing to the centre of the storm."

Adam put his back to the wind and lifted his arm. It pointed toward the northwest. He knew that the big tropical storms that blew with some regularity into the northern coast of Australia swung, eventually, toward the southeast. The storm was moving on a path that would put the centre directly over them if they continued on the present course toward Samoa.

"The big cyclones are rare, out here," Seymour continued, talking calmly over the steady whistle of wind. "Damned odd that we'd run into one, and most unfortunate. I can't guess how severe this fellow is, but we can't afford to risk the men and the ships in winds of even one hundred miles per hour, and these cyclones sometimes blow two hundred—although as far as I know, no ship ever lived to talk about winds above force twelve."

"You're saying then, that we'll have to alter course?"

Seymour smiled, as if pleased by Adam's inference. "We're already turning toward the northeast, actually. We'll try to run out of this fellow's path, let him pass, and then come down from the north into Apia Bay."

By midnight the winds were whipping blinding spray from the tops of some of the tallest waves Adam had ever seen, but the convoy's ships, demonstrating a seaworthiness that surprised him, kept a dogged course toward the northeast, heading out of the path of the storm. For once Adam was grateful to be aboard a steam-powered vessel and not at the mercy of the winds, and in his preoccupation with the safety of the men in his charge, it did not occur to him that the storm from which they were fleeing for their lives was headed, in all its destructive fury, straight for Apia Bay.

The steamer *Antony* rode on her anchor cables just offshore from one of the uninhabited, rocky Samoan islands northeast of Apia Bay. She had been there for long weeks, since having put Marcus Fisher and Maxim Stoltz off on the motor launch to make their way to Apia Bay. The *Antony* had, in those weeks, become a slovenly ship. The crew, knowing that they were only a half day's steaming away from the pubs and the women of Apia, were a grumbling, unhappy lot; and the captain, far from instilling the discipline that was wanted, was himself drunk most of the time.

Day after day she had lolled at anchor, the tropical sun heating her metal hull, making it unbearable belowdecks. Some of the men had braved the threat of sharks to swim in the cooling water, but most simply sought out the few patches of shade on deck and grumbled.

Harry Ryan ignored the complaints, when he was sober enough to hear them. At such times, when his mind began to swim up from the deadening effect of drink, he had the feeling that something had gone wrong with his life. But he had his orders, he told himself, and he was being paid well. As soon as this one last task was accomplished, he'd be given a ship of his own, Marcus Fisher had assured him, with *carte blanche*, and a loan from Fisher's company, to make his own trades, chart his own courses. That was all that he had ever asked. At the moment, his only real worry was whether the whisky would hold out until Stoltz sent word that it was time to take the *Antony* and her cargo into Apia Bay.

But this one morning when Harry had awakened with the usual vile taste in his mouth and the usual splitting headache, something different had seemed to be in the air. He had had his breakfast, washed down with hot coffee liberally laced with the whisky Marcus Fisher had so thoughtfully left aboard, and gone onto the deck. A few of his men were fishing over the rails, but most just lay about, hardly stirring. For a moment Harry considered putting them to work getting the *Antony* spruced up, but the thought quickly passed. What did it matter?

He walked to the stern and looked up at the barren rock of the uninhabited island. Here, at least, it was not at all the paradise that lubbers dreamed of when they thought of the South Seas. Apia, now, might be different. He yawned and stretched, then raised his face to look at the sky. Overhead the arch of the heavens was cobalt blue, and the sun was dazzling. But far off, low on the northwestern horizon, lurked a dark band of cloud. His first thought was that it was a squall line, but then he realized that the band stretched clear across the horizon, with a darkness that sent a shiver of dread through his half-besotted mind.

No seaman who had ever been in a tropical cyclone, or even been brushed by one, could ever forget the look of the sky, the dense, oppressive feeling that was in the air. Harry ran his hand across his face as if to clear his vision, but when he looked again the low band of cloud was still there. And now other members of the crew had noticed it, too.

Harry tried to think clearly. The run out from the last coaling station in the Fiji Islands had left *Antony*'s stock of fuel low, so low that it would be necessary to go into Apia to the German coaling station before departing the islands. Harry went into his cabin to consult his charts. When he came back out on deck, the band had perceptibly widened, and the crew, all of them now aware of what was coming their way, snapped to at his orders. Soon the decks were cleared, all loose items secured or stowed for a blow, and steam was up in the boiler room.

The crew was waiting anxiously to get under way. Harry paced the deck in an agony of indecision. He had strict orders not to show the *Antony* in Apia Bay in daylight and not to come in, even in darkness, until he got the word. Her cargo was of too sensitive a nature to risk discovery.

Suddenly Harry stopped pacing. He would give Stoltz until early evening. If a boat had not come with a message by then, he would up anchor and steam into Apia after sunset, take on coal, and, if Stoltz was still not ready to unload the guns, run the ship back to sea to get out of the path of the storm that was moving toward him. If Stoltz didn't like that, to hell with him. Harry had a ship and a crew—and himself—to protect. The best place to weather a storm was at sea, and to remain with land to leeward would be disastrous.

By early evening, the *Antony* was rolling on the broad backs of heavy swells that, having passed under her, thundered into the rocky shoreline in the form of foaming breakers. The sky was now totally overcast, with the bottom layer of clouds overhead rushing in a great spiral toward the low pressure in the centre of the storm.

"All right, Mr. Mate," Harry called out, "up anchor, if you please. We're setting a course for Apia Bay."

The *Antony* steamed through gusting winds and rain squalls, and by late evening she was off the mouth of the bay. With conditions worsening, there was no question of getting a pilot, but Harry didn't really need one. The entrance to the bay, according to the charts, was broad and safe, one of the assets that made it a strategic prize. He took the ship directly to the coaling pier and surprised the sleepy watchman who, with truly Germanic arrogance, told him that he would have to move away from the pier until permission was obtained.

Harry, stone sober now and not in a good mood, stepped

around the man's desk, seized him by the collar, and said, "I want you to go now and awaken whoever is in charge of this place. Tell him that if he doesn't have a crew at work filling my bunkers within a half hour, I will break down the doors and do it myself. Do you understand?"

"This is highly irregular!" the man protested.

"If there's any question, tell them that they had best contact Maxim Stoltz," Harry said, giving the watchman a shove to send him on his way.

He waited impatiently. He saw lights being lit, and soon men, yawning and gaping sleepily, were preparing to load coal. He was on the deck, looking down from the rail, when Maxim Stoltz and Bartholomew Jamison came striding quickly onto the pier, mounted the gangway, and confronted him.

"Why have you disobeyed my orders?" Stoltz demanded furiously.

"Listen," Harry said.

Stoltz cocked his head in puzzlement. There was, over the clank and clatter of the coaling equipment and the voices of the workers, a whine of wind around the *Antony*'s superstructure. A squall of rain came, even then, and skipped its way across the water to strike the *Antony* at a windblown slant.

"So?" Stoltz asked.

"In about six to eight hours," Harry said, "you're going to have winds of force eleven or above."

"You're crazy," Jamison said. "You're talking cyclone, and they don't move this far east."

"Believe what you like," Harry said, "but I don't intend to sit here in the harbour to find out, nor can I go to sea without coal."

As he spoke, coal was rumbling down chutes, adding choking black dust to the heavy air. Stoltz was red-faced. "You have endangered our entire mission," he said. "I shall remember your insubordination. Get your coal, but be out of this harbour before daybreak."

"I plan to," Harry said. "And about the cargo—I don't relish skirting a hurricane with that much weight in the hold. If just one of those monsters broke loose in heavy seas it would tear the ship apart. Any possibility of unloading them? I reckon we have time, if you can muster a crew."

"No possibility," Stoltz said. "Our troopships have not yet arrived."

Troopships? Harry thought.

Stoltz, realizing that he had revealed information best kept to himself, hastened on. "If you are right about this storm, the work may be delayed. Do what you must to protect the ship, and when the storm is past, anchor in the appointed spot and wait."

Harry nodded dully, although he was still thinking about troopships. He had heard rumours that Australian troops were destined for Samoa, but they were not in evidence. Could it be that a minor war was indeed being planned? There were German and American warships, one British cruiser, and a few merchantmen in the harbour.

"Stoltz," he said, "you might want to pass the word to your people that as good as Apia Bay looks, it's no place to weather a hurricane."

"I am sure that our captains are as skilled in seamanship as you," Stoltz said, sounding annoyed. He made a curt bow, turned on his heel, and strode stiffly off. Jamison followed, only to be pulled to a halt by Stoltz as they reached the head of the pier. Harry watched them and saw Jamison return. The black-bearded man came back up the gangway and explained that he had been asked to accompany the *Antony* to sea, in case Harry required any assistance. Harry did not like the idea one bit, but he could not refuse.

When the *Antony* steamed into the open sea, just before daybreak, she butted head on into forty-five mile-per-hour winds and growing seas. Harry set a course north-northeast, toward the open sea and well clear of the reefs around a small speck of land appropriately called Danger Island. Intending to keep an eye on Jamison, he invited the big man to his cabin and offered him a drink, which was eagerly accepted.

"Not drinking, Captain?" Jamison asked.

"I might need a clear head before this is over," Harry answered. He waited until Jamison had downed an entire glass of whisky, then spoke again: "Stoltz mentioned troopships. The Germans are going to have a go at it, eh?"

Jamison nodded. "If the Germans get their troops here first and get those guns mounted, it'll be all over. The Yanks won't be able to stop them, nor will our one cruiser. Samoa will be German."

"Does that bother you, Jamison?"

"Bother me?" Jamison chuckled. "What difference does it make? A few islands in the South Seas, a bunch of lazy kanakas." He eyed Harry sharply. "Maybe it bothers you?"

"Why should it?" Harry shrugged. All the time and effort he had spent setting up a purported commercial spy system for Marcus Fisher, he now realized, had been helping toward this end, toward a German takeover of Samoa. True, Fisher had benefited commercially by knowing the sailing times and cargoes and destinations of other traders, but the real information that Fisher—no, that *Stoltz* had wanted was the disposition of British forces . . . and he, Harry, fool that he was, had complied, noting the comings and goings of ships of war. Now, at last seeing the fruits of his labours, he felt an angry blackness in his heart. He had never pictured himself as being a traitor to his country, to his heritage.

"Well," Jamison said, "I am here, as you might imagine, to see to it that it doesn't bother you *too* much. Not enough for you to throw a monkey wrench into the works, at any rate."

"Jamison," Harry returned with a grin, "I have to admit that I've had prettier nannies in my day."

Aboard the *Maori* the young captain, Robert Farrington, was growing increasingly nervous as the barometer continued to plummet and the gusting winds and blowing rain worsened as the day advanced. He sent two crewmen ashore to look for Jon Fisher, to tell him that it was high time for the ship to seek the open sea and sail out of the path of the coming storm. When one of the seamen returned with Jon, Farrington breathed a sigh of relief and informed the supercargo of his plans.

Jon thought rapidly. On his second day searching for Misa, he had encountered a Samoan man who had told him that a young mission worker was being held somewhere in Apia. But that was as much as he had learned, and if Farrington was right and a severe storm was coming, the *Maori* should not be kept in harbour. Part of her cargo had still to be loaded, but that could wait. Misa was another matter, and Jon could not abide the thought of leaving her any longer in Marcus Fisher's hands.

"Give me two hours, Captain," he said. "Prepare the ship for sailing, and if I'm not aboard in two hours, leave without me."

For two days the birds around the mission had been acting oddly. The forest birds had been noisier than usual, with nothing observable to alarm them; and the seabirds cluttered the air over the high ridge, squawking, diving down, swooping seaward, to fly low over the waters of the bay only to soar again. Jane McDougall had called her husband's attention to the odd behaviour, but the missionary had other things on his mind. Misa's absence preoccupied him. He had been hoping and praying that the young Australian who had come looking for her could, somehow, save her from being shipped back into indenture, and in the past days he had been composing a strong letter denouncing the practice, to be sent back to England to the elders of the church. Other than that, he felt helpless, for he was not a man of violence, much as he would have liked to be if it could help Misa.

When the winds and rain arrived and the seabirds vanished from sight, Kevin looked at his wife and said, "There's your answer, my dear. The birds were feeling a drop in atmospheric pressure. We're in for a storm, I fear."

"Oh, dear," Jane said, "and just when we've finished the new *fales* for the children."

The thatched, open huts for the children were not among Kevin's main concerns; a few hours' work could replace a *fale*. Although he himself had never experienced the brunt of a hurricane, he had heard the natives talk of the huge storms that uprooted the strongest trees, flooded low areas, and sent debris flying through the air with a force sufficient to make a harmless twig a deadly missile. "I think we'd best keep a close eye on the situation, dear, and if it appears that we are in for the worst of this storm, we'll move everyone down the ridge into the caves."

Jane's apprehension was quickly overcome by her practical nature. "In that case I'd better get busy. We'll have to have food, water, clothing. Someone must think of these things."

Soon Jane had the children organized and carrying provisions to the schoolhouse, from where they could be swiftly transferred to the caves. In the midst of the hurried preparations, an old Samoan man came up the trail from Apia and asked to see the missionary. Kevin greeted him impatiently, for the weather was steadily worsening, and one gust of wind had already claimed his hat irretrievably.

"Reverend sir," the Samoan said, "I have a niece, Ota, who works for the Germans in Apia."

"Yes, yes, what is it you want?" Kevin prompted. "We're quite busy."

"That, reverend sir, I can see," the man said. "And you are wise to prepare. As I said, I have a niece, Ota, who works for the Germans in Apia."

"Yes, yes, go on."

"There is a young woman there, named Misa, who has been beaten."

"God help us," Kevin muttered.

"And Ota tells me that the man Fisher, who is not German—"

"Yes, I know," Kevin interrupted. "What about Misa?"

"—but Australian or possibly British, that the man Fisher intends sending her to a brothel."

Kevin was speechless as the rain spattered him.

"This girl, this Misa, whose brother, Tui, fights against those who support the Germans, asked my niece to send a message to you."

"What is the message?" Kevin demanded.

"She is in the German warehouse to the east of town, and she asks your help," the man said. "A single soldier guards her. That is all I know."

Kevin thanked the Samoan, who lingered long enough to warn that the coming storm would be a bad one, and then he was gone, leaving Kevin to find Jane and press forward with preparations. He worked with her until everything was in readiness and all the mission's charges, each carrying a box or a bundle, started toward the caves, through winds that whipped hair and clothing and were already blowing forest debris through the trees. Jane, one of the last to go, had an infant in her arms.

"Well, come on, then," she called to him.

"My dear," Kevin said, "I have received word of Misa, and she needs me desperately. You go with the others, and stay in the caves until it is safe to come out."

"You're not going into Apia in this?" Jane gasped.

"For Misa, I must."

She saw the determination on his face and knew it was useless to argue. "Then God bless you—I suppose you must." She kissed him on the cheek. "You will be careful?"

"On that you can rely."

Already soaked to the skin, he set off down the trail. At first the winds impeded his progress, whipping branches across the narrow path and blowing grit and rain into his eyes, but then he was in the shelter of the ridge and made good time. To his surprise, the warships still lay at anchor in the bay. Two merchant ships under sail were leaving the mouth of the bay for the open sea. Only one sailing ship remained, anchored in the inner harbour. He prayed that the ship was the one belonging to Jon Fisher, for he would need Fisher's help if he were to rescue Misa.

There had been nights when Caroline had longed for a snifter of brandy to the point of becoming dizzy at the thought. On such nights her dreams had been chaotic, filled with images of her son, and of Adam Vincent, sometimes nightmarishly distorted by hideous visions of Marcus Fisher. During waking hours, however, she had felt well, surprisingly well, and she had come to think that Jon had been very wise in forcing her to accompany him on the voyage. However, the idle hours had lain heavy on her while the *Maori* was at anchor in Apia Bay. Caroline had made a quick tour of the town on the first day, escorted by the ship's willing young second officer, for Jon had been busy elsehwere. She had no further desire to spend time ashore in Apia, and she longed for the ship to leave, to be on the green waters of the Pacific, where everything seemed so serene and cleanly beautiful. The onset of heavy weather dampened her spirits, and she spent most of the time reading in her cabin. As the approaching storm began to send squalls of rain over the bay, she could not help but note the agitation of the crew and their young captain. She had heard Jon's voice, once, and then he was ashore again. She went out into a blowing rain to meet Robert Farrington, who was on the way to her cabin.

"I have come to tell you, madam, that we are sailing in a half hour," Farrington said.

"But the cargo—" Caroline knew that loading operations had been stopped as the weather worsened.

"We'll have to come back for the cargo," Farrington said.

"Is it because of the storm?"

"Yes, ma'am. We'll weather it best at sea, and there's no time to lose. I suggest that you stay snugly in your cabin, for we'll hit some heavy seas as we leave the harbour."

"Where's my son?" she asked.

Farrington looked distressed. "Ma'am, Mr. Fisher gave orders for the ship to sail without him, unless he was aboard at a certain time. That time has now expired. In fact, I've given him an extra half hour."

"You can't sail without Jon," Caroline protested.

"Those were his express orders," Farrington said. "I'm sorry. I have the ship to consider."

"But where is he? Why isn't he aboard?"

"That I can't say. Now, if you'll excuse me, ma'am. I have my duties."

Caroline went back to her cabin to fetch a light wrap, to protect her somewhat from the blowing rain. She stood at the rail, looking toward the docks, watching for Jon, while final preparations were being made. It was not until the crew was gathered around the capstan to start weighing anchor that she made up her mind. She sought out Farrington.

"I want you to put me ashore," she said. "If my son stays, I stay."

Farrington looked doubtful and started to protest.

"I'll hear no objections, sir. I will be put ashore immediately. I'll find my son and stay with him."

Farrington seemed to come to a quick decision; it was evident he had no time to lose.

"Very well, madam," he said. "If you insist." He called two seamen. Caroline, having quickly gathered a few necessities, was helped down into the gig and rowed the short distance to shore. She made her way through the rain to the quaint, wood-framed hotel facing the waterfront and had her things taken to a room by a nervous Samoan boy who kept cocking his head to look out toward sea. Caroline glanced back once, to see that the *Maori* was under way, moving with bulging sails toward the mouth of the bay. She considered going into the streets to look for Jon, but the rain was becoming heavier, and she decided to stay put. Apia was not a large town; sooner or later Jon would find her at the hotel.

She left a message at the desk and asked to be shown to her room. She was at the foot of a flight of bare, plain wooden steps when Marcus Fisher came down and halted in mid-stride to look aghast at her.

"What in the name of Hades," Fisher asked, "are you doing here?"

Kevin McDougall arrived in Apia soaked and exhausted. He had watched the last sailing ship in the harbour put out to sea, as he made his way along the beach toward the town; he was not hopeful. He had no idea what he could do alone, but he was going to try. The streets of Apia were empty, save for a few men who were putting up boards over the windows of the wooden buildings. There was no evidence of German, American, or British sailors, and he assumed that they were all aboard their ships. Still the warships remained at anchor.

McDougall was fairly certain he knew which warehouse the Samoan had been referring to. It was not far past the other end of town, on the waterfront. He was inclined to go there directly, but he was only one man. The Samoan had said that a soldier stood guard there—probably a German. He would, he decided, appeal to the civil authorities. Hurriedly he made his way toward the building housing the *aumaga*, holding his hand over his eyes to ward off a stinging, blowing rain. He found the offices closed and boarded, however, and after standing indecisively in the rain for a few moments, he decided to go to the hotel. The hotel was the centre of the town's social activities. There would be people there. He would ask the whereabouts of the local authorities, then put to them his request for the release of Misa. That was the only forlorn hope that remained to him.

He was almost at the hotel when he recognized the Samoan man who had carried the message to him only hours ago. The man was putting the final nails into planks over a store window. McDougall ran up to him.

"So you have come," the man said.

"I have come. I'm looking for the civil authorities."

The man frowned. "They hide from the winds." He pointed to a seaman's pub. "But the young Englishman who also looks for

Misa is there." McDougall's heart leaped, and whispering a prayer of thanks, he made his way to the pub, pushed open the door, and looked in. A few Samoan men were there, and Jon Fisher was talking to them.

"Mr. Fisher," he said.

Jon turned. "Reverend McDougall?"

"What's left of me," Kevin said. "May I have a word with you?" He led Jon into a corner. "I know where they're keeping her. She's guarded by a German soldier. I can't locate any of the authorities."

"Forget the authorities," Jon said. "Take me there." He went over to the bar, where the owner had on display a collection of belaying pins, neatly arranged in a rack.

"I would like to buy one of those," he said, pointing.

"No for sale," said the Samoan behind the bar.

Jon put out a silver coin, and the bartender, after inspecting it, took one of the pins and handed it over with a grin. Then Jon was moving toward the door, beckoning, and Kevin, with serious doubts now, followed. Sheets of rain hit them as they gained the street.

The building where Misa was being held was not far off, but it seemed to take forever to get there as they fought wind, rain, and spray that all but blinded them. The front doors were locked. Jon led the way around the side of the building, until he found a window. The howl of the wind was so loud that McDougall did not even hear the glass shatter as Jon punched out a pane with the belaying pin. Jon reached in, undid the latch, and opened the window; then after looking around to see if it was safe, he hoisted himself up. Once inside, he turned and held out a hand.

They found themselves in a dark, closed, empty room. The door opened to a hallway, which they walked down until they came to another door, this one locked. Jon put his shoulder to it, and the lock gave. They entered a large area stacked with crates and boxes. On the far side, light showed through an open doorway.

The noise of the wind outside made their footfalls inaudible as they crossed the darkened warehouse. Carefully, Jon peered through the open doorway, which gave onto another hall, like the one opposite it. A German soldier, clearly uneasy, was pacing up and down, in front of a barred door. The German wore only a holstered pistol. Jon motioned McDougall to be silent, and as soon as the German was pacing toward the other end of the hall, his back turned, Jon made a dash for him. The German heard and turned, his hand reaching for his weapon, but he was too slow, and the deftly wielded belaying pin struck the side of his head with a force that crumpled him to the floor.

Kevin called out: "Misa, are you there?"

A weak voice answered, but it was clearly Misa's. Jon unbarred the door, found it still locked, and kicked at it furiously until it gave. The room was dark. He saw movement, heard Misa's voice, and rushed toward her.

"Who?" she asked.

"Quickly," he said, taking her arm to lead her into the lighted hall.

"Reverend McDougall," Misa said. "Oh, thank God." Her face and arms were bruised, Jon saw with anger as she collapsed into the minister's arms. Only after a long moment did she look up at him.

"Jon?" Her eyes were wide with disbelief.

Jon didn't answer. He was thinking of what he would do to Fisher and Jamison when next he encountered them, and in his unreasoning rage, he dared not speak.

"We must go," Kevin said. He led the way back, holding Misa's hand, and climbed out of the window first. Jon helped lower Misa down to him. As they stood outside in the blasting wind, however, Misa came to Jon and clung to his arm, and her touch raised such emotions in him that he had to force himself to go on, to follow McDougall's lead. He had found her, and despite her sad condition, she was more lovely than she remembered.

"Hurry," McDougall said.

"Where are you going?" Jon asked.

"We must leave Apia," McDougall shouted over the wind. "The penalty for attacking a German soldier is severe. We must be far away when the man regains consciousness or is discovered."

The storm had brought early darkness, and now the wind was behind them, speeding them on their way. They crossed the deserted streets of town, and as they reached the beach on the other side, the coconut palms were swaying perilously, the fronds crashing down to the ground, and the rain was blowing almost horizontally.

McDougall halted, put his face close to Jon's, and shouted: "I'd hoped to make it back up the ridge, to the caves, but we can't—not in this."

"There is a place," Misa said. She led the way, turning inland, beginning to climb the slope. The path beneath their feet was muddy now, and once Misa slid and fell back into Jon's arms. He held her for a moment, as they stared at each other and she caught her breath.

"It's only a little farther," she said.

They struggled over the top of a terraced field, then down into a gully. Misa led them off the path to a small cave, the entrance to which was almost hidden by wind-whipped vegetation.

It was pitch-dark inside, and Jon took her hand to keep her near him. The wind howled past the opening, but it was dry and snug.

"Well, this will do nicely," McDougall said from the darkness. "We might as well make ourselves as comfortable as possible. I fear we'll have a long wait."

"Sit here," Misa told Jon, pulling him down beside her. He sat on what seemed to be fine, dusty soil and felt the warmth of her next to him. He began to feel a chill from his wet clothes, and beside him Misa shivered.

"It is a bit cold," he said.

"You came," she said softly, and the sound of her voice made him forget his discomfort.

"It was the Reverend McDougall who found out where you were being held."

"We'll have to find a place for you two to hide," McDougall said, "until this Fisher fellow leaves the island and things settle down."

"No," Jon said fiercely. "She will *not* have to hide. Not from Fisher, not from anyone."

"The children?" Misa asked.

"They're safely tucked away in the caves," McDougall said, "with Jane and the other women and plenty of food and water." He sighed. "Now, if you two don't mind, I'm going to try to have a nap. I'm getting too long in the tooth for running up and down hills and attacking German soldiers and rescuing fair maidens, it would seem."

Neither Jon nor Misa spoke for a long time, until they could

377

hear McDougall's quiet snoring. Jon's clothing was still cold and damp, and he had put his arm around Misa to stop her from shivering. Now, forgetting his own discomfort, he reached out with his other hand and gently touched her cheek, and she did not pull away. He found her lips and kissed her.

"You said you would come," she whispered, giving him her mouth again.

He drew away, confused and shamed. He knew that he could not keep her with him forever, as much as he longed to do. He was English, and she was Samoan, and therefore he could never take her as his wife; it was as simple as that. And he could not take advantage of her again.

"Perhaps we, too, should try to sleep," he said.

"Yes," she whispered, leaning her head against his shoulder.

Earlier in the day, the American squadron commander at Apia had called a conference of commanding officers aboard his flagship anchored in the bay. The two captains from the other ships had arrived in shining wet oilskins, accepted the offer of hot coffee gladly, and settled down to hear what their superior had to say.

"Gentlemen," Commander Grey began, "we are caught in a difficult situation. Here we sit, three fat ships, with a blasted hurricane bearing down on us, and we don't dare move."

"With all respect, sir," one of the captains said, "if we don't move, the storm might move *us*."

"That is a possibility," Grey said. "I don't like it any more than you, but if we leave the bay now, it will be as if we're obeying the German ultimatum. The Germans are sticking it out so far, and if the storm merely brushes Upolu, when we come back we're going to find Germans everywhere—in possession of the town, the entire island. I do want to hear your opinions, however. Can we weather a hurricane here?"

The other captain said, "If the winds don't hit much over a hundred miles an hour, we might come through. I've put out anchors fore and aft in pairs, as you gentlemen have. We've got good coral bottom. They'll hold, but only to a point."

"As you've mentioned," the first captain added, "it's evident that the Germans are staying. On the way over I saw the *Adler* putting out extra anchors."

"I don't hesitate to admit," Grey said, "that I'd rather be at sea, steaming at full speed away from this storm. But, gentlemen, we have our directives, and I intend to carry them out. Make your ships as secure as you can, because we're staying."

CHAPTER XXIII

Caroline Fisher lay across the bed in her hotel room, fully clothed, listening to the sound of the wind, which reminded her of the home she had known before she had married for the first time. It had been a snug house, where in winter the huge storms from the Atlantic howled around the chimney pots. She had put her encounter with Marcus on the stairs firmly out of mind, for it was too unpleasant a subject to think of; she had been surprised at her own courage in telling him to get out of the way, and she had swept past him almost regally. But now her half-dreams of home gave her a false sense of security, and she was reawakened to reality by a giant crash of glass and a roar of sound. Wind and rain were rushing in through the smashed windows of the hotel room, and she leaped from the bed and was bowled over by the force of the wind. The dresser overturned, crashing to the floor with a sound scarcely heard over the continual roar of the storm. The bed-clothes were whipped away, to be plastered wetly against the wall. And even as she fought her way toward the door leading into the hallway she heard strained, cracking sounds over her head, as the roof of the building was lifted and ripped away.

Tbe blackness of hell seemed to close in on her. She was in the hallway, desperately trying to remember the direction to the stairway. She had to fight her way against the wind that dipped down and seemed to want to lift her. She crawled over broken things and was being drenched by the torrential rain, until her hands encountered the stairs and she tumbled down to the first landing, into a less chaotic condition. The floor of the second storey of the hotel was giving some protection, although the entire hotel shook with the fury of the winds. She walked in near total blackness, feeling her way, bumping into the furniture in the lobby. She had no real purpose, only to move farther away from the stairwell, down which the wind and rain were pouring. She felt herself encounter the desk, a tall structure that came just above her waist. Behind it there would be some shelter.

As she rounded the end she heard a new sound, made faint by the bellow of the winds. It was the sound of some small, trapped animal. Alarm caused her to feel faint.

"Who's there?" she cried. "Is there somebody there?"

"Caroline?"

She knew that voice, even as it cracked weakly.

"Marcus."

The sound she had heard was a man weeping. "We're going to die," Marcus whined. "We're all going to die."

The strongly built desk was cutting off the wind. Caroline let herself sink to the floor. Her husband was near, sobbing and moaning in his fear. She felt a great surge of revulsion. Only a few people knew that Marcus Fisher was, at heart, a craven coward. There had been a time in her life when she had tried to deny it, to herself, when she rejected the whispered stories of how he had panicked during the shipwreck that had ended his first trip out to Australia. Adam Vincent had, during that incident, incurred Fisher's hatred by keeping his head and saving most of the ship's passengers, only to have Marcus steal credit because Marcus had been after all, an officer and Adam only a common soldier. But then, shortly after their marriage, Caroline herself had witnessed Marcus's cowardice when, during a Maori attack, he had refused to fight with the men, choosing to hide, instead, with Caroline and Kitty Broome. Looking back, she knew—there in that crumbling, wind-battered hotel at the head of Apia Bay—that she had been, even then, far gone into the near madness from which her son had saved her, for only a madwoman would have continued to live with a man like Marcus Fisher.

"We're going to be killed," Marcus whined. He crawled to her, seized her, and put his head into her lap like a small boy seeking comfort.

"Oh, do hush," she said, her voice harsh. His touch revolted her. How could she have sunk so far? How could she have changed so much from the young woman who had married John Omerod, who had loved Adam Vincent? Was it, after all, divine retribution that she had been cast with this man, with Marcus Fisher.

A thundering crash sounded over the storm, and Caroline expected that the entire hotel was going to come smashing down atop them. Fisher whimpered and clung to her, burying his face in her sodden skirts. She could almost feel pity for him. She felt no fear now, only a great sadness that she was to die just when she had begun to discover a new life, and when she had just begun to know and appreciate her son.

"Hush, now," she said, and she patted Fisher's head. "Hush."

She sat there patiently, and it seemed to her that the storm went on forever, with a gradual increase in fury that she thought she half imagined until, with a din that caused her to scream for the first time, the battered structure gave way, sending what was left of the second storey down on them. Her scream was echoed by Fisher's hoarse wail, and his fingers dug into her thighs painfully. Something struck her a glancing blow to the shoulder, and that part of her went numb. Windblown water slashed at them through the debris, but they lived.

"We've got to get out of here," Fisher croaked, crawling to encounter a jagged mass of broken timbers. Caroline moved her right arm. She had little feeling in it, but she did not think it was broken. She, too, explored, and found that they were trapped in a small space between what remained of an outside wall and the reception desk of the hotel. The timbers atop them were far too heavy for her to lift.

With suddenly renewed fury, the wind shifted the rubble, and blowing objects crashed into the remains of the hotel. Marcus gave up all hope and clung to her again, making his odd, animal-like sounds of fear. He kept saying that they were going to die.

"Marcus, shut up," she said at last. "We're still alive."

"It's God's punishment," he whined.

"Perhaps it is. We've neither of us been saints."

"It's retribution for what I've done," he said, between childlike sobs. "It's my punishment."

"For what, Marcus? For being greedy, for being a liar and a coward?"

"How can you say such things, at a time like this?"

"It's quite easy, really." Caroline felt as if she, and not the storm, held the power of life or death over him.

"You've always hated me."

"No, not always."

"You were always in love with Adam Shannon," he accused.

"Oddly enough, you're wrong, Marcus. There was a time when I truly admired you, when I thought you were dashing and handsome."

"Is that true?" he asked, lifting his head.

"Yes, it's true."

Marcus's voice became eager. "If we live, perhaps it is not too late for us."

Caroline shuddered at the thought but said nothing.

"I'll make it up to you," he said. "I can give you anything you want. I'm going to be one of the most powerful men in the Pacific, Caroline. I have made plans, you'll see. I'll have a corner on trade with all the German-held areas—"

Caroline had not been greatly interested in what he was saying until he mentioned the Germans. She had, of course, heard the talk of impending war with the Germans, and now her husband's comment intrigued her. "How will you manage that, Marcus?" she asked.

"Never mind," he said; but in the next moment, as if to prod him on, a gust of increased power rocked their fragile shelter, and he cried out. In his fear he began babbling, making his confession to Caroline in the form of a prayer, but still not admitting to himself that he was a traitor to his country, not even when she, hearing of his spying for the Germans, of his cooperation with Stoltz in bringing the huge guns to Samoa, said, "But that's treason!"

"It's business," he defended. "It's nothing but good business. It is no crime to seek an advantage in business."

She sat there dumbstruck, sickened by his account, wishing that God would strike him down, taking her with him if necessary— anything to rid the earth of Marcus Fisher.

The men aboard the warships in Apia Bay began to realize, just after midnight, that their commanders had made a grave mistake. The usually serene bay had become a seething, heaving deathtrap. The power of the storm, pushing great masses of water before it, sent a tidal surge into the mouth of the bay, flooding the low-lying beaches. Palm trees, the ground beneath them already saturated, were uprooted and became juggernauts of destruction as they were hurled on the breakers. The native *fales* were, of course, long gone. Most of the town of Apia had been reduced to blowing, floating shards.

In that howling, debris-filled air there was almost no visibility, and the men of the anchor watch aboard the ships had to struggle against winds that would rip them bodily from the deck if they were not secured by lifelines or failed to hang on with both hands. Anchors began to slip. No one saw when a German man-of-war snapped the last anchor cable and was lifted by the surge of water to be smashed onto the shore. However, in the midst of the chaos, men aboard the American flagship, James Grey among them, caught a glimpse of a remarkable sight. The British cruiser, *Calliope*, had steam up and was beating her way against the winds toward the mouth of the bay. As she passed within a cable's length of the American ship, her lights gleaming through the Stygian blackness, men cheered and shouted well wishes to her, although their voices were carried away by the howling winds.

The tidal surge that inundated Apia's waterfront had fallen just short of the hotel, although its churning breakers smashed into the space where Caroline and her husband crouched, the water buoying and shifting the timbers. Marcus began to scream: "We'll drown! We'll drown!"

For some reason, his words renewed her resolution to live, and she attacked the tangled mass of broken timbers, clawing and tugging. "Help me, damn you," she yelled at him, and he, in panic, began to rip and tear at the mass. The water had risen to their waists before Caroline thrust her head into a miasma of blown rain and sea spray. Soon she had the hole enlarged and crawled out. Marcus scampered up behind her. The wind sent them tumbling, and Caroline felt her body being punctured and torn by the jagged debris, but she was still alive. Marcus was blown toward her and seized her, and they went down in a heap just as a sheet of corrugated metal roofing sailed over their heads with a force that could have decapitated them. Over the wind, they now heard the crashing thunder of breakers. A huge, dark mass loomed near, and with a shock Caroline realized that the object was a ship, one of the warships that had been anchored in the bay.

"We've got to get away from the waterfront," she shouted. She forcibly broke Marcus's grip on her and began to crawl. And then, incredibly, the winds slowly began to lose their force. The pelting rain ceased. The transition was not instantaneous, but so quick—in comparison with the seemingly endless hours of storm—that when a gleam of morning sun came, bringing with it blessed light, Caroline was stunned into immobility. She stood and looked around as the last gusts of wind died and the sun shone brightly on a scene of devastation. The sky overhead was clear blue. There was only the sound of the still-disturbed bay, of waves breaking into the debris along the waterfront. Of the other warships she saw nothing at first, and then, to her bewilderment, she realized that a large, whalelike object in the distance was an upturned keel. Beyond, in the same direction, on a coral reef not far from shore, was the wreckage of another metal ship—the German *Adler*, she realized.

Marcus stood, dazed and, like her, unable to comprehend the totality of the destruction. "The ships . . ." he muttered. "They're all gone."

"The water is still rising," she said.

"We've got to get to high ground," Marcus agreed, his voice almost normal. He looked up toward the heights and began to walk, picking his way through the debris. Caroline followed. Oblivious, or so it appeared, he stepped directly on the arm of a dead German sailor. Caroline gasped and went around the body. Soon they were climbing, having to bypass the upturned roots of huge trees and clamber over heaped masses of branches and trunks. Marcus seemed driven to get as far away from Apia as possible, and Caroline, nearing exhaustion, followed him without question. They struggled up a steep slope and paused to look down. From here they could see the wreckage of six warships.

"There's a mission up there somewhere," Marcus said pointing. "Perhaps we can find shelter." He led the way, seemingly confident now, walking quite close to the edge of a sheer cliff that fell hundreds of feet toward the bay. After a few minutes he paused again, turned and held out a hand.

"Come to me, my dear," he said. "You're exhausted. Let me give you some support."

Caroline was too tired to resist as he took her arm and held her.

"I said some things during the storm—" he began.

A feeling of dread came over Caroline, a warning that made her forget her exhaustion. She knew Marcus well, and there was a different cast to his eyes, a grim look on his face.

"I don't remember," she said.

"I think you do. I told you things about my business affairs—"

"Your treason?" Her anger flared. "and now you're afraid that I'll tell?"

He laughed. "No, I don't think there's any possibility of that." He had his hands on both her arms and was pushing her backward, toward the cliff. Aware of his intentions, she dug in her heels, threw her arms around him, and clung tightly.

"You will go with me. That I promise you."

He loosened one hand and struck her. She lifted her knee suddenly and rammed it into his groin, and he doubled up in pain but somehow managed to keep his grip on her. Then his free fist rained blows on her face, her head. Sobbing in frustration and pain, she hit back feebly, then managed to grab him around the knees and cling as he tried to force her over the cliff.

He stood, panting, looking down at her. To her surprise, he began laughing.

"I have a better idea," he said. "I won't kill you. I can very easily document that it was not Marcus Fisher but Jon Fisher who sold information to the Germans. Now, *that* would be fitting. I'll be rid of you and that ungrateful pup in one blow."

She released her hold on his legs and stood up. Her mouth was bleeding, and one of her eyes was beginning to close. She said, "You'll have to kill me to get away with that."

He laughed again. "Oh, no I won't. It will be your word against mine. The word of a woman who is a known drunk, the mother of the traitor."

He was still laughing at her, looking at her with triumph, when, from a great distance, there came the too-familiar roar with which they had lived for hours. A wall of black, drawn inexorably behind the calm, central eye of the storm that had taken more than an hour to move over the bay, was almost upon them.

"It's coming back," Fisher said, his voice cracking. "It's coming back!"

"This time I hope it kills you," Caroline said, with grim satisfaction.

A breath of wind gusted, and the sky was darkening rapidly.

"We've got to find shelter," Fisher said. He was trembling.

Caroline was thinking furiously. She knew that the threats he had made against Jon were not empty, that he probably was fully capable of casting his own guilt onto the son she had come to love and admire. But she herself had almost ruined the life of one good man, Adam Vincent. Like Marcus, she was not without guilt.

"I know a place," she said, holding out her hand.

He was doubtful, and he took a step in one direction, then the other. The wind was picking up, blowing their wet clothing and hair. A rain squall pelted them.

"Come Marcus," she said, holding out her hands. "I know a place where the storm will not bother us further."

With a resigned bleat of fear, he took her hands. Acting quickly, she turned him so that his back was to the cliff and, with her arms locked around him, threw all her weight against him.

In the brief seconds it took them to fall to the base of the cliff, Marcus Fisher's last sight on earth was his wife's calm, smiling face.

The *Antony*, steaming steadily northeastward, had encountered heavy seas and winds approaching hurricane strength, but she was a stout ship, and now the worst of the storm was behind her. Still, it was no picnic aboard, and it pleased Harry Ryan to see Bartholomew Jamison, in spite of his experience at sea, attempt to drown his uneasiness in drink.

On two occasions, after the *Antony* had pitched wildly, Harry had gone below to check the lashings on the huge cannon. He knew that if one of the guns somehow worked loose of the hempen cables holding it in its cradle, its sheer weight, even with the shift of only a few feet, could punch a hole in the hull. But the lashings remained secure. He had seen to them himself when the cannon were loaded.

Jamison's presence worried him more than the storm. He dogged Harry around the ship, staring at him from those squinted eyes, his facial expression unreadable behind his bushy black beard. Jamison continued to drink, but he stayed steady on his feet. His comments, when he made them, were singularly unhelpful and annoying.

"Seas falling off a bit?" Jamison asked, as he stood beside Harry on the bridge. They were alone.

"They have been for some time," Harry answered.

"We're out of it, then, eh?"

"The wind's changed. The storm is south of us now," Harry said.

"Good—that's good." Jamison moved to stand directly behind Harry. After a period of silence, he said, "I've taken over the ship, Ryan."

Harry turned. Jamison had a pistol pointed at his belly.

His first reaction was to curse himself for being a fool. "Hell man, if you want it, I'll give it to you. We work for the same employer, after all."

Jamison chuckled. "You don't quite understand. Our friend Stoltz thinks you've lost your stomach for this job. It's going to give me a great deal of pleasure to first put a hole in your gut and then toss you over the side. The brave captain, lost at sea in a terrible storm—"

Harry moved with desperate speed, seizing a heavy roll of charts from the chart table and swinging it at Jamison even as he threw himself to one side. Jamison's reactions had been slowed by drink, and the bullet from the pistol shattered glass, letting in the roar of the storm. The second bullet whizzed past Harry's head as he kicked open the door and dived onto the rolling, pitching walkway beside the bridge. He scrambled over the low rail and dropped to the lower deck as Jamison leaned down and fired ineffectually.

Harry dashed around the superstructure, through the rain and wind, found a nook, and paused to catch his breath and think. The odds were not at all favourable. The *Antony*'s crew were a scurvy lot, and most of them had been under Jamison's command for a long time and were dumbly loyal to him. They would, most probably, follow Jamison's orders. His suspicions were quickly borne out as he spied two crewmen coming down a ladder. They were armed with knives.

He ducked into a passageway, then into a paint locker, where he armed himself with a fire axe. He knew it would be suicide to head for his cabin, where he had a pistol; and he wouldn't last five minutes if he jumped overboard in these seas. Harry tried to think calmly, but he knew it was no use, that he was finished. Somewhere

388

along the line, things had gone wrong for him, very wrong. But then, he thought, they had started going wrong a long time back. They had gone bad when Jessica had chosen Sam Gordon instead of him, and then when he had lost himself in a cloud of opium and drink. Yes, he had done a lot of things wrong, but . . . with the help of God, he vowed, he could still set a few things right. It was a heavy sadness to realize that he would never get off the *Antony* alive, but it was past time to be sad.

With the axe in hand, Harry slipped into the passageway and paused at the door leading out onto the main deck. Through the grimy, rain-spattered window, he took a last look at the sea, magnificent in its anger, and thought of it on calm, golden, sunny days, thought briefly of Jessica and, with a wry grin, of all the other beautiful women that, now, he would never have the opportunity to appreciate.

He went on deck and was almost immediately spotted by a party of four sailors. But he nimbly slipped through the access hatch to the main hold, slammed and bolted it shut behind him, and was alone in the darkness. He continued down the ladder and lit the safety lantern.

The four huge guns were still riding snugly in their cradles. As his pursuers banged futilely on the hatch, Harry spit on his hands—a ridiculous gesture, he realized, since he was thoroughly wet already—then hefted and swung the axe at the hempen cable holding down the nearest cannon. Again and again he swung and the thick taut rope sang with the impact. It took a half dozen blows to sever it, and then he moved on to the next cable.

When he had severed all the cables on the lee side, he stood back, but he did not have long to wait. The *Antony* was running a quartering course to the waves and rolling considerably, and after she topped one big swell, the nearest gun jumped its cradle and shifted perilously. Harry started up the ladder. He would not die in the hold but would rather face the open sea. He began to unbolt the hatch as the *Antony* pitched heavily.

This time the cannon rolled without hindrance toward the side bulkheads. It crashed to a halt with a deafening, echoing boom that shook the entire ship, then rolled back to smash into one of its brothers. The impact shattered the wooden cradles and snapped the next set of cables, and now two cannon were loose. Harry clung to the ladder, with one hand on the hatch, watching with grim glee. On the next roll, both cannon struck the bulkheads, smashing through the inner hull. Still the *Antony* recovered, heaving herself up from the severe roll to send the pair of cannon back into the two still in their cradles. It would not be long now, Harry knew, and surely the men on deck were aware of what was happening. He opened the hatch, stuck his head up into blowing rain, to see the crewmen gathered in panic around the lifeboats. With the next roll, the *Antony* began her final list, the weight of four huge cannon crashing into her hull on the lee side, popping rivets, letting a cascade of seawater enter the hold through the battered plates. She was going, and Harry leaped onto the swiftly canting deck, dived to meet the oncoming wall of white water gushing over the rail, and fought to clear the ship before she turned turtle.

Seas smashed down on him. He surfaced, gasped for air, and got a mouthful of salt water. Even though he knew he was as good as dead, he was not yet willing to give up the fight.

He lived to see the *Antony*'s bottom thrusting up from the waves, and to see the last of her as she lifted her stern and slid under. He heard a faint cry from a drowning man before he was submerged by the huge waves. Then, suddenly, it was very peaceful.

On Upolu, the trailing edge of the storm was not as powerful as the hurricane's initial onslaught, but trees, weakened by hours of winds blowing in one direction, gave way to winds blowing in the opposite direction. Once more torrential rains scoured the mountainous islands, and then, as the winds began to diminish again, the survivors emerged warily from hiding.

The elemental forces of nature, as it turned out, had accomplished what man had not been able to do. Forgetting their differences, all the people, both native and white, pitched in to rescue stranded survivors from the sunken warships, to search the hills and fields for bodies, and to get food and water to stranded victims of the storm. The Americans and Germans had lost all their ships and hundreds of lives, and the Samoans, regardless of which side they supported, had suffered nearly as much. For a time, no one was thinking of war.

CHAPTER XXIV

Jon had known enough about hurricanes to realize that the sudden clearing they experienced had been but the eye of the storm, and so he had kept Misa and Kevin close to the cave, into which they had retreated once more when the rains and winds resumed the assault. When they emerged again it was morning, and the sky had been washed clean. Clouds lingered low in the southeast, but the sun was bright, and the air so pure that it seemed heady. The heat of the day was pleasant after the long night in the cave.

Kevin led the way to the top of the ridge, to a vantage point overlooking the bay, where the three of them took in the scene in shocked silence. The now-placid waters were spotted with floating debris, and the town of Apia was gone, along with its wharves and coaling facilities.

"Look," Misa said, pointing to a ship that lay on its side, high and dry on the shore. "Gone. All the warships are gone."

"Some of them may have made it to sea," Jon said.

"No, look." Kevin pointed to the wreck of the *Adler* on the reefs, just beyond another wreck, and then, in turn, at three long, unmistakable shadows beneath the waters of the bay. That left only one warship unaccounted for. "Lo, how the mighty have fallen," he whispered.

Misa was clearly anxious to get back to the mission, and since there was no place for Jon to go in Apia, he went along. He was worried about the *Maori* and his mother, but he had confidence in the seamanship of Robert Farrington, and all he could do was await the ship's return. There wasn't much chance of loading more cargo, of course, with everything in Apia destroyed.

The walk to the mission was difficult. The forest paths were blocked by fallen trees in many places, and they had to make their way through tangled masses of vegetation. Finally, after they had reached the top of the hill, they heard the voices of children, and Misa ran ahead.

The site of the mission had been swept clean. Jane McDougall and the Samoan women, among a crowd of children, were picking through the debris, to salvage what they could.

"Praise God," Kevin said, halting to get his breath. "They all seem to be safe."

"But you've lost everything," Jon said.

"No, on the contrary—we *have* everything." Kevin gestured expansively. "We're all safe, aren't we? And we have a new challenge, to rebuild better than before. Why, we've plenty of material, and the trees have already been felled for us."

"I do admire your optimism," Jon admitted.

"It has occurred to me that you're going to be at loose ends until your ship returns," McDougall said. "I'm sure we can find you something to eat, and we can certainly use a strong young pair of hands."

"Invitation gladly accepted."

Jon was astonished at how soon the women, working in the midst of apparent chaos, fashioned a satisfying meal. There was breadfruit and fish, and Jon, who was famished, had never had anything more delicious. To his amazement, many of the mission's pigs and chickens had survived the storm and began to wander back even as he, Kevin, and the older boys set about the work of rebuilding.

During the remainder of the day and into the next, as Jon laboured with rolled-up sleeves, swinging an axe and lifting the heavier frame timbers into place, he saw Misa only occasionally, at a distance, but she did not approach him. Her apparent shyness bothered him, yet he thought it best, in spite of Kevin McDougall's questioning looks, to avoid her. It would be easier for both of them in the long run. Still, it was torment for him to be so near her and not to take her in his arms.

By the end of the first full day of work, the new *fales* were already beginning to take shape. Some of the younger women were thatching roofs. The children were being fed around a fire, and Jon and Kevin, resting from their labours, lounged on a pile of palm thatch, sipping coconut milk.

"I've noticed that many of your children are of mixed blood," Jon remarked idly.

"Yes, the Samoans are a passionate people, you see. The young women fall easily for visiting sailors. Some of the children are German and Samoan, some half American, some half British." He looked at Jon oddly for a moment, but Jon thought nothing of it.

"Do the Samoans abandon children of mixed blood?" Jon asked.

"Oh, they have their taboos, of course, just as we do. It's somewhat shameful for a Samoan woman to cohabitate with a white man, and there's a certain amount of stigma attached to a woman who has a half-breed baby—but nothing serious. They don't abandon the mixed breeds. They *give* us a lot of them, however, in the hope that we can educate them to be as rich and powerful as their fathers."

"I admire what you've done here," Jon said.

"It's a beginning. We could do much more."

"When the *Maori* comes back, I would like to make a contribution, in cash, to help you in your work."

"That will be greatly appreciated, of course." Kevin's stiff tone belied his words, however, which puzzled Jon.

"Do I detect some form of disapproval?" he asked. "I hope that I didn't insult you with my offer."

"No, not at all." Kevin was appraising him with squinted eyes. "I was just wondering if the offer was made freely, or as a salve for your conscience."

Jon blushed. "I gather you mean Misa. That was a long time ago," he said. "I was under the impression that she was trying to repay me for helping her and her people. I suppose that I did take advantage of her, but it won't happen again."

"Thunderation, boy!" Kevin's outburst was so out of character that it alarmed Jon. "Are you trying to tell me that you don't know?"

"I beg your pardon?" Jon asked.

Kevin leaped to his feet and strode away, leaving Jon sitting there, perplexed. The minister was back in less than a minute, however, with a dark-haired, light-skinned boy of tender years walking proudly at his side. "I want you to meet Tolo."

Jon, puzzled by Kevin's actions, looked at the boy for several uncomprehending seconds before realization finally surfaced, setting his face on fire and causing a pain in him that made him want to cry out.

"How do you do, sir," the small boy said in beautiful English.

Jon looked at Kevin with a face that revealed his shocked emotional state.

"This is Misa's boy," the missionary said.

The boy had blue eyes, like Jon's. And like Adam Vincent's, Jon realized.

"I'm pleased to meet you," Jon said, extending his hand, which the child shook solemnly.

"Run along now," Kevin directed. The boy gave Jon a fleeting, white-toothed smile and ran away.

"Your son," Kevin said.

After a sleepless night, Jon had walked in the predawn light to stand on the cliffs overlooking Apia Bay. Throughout the long night he has agonized over his choices. He had still formed no conclusion when, with the sun's first rays making a red glory of the eastern skies, he saw three ships in line steaming toward the mouth of the bay, the flag of Great Britain flying proudly from their mastheads. He recognized the lines of the *Royal Victoria*, the flagship of the Australian squadron. As the ships drew nearer, he could see that they had not escaped damage from the storm, for the *Royal Vic* had lost her foretopmast, and the other two vessels displayed comparable damage. In his inner confusion, Jon seized upon the appearance of the ships with perhaps more enthusiasm than the occasion warranted, and he hurried back to the mission, to tell Kevin McDougall that he was going down to the bay to talk to the commander of the Australian squadron.

"I'll be back," he promised; but Kevin only nodded and said not one word in parting.

The native population, in their comings and goings, had already cleared the tracks of storm debris, but still it was a distance to Apia, and by the time Jon reached what had been the outskirts of town, the three ships were at anchor and longboats were heading for the ruined docks. Jon had to wade through water left from the storm to cross the site of the former town. As he neared the docks he heard the welcome accent of Australians, hailed a group of sailors who were questioning some Samoans, and was examined with great curiosity as he approached. His clothes were tattered, wrinkled, and soiled, he realized, and he had not shaved in days. He introduced himself to a noncommissioned officer and stated that he wished to make a report to the officer commanding the Australian force.

"You were here during the big blow, sir?" he said.

"That I was."

"We saw three of the American and German warships," the rating said. "What happened to the others?"

"They're at the bottom of the bay."

The sailors looked at one another in disbelief, until the rating shouted orders to have Jon rowed out to the flagship.

He was met at the top of the accommodation ladder by a smart young lieutenant who escorted him to the captain's saloon. Jon introduced himself to Commander Seymour, who graciously suggested that he have a drink and make himself comfortable before he began his account of events on the island.

Jon sat down, accepted a glass of brandy, and felt its bracing warmth. "I can tell by your rigging, sir, that you didn't miss the storm," he said.

Seymour nodded. "We avoided the worst of it, fortunately. Still—"

A knock on the door was followed, to Jon's utter astonishment, by the entry of Colonel Adam Shannon. Jon leaped to his feet, almost dropping his drink.

"Jon—Mr. Fisher," Adam said, also clearly surprised—and just as clearly pleased. "I did not expect to see you here."

For some reason Jon could not meet his father's gaze, and he let his eyes shift away. "It's a long story, sir. I came to do some trading, and to look for someone, and found myself in a hurricane."

"I suspect you'll be as eager as I am to hear this gentleman's story," Seymour said. "Obviously the two of you are not unacquainted."

"Indeed," Adam said, "we have met before." He must have sensed Jon's discomfort, for he did not elaborate further. "I am, needless to say, curious about what happened to the German forces and to the other warships."

They all sat down, and Jon began talking. He told of the

shadowy forms of sunken ships he had seen from the cliffs, and that, as far as he could tell, only one warship had escaped devastation. He mentioned the rumours he had heard, that German troops were on the way, that the Germans had fully intended to annex Samoa.

Later, after Commander Seymour had dispatched longboats to investigate the sunken wrecks, Jon asked a question of his own. He was told that the convoy had seen no sign of the *Maori*, or any other ship, on the approach to Samoa, but no sooner had Seymour imparted this information than word came down from on deck that a sail had been sighted, heading toward the bay. The three of them went on deck, and Jon, to his intense relief, recognized the familiar shape of the *Maori* through Commander Seymour's glass.

"Commander," Jon requested, "I'd be much obliged if you would provide me a boat so that I could board her straightaway. They'll be worried about me."

"I can imagine," Seymour said. He stepped aside to arrange the favour, and for a few moments Jon stood at the rail alone with Adam.

"I'd be honoured, Jon, if you'd come back aboard and take the evening meal with us," Adam offered.

"Thank you, sir, but I'm afraid I cannot accept, at least not tonight. There's someone on the *Maori* who will be, I think, requiring my company." Jon felt guilty at turning down the invitation, and standing next to his father, he realized that he no longer felt uncomfortable in the man's presence. Indeed, he felt quite at ease.

The comfortable sensation, however, did not last long.

"May I ask who it is you will be joining?" Adam ventured.

Jon saw no reason to lie. "Yes, sir. My mother."

"Caroline?" Adam looked baffled. "I—I suppose I shouldn't be surprised, but I am."

"She has left Marcus Fisher," Jon explained, "with my encouragement. The voyage here was good for her. I'll be taking care of her from now on."

"Good—that's good," Adam said, and Jon believed he meant it.

The words they exchanged came easily enough, sounded almost natural, but still there was a gulf between them. Then, not really knowing why—perhaps because talking with Adam kept his mind

396

off Misa—Jon began to bridge that gulf. "She was wondering, sir, just the other day, if you could ever forgive her."

Adam started visibly. He looked up, and then away. "Her? Forgive me?"

"Those were her words," Jon said.

"Well—bless her," Adam said. "I mean that." He looked at Jon with a smile. "Perhaps it's time for a mutual forgiveness. May I have your permission to come aboard the *Maori* after you've had your reunion with your mother?"

"Yes, of course," Jon said. "I would be honoured."

The longboat ferried Jon to the *Maori*, and Robert Farrington met him at the rail. "Well, thank God you're safe," he said. "What a pounding this place took!"

Jon shook the man's offered hand. "Where is my mother?" he asked.

Farrington's face fell, and he drew away. "Ah—"

"What is it, man?" Jon demanded, fearing that the storm had made Caroline ill.

"My God," Farrington said, "she's not with you?"

Misa sat in the shade of a newly constructed shelter, weaving a mat for the floor of her *fale*. Because of the work of rebuilding, formal classes had not yet been reinstituted for the children, who were taking full advantage of their moments of freedom. A rowdy group of boys were playing at the odd English game taught to them by the Reverend McDougall, doing seemingly senseless things with a flat bat and a hard, small ball. Her son, his voice as strident and forceful as that of the largest of the boys, had the bat and was hitting the ball with regularity.

Misa never tired of looking at Tolo. He was slightly smaller than other boys his age, more wiry, but graceful in his movements. Although his hair was like hers, his skin was lighter than even that of the other half-bloods. She had always been aware that her son's features favoured his father, but in the long absence of Jon Fisher, she had actually forgotten the details of Jon's face. Reminded, after the relief and joy of seeing him in the German building in Apia, she now realized just how much Jon Fisher had contributed to Tolo's appearance. It was as if, as she watched the boy at play, she was seeing a miniature version of the man who had appeared in

her life twice now, so briefly and, the second time, so enig-
matically.

Once and only once had she taken a man. In all the long months
and years since that night in the grove in Australia, she had not
yielded to natural temptations. She had turned aside Tui's urgings
to be with him so many times that, at last, she feared, she had
estranged him, her best friend, and a man she looked upon almost
as a brother. And now Jon Fisher had come and gone. Once, in the
cave, he had kissed her, and that kiss had made joy, had made her
glow with love for him. But it had been only once. And then,
during the rebuilding, he had hardly looked at her.

He was gone now, perhaps forever, and with no words of
farewell. It was best that Tolo did not know that he had, for a
little while, been in the presence of his father. It would be best for
her to wipe Jon Fisher from her mind. After all, she had a good
enough life at the mission and what she did was important. She
had seen enough of the world of the Europeans to understand that
they were powerful—if not always wise—and to know that, as
Kevin McDougall had told her, Samoa would never be the same,
that the Samoans would have to change, to conform with the white
men's way of life. Misa wanted her son to become not a warrior or
a village *matai*, but a rich and powerful man, like the Europeans, a
man who would be respected and could not be taken advantage of.
For this, a good education was necessary, no matter how much
Tolo begged to be allowed to play with the other Samoan boys and
wander off to the bay to fish and collect shells. She would see to it
that he learned all that the McDougalls could teach, and she would
do her best to teach the other children at the mission as well.

Misa returned her attention to the half-finished mat on her lap.
She herself could never become a member of the Europeans'
society, she realized. She knew well that even the kind and decent
missionaries looked upon her people as somewhat wayward but
lovable children; that was the best that could be expected from
whites. In Apia, before the storm, the Germans had treated all
Samoans as inferior beings, and Misa had personally experienced
the contempt that Australians had for the people they called
kanakas. To have dreamed of love with Jon Fisher—other than
the fleeting, temporary encounter—had been foolish and childish.
But, oh, God, she thought, how sweet had been that kiss in the cave,

with the storm roaring outside, and with the warmth of his body next to hers.

Two days, three days, then four passed following Jon Fisher's departure from the mission. The rebuilding work had continued unabated, and Misa, like everyone else, was always too busy. Before the middday meal, nevertheless, she gathered her reluctant scholars and seated them in the shool *fale*, to remind them of the rules of English grammar.

He came a short while later, when the children were eating. She saw him appear in the central compound, wearing new clothing, tall and so handsome that she felt her throat tighten. Not seeing her, he went directly to the veranda, where Kevin and Jane McDougall were having their meal. Misa, seated with the children in the shade beneath the dining *fale*, could not hear their voices clearly but saw Jane look toward her and then quickly back at Jon after some talk. Her pride told her to be aloof, to ignore Jon Fisher, but it was she, apparently, who was the subject of the talk, for now Kevin looked her way, an odd expression on his face. She pushed aside the plate with the remnants of her food, excused herself, and went casually into the school *fale*. There, hidden from view of those on the veranda, she walked closer until, when the children's happy voices subsided for a moment, she heard words that froze her heart.

"I will not leave the boy fatherless," Jon was saying. "He is flesh of my flesh. When I leave here, he will be with me."

In sudden terror, Misa darted away. He was going to take from her her only reason for existence, her son. She ran back to the dining *fale* where Tolo was seated among a group of his friends. She gave the peculiar whistle that was a signal to him that she wanted him. He looked up and said, "May I please finish my food?"

She gestured, with a stern face. With a sigh, he put aside his plate and rose.

"I wasn't finished, Mother," he said.

"Be silent. Come. Follow me."

Tolo was puzzled, but he was an obedient boy, and he hurried to keep up with her. "But where are we going?"

"Hush," she said, leading him into the trees behind the mission.

"Mother," he repeated, "why are we leaving? You have your afternoon classes."

She had led him in a circle, and now they intersected the trail leading to the far end of the bay, toward the village of her father, Molo. She was half running now, covering the ground quickly, so that Tolo had to struggle to keep up with her. "I'm getting tired," he complained, after a few minutes.

"We will rest, then," she said. He immediately threw himself down on his back, with his hands under his head. She sat on a tree blown down by the storm.

"Where are we going?" he asked.

"To visit your grandfather."

"Good, I like that." Once before, within the last year, Misa had taken him to visit Molo, who had let the boy go fishing with the men, riding in one of the many-oared *fantasi*.

"Perhaps we will see Tui," she said. "Would you like that?"

"Maybe I would," Tolo said noncommittally. Misa knew he had not liked Tui, perhaps because of the way Tui had looked at her with longing.

"Perhaps we will live with Tui," Misa said. "Perhaps he will be your father. Would you like that?"

Tolo sat up. "My father is a white man. You have told me that."

"I know," she said, her heart aching. "But a boy needs a father here, does he not?"

"The Reverend McDougall says that I have a heavenly father, and I have a white father. So far I have done well with only two fathers."

"We will speak of this later," she said. "Are you rested?"

Tolo's interest in the surprise visit to see his grandfather had all but evaporated. He shrugged sullenly.

"We will rest only a little longer," she said.

Misa had heard only a small portion of what Jon had said to Kevin and Jane McDougall. He had begun the talk by explaining that his absence had been prolonged because of the search for his mother, whom he had not realized had come ashore. Jane hugged him with motherly affection when he told them that Caroline's body had been found, with her husband's, and given Christian burial.

Jon's emotional state had been understandably troubled, and the McDougalls had reacted with caution, therefore, when he announced, almost impulsively, that he had come to ask Misa to marry him, and to take her and their son to Australia.

"Jon, are you sure you know what you're proposing?" Jane had asked him.

"I am proposing to be a father to my son, to marry the woman whom I love."

"Perhaps you should not be precipitate," Kevin had counseled. "Intermarriage is a serious matter. As intelligent and attractive as Misa is, she's still Samoan, and no one knows better than I that Samoans are different from us."

Jane had supported him. "She has been reared in a culture so different from ours. To bridge that gulf would not be easy."

"And you, as missionaries, are advising me to abandon her?"

Kevin had bristled. "I didn't say that. It's just that we know these people, Jon."

"And I know Misa."

"How? From one chance encounter in Australia?"

Thus the conversation had gone, until Jon, angered, had said, "I had hoped that you would perform the marriage ceremony. If, however, you don't wish to do so, and if Misa will accept me, then I will have the captain of my ship do it, and make it more official, in a church, when we reach Australia. I'm taking them with me, if I can, sir. I hope, with your blessings."

It was at this point that Misa had begun to overhear, and Jon, frustrated and upset from his reception by the McDougalls, had all but given up on the couple when Jane, to his astonishment, had broken into a wide smile and again thrown her matronly arms around him, kissing him on the cheek. "For Misa's sake," she said, her voice breaking with emotion, "I've been praying that you would come to this conclusion."

Puzzled, Jon looked at Kevin, who spread out his hands. "Congratulations, Jon. For a long time I didn't think you had it in you."

"What?" Jon asked.

"We were giving you, shall we say, a small portion of what you're sure to get when you take a Samoan wife and a half-breed son into respectable society," Kevin said.

Jon was slow to recover from his discomfiture. "My apologies, then." He grinned weakly. "You had me greatly concerned, I must admit, for the motives of our entire missionary effort."

"She must love you very much," Jane said. "She has been courted by several fine men, and she has turned down them all. Go to her now—she's with the children."

Jon walked toward the dining *fale*, his heart pounding, and, with every step, his doubts growing that he would be accepted. After all, he had practically ignored Misa for days. What would he do if she would not have him?

"Where is the teacher?" he asked a group of children. "Misa?"

A smiling girl pointed toward the forest. "She has gone there, you see."

"There? Into the forest?"

"She was much disturbed," a boy said. "I saw it. And she took Tolo with her."

Jon ran back to the veranda. "She's gone," he said. "The children said she'd gone into the forest."

"But why?" Jane asked.

"I don't know. The children didn't know," Jon said, but in his heart he had a suspicion of why she had left. "Perhaps she was hurt because I had not spoken. Where would she go?"

Kevin mused for a moment. "She would have only one place to go. To her father's village."

The trail was pointed out to Jon, and instructions given on how to reach Molo's village. "If you don't catch her before she gets there," Kevin advised, "be careful. Don't go rushing in, demanding things. Molo is a great *matai*.

"Keep your temper. Take your time," Jane added.

And then Jon was off, running down the sometimes slippery trail, losing his footing more than once in his haste, so that his clothing was soon soiled with mud.

It was Tolo who first heard his approach. "Someone's coming," the boy said, though not in fear.

Misa leaped to her feet as Jon spotted her. She seized her son's hand. "Hurry, run."

"But he's a friend," Tolo protested, recognizing Jon. "He won't harm us."

"Come," she said, jerking him into a run.

Jon called for them to stop, but Misa ignored him. "Misa, wait," he panted. "Misa!"

He overtook them quickly, for Tolo, in his curiosity, was holding back. Jon seized Misa by the shoulders and halted her. She wheeled, her eyes slitted in defiance.

"I must talk with you," he gasped. He was winded, and he bent, hands on his knees, to take deep breaths. Misa seized the moment to run, again dragging Tolo after her. Jon bolted after them and caught her by the arm. She struggled and his feet slipped, causing him to tumble with her to the matted floor of the forest. Misa flailed at him, but he managed to catch her hands. Before he could say a word however, a miniature fury landed on his back. Tolo's small fists pummelled his head and shoulders, and Jon rolled over, grabbed the boy, lifted him, then plopped him down beside his mother.

"Hold on," he said, raising his hands and backing off. "I surrender."

"That is good for you," Tolo said heatedly. "If you hurt my mother . . ."

"I never want to hurt her," Jon said.

"I will not let you take my son from me." Misa put her arms protectively around the boy.

"Take him from you?" Jon understood now. He reached out cautiously, slowly, and touched her cheek, wiping away a damp bit of leaf with his fingertip. "No, I never intended that. To take him with me, yes, but with *us*, Misa. With us, if you'll have me. If you'll come with me."

Her eyes widened. Tolo sat up and regarded the two mad adults with perplexity.

"But you said—I heard you say you would take him." Misa brushed at her hair and tugged her clothing back into place as she sat up to look into his eyes.

"Misa, my darling," he whispered. "To me you are by far the most beautiful woman in the world, and you would do me great honour to be my wife."

"Wife?" A slow smile spread over her features.

"Yes. Will you say yes?"

She frowned. "It has taken you a long time."

"I know, and I am sorry. I came as soon as I could get a ship."

403

"And then, for days, you ignored me."

"I had to know if you still wanted me," he temporized, for he could never admit to her that he had had doubts about taking a Samoan wife. "I had to know if you, perhaps, had committed yourself to another man. I didn't know about this one." He looked at his son, who was following the talk with evident curiosity.

"In my life, only one man has touched me," she said, lifting her face haughtily. The movement emphasized the beauty of her neck. "But yes, I will marry you."

Jon took her in his arms, and this time Tolo did not interfere. There still were explanations to be made, however.

"I have told you that your father is a white man," Misa said to Tolo, pulling herself away. "This is he."

Tolo regarded Jon for a moment in silence.

"Would you like to come with me?" Jon asked. "Aboard a great ship, to see faraway lands and to live in a proper—well, a different kind of house?"

"This one is my father?" the boy asked suspiciously.

"Yes," Jon and Misa replied as one.

Tolo frowned and turned his head away.

"You don't approve?" Jon asked.

The boy looked back at him. "Are you good at cricket?"

"I've batted my century," Jon said.

"I had hoped—" Tolo paused.

"You had hoped what?" Jon prompted.

"Oh, nothing," Tolo said, then he smiled. "I had dreamed that you would be big and strong, with a fierce beard."

"Well, I could grow a beard." Jon fingered his bare chin.

"No, you don't have to do that," Tolo said. "If you can bat a century, I suppose you'll do."

Misa, in a white dress, stood beside Jon in the thatch-roof chapel of the rebuilt mission. Adam Shannon, in full-dress uniform, was standing to one side, in the role of best man, and Tolo, seated in the front row of the small congregation, looked on with precocious patience as the ceremony neared its end.

To Adam's eternal credit in Jon's eyes, he had received with total aplomb the announcement that Jon was going to marry a Samoan woman; and indeed, once having met Misa, he had been

404

effusive in his praise of her poise and beauty. Adam had been visibly moved upon seeing the boy, and despite the gap in years and experience between them—or perhaps because of it—grandfather and grandson had been totally at ease with each other after only a few minutes' acquaintance.

Kevin McDougall's voice had, it seemed to Jon, a heartfelt authority as he read the solemn vows, and it carried strongly even as a soft breeze blew through the sideless chapel, gently ruffling Misa's dress. Behind him, Jon could hear Jane McDougall weeping softly while he repeated the age-old words: ". . . to have and to hold . . . from this day forward . . . for better for worse . . . for richer for poorer . . . in sickness and in health . . . to love and to cherish . . . till death us to part . . . according to God's holy ordinance."

A kiss sealed the covenant, and then there were congratulations all around, followed by a full-scale Samoan feast prepared by the women of the mission, and talk and celebration until long after dark.

The days that followed were the sweetest Jon had ever known, and they passed so swiftly that the time to leave was all too soon upon them. Molo—who, since the hurricane, was no longer at war with the neighbouring villages—had arranged for a gathering of *matais*, and the result was a flow of native crafts that more than filled the holds of the *Maori* when, finally, she sailed out of Apia Bay. The colonial volunteers under Adam were staying, to help in the rebuilding of the town, with able assistance from sailors of the British cruiser *Calliope*. The *Calliope*, to everyone's amazement, had reappeared a full week after the storm, which miraculously she had weathered, although she had been blown nearly a hundred miles off her course.

As the *Maori* cleared the entrance to the bay, Jon with Misa at his side, took one last look at the wreckage that had once been Apia. His gaze wandered to higher ground, to the churchyard where his mother was buried, and sadly he said a silent good-bye. It was odd, he thought how so many of the people who had a direct effect on his life had come together on this tiny island, so far out in the vast Pacific. His mother . . . Marcus Fisher, who was also buried in the churchyard, although the manner of his death, as well as that of Caroline, would always be a mystery to Jon . . . and

Adam Shannon—father, and now friend. And the woman who had inserted herself so accidentally into his life, Misa, at his side, to stay by his side until, as he had vowed at the marriage ceremony, "death us do part." And his own son, bright and agile, though still a bit wary of his father.

"He will fall," Misa said, looking worriedly upward into the rigging, where Tolo had insisted on climbing.

"Boy," Jon yelled, "come down!"

Tolo obeyed. He hurried to stand at Jon's side, leaning over the rail to look down as the *Maori*'s billowing sails pushed her ever more rapidly through the water.

'We'll see England soon," Jon said. "We'll buy you a proper gentleman's clothing there, son."

"I want boots and a great hat," the boy replied.

"And you shall have them," he said. "And beautiful gowns for your mother, and jewels too. Nothing too ostentatious—pearls, perhaps." He looked down into Misa's smile. Her beauty, he decided, needed no ornamentation.

EPILOGUE

There was a new head at the Broome table in Sydney, and occasionally new faces appeared at the dinners that had so long been a tradition there. Lieutenant Rufus Broome, who had been uneasy, at first, as acting head of the household while he was on shore leave, had soon fitted in well, and his opinions were respected by the old, familiar faces that were, most often, in evidence at the dinners.

Times were changing, but the conversation at table was essentially the same, reflecting a lively interest not only in what was happening in Sydney and New South Wales, but also in the great events of empire, and in the development of Australia since Justin Broome, Red's father, had been involved in the exploration of the Blue Mountains. The talk was of the newly recognized British protectorate in Burma, the sinking of the British ship *Kowshing* by the Japanese, and the brief Sino-Japanese War. Japan, Johnny Broome said, was going to have to be reckoned with as a legitimate power in the Pacific.

The growing brood of children associated with the Broomes and their friends had accepted Jon and Misa's son without question. Jon Fisher had changed his own surname legally to that of his maternal grandfather, Mason, and at Misa's behest, Tolo was now addressed by his Christian name, Thomas. Mrs. Mason, as Misa was so proud of being called, looked lovely in her favourite white dress, with a single strand of pearls the only ornament to her striking, exotic features. Sometimes she would be asked to recount one of the various legends of her native islands, and Jessica Gordon's favourite was the tale of the love-stricken king of Fiji who changed himself into an eel to woo a Samoan girl on the island of Savaii but lost his magic power, could not change back to his human form, and died as an eel, to sprout into the first coconut tree.

It was, during one such family gathering in the closing years of the nineteenth century, an evening that made Magdalen wish that Red were still alive, for all of his best friends were present: Adam and Emily Shannon visiting from Wellington—Adam and his new brigadier's stars on his shoulders—Sam and Jessica, with Sam's ship, the *Cutty Sark*, anchored in the harbour, waiting to take them and little Java, who was no longer quite so little—back to England; Johnny and Kitty, of course; Claus and Mercy Van Buren, also visiting from New Zealand, so that Claus could confer with the new business partner in his firm, Jon Mason. Magdalen, for one, wished that the males in her life would stop changing their names; it made for an awkward moment when she forgot and introduced Jon as Jon Fisher.

Sam, at the urging of Claus and Rufus, had been recounting with colourful detail his last encounter with the *Thermopylae*, which no longer sported the boastful cock at her masthead, but instead looked on in envy at the *Cutty*'s new ornament—a gilded witch with a horse's tail in her hand, a miniature of the figurehead but perched proudly on the tip of the mainmast, proclaiming the *Cutty*'s now undisputed claim as the fastest clipper on the high seas. The *Cutty* had, in fact, in the race following Red's death, overtaken the *Thermopylae* somewhere in the vicinity of Cape Horn and arrived in the Downs a full week ahead of her archrival, in a record-smashing pace of seventy-three days from Sydney to the mouth of the Thames. Jock Willis had been so excited that Sam had feared for the old man's health.

Rufus, too, had much to tell of his education in England, and of the changing navy, run now by bureaucrats and engineers, and a far cry from the sailing ship days of his father's youth. Indeed, the world seemed to be changing too fast for Magdalen's liking, and she was relieved to leave the men to their port and cigars as they discussed the idealistic rebel Sun Yat-Sen's efforts to overthrow the Manchu dynasty in China and the continued unrest there; the victories of the Liberal Labour Party in New Zealand; the Treaty of Federation of the Straits Settlements in Malaya; France's strengthened position in Southeast Asia with the acquisition of a protectorate in Laos; the annexation of Pondoland to connect the Cape Colony in South Africa with Natal; the pacification of Nyasaland through Sir Harry Johnston's defeat of the Angoni blacks and the Arabs.

But it was the Germans who gave Johnny Broome the most concern. To the consternation of Adam Shannon and many of his fellow colonials in both New Zealand and Australia, the governments of Great Britain, United States, and Germany had signed an accord ceding to the Germans control of Western Samoa, after all. The Americans had kept control of the easternmost islands and the harbour at Pago Pago.

"They've had a taste of international power," Johnny said. "They've whipped the Wahehes in German East Africa. They won in Samoa, despite the ships they lost."

"Delusions of grandeur," Adam commented.

"Perhaps not," Johnny said. "Their armament industry, under the Krupps, is reportedly second to none in the world. They've not tasted defeat, the Germans, as we have, as we did, for example, at Khartoum."

"I find them to be quite cooperative in Samoa," Jon put in. He was engaged in a growing trade, with three ships of his own now, in the South Pacific. "If, that is, one can overlook their occasional arrogance—a fault that the British are not entirely lacking, I should add." He sipped his drink. "Incidentally, on the last trip out I ran into that Maxim Stoltz fellow. He was in full uniform—a general, I believe. Military governor of Samoa. I heard that he swam ashore from the *Adler* after she was tossed on the reef."

"Perhaps we should be relieved," Rufus said with evident cynicism, "that our German friends are willing to shoulder their share of the white man's burden. Some would say that our good Queen's empire is quite big enough. I, for one, question this dispute with Russia over territories in Manchuria. I say let the bloody Russians build the railroads there. We should be concentrating on lands like India, making a greater effort to bring them into the nineteenth century—indeed, into the coming twentieth century.

"Hear, hear," Sam Gordon said.

Claus Van Buren, who had been showing his age by nodding in his chair, revived. "If you ask me, we should forget all the little quarrels of the European powers. There have always been war and rumours of war in Europe. Let's concentrate on our own

409

economy, our own problems, and end this slavish dependency on the home country."

This successfully turned the conversation to British colonial politics, which, in New South Wales, inevitably translated into the heated topic of Australian unification.

"Here we've solved the problems of the entire world," Johnny put in wryly, "and we haven't touched on unification at all."

"It will come," Claus said. "It has to come."

Jon, who usually listened more than he talked in such gatherings, said, "It had best come, and a unified government must do something quickly about the land problem or we'll not have to look to Europe and Asia for a small war—we'll have one right here, between the squatters and smallholders and those who are hungry for land."

"A touchy subject, indeed," Johnny agreed. "How do you tell a man whose grandfather trekked through unknown wilds to find a place to pasture cattle and sheep that he's got to give up some of the land that has been in his family for three generations to an immigrant fresh out from Liverpool or London?"

"How do you tell a man who has been promised land that there is none for him," Jon asked, "when there are landholders sitting astride tens of thousands of acres?"

"What we need to do," Rufus said, "is run Uncle John for public office. He'd straighten things out."

"Deliver me from such a fate!" Johnny joked. "I think I can have a stronger voice, and certainly a more unbiased one, in my newspaper."

Adam Shannon rose. "Gentlemen, it's been a long day. And as much as I enjoy your conversation, I have a yen to find my bed."

"I'll second that," Claus said. Like Adam and Emily, he and Mercy were spending the night in the Broome house. He turned to Jon and said, "Before you sail, I'd like to have another talk with you. I think we've let the English and Americans dominate the wool trade long enough. Perhaps together we can devise a way to do something about it."

"I'm afraid my ships can't compete with the *Cutty Sark*," Jon said, looking at Sam Gordon. "They're only slow steamers. But I'm open to ideas."

Jon walked with Adam and Emily to the base of the stairs. "I haven't had a chance, sir," he said, "to officially congratulate you on your promotion."

"Thank you," Adam said. "I'm afraid it's just a bone they've thrown to an old dog, since I'm due for retirement."

"Now, how can Australia be defended without you?" Jon asked with a laugh.

"They'll manage."

Back in the drawing room, Misa was still seated with Jessica Gordon. Java Gordon and little Tom Mason had been brought down from the nursery, sleepy-eyed. Jon looked at his son with great pride. He was growing to be a strong lad. Java, standing beside the boy, had her mother's beauty.

"Mr. Mason," Java said, "I've told Tom that you're to take him to visit the *Cutty*, so he can see that she's the most beautiful ship in the world."

"My father's ships are just as beautiful," the boy said defensively.

'Well, son," Jon said, crouching to speak with him, "the *Cutty Sark* is the queen of them all, really."

"Then I have to see her," Tom said. "Will you take me there? Tomorrow?"

"We'll see. I do have to go down to the harbour."

Jon was not sure if it was his imagination, but he thought he detected a look of disapproval briefly touching Jessica Gordon's face. If so, she recovered swiftly. "If you come, Jon, please bring Misa as well. She's so lovely, and such good company."

"We'll see," Jon replied somewhat stiffly, for far too often he had heard people, mostly female, speak of Misa with condescension. He couldn't believe that Jessica, of all people, harboured such prejudices, but there was that tone in her voice. Or perhaps he had imagined it, being oversensitive to any slight directed at his wife or son.

On the way home, he put his arm protectively around Misa's shoulders. Little Thomas was up front with the driver, being allowed to hold the reins under careful supervision. Not once in the years since he had spoken the marriage vows at the mission on Upolu, Jon thought, had he regretted it. This beautiful woman at his side, and the son she had borne him, were worth the rest of the world combined.

THE EMPIRE BUILDERS
Volume 9 in the bestselling
Australians series

Vivian Stuart writing as
William Stuart Long

THE EMPIRE BUILDERS – they sailed towards new
horizons to claim a land with their courage and their
blood. With the vast Australian continent behind them
they set their sights on the exotic landscape of New
Zealand, driven by a vision of one glorious empire united
under the Union Jack.

For young Adam Vincent, the Maori Wars offer a chance
to prove his true worth, by death-defying risk and valour.
For Lady Kitty Broome, the stage is set for a dramatic
confrontation between illicit temptations and sacred vows
as the New Australians fight a war between cultures,
between friends and lovers, for the future of their world.

THE EMPIRE BUILDERS – volume nine in the
majestic saga of the pioneer Australians.

FUTURA PUBLICATIONS
FICTION
0 7088 3985 1

SUMMER HARVEST

Madge Swindells

'a spellbinding read' Sarah Harrison

Set between 1930 and 1968 in a land where gruelling poverty rubs shoulders with remarkable opulence, and moving from the Cape to London and the West Coast of America, SUMMER HARVEST is a family saga in the finest tradition.

At the heart of the story is Anna, a woman as strong and passionate as she is ambitious, who fights her way up from near destitution to become one of the Cape's most prominent and powerful businesswomen. Only love eludes her. For Simon – a poor farmer when they marry – has too much masculine pride to stand on the sidelines while Anna plunders her way to a success that threatens tragedy and loss.

'Anna van Achtenburg mirrors the strengths and the weaknesses of her beautiful, harsh country: the toughness, the dazzling material success, the moral dilemmas, the tragedy. I was gripped from start to finish. Kate Alexander, author of *Fields of Battle*

FUTURA PUBLICATIONS
FICTION
0 7088 2528 1

SAMSARA

Alexandra Jones

Tibet in the late nineteenth century – an untamed and mysterious land. Lhasa, the residence of its god-king the Dalai Lama, is a forbidden city – and death at the hands of his fierce soldiers is the fate of any foreigner who dares set foot inside its sacred walls. But for the mighty British and Russian empires Tibet has become a strategically vital country to be conquered at all costs.

Into this turbulent, dangerous realm come two young people, drawn together by deepest emotions yet torn apart by conflicting loyalties . . .

Lewis Joyden

is a handsome Englishman who travels disguised as a Buddhist monk to survey this wild and mountainous land in preparation for a British invasion.

Sonya Vremya

is the fiercely independent Russian princess who first bewitched him many years ago at home. Her quest is to find her brother who was sent on a mission by the Tsar . . . but has vanished without trace . . . and to track down her unloving husband and beg him for a divorce.

Though separated by national conflicts, they are forced up against all the dangers and uncertainties of a strange and magical country, and drawn ever closer by the constant perils which threaten them.

FUTURA PUBLICATIONS
FICTION
0 7088 4204 6

<u>ALWAYS A STRANGER</u>

Margaret P. Kirk

The tranquil Yorkshire countryside in the summer of '39 offers Lallie Wainwright, adored only child of a wealthy foundry owner, blissful happiness: as long as she has her family, dogs and Neil, her childhood friend, her life is complete.

But the war brings more than upheaval – it brings Jan Kaliski, a Polish pilot in a strange land, into Lallie's home and into her heart. Then the war, and the chaos that is war's aftermath, forces them apart. Only after heartbreak and tragedy do Lallic and Jan learn the bittersweet lesson that home is not always where the heart is . . .

'a love story in the old, grand manner – heroic and emotionally charged. She deals with big themes in the stylish and deceptively simple manner of the born storyteller. Have your handkerchiefs ready. You won't just read. You'll care.'
Sarah Harrison, author of *A Flower That's Free*

'vivid and real . . . an irresistible read of passion and heartbreak. I couldn't put it down.'
Madge Swindells, author of *Summer Harvest*

'a really heartwarming story with flashes of brilliance'
Cynthia Harrod-Eagles, author of the *Dynasty* series

FUTURA PUBLICATIONS
FICTION
0 7088 2723 2

All Futura Books are available at your bookshop or newsagent, or can be ordered from the following address:
Futura Books,
Cash Sales Department,
P.O. Box 11,
Falmouth,
Cornwall TR10 9EN.

Alternatively you may fax your order to the above address. Fax No. 0326 76423.

Payments can be made as follows: Cheque, postal order (payable to Macdonald & Co (Publishers) Ltd) or by credit cards, Visa/Access. Do not send cash or currency. UK customers: please send a cheque or postal order (no currency) and allow 80p for postage and packing for the first book plus 20p for each additional book up to a maximum charge of £2.00.

B.F.P.O. customers please allow 80p for the first book plus 20p for each additional book.

Overseas customers including Ireland, please allow £1.50 for postage and packing for the first book, £1.00 for the second book, and 30p for each additional book.

NAME (Block Letters) ....

ADDRESS ....

....

☐ I enclose my remittance for _____

☐ I wish to pay by Access/Visa Card

Number ☐☐☐☐☐☐☐☐☐☐☐☐☐☐☐☐☐☐☐

Card Expiry Date ☐☐☐☐